Alley Rehfeldt

Second edition, 2024

Published July 18, 2023

This novel is entirely a work of fiction. The names, characters and incidents portrayed in it are the work of the author's imagination. Any resemblance to actual persons, living or dead, events or localities is entirely coincidental.

Alley Rehfeldt asserts the moral rights to be identified as the author of this work.

Alley Rehfeldt has no responsibility for the persistence or accuracy of URLs for external or third-party Internet Websites referred to in this publication and does not guarantee that any content on such Websites is, or will remain, accurate or appropriate.

Designations used by companies to distinguish their products are often claimed as trademarks. All brand names and product names used in this book and on its cover are trade names, service marks, trademarks and registered trademarks of their respective owners. The publisher and the book are not associated with any product or vendor mentioned in this book. None of the companies referenced within the book have endorsed the book.

CROWN OF BLOOD

To Madi —

My sister and best friend.

Love, Squid

Preface

The idea for *Crown of Blood* originally came to me as a wee little middle schooler back in 2009. I had always known that I wanted to write a story about the natural elements and their evolution into magic that characters could manipulate from birth. When I first started comprising this story in my head, I had wanted the characters to attend a sort of Elemental boarding school where they learned to control Elemental manipulation and other abilities. However, as I began to grow up and mature, so did this story.

The process of writing *Crown of Blood* took about two and a half years from the moment I wrote the first word to the day my debut novel was published. During that time, I went through multiple drafts of the storyline and characters until what ran through my mind was perfectly laid out in words.

Since the layout of the continent where Creobe and Visaran are located is fiction, most of the research that I had to do for this story was about landscapes and which plant life, trees, and bodies of water could thrive in different locations with very different climates like the City Center and the Creobian Palace.

After a long and incredibly exciting two and a half years, I am so excited to bring this story into the world and share it with you all.

NORTHERN
SECTOR
KELT
ABELFORTH
ROYAL
SECTOR
WESTERN
SECTOR
CREOBE
WESTERN
PALACE
THEROD
THE OBSIDIAN COAST
EASTERN
SECTOR
SILIA RIVER
DRISTOL
SOUTHERN
SECTOR
HOWE
THE BALTIC OCEAN

ATHAR
NORTHOW
TALLUH
VISARAN
THE GRASSLANDS OF VISARN
PASTOLE
EASTERN PALACE
CITY CENTER
THE GREAT NATIONS OF
CREOBE
AND
VISARAN

Sayr's head throbbed as she hit the ground, her body sprawled against the earth and a spear at her throat. She kept her eyes squeezed shut, waiting for the throbbing pain to cease and finally opened them to stare up at her opponent. Standing above Sayr, the tip of their dulled spear dug harder into her neck. A sliver of the sun rose over the grassy plains in the east, casting a bronze glow over her opponent's silhouette. They lifted a hand, and flames shot at Sayr, landing in the dirt just to her right with a sizzle.

Sayr could feel the heat of the sizzling flames lick her cheek. She craned her neck to peer at the scorched earth just inches from her dirt-caked hair, then glared up at her opponent.

"And just like that, you're dead," Marenda taunted.

She took a step back and offered Sayr a hand, lifting her off the ground with ease. While Sayr brushed the dirt off her training uniform, Marenda cocked her head to one side, inspecting her mentee.

"You're distracted again, Sayr," Marenda said. She twirled her spear and planted her feet for the next round.

Sayr picked up her own daggers lying in the dirt, much smaller than her mentor's spear, and took a defensive stance. She'd always favored the two smaller blades; they were easier to control with her body than the elongated weapon Marenda preferred.

"I'm not distracted," Sayr shot back. "That kick was a foul move."

Marenda let out a short laugh before facing off against Sayr. "Everything's fair play when you train with me."

The two shuffled around each other. Sayr spit out a piece of hair that had lodged itself in her mouth during the fall and inspected Marenda. Her braided hair was twisted into a high bun out of her face. Sayr gripped both daggers between her teeth to tie her own wavy brown hair into a low ponytail before taking a defensive stance once again.

Marenda twirled her spear so that the dulled end pointed directly at Sayr and lunged. Sayr twisted left to avoid the attack and swung her dagger at her mentor's thigh. The blades were dull enough that their hits wouldn't render their opponent immobile, but they would certainly leave a nasty bruise. Their training uniforms were no source of protection, either. They wore no more than a fitted long sleeve top, tight pants with a thick belt to hold their weapons, and heavy boots.

"You're too heavy on your left foot," Marenda advised.

The two continued to strike and dodge each other's attacks. As a member of the Queen's Army, Sayr was supposed to train with the other soldiers in the barracks. Yet

Her Majesty had ordered her to train privately with Marenda, too, who was one of the most skilled fighters in Visaran, and the Eastern Queen's personal guard.

Marenda pounced at Sayr and swung down her spear. Sayr instinctively lifted both daggers above her head, blocking Marenda's attack, and swiped the spear down into the dirt. Sayr was within Marenda's defense circle, she had the advantage. She aimed one dagger at her mentor's ribs while Marenda's spear was still lodged in the earth. Marenda shifted her body away from Sayr's attack, missing the dagger by mere inches.

Marenda danced around Sayr, looking for her weak spot. Sayr shuffled her feet as she waited for her mentor to advance. Marenda twirled the spear around her body. Her moves were fluid while she advanced, striking Sayr's knee with the blunt end of her spear.

Sayr stumbled from the impact. Her right leg threatened to give way, and her focus sharpened on her balance. She took one step back with her good leg, keeping her weight on one foot, and looked at her mentor.

Marenda was closer than expected. Sayr tried to move out of reach, but it was too late. Marenda took the advantage. She dug her spear into the ground and used the momentum to fling her body into the air. She kicked out, slamming Sayr square in the chest. Sayr fell backwards, her back slamming into the dirt. Marenda pulled the spear out of the dirt and dug the point right above Sayr's heart.

Panting with exhaustion, Sayr lifted her hands over her head and dropped the daggers to the ground in surrender. Marenda didn't look at all pleased, even though she had just bested her mentee.

"What's going on?" she asked. She placed one hand on her hip in annoyance and leaned against her spear. "You aren't even trying to strike me."

Sayr gritted her teeth and rose from the ground, meeting her mentor's stare. She'd been trying her hardest to land a solid blow against her mentor but only managed to get a few cheap hits in.

Her gaze softened as she looked at Marenda for another moment. Was now the right time to tell her? Marenda had been Sayr's closest friend since she had become a part of the Eastern Court, and one of the very few people she trusted completely.

"Okay, listen." Sayr backed away from her friend and took a seat in the dewy grass. Marenda followed close behind and settled down next to her.

"I keep seeing something," Sayr admitted. "I don't know what it's supposed to mean or where it's even happening, but it feels so real and it's the same vision every time."

She looked over at her friend sitting next to her. The rising sun made Marenda's bronze eyes look like glowing embers as she stared wide-eyed at Sayr.

"What exactly do you see?" she whispered.

Sayr closed her eyes to recall the vision she had seen so many times before. "At first, I'm alone. I'm standing in some sort of forest, but not any forest I've seen before. It's like a wasteland; bare and cold. Trees surround me in every direction, but their trunks are dead and blackened and covered in ash."

Her brow creased in concentration as the vision began to take form behind her closed eyes.

"There is ash everywhere, covering the ground, the trees, falling from the sky. I turn around and I can see someone standing in the tree line in the distance, watching me. I move towards them but every step I take feels like I'm stepping through thick mud. I can't make out any features of this person, but something about them feels important to me. They move farther and farther away from me, until I can't help but run after them. I call out to them, but they never slow down. I keep running and running but they never get any closer. The ash comes down thick like black rain, filling my mouth and nose as I'm running until I am suffocating on it. I collapse to the ground as they vanish into the dying trees in the distance. That's when I wake up."

Her voice was barely above a whisper when she finished. She stood from her spot in the grass and hugged her arms tightly around her body to ward off the shaking from the memory.

She was used to having visions, and they were often unpleasant, but they never occurred more than once or twice. She had never been the main focus of a vision before. They always revolved around her observing others, not her interacting with them.

This time she was the focus of the vision. She and the stranger that ran from her. And in the past two weeks, she'd had the vision three times.

Marenda slowly stood and put a hand on each of Sayr's arms in a comforting hold. Her touch held its usual unnatural warmth, easing the chills that ran down Sayr's spine.

"You said you keep seeing the same vision," Marenda noted. "Does Her Majesty know?"

Sayr shook her head, hating the weight that the secret held over her. "I've requested to meet with her, but I haven't told anyone about the details of the vision yet, besides you."

Sayr saw the disapproving look rise in Marenda's face and lifted her hands in defense, knowing she would be furious that Sayr hadn't told the queen yet.

"I have a meeting with Her Majesty and the Council later this morning." The words shot out of her as quickly as possible. "I plan on telling them everything then."

"The Council meeting this morning?" Marenda repeated. "I've been ordered to attend, too."

"Really?" Sayr asked. "What for?"

"I have no idea. I didn't ask any questions when Her Majesty demanded my presence." Marenda gave Sayr a reassuring smile, the tension dissolved from her face. "I'm sure everything will be okay; Her Majesty will know what to do and the Council will help."

Sayr huffed out a laugh. "You haven't been to a Council meeting before," she said. "You have too much hope in the Council if you think their best interest is in helping me decipher these visions."

Marenda steadied a hard look at Sayr. "You are the Queen's Seer, Sayr. I have no doubt that the Council recognizes your importance to the queen and her Court."

She gave Sayr's arms a final squeeze and turned to retrieve the discarded weapons in the training circle.

"We'll end training early today," she called over her shoulder. "You clearly have a lot on your mind and it's not as much fun kicking you into the dirt when you're not fully committed."

Sayr grinned at her back and headed in the opposite direction towards the Eastern Palace.

The East Wing of the palace was home to the more permanent members of the Court, including Royal Guards and high officials. The Eastern Queen wanted everything and everyone in her Court where she could monitor them.

Sayr's suite was conveniently placed in this wing as well. She didn't mind its location, though she stayed away from any high officials in the halls. The location kept her away from the rest of the Court guests and aristocrats that often whispered about her when she passed. She preferred sticking by the people she saw daily during drills. Plus, Marenda bunked with three other Royal Guards just down the hall, though she usually stayed in Sayr's much more spacious suite.

The rest of the Queen's Army bunked in the barracks located between the North and East Wings. Marenda had been sleeping in the barracks before her promotion as the queen's personal guard and Sayr had spent much time there with her best friend in those days.

As much as Sayr had wanted to bunk with the other guards and trainees, Her Majesty had prepared a separate suite for Sayr when she first arrived at the palace to help disguise her real reasons for entering the Court.

Most of the Court believed Sayr was an apprentice to one of Her Majesty's Councilmen. Her duties consisted of taking notes during Council meetings and acting as Councilman Danil's personal assistant. Her duties also consisted of training with the Queen's Army, which stunned many Court officials. No one dared question the queen, though, and after a couple years, the lie stuck. No one knew about Sayr's true abilities other than the royal family, the Council, and Marenda.

Sayr swung the doors to her suite wide open. The morning sunlight streamed in through the two enormous windows that took up most of the wall space across from the doors, showcasing Visaran's glowing City Center just a mile outside the palace grounds.

Visaran's palace sat atop the rocky cliffs of the ocean shore at the southernmost tip of the country. The road between the City Center and the palace was surrounded by stretches of grassland that covered most of the country's terrain.

Sayr spent the early morning hours in the bath, scrubbing the dirt and sweat from her body, and ordering breakfast from the servants in the East Wing. She pulled a pair of cotton trousers and a sleeveless linen shirt out of her wardrobe. She tucked the loose shirt into her trousers and slipped on a pair of sandals.

Sayr sat on the loveseat, nervously touching each finger together one by one while she waited for the knock at her door.

Finally, a light rhythmic knock sounded, and she rose from her seat to open the door for the guard that would escort her to the Council meeting.

Marenda stood outside the door instead. She had also changed out of her training clothes and into her Royal Guard uniform, or an unofficial version of the uniform. Sayr noticed that the armor and weapons that went with the official uniform were missing, indicating that Marenda wasn't currently on duty.

She wore thick leggings that faded from black to deep blue at her knees, disappearing into her knee-high boots, and a long sleeve, fitted royal blue top. Visaran's swirling insignia was displayed on her left shoulder and a black mesh halter finished off the uniform. Her hair was no longer in a braided bun and now flowed down her back in black and deep red braids, a small tribute to her element. A long scar ran along her jaw on the left side of her face, contrasting with her medium-brown skin. Her bronze eyes ignited with light while she looked Sayr up and down.

Sayr typically stuck to the trendier Visarian clothing, light, loose pants and breezy tops. Many Visarians wore lighter colors of white, yellow, and tan along with various shades of blue in support of the royal family. The Eastern Palace was located so far south that the Court rarely ever experienced cold climates.

Marenda gave her an approving nod and closed the distance between them. She linked her elbow with Sayr's, and they walked down the halls of the East Wing.

The palace buzzed with life. Court guests hurried by the girls in the public halls of the palace towards the gardens for morning tea. Officials gathered in the halls, speaking quietly with one another about business that Sayr had no interest in. Servants and ladies-in-waiting followed noblewomen throughout the halls or into the gardens for tea and breakfast.

Royal Guards were stationed all around the halls of the palace. Each guard straightened a little more when the girls passed, refusing to meet Marenda's gaze. Marenda was a high-ranked soldier in the Queen's Army as well as a personal guard. Her position, and her fierce attitude, demanded respect from just about everyone around her.

Marenda walked with a silent confidence that made her appear far beyond her twenty years. She held that confidence with her everywhere she went. She was a striking force to be reckoned with.

The girls remained linked at the elbow until they reached a door to a private chamber just outside the Royal Wing. Marenda gently squeezed Sayr's arm before letting go to open the door.

Sayr entered first.

The long room was mostly bare besides a few small tables and chairs placed neatly around the room. A long table was placed in the center of the room where multiple people were already seated. Large-paned windows separated the room from the grassy plains down below. Both girls gave curt nods to the other members and took two empty chairs next to each other. An elaborate chair was set at the end of the table farthest from them.

Two men sat across from Sayr, whispering to each other in deep conversation. One of the men—Sayr had nicknamed Baldric—was bald and looked to be in his mid-forties. His brow furrowed in thought while he listened to the other man talk, who looked as if he had been alive for the better part of a century. The other man had long, white hair and beard, and small rimmed glasses that rested at the tip of his nose.

The aging man's name was Danil, the Councilman Sayr was posing to be the apprentice of. Danil gave Sayr a soft nod and smiled when he spotted her across the table.

A few seats down from them sat Velda, a woman whose thin, greying hair was styled in a tight bun. Her hands were clasped tightly in her lap, and she sat stiffly, looking ahead at one of the massive portraits of some royal ancestor displayed on the wall. Another man and woman, Larse and Victoria, sat across from each other closest to the queen's chair and exchanged quiet conversation.

Sayr recognized all the Council members from previous meetings. Council members were some of the wisest and most educated people in the country, though Sayr thought some of them were also the most boring people in the country. They only attended certain meetings that required their extensive knowledge. Apart from Council meetings, Sayr never saw any of them around the palace.

Sayr became a Council member almost two years ago, when she was just fifteen. Her Majesty believed her gifts were unique and rare. As far as anyone knew, she was the only Seer in Visaran. There was no surprise that once her abilities began to grow, Her Majesty began to take more interest in her and her visions.

Her first Council meeting two years ago was still one of the worst days of Sayr's life. Sayr had finally begun to feel confident in her abilities, and her training as a soldier were earning her support amongst some of the other trainees. But when she was introduced to the Council that day and asked to show her abilities to them all, she had failed. She was not able to conjure up a vision for them. Her visions often came to her more than she could call on them. The Council had reprimanded her in front of the queen, who in return scolded her harshly afterwards.

"Your worth in this palace is determined by those around you," the queen had told Sayr. "If the people of my Court do not find you worthy, why should I find you worthy enough to remain in my palace?"

Sayr was too lost in thought of the past to realize the Council members had all stood when another door opened, and three more people entered the room. The Council all bowed their heads and Sayr quickly stood and did the same. After a respectable amount of time, they all lifted their heads and faced the Eastern Queen, flanked by two Royal Guards.

Queen Cheralin was terrifyingly striking in her floor-length, royal blue gown. She had pale, ageless skin and piercing grey eyes that scanned over every person at the table. Her shoulder-length, platinum hair was pinned up off her neck and around her sharp face. A silver crown decorated with blue crystals of every possible shade sat atop her head.

The Eastern Queen was an intimidating sight. She walked gracefully over to the head of the long table and sat down. The other Council members followed.

"Good morning, everyone." Her Majesty's voice was soft yet confident as she addressed the Council. Queen Cheralin locked eyes with each member before she settled her stare directly on Sayr and gave her an emotionless smile.

"Let's begin."

Queen Cheralin looked over the papers displayed before her on the table. Only when the papers were approved and piled high did she look up at the Council.

"I appreciate any and all updates you have given." The queen turned her attention to Velda. "I suspect we remain on track for a prosperous harvesting season, Velda?"

Velda stiffened as she spoke. "Yes, Your Majesty." Her high-pitched voice scratched in Sayr's ears. "I believe the City Center will be set by the end of next month."

"Excellent," Queen Cheralin said. She focused back on the pile of papers before her. "We can begin to prepare for the Harvest celebration as well. I will send my ladies to begin planning the events and invitations."

It took a good amount of Sayr's restraint to not roll her eyes at Marenda while the Council took turns giving their opinions on this year's color scheme for the Harvest Ball, what caterers should be employed for food, the important families that should be invited, and any other insignificant detail that Sayr stopped listening to.

The Harvest Ball was Visaran's biggest celebration of the year. Most villages outside the City Center celebrated the Harvest Festival with a feast, dancing, and the company of friends and family. In the palace, the royal family hosted the Harvest Ball for the most important families in the country, including any and all Court members.

The ball celebrated the end of the country's harvesting season, the busiest season of the year. It also wasn't supposed to take place for another four months. Sayr saw little reason to be discussing the color of tablecloths when she had more pressing matters to discuss with Her Majesty.

"Well then." Queen Cheralin smiled at Velda before turning her attention to Sayr. "If there is nothing else, I believe now is a suitable time to address why we are all here this morning. Sayr Rieve, I call on you to speak."

Her Majesty lifted a hand in Sayr's direction and Sayr rose from her seat to address the Council.

"Hello, Council." Her voice shook slightly, and she took a moment to ease her nerves before continuing. "I asked Her Majesty to assemble this meeting because I've recently had another vision."

The Council immediately deflated, a few members eyed her in disbelief and boredom. She lifted her chin and stared them down, unwilling to back down. She'd felt a lot of frustration towards the Council over the past two years. Few of them had any faith in her gifts and even fewer accepted her as a true Council member.

The queen had ordered that she bring all of her visions to the Council, and many times her visions held so little detail or were so brief that she had little to no information to offer the Council. In turn, many of them believed her gifts did not exist at all, and that she was simply a non-Elemental posing as a Seer to gain the queen's favor. She'd had a handful of visions that proved her gifts were both real and useful to the wellbeing of the kingdom, but still the Council refused to take her seriously.

She tried to swallow her growing anger and continued, "This vision isn't like any other that I've had before. Recently, I've been having the same vision over again for the past couple weeks."

She took a quick breath to begin retelling what she had seen when Baldric raised a hand to stop her. "If you've been having repeating *visions*," he spat out the last word, "then why are we just now hearing about this?"

Sayr turned to look him in the eye. Her thoughts ignited with vicious words that she wanted to spew at him but swallowed them down. Her position in Court was fragile enough. She wouldn't let him get to her, not if she wanted to keep her position in the Queen's Court, and her life here.

"I can't call on my *visions*," she spat back at him, "whenever I want. Many times, they come to me before I can call on them. I don't have full control over what I see or how often I see it."

Baldric barely glanced at her, and Sayr's irritation turned her cheeks red. "You say this has been happening for weeks, and yet you have just now decided to tell us? If you can take this long to address it, I do not see how it can be of much importance to us."

Rage burned up Sayr's throat, her patience dangerously thin. None of them understood how much convincing it took to request a meeting with the Council or that she'd had the vision twice during the time it took for them all to come together.

"If you'd let me finish," she spoke through gritted teeth, "then maybe you can decide that for yourselves."

"Yes, please tell us more," Victoria spoke up. "Where exactly do you see this vision taking place?"

Sayr hesitated a moment and braced herself for the reaction she was about to receive. "I'm actually not sure exactly where it takes place, but I know it's not—"

Baldric barked out a laugh, cutting Sayr off, and turned his attention towards the queen. "Your Majesty, the girl is having daydreams, not visions that can be of any use to us."

Marenda slammed a hand on the table. Her voice seethed as she spoke. "You dare disrespect Her Majesty, who chose to put Sayr on this Council? You know nothing about her gift, and because of that you ignore all of this? Shut your mouth and let her speak, then let the Council decide what to do next."

Baldric looked at Marenda, aghast. His face turned red with embarrassment and anger. "Why, you little—"

Queen Cheralin shot up from her seat. The Council became silent as they all turned their attention towards her. She shifted her gaze to Baldric before speaking loud enough for every member to know she was addressing them all.

"Sayr's gifts may be unknown, but these visions are useful in understanding what lies ahead for my kingdom." The queen's gaze flitted over each member of the Council.

"I do not think I need to remind any of you which of her visions have come true, and the urgency that these visions should be dealt with. If she is having this vision repeatedly, as she says she is, then I suspect these coming events are more urgent than we know. Now, I suggest we all give her enough patience to tell us what this vision is, *without interruption.*"

The queen's voice was sharp as she finished. Each Council member nodded in agreement, mumbling apologies. None bothered to apologize to Sayr. She gave the queen a small nod of thanks before continuing and described her vision to the Council in as much detail as she could muster. Once she had finished, she bowed her head and sat back down.

The Council discussed back and forth about when and where her vision was most likely to occur based on the information she gave and what they could do to spin the upcoming events in their favor.

"Northow is the only city in Visaran that is remotely close to large expanses of forests, these events must be taking place there," Danil said.

"The vision does not seem to be happening anywhere near civilization," Victoria noted and pinched the bridge of her nose. "We cannot look solely at locations near Visarian cities or towns."

"We've already passed the driest season of the year," Larse spoke up. "These events may not even take place until next summer!"

The Council decided that each member be assigned a piece of the country's map to locate any possible threat of wild or man-made fire that could burn their crops or trees to ash. Evidently, nothing useful came out of the meeting.

Ridiculous, Sayr thought. There was no doubt in her mind that the Council had been so lenient about finding a solution because the vision only consisted of her and a complete stranger.

"There is one last topic that I must discuss with you all before we disband." Her Majesty massaged her temple with two manicured fingers. "I delayed this meeting until I was certain of what is to come. I have requested that my personal guard be present to this meeting for this specific topic."

Everyone turned their attention to Marenda who sneered right back at them, clearly still unhappy with them all.

"I have spoken with the Western King," Her Majesty announced. "King Mylan of Creobe has requested an audience here in Visaran. The king entered Visarian territory eight days ago and he and his Court will arrive here in two days."

Everyone's heads snapped from Marenda back to the queen. Velda gasped loudly and quickly clamped a hand over her mouth. Others began murmuring questions and words of disbelief to one another. Sayr couldn't completely hide her own shock. She couldn't remember the last time anyone from Visaran had visited the Western Kingdom, or anyone from Creobe had entered their own territory.

The two kingdoms had coexisted peacefully enough for centuries as far as Sayr knew, although the citizens from both countries were forbidden from traveling back and forth to either kingdom. She'd heard stories of the royal families meeting within each other's borders but never expected to witness the royals' meeting, especially within the Eastern Palace where she would no doubt get a glimpse of the Western Court, herself.

"I understand this turn of events may not be welcomed by everyone in my Court; however, I believe it would be best not to anger King Mylan by denying his request. Therefore, my decision to meet with the Western King is non-negotiable."

Her Majesty turned her attention back to Marenda. "I have asked you here to inform you of this news, and to warn you not to tell another being outside of these walls. I also have a private order for you. I am giving the order to double your shifts as my personal guard while the Western Court is here, and to select an additional Royal Guard for both the crown prince and princess. We must ensure safety more than ever while the Western Court is within my palace."

Marenda discussed soldiers with Queen Cheralin and eventually gave two names for who would personally guard the prince and princess; Ajax, a recruit who had joined about eight months ago but climbed the ranks quickly, and Marcel, a soldier who had been in the Queen's Army for a little over a year before being initiated into the Royal Guard.

Queen Cheralin looked at Sayr again. "I am giving you an order as well. Your gifts are rare, if not completely unique to you and you only, and you are one of my stealthiest and most skilled soldiers. I have no doubt that part of the Western King's intentions in coming here is to see my Court in its entirety for himself. He will likely deploy members of his own Court to inquire about my people. I want you to do the same for me. Watch the Western Court as much as you can without raising suspicion. Find out who in King Mylan's Court are most valuable to him and what their positions are, and report back to me."

Sayr picked at her nail while she thought. She'd heard stories of the cruel king in the west since she'd arrived in the palace eight years ago. "Do we have any idea how big his Court is? How many people may be traveling here with him?"

Queen Cheralin nodded. "I approved only the king's inner Court, though he only listed five other names coming with him. The king has six royal carriages carrying him and his Court, footmen, guards, and a few servants."

"Still, six royal carriages seem like a lot for such a small group," Sayr noted. "It's certainly something to keep an eye on."

A new thought stirred in Sayr's mind. "I will watch these people, and report everything back to you, but what if they get too close and start asking about my abilities? I can't exactly show off any Elemental abilities to keep them from getting suspicious."

"The king and I have an agreement that none of our people will use any sort of abilities on the other's Court," Cheralin answered. "Anyone who does so will be severely punished, especially if Mylan disregards our agreement while in my palace. I will not have him come into these walls and create havoc among my people."

Sayr nodded. "Of course, Your Majesty."

The queen stood from her seat at the head of the table. The rest of the Council stood quickly after and lifted a hand to their chests just above their hearts.

"There is strength in duty," the queen recited the kingdom's proverb.

"There is strength in duty," the Council repeated.

Her Majesty's guards followed her out of the room and the rest of the Council made to leave as well.

Sayr pondered everything the queen had said while the rest of the Council parted ways. Her Majesty said the king would likely try and gather intel on their Court, just as Sayr would do for her queen. She needed to gather information before they arrived, which guest wing they would be staying in, what their daily routines would be, and if anyone knew what sort of Elementals would make up the Western Court.

Sayr turned back towards the exit. There was one person she knew who may be able to offer some of that information to her.

She quickly made her way down the twisting halls towards the outskirts of the palace. The farther she got from the center of the palace, the more the halls transformed from white quartzite to thick glass. Each hallway was lined with floor-to-ceiling windows and domed by impenetrable glass, reflecting the bright sky above.

If her predictions were correct, as they usually were, the person she was looking for would be heading towards the royal gardens. She made her way through the halls until she could just make out a figure walking through the halls adjacent from her, their figure distorted through the many glass panes separating them. Sayr smiled and slunk past a corner, down the hall, and rounded another corner to the hall where a man was walking, his back towards her.

Sayr's footsteps were silent as she snuck up on the man. She was within arm's reach of him before he sensed her presence, and she swiped the dagger from its hilt at his hip just as he turned in her direction.

"Hey!" the man cried out and turned toward her. Sayr dipped under the man's arm and stepped around him. He turned again and looked at her in surprise.

"I've always envied this dagger," Sayr sighed in admiration. She weighed the dagger perfectly on one finger, examining the long, slender blade and thick hilt.

"I'll never understand how you manage to do that." Everett frowned at Sayr. "I'm going to have to start watching my back constantly or have a guard walk with me to keep you from snagging my weapons."

He swiped at the dagger and Sayr let him take it back. Everett began walking again and Sayr kept pace next to him. "I came looking for you," she told him.

"May I ask why?" he teased.

Sayr looked around the open halls. This was not the place to talk so openly, where their voices could easily echo through multiple halls.

"Are you heading to the royal gardens?" she asked. "Mind if I tag along? We can talk there."

Everett's frown dissolved and a wide smile took its place.

"I don't mind at all." His voice offered the same excitement that showed on his face. "I'd appreciate the company."

Everett took a small step away and offered her his arm, which she gladly took. She smiled back at him, and they continued through the glass hall together. They walked side by side, turning down another glass hallway. He put his hand against an ornate glass door and pushed.

The warm, late-summer air swept into the hallway and the sound of the ocean waves crashing into the cliffs was music to Sayr's ears. She bounced down the steps and into the royal gardens.

The gardens were stunning. The colorful flowers were so vibrant that they often gave Sayr headaches if she stared at one spot for too long. The perfectly trimmed bushes that lined the exterior walls of the palace were thick with flowers of every color Sayr could imagine. She inhaled deeply; the almost sickeningly sweet scent of the florals and salty ocean air made her senses spin with delight.

Everett led her down one of the many cobblestone paths into a grassy area surrounded by white and pink hydrangeas. To the right sat a bench carved from pale stone and a beautiful fountain just behind it. The fountain calmly bubbled as the water poured down three levels and into the basin.

Sayr expected Everett to lead her towards the bench, but he veered off the cobblestone path into the grass and sat down. Sayr plopped down across from him and crossed her legs. Her eyes scanned his face as he leaned back, closed his eyes, and lifted his face to the sun.

Everett was paler than Sayr, most likely from being forced to spend most of his hours inside. His blond hair glinted in the sunlight. His broad nose was tipped towards the sky as he soaked in the sun and Sayr couldn't help herself as her eyes scanned down to his strong jaw, his lips forming a small smile. He had a strong build to him, but Sayr had no doubt that she could take him down in a fight. She let her own smile form at the thought of someone as regal and formal as him lounging in the grass of these gardens.

He brought his face back down and opened his eyes to look at Sayr.

"Now." He pulled one knee up to his chest. "What purpose do you have for sneaking up on me like that?"

Sayr leaned back and twined her fingers through the soft grass. She surveyed the garden, looking for any extra eyes or ears on them. When she didn't see anyone else in the gardens, she turned her attention back on Everett.

"I just had a lovely conversation with your mother, actually," she said.

Everett's smile faltered a bit. "So, you were coming from the Council meeting?"

Sayr nodded in response.

"She told me about the Western Court coming to the palace," Everett added.

"What do you know of the Western Court?" Sayr asked.

As the Crown Prince of Visaran, Everett knew almost as much as his mother when it came to the Western Court, if not more. Everett commanded his own troops within the Queen's Army and attended political meetings with his mother. He also had a much deeper interest in the kingdom to the west of Visaran and its people, which made him the perfect resource for Sayr.

Everett let out a small breath. "The Western Court is a complex web of people," he started. "It appears the king has Courts within Courts. I believe he is bringing one of these smaller Courts with him."

"That must be the Court that's closest to him, then," Sayr assumed. "The Court that is most loyal to him or answers only to him, at least."

"Every Court answers to their throne," Everett countered.

"Yes, but people within many Courts have other priorities like political gain or status," Sayr countered. "If the king is bringing his closest Court with him, that Court would likely be filled with people already given the highest positions and therefore will do anything to keep those positions."

Everett grinned at Sayr. "You've been spending far too much time in those Council meetings. They've turned you into a political machine."

Sayr grinned back proudly. "Do you know what kind of Elementals make up this inner Court? And which guest hall they'll be staying in?"

"My mother is having the guest halls in the North Wing prepared for the Western Court," Everett answered. He turned his attention away from Sayr and towards the hydrangea bushes. "As far as their elements, I'm not exactly sure what sort of Elementals make up this group."

He glanced back at Sayr. "But I know they are not like you."

The two shared a knowing look. Sayr knew they would not be like her. There was no one else like her on the continent, with abilities outside of the natural elements; air, earth, water, and fire. The queen held her and her gifts in high regard, offering her protection in the Eastern Palace from those who would try to kill her for her unnatural gifts, so long as she continued to be useful to the Eastern Crown. Others hated her for her position in the Court, believing she was a non-Elemental.

The Eastern Court still held a lingering prejudice against non-Elementals. Non-Elementals happily lived all over the country as farmers, shop owners, and obtained other jobs that were available outside of the palace, but Her Majesty only kept the strongest Elementals in her Court. Every Royal Guard, high official, and aristocrat in her Court was a Fire, Water, Air, or Earth Elemental. Apparently, Sayr's gift had passed the queen's test, and she was permitted into the Court as well.

As far as the Court knew, a seventeen-year-old girl with supposedly no ability had been offered the position of a Councilman's apprentice and a well-ranked soldier within the Queen's Army. Many of the Court officials envied her even more for the fact that she had gotten the position with no special abilities, or so they thought. The Queen's Court was supposed to be built from the strongest Elementals, not someone like her. They did not know how much of a lie her position, or her life, truly was.

But Everett was her oldest friend and because of him, she could never refuse his mother. She was fully aware that Her Majesty kept her close only to keep an eye on her, but Everett was different. He was only a year older than her and the first child she had met when she moved into the palace eight years ago. She had visited the palace many times before then, but no one truly believed that she had a gift outside of the elements.

Until she had a vision of King Luzan, Everett's father, falling ill with fever. She could remember as clear as day coming to the palace with her father to tell the royal family what she had seen. No one had taken her seriously during any of her previous visits, but this time was different. She wasn't even a decade old yet and His Majesty was in perfect health.

Four months later, the symptoms of fever began to show, and nearly eight months later the king had succumbed to the illness. After the king's death, the queen became the sole ruler of Visaran and Everett quickly had to prepare for kinghood at such a young age.

Visaran's rules for the monarchy stated that both king and queen were equal rulers of the country. Once King Luzan married Queen Cheralin, they became equal rulers. When a ruler died, their power fell to their spouse before their children or siblings. Therefore, Queen Cheralin remained the Eastern Queen after her husband's death, and Everett would not become king until his mother's death or her descent from the throne.

Everett never blamed Sayr for his father's death. He never blamed her for the outcomes of her visions. He was not afraid of her visions. When she was around Everett, they could pretend like they were normal friends, not a crown prince and a Seer.

Sayr pushed the darkening thoughts from her mind.

"Of course they are not like me." She pushed the small kernel of disappointment deep down. "But it would help to know what sort of Elementals they are before they arrive."

"It would," Everett admitted. "But both royals agreed that their people will not use any Elemental abilities against one another while the Western Court is here."

"I don't like to put all my trust in the words of others," Sayr challenged. "I'd like to be prepared just in case."

"Is this another order from my mother?" Everett asked. "To learn about them?"

"And to watch them while they're here," Sayr admitted. "Do some investigating for Her Majesty."

Everett raked a hand through his hair. "I admire your dedication to always do as you're told, but I hope you're taking care of yourself, too."

"I'll think about myself when I'm accepted in Court, just as I am." Sayr's voice had turned icy.

"You are accepted, Sayr," Everett countered.

"Not as I am. Not by everyone in this Court." She sighed and leaned back further into the grass. "I wish I could be like you. It'd make acceptance much easier."

He raised an eyebrow at her. "You wish to be a prince who spends most of his time in war rooms and political meetings? That doesn't sound like you at all."

Sayr laughed. "No, it doesn't, and that's not what I meant. I wish I could be like you, and Mar, and everyone else. I understand my importance to the Court and to your mother, and I am forever grateful to her for giving me a position in her Court, but sometimes I wish for a normal life as a normal Elemental."

Everett gave her a reassuring smile. "I'm more than happy to help you with that. After all, I happen to come from a pretty strong family of Water Elementals."

Everett made a show of flexing his muscles and Sayr let out a small laugh. She watched him stand from their comfortable spot in the grass and make his way towards the fountain.

"You want to feel like a normal Elemental?" he called back to her. "Your days as a Water Elemental start now."

The water falling from the massive fountain glittered like liquid diamonds under the summer sun. Sayr stood next to Everett at its base, watching him focus on the water.

He took a settling breath and reached his hand into one of the falls of the fountain. When he brought his hand out, the water followed, and a liquid orb floated just above his palm. He smiled and looked from the makeshift sphere to Sayr.

"Water is always flowing," Everett explained as Sayr peered through the orb. "It doesn't take a single form, so you can will it to take any form you wish. Elemental manipulation is not the same for everyone, either. While I can manipulate and create water easily, there are many Water Elementals that can only manipulate already existing water."

Sayr inspected the orb. The water flowed in circular motions just above Everett's hand. She reached a finger to touch the manipulated water.

"Is this your gift?" Sayr asked. "To manipulate and create small forms of water?"

"Not exactly," Everett answered. "Water is different than the other elements. While Earth, Fire, and Air Elementals are limited to a piece of their element, many Water Elementals can manipulate or create water to a specific limit. My gifts extend beyond this, but I don't want to impress you too much too quickly."

Sayr elbowed Everett in the side. He let out a laugh and she smiled while she inspected the orb closer. Sayr knew Elementals had their limits on their gifts. She knew Earth Elementals in the Queen's Army who were limited to only manipulating small masses of dirt or rock, and others that could create entire pillars from the earth. She'd often trained against a Fire Elemental that could create and manipulate sparks but couldn't get them to grow into actual flames. Marenda's gift was the strongest gift she'd ever seen, though she suspected Everett's were just as strong, if not stronger.

Everett tossed the watery orb back into the basin of the fountain. "Your turn," he said to her.

Sayr's eyes snapped up to meet his. "I'm a Seer, Ev. As much as I'd like to possess Elemental abilities, I don't think this is how we change things. I can't just manipulate water simply because I wish it."

Everett nudged her shoulder and moved behind her to put his arms around hers. "I know that, but I can help make you feel like a normal Water Elemental, at least for a few moments."

He wrapped his arms around hers so that his hands cupped her own and led them into the fountain's basin. The water was cool and refreshing. Sayr closed her eyes and let the sensation come over her.

"Now, watch," Everett whispered into her ear and began pulling their hands out of the basin.

Sayr squinted one eye open while they slowly brought their hands out of the water. Another perfect orb of water floated just inches from her palms. The surface of the ball was so flawless that she could see her own reflection in it, and Everett's reflection standing right behind her. She let out an astonished breath of laughter and looked up at Everett for approval.

"See, that's all it takes to be a Water Elemental," he said and looked from the ball of water to her.

"It's pretty simple when you're doing all the work," Sayr teased.

Everett's grey eyes bored into Sayr's own sea blue eyes, and his smile grew bigger as they stood there, the ball of water still floating in their palms.

The watery orb began to shift in their hands. Sayr jolted and withdrew their hands to drop the ball back in the water at Everett's command, but it did not fall. The orb remained floating, stretching and warping itself into a thin line and zipped past them.

The two broke apart and turned to follow the thin stream of water as it swam through the gardens and settled into the palm of a slender girl in a baby pink dress standing next to the rosebushes.

The water shifted midair into a wide ring shape. With one hand on her hip, the girl stuck her other hand through the ring of water and snapped it around her wrist like a bracelet.

"Lanni!" Everett shouted and he waved his younger sister over.

Lanni extended a long leg and breezed down the garden path towards Everett and Sayr. Sayr glanced down at her wrist where the ring of water still spun as she approached.

"Impressive," Sayr remarked.

"Thank you." Lanni stretched her hand up towards her brother to show off her new piece of liquid jewelry.

"So, what reason do you have for Everett showing you his water tricks?" she asked and tossed her long, silver hair back over her shoulder. "Isn't being the sole person with an unnatural gift enough for you?"

"Lanni!" Everett thundered at his sister, but she only smirked at Sayr, who paid no attention to the harshness of her words.

Lanni typically came off a bit rude when she spoke, but Sayr appreciated the way she never filtered her thoughts. At least she knew how Lanni really felt about her, something she couldn't say for almost every other member of the Court.

Sayr knew Lanni was not afraid to speak her mind. After all, she doubted anyone would go against the Eastern Princess's word. While Everett was mostly bark, Lanni truly was all bite.

"Our mother has guests coming to Court," Everett started. Sayr quickly elbowed him in the side. Her Majesty hadn't mentioned whether or not Lanni knew about the Western Court yet.

"Ev was just showing me what it's like to be a Water Elemental," Sayr explained.

Lanni arched a perfect brow and lifted her wrist again to show off her bracelet. "Well, it just so happens that my lessons have been canceled today and I'm available to offer my expertise."

Everett snorted in response, knowing Lanni's 'canceled' lessons meant she had chosen to skip out on them. With a flick of her wrist, Lanni's bracelet transformed into a thin water whip that she slung at Everett's ear.

"Ouch!" He rubbed his sore ear and scowled at his sister. Sayr put a hand to her mouth to hide her smile.

"I'd start by showing her more than how to manipulate a pathetic ball of water," Lanni scolded her brother. "Really, Ev? You're the Crown Prince of Visaran, you're supposed to be the next strongest Water Elemental in the country and *that* is what you choose to do with your gift?"

Lanni flung her hand out towards the bushes and the water whip followed, slicing a bushel of roses off their stems. She turned to Sayr and crossed her arms.

"If this has anything to do with King Mylan coming to our Court, then I assume my mother has asked you to remain in hiding?" Lanni asked.

"The opposite, actually," Sayr said. "Her Majesty has asked me to spy on them while they're here, to learn about them and report any findings back to her."

"That's dangerous," Lanni warned. "Especially if they were to find out about your strange abilities."

Everett opened his mouth to reprimand his sister again, but Sayr spoke up first. "Both Courts are forbidden from using any abilities against each other. They won't get the chance to see if I possess any sort of Elemental abilities."

"Yes, I'm sure the king agreed to that, but you'd be surprised at how easily royals can find loopholes in their agreements." Lanni looked between Everett and Sayr. "I recommend you keep your distance. Even if you are being ordered to spy on their Court, you don't want them finding out more about you than you find out about them. And if that doesn't work, tell them you're a distant relative of the royal family and that is why you're here in the palace. Only as a last resort, though. Our mother would be furious to hear you're telling others that she is a distant relative of a non-Elemental."

With that, Lanni turned to walk back towards the palace. Sayr looked over at Everett, who only shrugged his shoulders. "She does have a point."

"Your mother would gut me if she found out I was posing as a non-Elemental relative of hers," Sayr said and nudged her shoulder against Everett's arm. "But she's right, I will need some sort of cover. Until the Western Court leaves, I am not a Councilman's apprentice or have any position worthy of a royal's attention. I am nothing more than a soldier in the Queen's Army."

The next two days flew by in a blur. Court guests were buzzing at the news of the Western Court's visit. Her Majesty had experts of every trade come to the palace to prepare. Polishers made the tiled floors of the palace shine like crushed jewels, the gardeners trimmed and planted new bushes in the tea gardens, servants dusted out the vacant guest rooms, and the kitchen staff were busy preparing only the best Visarian dishes.

Sayr spent most of the days at drills or attending brief meetings with Her Majesty. She rarely saw Everett or Marenda at all. Marenda was stuck with double shifts and Everett had other duties to tend to as the crown prince. Plus, the queen had ordered an official check up on her twice a day to see if she had any updates to offer Her Majesty, which Sayr knew quite well meant the queen was asking for any new information on her vision. Which, of course, the answer was a hard 'no' every time.

Sayr sat cross-legged on the floor of her bedroom facing the large windows. She kept her eyes closed to block out the setting sun. Her hands rested on her knees, and she kept her back straight. She slowed her breathing and kept her mind empty.

She waited in darkness, willing for something to happen. All thoughts left her mind as she focused on breathing in and out, in and out. Her senses began to fade as she felt the familiar tug at her core. A dim light appeared behind her eyelids in the distance, growing brighter and brighter until it was nearly blinding, and her eyes unwillingly flung open.

She found herself sitting in the middle of a decrepit forest. Trees surrounded her, burned and blackened and dead. She looked down at where she sat, there was no lush grass beneath her like in the palace gardens. Instead, grey ash covered every inch of the earthy floor for as far as she could see.

No breeze swept through the decaying trees or moved the ash that piled onto the ground. She stood and looked around the bleak forest, searching for someone.

She trudged through the ashy forest, reaching out to touch one of the blackened trunks of a tree. The blackened bark immediately began to dissolve under her touch, giving way piece by piece until the dead tree crumpled into ashy dust.

Something in the distance caught her eye, and she peered past the tree line. A figure stood far off in the trees, facing her. Watching her. A surge of familiarity hit her as the same vision began once again.

Without hesitating, she sprinted towards the figure, not willing to let them get away from her again. This time, she would catch them. She would not let them get away.

The figure ran, but Sayr was ready, and she sprinted full force in their direction. She inched closer and closer as the figure ran away from her. Her legs felt weak as she trudged through the muck and ash but her determination to reach the stranger grew with every inch that she neared. Panting hard, she was almost within arm's reach when she lunged for them.

Her hand wrapped around their dusty coat, her body still in midair, and she slammed into the person's back as they hit the ground.

The solid figure turned to ash and dust on impact, and she tumbled a few yards before landing on her back.

Breathing hard, she shot up to her feet. Black ash smeared across her face and hands and covered her clothes. She had never gone this far in the vision before. Every vision before this, she woke up chasing the figure, suffocating from the ash that stuck in her throat. She turned frantically, looking for the person she was supposed to be running after. She was supposed to wake up by now.

Only she was not waking up.

Her breathing turned shallow as her heart raced. She turned once more and nearly crashed into a man. She stumbled and fell back into the ashy earth.

Unlike the figure that was usually in her visions, she could make out every feature of this man's face, ruthless dark eyes, the scruff of a beard starting to grow in, and long chestnut brown hair. He looked down at her on the ground and let out a low, guttural laugh so deep it shook the ground beneath her.

"Who are you?" she asked frantically, scrambling against the ashy, decayed earth.

She should not be here. The vision was supposed to end.

She was *not* supposed to be here.

"Why am I still here?"

His grin turned sinister, and he opened his mouth to speak—

Sayr was suddenly yanked back by her core and out of the vision. She gasped as her eyes flung open and reality set in. She looked around, frantic, trying to take in the space around her. She was back in her bedroom still sitting on the floor. The sun had almost settled beneath the horizon.

Each of her senses began to come back to her one by one while she recalled where she had just been in the vision. Her arms and legs had grown numb and now a static, tingling sensation ran up and down each limb. Her eyes began to adjust to the lighting around her. Her tongue felt too big for her mouth, and she swallowed a few times.

Fog clouded her mind as she tried to remember where she was, who she was, and what she had been doing before the vision. Her hearing returned to normal, and she registered the faint sound of bells ringing in the distance. She focused on the bells, trying to remember the meaning for their ringing.

All at once, the realization hit her. She shot up to her feet, ignoring the numbness still in her legs. She pressed her nose against the windowpanes and looked out into the distance.

The City Center reflected the bronze light still lingering from the last few rays of setting sunlight. Her eyes trailed over the array of buildings and followed the main road that led to the palace, and widened when she spotted the parade of sleek, long carriages and the dozens of horses drawing them nearer to the palace.

Move, she screamed in her head, *Find Ev, get to the queen!*

She bolted for her wardrobe, threw on a pair of loose trousers and a tank top, strapped on a pair of sandals, and opened the door to the halls. No one had sent word yet, but she already knew what was happening.

The Western King had arrived at the Eastern Palace.

The throne room was overflowing with the Court's aristocrats and officials observing high up in the balconies. A heavy railing separated the spectators from the main floor below.

Sayr stood in a small space with the rest of the officials on the second level balcony. White stone pillars held up the stacked balcony levels on each side of the room. To her right was the only entrance to the throne room, two large doors that met at a sharp point at the top. The wall adjacent to the entrance was made up of three giant windows that looked out over the rocky cliff shores and ocean beyond.

The sun had set over the horizon and the candlelit chandeliers above ignited the large room in yellow light. Three golden thrones sat atop an elevated dais in front of the large windows.

Queen Cheralin sat on the middle throne. Her throne was the tallest and most intricate with golden armrests that twisted and flowed up into the back of the chair, settling into two sharp points at the top. She tapped a perfect nail against the armchair in clear impatience.

Everett and Lanni were seated on each side of the queen. The candlelight shone in the crystals of the chandelier above, warping shadows on each member of the royal family and twisting their features into something sharp and fierce.

Marenda stood at the base of the dais, dressed in her Royal Guard uniform and heavily armed. The tension in the room was suffocating as they all waited for the Western Court to appear through the large doors. Whispers floated through the balconies as Court members became restless, exchanging rumors and gossip that they had heard of the Western Kingdom.

"I heard that most of Creobe's population is made up of non-Elementals," one woman whispered behind Sayr.

A quiet giggle came from her left. "I heard that the king has no wife because of his many mistresses that he keeps in his Court. They all fight one another for the king's permanent attention."

"He may not have a wife," the first voice laughed softly, "but he likely has *many* heirs, then."

"The Western King is cruel to his subjects," a shaky voice added. "I hear he tortures his servants and lets his mistresses do whatever they please with non-Elementals for amusement."

Sayr rolled her eyes and looked around at the rest of the audience. Everyone had arrived in the throne room to get a peek at the Western King and his entourage. Some people had looks of giddy excitement on their faces while others appeared petrified by the incoming guests. Several long minutes passed before the giant doors opened and every person in the room held their breath in anticipation.

A small group entered the throne room; two men and three women. The women all wore the same floor-length gown. The material of the dresses climbed all the way to their throats and wrapped tightly at their necks. The sleeves were thick and drifted down to each girl's wrists, and the skirts of the dresses wrapped around their legs like wisps of smoke. The only difference was the varying pastel colors of each dress, pink, white, and light green. The men were dressed in thick shirts, pants, heavy boots, and heavily decorated in different leathers.

Sayr's eyes quickly flitted over each person in quick inspection. Her eyes lingered on one of the men in the group as he turned and claimed a spot beneath the balconies across from her.

The man leaned against one of the stone pillars while the rest of the group hung tightly together. None of them paid any attention to the guests on the balconies or the royals seated ahead of them, except for him.

His skin was tanned, and his raven black hair was shaved short on the sides and left longer at the top. A few strands toppled over his eyes while he stared ahead at the three terrifying thrones. A sneer formed on his lips when he took in the royal family, keeping his arms crossed over his chest as he stationed himself against the pillar.

A surge of fear hit Sayr as she watched him. The man's expression was fueled with hatred, and she suddenly became very afraid for the people in the room, especially Everett as he met the man's challenging glare with his own.

A second group entered through the doors and everyone's attention once again turned to the entrance.

Four Creobian guards entered the throne room, all surrounding one man. Once they had all entered, the doors to the throne room finally shut. The Creobian guards all stepped to the side, leaving the man in the middle to stand alone in the center of the throne room.

The man had deeply tanned skin and neatly trimmed, coffee brown hair. He wore a decadent black suit that was heavily embroidered in bronze-colored threads. His crown was the size of Lanni's tiara and about half as decorated with jewels. Instead, his was simpler, a few thick strands of gold entwined together to fit his head and dipped into a V-shape at his brow. His deep brown eyes creased in the corners as he smiled and spread out his arms to address the crowd around and above him.

"Ladies and gentlemen," he bellowed and made his way towards the thrones. "It is an honor to be in your beautiful country."

The man's voice held an odd, yet admittedly appealing, accent. He spoke quicker than most, connecting his words. The letters that Visarians hardened when speaking, he softened to create a more fluid sound.

"I am King Mylan."

The king remained standing in front of the dais, looking up at the thrones. The crowds standing in the balconies chuckled at the king's informal introduction. Sayr's gaze shifted from the king to the royal family still seated on their thrones.

Queen Cheralin simply offered the king a tight smile. To her left, Lanni seemed to enjoy the display before her. She chuckled along with the rest of the Court, her chin resting casually in her hand. Everett frowned down at the king. His hands tightly gripped the armchairs of his throne, and he sat pin straight.

A guard stationed by Marenda stepped forward in front of the dais and announced, "The Eastern Kingdom of Visaran presents Her Majesty, Queen Cheralin Lemay, and her children; Crown Prince Everett Lemay and Princess Elanor Lemay."

The royal family all stood when their names were announced, Lanni huffed when her introduction included her full name. Queen Cheralin finally stepped forward to address the Western King.

"Welcome to Visaran, King Mylan." She dipped her chin in greeting and both of her children mirrored the action. "We are thrilled to have you here in our Court."

The queen's words held as much warmth and welcoming as the ocean waves that crashed in the distance.

Sayr stopped listening to the royals exchanging fake pleasantries with each other. She craned her neck to get another look at the group that was undoubtedly King Mylan's inner Court. They were all still huddled together under the balconies. The three women all whispered to one another while the two men continued staring at the thrones, their eyes flicked back and forth between their king and Sayr's queen.

Sayr meandered through the glass halls of the palace. Marenda's double shifts with the queen left little time for her and Sayr to train so Sayr had decided to attend a training at the barracks with the rest of the Queen's Army. The Western Court had arrived at the palace just yesterday, she needed a distraction to keep her from seeking any of them out too soon.

She rounded a corner into a second glass hallway that peered into one of the many gardens in the palace. The garden was filled with leafy bushes and pearly white furniture, though no one sat at the tables. The gardens appeared completely empty, until Sayr's eye caught a couple tucked behind the tall bushes in one corner. Sayr rolled her eyes and paused a moment to look at the couple. If this was meant to be a secret rendezvous, the couple certainly wasn't doing a great job at hiding.

A young man was nestled up against a woman, his head tucked against her bare neck. Sayr couldn't see the man's face, but she immediately recognized the brown short cut hair, stocky shoulders, and pink-tinged skin from training long hours in the sun. Vic, a soldier in the Queen's Army, had his face burrowed against a girl and hands gripped around her wrists at her side. Sayr didn't recognize the girl and would have brushed her off as a sweetheart of Vic's if she hadn't taken notice of the girl's frightened face. Her hands were clenched into fists, and she kept yanking them to get free from Vic's grasp.

Sayr did not think before she opened the glass door to the gardens and prowled over to the couple. She made no noise as she approached Vic from behind. His face was buried so deep against the girl's neck, and the girl's focus was devoted to freeing herself from Vic that neither of them heard or saw Sayr.

"Please," the girl begged. "Just let me go."

Vic's voice came out muffled and quiet. "We're having fun, dear. And I haven't even started, just you wait."

Sayr forced herself not to lunge at Vic right then. She took out the dagger sheathed at her hip, twisting it in her fingers as she neared. She was directly behind him when she lifted the blade to Vic's neck, the sharp point pressed against his jugular. Vic's body stiffened and the girl's wide eyes flicked to Sayr.

"She said let her go." Sayr's voice was sharp. "I suggest you do just that."

Vic tried to crane his neck, then stopped when the tip of Sayr's blade pressed harder against his skin.

"Move back slowly, do not turn or I'll dig my blade in harder," Sayr ordered.

Vic released his grip on the girl's wrists and the girl immediately pushed her body away from him, backing further into the bushes behind her. Vic lifted his hands above his shoulders and took one, two, three steps away from the girl. He did not dare turn and look at Sayr.

"Unstrap your belt and set your sword on the grass," Sayr instructed.

Vic didn't utter a word while he did as Sayr ordered. He unslung the belt that held his sword from his hip and threw it to the ground.

"Now kick it away."

Vic paused and Sayr pressed the dagger further against his neck until a bead of blood dripped down the blade. Vic kicked the sword and belt away from him. The sword landed in the dirt at the bottom of a bush.

Sayr turned her gaze from Vic to the girl still standing in the bushes. Her arms were held tightly to her chest and her whole body shook. The sword rested just a few feet from her. Sayr flicked her gaze from the girl to the sword and back again. The girl's eyes looked down, locked on the sword, and flitted back to Sayr. Sayr nodded, and the girl bent low to pick the sword up and clutched it close to her body. Sayr reached out an arm towards her and opened her hand. The girl glanced at Vic and then back to Sayr. She pried herself from the bushes towards Sayr and lifted a shaky hand to grab Sayr's own. Sayr softly pulled the girl behind her.

"Now turn," Sayr ordered Vic.

She released the pressure of the blade just enough for Vic to turn and face her. His eyes narrowed in a heated glare as he looked down at Sayr, then at the girl standing behind her.

"The fun's over," Sayr said. "You're going to go back to the barracks and *have fun* by yourself. And if I see you bothering her again, or anyone else against their will, I won't give a second warning before my blade hits an artery."

Vic's nostrils flared as he remained still. "You wouldn't dare," he challenged. "General Kline would have you flayed, himself, for killing a member of the Queen's Army."

"I'm sure Councilman Danil would forgive his apprentice for defending a helpless girl and defend me against the general. After all, a Councilman's word goes much farther than a general's." In one motion, Sayr lowered the dagger and took several steps back. She kept the girl behind her. "We're going, but if you go looking for her again, I will know. And then I'll come looking for you."

Vic glared at Sayr and the girl as they retreated but did not say a word or move a muscle while Sayr guided the girl back into the glass hallway. She kept her eyes on Vic while they walked. Once she could no longer see him through the glass, she sheathed the dagger and released the girl's hands.

"What's your name?" Sayr asked. "And what's your position in Court?"

"Carla, milady," the girl said. Her whispered voice shook just as much as her body. "I–I am a lady's maid for Lady Paloma."

Sayr nodded. She knew of Lady Paloma, and though she did not know her well, she knew Lady Paloma was one of the kinder members of the Court. If she heard this girl's story, she would likely offer her protection, at least for today.

"Go to Lady Paloma's rooms and tell her what happened, as much as you're comfortable with sharing. She will offer you protection and keep you there," Sayr said. "If she doesn't, then get to the kitchens and find Neil, he is a chef. He will keep you hidden and protected."

Carla nodded. "Go on," Sayr assured and gave the girl a small push in the direction of the West Wing where Lady Paloma's rooms were. Carla hurried off down the hall.

Sayr remained in place, watching the girl until she was out of sight. She let out a deep breath and ran a hand over her face.

Vic would come after her, not now but certainly later. Sayr knew she could handle him, but if he ran his mouth to another soldier or General Kline… she wasn't so sure Councilman Danil or Her Majesty's protection would fully prevent any sort of punishment that would come her way. Sayr would have to be careful over the next few days. Most of the soldiers in the Queen's Army knew of her position as a Councilman's apprentice, but that did not protect her from anything that could happen to her outside of Council meetings. As long as she was able to attend the meetings, any ill-treatment would be overlooked.

"That was very noble of you." A voice came from behind Sayr, and she whipped around, one hand back on her dagger.

Three girls stood in the middle of the hall, staring at Sayr. One stood in front of the other two with a sly smile plastered on her face.

"We didn't want to interrupt," the leader said. "But I believe we're a bit lost."

Sayr recognized the girls. They were part of the Western Court, part of the first group to arrive in the throne room. These were the girls Sayr had been ordered to follow and spy on, and yet they had been the ones following her.

The leader stepped closer. She was about eye level with Sayr and had thick, ash brown hair that hung past her shoulders. She had thick brows and angular dark eyes.

"Where are you headed?" Sayr asked. Her eyes moved from the leader to inspect the two other girls behind her.

The girl on her left had deep brown skin and short, coiled hair. She had a small nose and eyes that looked out into the gardens. The girl on the right was much shorter than the other two. Her skin was paler, and her fire-red hair was pulled into two long braids over each shoulder.

"We were just on our way to the tea gardens, but we can't seem to find where they might be," the leader said. Her eyes slunk past Sayr down the hall where Carla had gone. Sayr took a step towards the middle of the hall and widened her stance, making it impossible for the girls to get past her.

"You're heading away from the tea gardens; they're back that way." Sayr jutted her chin past the girls. "You should've passed them if you've made it this far through the outskirts of the palace."

The leader squinted as she examined Sayr. "You're angry," the girl thought aloud. "And anxious."

"I'm sorry?" Sayr said in surprise. She *was* angry after encountering Vic with the girl, but she thought she'd hid her anger well.

"No need to apologize," the girl assured Sayr, but her pleasant smile turned sinister. "But you can beg for forgiveness, anyway."

The two girls behind her giggled as they all stared Sayr down. They all stood frozen for a moment. Sayr had no idea what to say. What was she supposed to be asking their forgiveness for? She hadn't done anything wrong, and her apology was for clarification, not forgiveness.

"Go on," the leader prompted. "Don't you feel sorry? Get on your knees and beg me for forgiveness."

Sayr felt a strange tingling sensation in her limbs and a familiar, faint tug at her core. Her pulse quickened and her body broke into a cold sweat.

Not now! Her mind screamed as the familiar sensation of an oncoming vision came over her. She was supposed to hide her gifts, if she were to be pulled into a vision now then these girls would certainly know something was different about her.

Only, no vision came to her. She hadn't realized she had still been staring back at the leader as fear and panic took over her. The brunette's sinister smile quickly dropped into a frown and her brow creased in concentration.

Sayr needed to get out of the halls. *Now.* A vision could still take over her, and if it did, she would only be safe back in her suite.

"Excuse me," Sayr said as calmly as she could muster before turning back around and traipsing towards the center of the palace.

She took one small glance back at the girls. The other two began walking in the opposite direction but the leader of the pack still stood in place, staring at Sayr in confusion as she walked away.

Sayr turned the first two corners quickly and looked through the windows of the hall to make sure she could no longer see the girls before breaking into a run. She sprinted through the palace, not caring about the Court officials that hissed at her as she ran past. In a matter of minutes, she was in the East Wing and darting to her suite.

She threw open the door and collapsed onto the floor of her bedroom. The cool floor eased her sweat-slicked body, and she stayed crumpled on the ground. Her panting breaths eventually evened out and the tingling in her limbs began to fade. The only indication of her hysteria was the shaking throughout her body that would not stop.

She hadn't lost her hearing, or her vision or taste, as she always did during a vision. The tug in her core had disappeared, leaving an empty feeling in her center. Nothing had come to her. Not a new vision or the recurring one she had been having for weeks.

Nothing.

5

$\mathcal{F}$our days had passed since the Western King had come to Court. The gossip and excitement had begun to die down and Sayr's daily schedule resumed as normal.

She spent the late morning back on the training grounds with her training unit. The first hour of training was spent refining combat skills and practicing new techniques.

An Earth Elemental trainee was positioned across from Sayr in the fighting pit. Sayr had never trained with her before, but she'd seen her face off with a few other soldiers and knew she often won more fights than she lost.

The two took their defensive stances, each waiting for the other to take the first shot. Sayr's muscles tensed with anticipation. She liked starting on defense, it gave her the opportunity to witness her opponent's skill and speed before she struck.

Her opponent quickly took offense, leaping into the air and slamming a foot into the ground. A low rumble shook the ground below them, growing stronger as the earth cracked in Sayr's direction. The earth shook so hard that she could feel the vibrations in her knees and hips. The ground below her split in two, a deep slit in the ground about two feet wide.

Sayr quickly stumbled back and rolled her body away from the attack. She looked over in surprise at the parted earth, her opponent was stronger than Sayr had presumed. When she looked up, the girl was already over her, swinging her blunt axe down on Sayr. Sayr met the axe with her daggers.

They pushed against each other. Sayr took one step backwards and leaned back slightly. Her opponent stumbled forward, not expecting Sayr to let go so suddenly. Sayr pivoted and turned as her opponent fell, facing the girl's back, and kicked her down to the ground. A faint voice yelled in the distance, but Sayr ignored it.

Another low rumble trembled through the earth. Sayr expected another slit to appear beneath her and made to move, but the ground rose with her. The dirt of the pit twisted and clawed up Sayr's leg. The Earth Elemental had her trapped in one spot.

Elements, the girl was strong. Sayr's opponent was able to manipulate the earth in the pits, and the ground was now twisting and trapping Sayr's leg. She was quickly losing the fight.

Another voice called again, closer this time. She paid no attention to it as her opponent advanced.

Sayr's right leg was consumed by the earth up to her knee. The dirt had solidified once again, making the trap inescapable in so little time as the Earth Elemental leapt at Sayr. She quickly lifted her other leg onto the dirt trap and bent so both legs were even and secure before leaning far back, her hair splayed against the earth as her opponent reached her.

The Earth Elemental had planned to attack Sayr at the head, not expecting her to be able to bend so close to the ground in her trapped position. The tension in Sayr's legs and abdomen tightened as she kept herself horizontal. Her opponent flew over her, and Sayr swung her blunt dagger at the girl's ribs.

The girl yelped and tumbled to the ground. Sayr took the extra moments to jab the hilt of her other dagger into the hard earth around her leg to try and free it. The hilt created a spiderweb's crack and the pressure on her leg loosened, but she'd used too much time.

Another deep rumble crept through the earth, splintering the ground around her. Sayr swiveled around as far as she could with her leg facing the opposite direction while her opponent neared. She bent low with her free leg to swipe her dagger into the girl's thigh just as her opponent swung her axe down at Sayr's shoulder.

"Sayr Rieve!" a voice shouted from the edge of the fighting pit.

The two girls instantly froze, their weapons still displayed. Sayr panted hard and silently thanked each of the elements for the distraction, as she had likely been seconds from getting an axe planted in her shoulder. The two turned their attention to the drill instructor standing at the edge of their training pit.

"You've been called to meet with the crown prince," the greying instructor barked at Sayr. "In fact, you've been called several times."

Sayr looked at the general, realizing where the yelling had come from. "My apologies, sir." She dipped her head in respect.

"I'm not the one you should be apologizing to. You should be apologizing to the Crown," the instructor scolded. "Pay more attention."

The instructor walked off, already shouting another soldier's name. Sayr looked over at her opponent and held out her hand.

"Good fighting," she said.

The Earth Elemental took her hand. "Good fighting."

The pressure on Sayr's leg disappeared as her opponent released her from the trap, settling the dirt back into place and mending the slit in the ground on the other side of the pit.

"You didn't use any Elemental abilities," the girl noted. "Are you a non-Elemental?"

Sayr's defenses sprang up. "I can fight just fine without the advantages of an element," she shot back.

"Never said you couldn't." The girl's tone was casual, as if they were exchanging training tips. "I don't doubt your fighting abilities, it's just rare to see a non-Elemental in the Queen's Army. You must be quite skilled if you've made it this far."

The girl didn't wait for a response from Sayr before twirling her axe over one shoulder and walking off the training pit. Sayr picked up her daggers and looped them back through her belt before jogging off the training grounds. She had made it past the weapons compartment before letting herself smile. She jogged up to the palace and entered through a door to the East Wing and into her suite.

She didn't have enough time to bathe and resorted to washing her face and neck before pulling on a pair of wide legged linen pants and a tan colored top. She strapped on a pair of sandals and headed out of her suite towards the royal gardens.

Everett was already waiting for her in his favorite garden. He was again lounging in the grassy area, this time next to the pink gardenias. His smile widened as she approached, and he rose from his spot in the grass. He wore brown trousers and a light cotton shirt under a thin, hooded cloak. He handed her a cloak of her own when she reached him.

"Your Highness." She gave a playful bow. "Thank you for taking the time to meet with me."

He chuckled at her as she pulled on the cloak. "Let's get going before anyone sees us."

※

The streets of the City Center were busy with people pushing in and out of shops and down the streets. The heat of the late summer sizzled through the Center, and its citizens were desperate to find any sort of relief from the sweltering sun.

Sayr and Everett sat at a small table at the Steam Room, Sayr's favorite café. She sipped her iced coffee and watched the shoppers pass by while Everett bobbed the tea bag up and down in his cup.

The people of the City Center had learned to combine their Elemental gifts with modern-day science to create amazing advancements in the capital. Many Elementals became rich off their new inventions; freezing mechanisms that let Water Elementals create ice instantly, temperature-controlled machines that let Air and Fire Elementals heat or cool entire rooms, and architectural advancements that made Earth Elemental's construction trades ten times easier and more efficient. While Sayr appreciated the advancements, she liked whatever invention allowed her to sip an iced coffee in the late summer heat the most.

Sayr kept the hood of her cloak around her shoulders to let the sun settle on her face. Everett kept his hood up well over his head, the cloak shadowing his features to keep him from being recognized.

The cloaks were light and thin, and offered refreshing shade as well as coverage from anyone recognizing their crown prince wandering through the streets. The people of the City Center were mild enough towards the Crown that neither of them worried about him being bothered if recognized, but Everett's personal guards always insisted they wear the cloaks and keep a dagger at each hip. The guards also insisted that they come along. Sayr snuck a look behind Everett where they sat two tables away and dressed very similarly to Everett. One pretended to keep his nose stuck in a book while the other made no motion of secrecy, watching Sayr and Everett with eagle's eyes.

"Thank you for bringing me here," Sayr started and focused her attention back on Everett. "You have no idea how much I needed to get away for a while."

Everett smiled at her and continued steeping his tea. "Of course. This week has been stressful for everyone, but I'm happy to help you find relief."

"Next time try getting me out of a Council meeting," she joked. "Those seem to be getting worse each time I'm called to attend them."

Everett's smile dropped and his features turned serious. "I don't mind taking you out of drills since you work with Marenda in the mornings, but Council meetings are important. It's an honor for Her Majesty to have put you on the Council, you should take it seriously."

Sayr rolled her eyes at her friend and watched the passersby in the streets, ending the conversation.

Queen Cheralin was Everett's own mother; he didn't need to address her as *Her Majesty* like the rest of them did. She continued watching the busy City Center when she spotted two familiar faces walking in their direction and her breath hitched.

Two of the girls that she'd run into in the palace halls were heading right towards her and Everett. One of the girls was missing from the group—the short, red-haired girl—leaving the brunette leader accompanied by the girl with short, coiled hair. Sayr watched them closely as they strolled along, shopping bags in each of their hands.

"Ev, have you seen those two girls in the palace?" Sayr asked and nodded in their direction.

Everett turned his attention towards the bustling streets and paled as he spotted the girls. He quickly hunched over the table, drawing his cloak farther over his face.

Sayr took the cue and pulled her own cloak over her head. Her body tensed at Everett's reaction, and she raised an eyebrow at him, waiting for a response.

"They are part of King Mylan's Court." He leaned closer to her over the table and whispered.

"That one there is Willa." He pointed to the dark-skinned girl. "I've seen her passing through the gardens."

"The royal gardens?" Sayr asked. "How does she have access to them? I thought they were restricted to certain members of the Eastern Court."

Everett nodded. "King Mylan requested that she have access to the gardens. He said she enjoys the outdoor spaces in Creobe and thought having access to our gardens would make her feel more at home, but I don't believe it. She lingers around whenever I'm there, always walking on the same path as me or following close by."

Sayr's eyes followed the girls as they reached the street corner and turned. A Royal Guard followed close behind them. Citizens of the City Center gawked at the guard as they passed, not bothering to look at the girls ahead of him. They passed by the café on the other side of the street, too busy looking in the windows of the shops to see her or Everett.

Once they were out of sight, Sayr finally spoke again. "I ran into them and another girl in the palace the other day. They acted so strange when I spoke to them."

Everett's head snapped towards her, his cloak almost falling off to reveal his face. His grey eyes were wide and unmoving as he looked at her, mirroring his mother's cold steel stare. "What did they do to you?"

"They didn't *do* anything. It's what they said that threw me off. I ran into them in one of the outer halls. They were nice enough, I guess, just odd. They asked me for directions and then the brunette told me I was 'angry and anxious'. I was, at the time, but she said it so strangely. Then she told me to beg for forgiveness and just stood there—like that was exactly what she expected me to do. She looked very disappointed when I left without doing so."

Everett's stare narrowed while she spoke, nearly glaring as she told him what had happened. He barely gave her time to finish before grabbing her wrist and standing, dragging her up with him.

"We're leaving." His voice was final.

"But I'm not finished yet." She reached back for her coffee, still half full.

Everett's grip on her wrist tightened as he pulled her from the table.

"*Now.*"

Everett nodded to his guards who immediately stood and followed closely behind while Everett hustled towards the streets, his hold still strong on Sayr's arm.

They blended into the crowds of the City Center. No one gave them a second glance as Everett pushed through the crowd. Anger blossomed in Sayr's chest, and she twisted to get out of his grip, failing with every attempt.

"Everett, let go of me!"

He turned into an alleyway and whirled her against the wall. She flinched at the impact of the brick against her back and looked up at him towering over her.

His eyes were wild with fear when he spoke. "I'm sorry, Sayr, but you have to listen to me. Do not speak with anyone from Creobe while they are here. Do not go anywhere near them, you're already at risk of being discovered with them in the palace."

"I haven't done anything wrong." Sayr shook her head. Why was she pleading her innocence to her oldest friend?

He let out a shuddered breath and closed his eyes, the two of them frozen against the alley wall. When he opened them, he looked far beyond Sayr or the wall behind her.

"You don't know these people, Sayr," he whispered. "They are not like us."

She shrunk away from him, her back digging into the brick wall. She glanced away from Everett and back towards the street to ensure no one was watching. She didn't want to make a scene in the city, especially with the crown prince. Where were Everett's guards? Why was Everett being so careless, pushing her against the wall of an alleyway in the middle of the City Center?

Without daring to look back at her friend, she asked, "Is there something that you're not telling me about them?"

Everett's body moved away from hers and he finally released his grip on her arm. "There's nothing that you're not aware of." His voice was deep and quiet and when she looked back up at him, he refused to meet her gaze.

"What is it? What are you not telling me?" she asked.

"I said there's nothing. Now, let's go."

He pulled farther away and walked back towards the main street. He didn't look back to see if she followed him. Sayr's heart raced as she peeled herself off the alley wall and followed a few steps behind him.

Everett's guards leaned against the corner of the alley, silently waiting for her to follow Everett and escort them back to the palace. She gave them a quick look over before joining the crowded street.

She watched Everett blend into the crowd of people around them. Everett had never been an aggressive man; she'd never seen him lift a violent hand to anyone. Her heart thundered in her chest as she thought of what he'd accidentally revealed to her in the alley, and when she spied his hand resting against the dagger at his hip as he walked.

Queen Cheralin tapped a finger against her lip as she listened to Sayr's report. Her vision had expanded, still the same vision as before but… more.

"And you are certain you have never seen this man before?" the queen asked. "Not in my Court or outside the palace at all?"

"No, Your Majesty," Sayr answered. Her hands were clasped behind her back, and she stood tall in front of the desk where Cheralin sat. "I have never seen the man before in my life."

The queen nodded. Why was the vision recurring for the girl? And why, now, had the vision expanded further than before?

"Do we need to arrange another Council meeting?" Sayr asked.

"There is no need," Cheralin answered. "Unless significant information is presented in another vision or you have a new vision entirely, I will deal with this myself. Councilwoman Victoria is up north investigating the lands furthest from the palace. When she reports back to me, hopefully after the Western Court has departed, we will schedule another Council meeting to discuss further."

"Yes, Your Majesty." Sayr bowed low.

"Have you found anything about the Western Court since their arrival?" the queen asked.

"So far, it seems the five members don't stick together much, save for the three girls," Sayr reported. "I've followed them but haven't seen them use any sort of Elemental abilities and the two men have all but disappeared since their arrival at Court."

The queen studied Sayr for a moment. The girl's posture was stiff, and she barely met the queen's gaze. "What else?" she asked.

Sayr's eyes flitted away from the queen. "I encountered the three girls in the hall and one of them said something odd to me," Sayr explained. "She told me to… get on my knees before her and beg for forgiveness."

Queen Cheralin's gaze slanted, and she dropped her hand from her lips. "And did you?"

Sayr shook her head. "No, Your Majesty. She seemed almost shocked when I didn't."

Queen Cheralin's brow creased in thought. The Creobian girl may have tried to use her influence on Sayr, but Sayr had not felt any effects. Either the girl hadn't used her abilities, or Sayr was able to fend off the manipulation in some way. Or could it have been both?

"I want you to go see Lord Ellis today," the queen ordered.

Sayr started. "The Spy Lord? I haven't visited him in months."

"Then I believe a visit is far past due," Cheralin shot back. "You could use a refresher lesson if you are going to successfully spy on the Western Court. I do not like that they have already been watching you. I need you to be stealthier, but if any of the King's Court approaches you, do not run. Do not back down."

Sayr bowed her head. "Yes, Your Majesty."

"That is all," Queen Cheralin dismissed Sayr with a wave of her hand. Sayr bowed low before leaving the queen alone.

78

6

$\mathcal{T}$he Eastern Palace was swarming with Court guests all making their way to the tea gardens or strolling through the palace grounds. The end of summer was inching closer, and it seemed that everyone in Court wanted to savor as much summer warmth as possible. The sky was a cloudless blue and a light, salty breeze swept through the open windows and into the palace.

Sayr decided to take advantage of the beautiful day, too. Escaping the palace walls, she ventured out past the training grounds and into the grassy fields above the cliffs that separated the grounds from the ocean below.

She sat at the base of a large weeping tree with its long, lean branches dipping towards the earth, swaying lightly in the wind and creating a haven to keep her hidden as she sat at the trunk of the tree. She kept her eyes closed and legs crossed as she breathed in through her nose and out her mouth. The tall grass shifted around her as a faint breeze swept through.

Sayr had spent all yesterday afternoon and most of the night with Lord Ellis. He circled her like prey while he drilled her on their past lessons, seeing what all she remembered. Afterwards, he ordered Sayr to hide in plain sight around the East Wing, using shadows and camouflaging herself against furniture, bookshelves, and other covers that she could use to her advantage. Her order was to hide well enough that even he could not spot her if he passed right by. She'd failed the first three attempts, and he'd struck her hands and knees viciously after all three.

"Your enemies will do worse to you if they were to find you spying around," he'd justified to her.

The Spy Lord had ended their lesson by bringing Sayr out to the tea gardens. "You may leave once you bring me a nightingale," he had ordered.

The hunt had taken several hours and even more failed attempts before she finally slunk up a tree and onto a branch where a nightingale perched. She snatched the small bird in both hands. By the time she had brought the nightingale to Lord Ellis, her arms and legs were covered in scratches and already blooming bruises.

Sayr shook the memory from her mind and focused on her breathing again. She breathed deeply, beginning her meditation routine. It had been well over a week since her last vision, and she still hadn't seen anything new since the Western Court's arrival. She hadn't felt the familiar pull of a vision or any of the tingling sensations she'd felt during her altercation with the Creobian girls in the hall, she'd felt nothing relating to her gift since then. She hoped the calming ocean waves below would help her relax and sink into herself to see something again.

An hour might have passed since she first sat under the weeping tree, maybe two, she couldn't be sure. She controlled her breathing and blocked off any thoughts, hoping something new would involuntarily find its way in.

The faintest padding of feet shuffled through the tall grass outside the weeping branches. A ray of bright light pierced through her shaded haven. She opened her eyes and held up a hand to block the sunlight streaming through the opening of the tree branches. She squinted at the man standing in front of her in the grass.

"I didn't realize anyone was down here." The raven-haired man from King Mylan's Court loomed over her. "I hope I'm not interrupting."

Sayr immediately recognized the Creobian accent, though this man's words weren't as connected as most, as if he were trying to speak slower for Sayr. She lowered her hand and looked him over. He was no longer dressed in heavy leathers, though a leather bag was strapped across his chest. A few strands of dark hair fell into his eyes as he looked down at her.

"Not at all," she said flatly. "In fact, I was just leaving."

He chuckled when she made to get up from her spot under the tree. "No please, don't leave because of me. I was just looking for a quieter place than the palace, too many people for my liking."

His voice was low and deep, as if he were speaking with a close friend.

Sayr settled back down in the grass and leaned against the tree trunk. She wordlessly watched while the man sat at the base of the tree a few feet away from her.

Sayr could reach out and touch him if she wanted, and the thought made her scoot a few extra inches away.

He pulled out a small notebook and pencil from his bag and began writing, ignoring Sayr. His brow creased in concentration. She knew she should get up and leave right then, yet she couldn't help herself as she opened her mouth and asked, "You're a part of the Western Court?"

The man looked up from his notebook at her. "If you mean to ask if I'm Creobian, yes. Though I don't consider myself a true member of the king's Court."

"Why not?" she pushed on. "You came all this way with your king, you must have some sort of position in the Court to be permitted on this trip."

The man laid the notebook in his lap and leaned towards her. "I prefer to keep my position private." He grinned at her again. "I'm sure you understand."

Sayr lifted her chin and closed her eyes again. "I don't know what you mean."

"I'm sure you do," he retorted. "What sort of high position could you have in the Eastern Court to live here in the palace?"

Sayr squinted one eye open. "What makes you think I live here in the palace?"

The man shrugged and opened his notebook again. "You train in the mornings with the Queen's Army, you attend private lessons with the queen's personal guard, and you're rather close with the crown prince. I have to say your position is very hard to understand based on that information. A Court member who trains with soldiers, I've never heard of such a position."

Sayr would have been surprised that she was being followed, if Everett hadn't told her the other day about Willa practically stalking him through the royal gardens.

"It sounds like you've been watching me far too much to not know that I was out here alone before you showed up." She opened her eyes fully and faced the man again. "What are you really here for?"

The man flashed her a charming smile. "What's your name?"

Sayr didn't answer. Being near a Creobian already violated Everett's rules for her, telling this man her name would only cause further harm. On the other hand, Her Majesty had ordered Sayr not to back down or shy away from the Western Court or raise any suspicions.

"What's yours?" she asked.

"Dimitri," he answered.

"Dimitri," she repeated.

"Now, will you tell me yours? Or maybe you could tell me about your position in the Eastern Court since you are so eager to learn mine." He twirled his pen in his hand, eagerly waiting for her to reply.

"You still haven't told me about your position in Court," Sayr stalled. "Why should I tell you mine?"

The man—Dimitri—huffed out an impatient breath. As much as Sayr knew she should probably leave, she found a sort of amusement dodging his questions and flustering him.

"At least tell me your name," Dimitri said. "I gave you mine. Aren't us Creobians and Visarians supposed to be showing camaraderie with each other? Forming bonds and friendships? How can I do that if I don't even know your name?"

Sayr doubted either of them felt any sort of bond of friendship forming between them. But would he become more suspicious of her if she refused to answer any of his questions?

She stood from the base of the trunk and pushed aside the dangling limbs to exit her shaded haven. Before she stepped out, she looked back at Dimitri. "My name is Aryn. I'm a soldier in one of the queen's special ranks. That's it. If you want to keep following me around, be my guest, but you will be very disappointed to find nothing more of interest."

With that, Sayr walked through the dangling branches, leaving Dimitri behind to do what he would with the fake information she gave him.

He didn't need to know that she'd used her mother's name instead of her own. And so what if there were no special ranks in the Queen's Army? If he'd been following her around since he'd arrived in the Eastern Palace and hadn't already gathered that information, she didn't feel worried that he'd be able to find any more information about her.

The sunny weather didn't last the rest of the week. Sayr trudged through the training grounds which were now slick with mud. The blue sky had turned an ugly grey and a constant drizzle had fallen for two days straight.

Marenda had shown up a little after Sayr had finished stretching. They'd thrown a few mediocre blows at each other, but it was obvious how tired Marenda was from her extra guard shifts. Deep purple bruised underneath her eyes, and she swayed back and forth a bit from exhaustion.

Sayr wiped away the wet strands of hair plastered against her face. They both stood in mud up to their ankles and the drizzle was turning into a steady stream of rain, Marenda's fire wouldn't be any good in this weather.

"Go take a nap, Mar," Sayr called at her through the rainfall.

Marenda surprised her with a sour look. "You brought me all the way down here and now you want me to leave after a couple rounds?"

Sayr twisted her daggers in each hand. "You're exhausted," she explained. "And it's not as much fun kicking you into the mud when you're not fully committed."

She gave her best friend a teasing smile, hoping to lighten the mood by repeating the words she'd said to Sayr not too long ago.

Marenda's spear landed in the mud a few feet in front of Sayr. She stared at it in surprise, mouth hung open, before looking up at her friend. Marenda looked exhausted but she flung an amused grin at Sayr before walking off the training grounds. Clearly, Sayr would be putting all their weapons back in their compartment by herself.

The small compartment room was warm and dry, easing the chill that was beginning to settle in Sayr's bones. She dumped the weapons into one of the bins for cleaning. The training weapons were meant to help soldiers with precision, not harm them, so there was no need to waste time sharpening them.

She walked back to the door and peered outside. The rain had become a downpour so thick that she could barely see past the entrance of the weapons compartment. She took a few seconds to gather in the warmth of the compartment room before giving herself a shake of encouragement and running back out into the rain.

She continued to sprint in the direction of the palace, planning to head to the entrance of the East Wing and drag in as little mud as possible. She thought of the trouble she'd likely get into with one of the servants for dragging around such a mess.

A hard mass slammed into her, knocking her off her feet.

She slid across the mud a few feet before coming to a stop, arms covered in mud up to her elbows. She managed to prop one foot back on the ground when another blow struck her in the side. She grunted in pain, clutching her side, and squinted up through the rain to see the figure standing over her.

"Hello, Sayr." Vic's eyes were wild as he looked down at her.

Vic greeted her with another kick directly in the stomach. She gasped and rolled her body to the side. She clutched her stomach, huddling inward to better protect herself from any more attacks while she willed more air into her lungs. Vic's boot landed on her head, digging one side of her face into the mud.

He leaned over and rested his elbow on his knee. "I never repaid you for your little interruption last week."

Gasping, she glared up at Vic with her one eye that was free of mud. His hair was as soaked as hers, he must have been waiting out here a while. Sayr's heart raced faster with each beat. Vic had been waiting for her. Waiting for this moment. She'd put all her weapons back in their compartment, she was completely defenseless.

"Oh well," Vic taunted. "Why don't we have some fun of our own?"

"Screw you, Vic," she gasped.

She let out a yell of protest and rolled her aching body sideways. Her face completely submerged in the mud as she rolled, setting Vic off balance. She could feel the pressure of his boot lift off her head as he slipped forward.

Grits of mud stained her tongue and filled her nose. She rolled just enough to reach around his leg and dug her arm into the back of his other knee. His leg gave out and he fell to the ground with a heavy grunt.

As he hit the ground, she propped herself up and swung her elbow into Vic's face. His nose crunched underneath Sayr's elbow and blood sputtered down his lips and chin. Vic screamed and reached up to clutch his face.

Her stomach and lungs still blazed in hot pain with every move she made, and the left side of her body was stiff from the collision, but she quickly got to her feet as Vic shouted curses at her.

She knew she wasn't going to get very far if she didn't make a break for it. She had nothing to defend herself with. Vic laid in her path towards the East Wing where she had planned to go, so she ran in the opposite direction. Her body throbbed as she sprinted for a simple door on the far side of the grounds, threw it open, and hurled herself inside.

Dimitri watched from the palace halls while the boy continued kicking Aryn, lying in the mud. His frown deepened, Aryn hadn't gotten up yet and the boy dug her head into the muddy earth with his boot.

"Well, he is clearly not an ally of hers," Lilith noted as she watched the fight next to him. "But why attack her like this?"

"Does it really matter?" Dimitri grunted.

"Of course, it matters. She is different. The high officials within the Eastern Court all stay away from her, and yet this low-ranking boy provokes her?" Lilith brought a finger up to her lips as she thought. They'd found a small window in the corner of the halls to watch the altercation without being noticed from the outside.

"Something isn't right with her, and I want to find out what it is. The Eastern Queen keeps her very close, too," Lilith thought aloud.

"Her name is Aryn," Dimitri added. "She's a special rank in the Queen's Army, or so she says."

Dimitri hadn't fully believed the girl when she gave up her name and position in the palace. Her confession was much more boring than he'd expected, and he knew it couldn't be entirely true. However, she did train with the soldiers almost every day and had private lessons with one of the queen's personal guards. She must have some rank in the army in order to be allowed so much access to the training grounds. None of that explained the queen's caution with her or the disdain the rest of the Eastern Court seemed to have for her, though.

Dimitri watched Aryn; half her body was completely covered in the mud. His nostrils flared as the boy pressed his leg harder onto her head.

"Careful, Dimitri. His Majesty warned you to keep your hatred at bay." Lilith slinked a hand over Dimitri's arm and up toward his shoulder.

Dimitri scowled down at Lilith and stepped away. "Can we leave now? We have enough to report."

Lilith waited a few more moments, watching as the girl rolled through the mud and pulled the boy to the ground. She slammed her elbow into the boy's face. Lilith's lips twitched upwards while she watched.

Finally, Lilith turned toward Dimitri. "Yes, let's go. I believe this will satisfy His Majesty for now."

Lilith turned and walked down the hallway. Dimitri glanced back out the window just in time to see Aryn sprint in the direction away from them. He turned from the window and followed Lilith down the hall.

Sayr leaned against a wall, panting and swearing at Vic and her aching body and the fact that she was too weak and had to run. She knew what would've happened if she hadn't gotten away. She hadn't known Vic very well, but would he really have taken advantage of her if she hadn't gotten away? And then what? Would he try and kill her to keep her quiet? Would anyone care about what he would have done to her?

She remained against the wall, trying to catch her breath when a door across the hall swung open. She pushed herself off the wall and looked down at her mud-caked arms and legs and her soaked clothes. Before she could make another break for it, someone walked through the door.

Lanni strutted into the hall, carrying a hefty stack of books. Her silver hair was tied back in a half-up style, the lower half of her hair cascading over her shoulder. Two guards filed into the hall behind the princess.

Sayr let out a sigh of relief, which caught Lanni's attention, and she turned to look at Sayr. Her big blue eyes scanned Sayr up and down, and her nose wrinkled in disgust.

"What in the elements happened to you?" Lanni asked.

Sayr shot her a look that she hoped told Lanni she didn't want to talk about it. Lanni gave a sigh of her own and walked over to her.

Sayr scanned the books in her arms. She didn't recognize any of the books, but one title caught her eye.

The History of the Continent; an Accurate Retelling, 476-530 P.E.

Lanni followed her gaze, shifting the titles away from Sayr's sight. "Reading is much more entertaining when I choose the material, not like the books my tutors try shoving down my throat," she explained.

"I didn't realize you willingly chose to read history books," Sayr said, noticing the dating on the spine of the book and the P.E., *Post Establishment.* The history book led up to 530 P.E., only twelve years before the current date.

"I am a princess," Lanni said. "Learning about history is good for me, and I occasionally get tired of reading only fiction."

She adjusted the pile in her arms before walking away. The clicking of her heels echoed down the hall. "Follow me," she ordered.

Sayr followed the princess down the hall, certain she was leaving a trail of mud and rainwater behind her. Lanni stopped and opened one of two large doors with her body, leading them into one of the palace's guest suites.

"Wait out here," she told the guards, and they obediently stood on each side of the doors. Lanni walked in, dropped her books onto one of the sofas and sat down in one of the plush seats.

Sayr remained in the doorway, staring at the beautiful rugs that she was about to ruin.

"I've dragged in worse than mud before," Lanni called. She grabbed a book from the pile and began flipping through the pages. "Come in."

Sayr walked into the room and shut the door behind her. "Do you come here a lot?"

"Only when I want to hide," she admitted and leaned her head against the plush headrest. "From my tutors, the Court ladies... my *mother*."

"I would appreciate if you didn't tell my brother or mother about this," Lanni said, and her hand passed over the stack of books. "I'm not so sure they'd approve of some of my reading materials."

Sayr nodded and took in the rest of the room. It looked as if someone had been staying here for quite some time, though she never thought Lanni would be one to want to leave her own exquisite suite in the Royal Wing.

"Take off your clothes," Lanni ordered.

Sayr looked back at Lanni, open-mouthed in shock, but Lanni just rolled her eyes and pointed to a door behind her. "Not in *here*. I'll call my ladies to start a bath and bring some clothes. You reek."

Sayr's cheeks burned but she made her way to the washroom to bathe. When she returned from the washroom, clean and mud free, Lanni was still seated in her chair, intensively reading one of her new books.

She was impressively far into the book. Sayr quickly took a seat in the chair across from her and waited. Lanni marked the book and clasped it shut. She glanced at Sayr, giving an approving look at her washed hair and clean clothes.

"So, what orders did my mother give you to have you dragged through the mud?" Lanni asked.

"Your mother's orders aren't what got me here," Sayr admitted. "My own stupidity over caring for other's well-being is."

Lanni raised an eyebrow at Sayr. "At least you still care for other's well-being, that's not something most can say in this Court. Either way, you're an asset to my mother and shouldn't let a man lay a hand on you."

"How did you know it was a man?" Sayr's voice was solid, unbreaking, but her heart stirred at the thought of what Vic had done, and what he had planned to do further.

Lanni's gaze softened. "You don't think I deal with the same troubles? Husbands of Court ladies eyeing me as I walk by, even some of the Royal Guards have built up enough nerve to try and touch me."

Sayr gaped at her in surprise, thinking about all the times she'd assumed Lanni had been interested in the new members of the Royal Guard or Court officials by the looks they had given her. She never bothered to look and see if Lanni had reciprocated those looks.

"Lanni, you are the Eastern Princess. No one should be able to get anywhere near you." Sayr's voice was soft and low.

Lanni gave her a withering look. "They can if my mother lets them. Sometimes having a high position in life can make you more vulnerable to those around you. I may be a princess, but I have no real power against anyone in this palace. That is given only to my mother and brother."

Sayr's throat tightened at Lanni's words. "No one's ever… harmed you, have they?"

Lanni's face turned to icy stone and the smile that she gave Sayr held no joy. "They would not be alive today if they did," she answered.

She sat up in her chair and placed the book in her lap. "You and I are very different, but there is one thing that links us together. We are dispensable. Everett will be king one day and I will likely play housewife to some high official somewhere in Visaran for our kingdom's benefit. I believe, someday soon, we will both be somewhere far away from this palace, and not by our own choices."

"And where do you think I'll end up?" Sayr asked.

"I honestly can't say for sure," Lanni admitted. "But I do know that the moment your visions are wrong more than they are right, or they no longer benefit the Crown, my mother will dispose of you quickly."

Her answer sent a shiver down Sayr's spine. Her visions were what gave her protection in the palace. She offered her visions to Queen Cheralin in return for a life in the palace and protection from those outside the capital that would want to harm or even kill her.

"I'm not saying this to frighten you." Lanni's voice dripped with sincerity. "This is something that I think you should be aware of, just as I am aware of my own situation. My point is you cannot continue to let these people walk all over you. Everyone in this palace feels entitled to something of importance, some of us more than others. You cannot let anyone think they are entitled to *you*. What is important is that you understand you belong to no one. No one is entitled to any part of you, and that includes my mother and your unnatural gift."

She smirked at her and opened the book in her lap again. "Now leave me alone." She lifted the book in her hands. "I have lots of work to do."

Sayr gave her a small smile as she stood from the chair and headed towards the doors. She turned the knob to leave but turned back towards Lanni.

"Thank you, Lanni."

Lanni waved a hand in her direction as Sayr shut the door behind her.

The drizzling rain hadn't let up all day or night. By the time the sun had risen the next morning, the hard dirt of the training grounds had turned slippery and large puddles scattered the grounds. Water and Earth Elementals were hard at work clearing the stagnant water and resetting the dirt.

Sayr remained inside her rooms, enjoying her steaming coffee. She sat on the loveseat while she scrawled her pen across the paper on the table in front of her. She needed to meet with Her Majesty. After she had left Lanni's hiding room yesterday, she had dedicated the rest of the day to spying on the Western Court.

She had followed the trio of girls for a couple hours, as they were easiest to track. The three of them were relatively boring, Sayr thought, lounging in the center of the palace near the gallery. The brunette had pulled a long chair over towards the glass windows to lay in the sun. The group stuck together most of the time. Willa left the other two to go off on her own twice, and the second time Sayr followed.

She had made her way through the halls towards the Royal Wing of the palace. Sayr had kept far behind the girl and had snuck into the servant's hall, hiding in the shadows to listen while Willa met with the blond Creobian man who had also entered the throne room as part of the Western Court.

They were planning to bring some sort of information to the king. Sayr couldn't make out every word from the servant's hall, but she knew that they had found something crucial about a member of the Eastern Court that their king needed to be aware of.

They had also mentioned the 'King's Court', a smaller Court Sayr assumed resided within the Western Court. She'd overheard two names in this King's Court that Sayr did not recognize: Mina and Ryon.

Yet no matter how much sleuthing Sayr did, she could not find a single member of the Western Court by those names. But if they were indeed part of the King's Court, why would they not be in Visaran with their king?

Sayr wrote everything down. She lifted the mug of coffee to her lips as she jotted her findings on the paper. Once she was finished, she would roll it up and personally hand it to Marenda to give to the queen.

The familiar pull of a vision ignited her core and Sayr stilled on the loveseat. In an instant, everything went black, as a vision overcame her.

A bright light encapsulated Sayr's vision. The blinding light faded slowly and everything around her grew foggy. She blinked rapidly and looked around her. She was in the throne room, but not in the balconies as usual. She stood on the main floor of the throne room in a corner underneath one of the high balconies.

Looking up, she saw the Court all standing on one of the balconies, the rest likely standing on the balcony above her. To her left, Queen Cheralin sat at the raised dais along with Everett and Lanni. The queen looked like she had been chipped from ice as she stared coldly at the large doors on the far side of the room.

"Bring her to the throne room," Queen Cheralin ordered, and two Royal Guards exited the room.

Sayr looked around, and her eyes landed directly on Dimitri. He stood underneath the balcony opposite her along with the rest of the Western Court. Her eyes darted back towards the thrones, and she spotted King Mylan standing at the base of the dais. Everyone stared at the queen in eerie silence, as if no one was willing to speak aloud besides the queen.

The Western Court was still in the palace, Sayr realized. The vision must be happening soon. Sayr darted behind one of the pillars holding the balcony, the shaded coverage blocking her vision. She reached a hand for the pillar to steady herself but felt nothing.

Sayr's hand went through the pillar, and she fell back into darkness. She plundered through empty space until she landed hard on her knees, finally feeling solid ground. Sayr blinked, she was back in her suite, crouched on all fours next to the loveseat. Her left hand had landed in something warm and wet. Sayr had spilled her coffee all over the floor, the remains of the shattered mug scattered across the floor.

She panted hard, waiting for the numbness to subside. Her head pounded, her limbs tingled, and her hearing slowly came back to her. She repeated where she was, who she was, and what had happened before the vision to keep her sanity intact.

A loud knock thumped at the door. Her head snapped up and she shakily lifted herself off the floor and to the door, expecting Marenda to be on the other side.

Only Marenda wasn't on the other side of the door. Instead, two Royal Guards stood there, the two she had just seen in her vision. What were they doing at her suite?

"Sayr Rieve," one of them addressed her. "We've come to escort you to the throne room."

Sayr looked between the two guards. "What's happening in the throne room?"

The other guard looked hard at her. "You are being called on to testify in front of Her Majesty."

7

Sayr willed her hands not to shake as they trekked down the hall, one guard on each side of her. Her blood ran cold, and she couldn't gain warmth back into her body. She crossed her arms tightly over her abdomen as they continued walking in silence.

All too soon, they reached the main entrance to the throne room. Two more guards were stationed at each door, and one turned to open it for her.

She peered up at the guard, recognizing him. Ajax: a tall, muscular young man who joined the Royal Guard just eight months ago. Marenda had taken him under her wing when he first arrived and Sayr had ended up spending a lot of time with the two of them on the training grounds and during meals in those first few months.

He nodded at her before nudging his head towards the throne room. Sayr wanted to stay outside with him, though she knew no one could help her. Ajax faced forward again. Sayr straightened and entered the throne room.

The throne room looked exactly as it had in her vision mere minutes ago. The room seemed so much bigger from the main floor. The balconies loomed high above, filled with Court guests and high officials all staring down at her.

As she walked farther into the room, she looked ahead towards the three thrones. Queen Cheralin, Everett, and Lanni all sat there, watching her. Her Majesty had her hands balled into fists in her lap and Everett's stare was furious.

Sayr glanced at the spot in the corner under the balcony where she had just stood in her vision. It was now empty, shaded from the large balcony overhead. Sayr turned her attention away from the balcony and approached the raised dais.

Marenda stood behind the queen's throne, wearing her Royal Guard uniform. She gave Sayr a momentary glance over before keeping her eyes glued to the main doors. Standing below them all in front of the dais stood King Mylan.

"Sayr," Queen Cheralin sweetly called her name. "This is King Mylan of Creobe." She gestured to the king, who smiled at Sayr and nodded his head in greeting.

Sayr took a shocked step back. She had expected the queen to publicly lash out at her for something she must have done wrong. Maybe she'd found out about her and Everett's trips to the City Center? It would explain Everett's anger. But why was King Mylan there?

She bowed her head to Queen Cheralin, then to King Mylan before looking back up at the queen with a thousand questions on the tip of her tongue.

King Mylan stepped forward and spoke instead. "I am sure you are curious as to why you have been called here. Allow me to explain. I have come to Visaran with my Court to request aid from the Queen's Army. There have been recent incidents within my country that my army cannot handle on its own. These soldiers that I have requested will accompany me and my Court back to Creobe, where they will continue to train with my own soldiers and offer aid when needed. Queen Cheralin and I have already agreed that this exchange will bond our two countries, bringing us closer to a stronger alliance."

King Mylan clasped his hands together excitedly. Queen Cheralin sat stiff and silent on her throne. Whispers drifted above from the balconies as the king turned to look up at Queen Cheralin.

"I am formally requesting, in front of both our Courts, that Lady Sayr be included in this exchange," the king said. "With your approval, she will travel with my Court back to Creobe where she will be cared for and trained until she is needed to aid my people and me."

Sayr's eyes widened as His Majesty finished speaking. The royals had this planned since the Western Court arrived. This was never a visit to bond their people, the king had come to ask for aid from Her Majesty, and now he wanted to take Sayr back with him to Creobe.

Her Majesty rested her chin in the palm of her hand, uninterested. "I see absolutely no reason why Sayr should accompany you to Creobe with my army. The agreement included my soldiers. Sayr is an apprentice, not a soldier."

"My Court has told me that she is a special rank soldier within your army. She told Dimitri so, herself." Mylan cocked his head towards the group standing underneath the balcony.

Sayr turned to see where Dimitri was standing with the rest of the Western Court. His eyes remained on the king, ignoring her.

Mylan's smile remained on his face as he lifted a hand to wave someone over to him. The brunette girl from his Court walked to stand next to His Majesty. She smiled at Sayr like she was her prey.

"This is Lilith, one of my ladies." King Mylan gestured towards Lilith and continued. "Not too long ago, Lilith and two more of my ladies encountered Lady Sayr. Their meeting was brief, I am told, but she was able to report back to me some very intriguing information."

Queen Cheralin's sudden glare could have pierced right through the king. She straightened on her throne, clenching and unclenching her fists against the arms of the chair, but she remained silent. Everett, on the other hand, looked as if he wanted to strangle the king and his *lady*.

"You see," Mylan went on, "Lilith is an Elemental like me, and she is very gifted. During her encounter with Lady Sayr, she used her gift to persuade the girl but failed. Lilith tells me that Lady Sayr had no reaction to being manipulated by such a strong Elemental, besides running away."

The Western Court all laughed and Sayr's cheeks burned with shame. The king gestured to Lilith, and she stood taller to look up into the balconies as she spoke. "I am one of the most gifted Elementals of my kind," she boasted. "Yet when I used my influences on Lady Sayr, she did not succumb to my commands."

The whispering grew louder. Those above in the balconies all came alive with concern.

"What could the girl mean by 'her influence'?"

"What commands had she given to Sayr?"

"I knew there was something wrong with that Councilman's apprentice."

"Enough!" Her Majesty raised her voice over the chatter above and the crowds immediately fell silent. The queen's icy glare shot at Lilith, who shrunk back and turned her attention away from the thrones. She then looked at King Mylan.

"We had an agreement," Queen Cheralin said through gritted teeth, "that our people were forbidden from using any abilities against one another."

Mylan's smile faltered and he stepped back, away from the thrones. "My apologies, Your Majesty, but I cannot watch over my Court and also meet with you and your Council so often. However, I will follow our agreement, and Lilith will face repercussions the moment we arrive in the Western Palace."

"No." The queen's voice was firm and unforgiving. "She will face public punishment here in my palace, by your hand, or our agreement to send my soldiers to your kingdom is off."

King Mylan's smile vanished, and he looked at Lilith. Lilith's eyes were wide with shock and fear. "I will not lay a hand on any member of my Court," the king said.

Queen Cheralin smiled wickedly. "Then a member of my Court will give her punishment. Three lashings. And I find it only fitting that the person your lady manipulated be the one to give the lashings."

Queen Cheralin's eyes drifted from Mylan to Sayr. Sayr stared back at the queen, silently pleading against the orders. Her queen wanted Sayr to publicly lash Lilith in front of both Courts. The queen's icy stare was unyielding. There was no room for discussion, Sayr was to do as she was ordered. Mylan turned, too, so that he could look at Sayr and she turned her pleading eyes to him. The king assessed her for only a moment before turning back to the queen on her throne.

"Three lashings are an extreme punishment," Mylan countered. "Lilith does not deserve such severity. There must be something else, a less physical form of punishment, which will satisfy you.

Queen Cheralin only shook her head. "These are my terms. Accept them, and I will give you my troops. Deny them, and you will not receive aid from Visaran."

Mylan's jaw twitched in anger. He looked back at Sayr. His eyes roamed up and down before he turned back towards the queen seated on her throne.

"We finish our business first," the king said, defeated. "Only after the troops have been given will Lilith be punished."

Sayr's heart plummeted, and she looked at each face around her for help when she met Lanni's gaze. Sayr could sense the understanding in her clear blue eyes. She knew something, they all knew something that Sayr did not.

She thought of the conversation they'd had just yesterday. *I believe, someday soon, we will both be somewhere far away from this palace, and not by our own choices.*

King Mylan continued. "Due to Lilith's findings, I am requesting Lady Sayr to accompany me and my Court back to the Western Palace where she will stay for the duration of the time agreed upon for the Queen's Army. I believe, if she is what I think she is, that she will be a great asset to helping stop these attacks in my country."

"Absolutely not!" Everett exploded off his throne and roared at the king. "How dare you come into our Court, ask for troops from us, and now demand to take a girl away from her home for *experimenting*?!"

The prince's rage rippled through the air, the floorboards, through every person within the room. Every soul shied away from the prince. Everyone except for King Mylan, whose feline grin remained.

"I would never demand." The king's tone remained casual, but his eyes hardened when they met the queen's. "I am simply requesting an extra body, one would say. A request that I believe Her Majesty cannot refuse. After all, I am told she is a soldier in the Queen's Army, and I am requesting soldiers. How much could you truly miss one girl?"

Queen Cheralin stared down her nose at the king and Sayr expected the queen to refuse King Mylan's request and throw him and his Court out of the palace for good. Everett, who still stood in front of his throne, took an angry step toward the king. Her Majesty rose from her own throne and put a hand on her son's arm, stopping him from moving any further. Her steel eyes remained on the king.

"Of course, Mylan." The words sounded forced from the queen.

Sayr's pulse thundered in her chest. Her legs shook, threatening to give way.

"Wait," she pleaded, her voice coming out barely above a whisper. She looked at the royal family. The only person still acknowledging her was Lanni, her gaze soft and sad.

"No," she tried again, her voice thin.

The queen didn't spare a single glance at Sayr as she raised her head high. "Sayr will accompany King Mylan back to the Western Kingdom."

8

Queen Cheralin dropped into her chair in the Council room. Only she and Sayr sat at the table. The young girl looked as if she was seconds from shattering to pieces in her chair. The queen lifted a hand to her face and let out a slow, frustrated breath.

She looked through her fingers at Sayr. "Do not think that I am abandoning you to serve in Creobe. I cannot deny Mylan his request, but I will not abandon you or let him do what he likes with you."

Sayr's stare remained locked on the table in front of her. "Did you know this was going to happen?"

"Not initially," the queen admitted. "I did not foresee this when King Mylan requested an audience here in my palace. But I suspected this may happen after you reported your encounter with the king's ladies in the halls."

Sayr barely lifted her eyes from the table to look at the queen. "Why does he want me?" she asked. "There are hundreds of soldiers here in the Eastern Palace, and thousands—tens of thousands—throughout the capital. Why has he selected me specifically?"

"The Western Court has been watching us just as much as we have been watching them," the queen answered. "From what you've told me about their private conversations, I have no doubt that you were also being followed and the girl's violation with using her abilities on you has certainly peaked the king's interest in you. No doubt, the king also wants to flaunt his power by showing both Courts that he can take whatever and whoever he wants."

"But he shouldn't be able to do whatever he wants, especially not when he is here in your Court," Sayr pushed.

"I have my reasons for allowing this," the queen retorted. "I trust you will not question my judgment. Since your report, I have been putting steps in motion to keep this turn of events in our favor. And I believe we will be successful if all goes as planned."

"Of course, Your Majesty." Sayr opened her mouth, then closed it, and opened it again. "Do I have to be the one to punish the king's lady?" Sayr's voice was quieter, softer. Weaker.

The queen leveled Sayr with one look. "It must be you," Her Majesty confirmed. "The girl tried to manipulate you. We cannot let anyone from either Court see any sign of weakness in my palace. I know something like this is not in your nature, but you are a strong soldier and member of my Court. We must show that side of you now more than ever. When the time comes for the girl's punishment, it will come by your hand."

"But she didn't manipulate me," Sayr pushed. "She didn't manipulate any sort of element against me."

"Yes, that is interesting," the queen pondered. Why hadn't the girl's manipulation affected Sayr? "It is likely that the girl's gifts are not as strong as the king says. Do not mind what he says. He is a liar, they all are. No matter, I have given you my orders."

Sayr lowered her head. "Yes, Your Majesty."

Cheralin rose from her chair and walked over to where Sayr sat. "I know how much I am asking of you, but I also know just how much you wish to prove yourself in my Court. This is how you prove yourself, Sayr. By obeying my orders for you. Remember, there is strength in duty, and this will only make you stronger. Focus on this task first, and once the punishment is given, I will give you my next orders while you are in Creobe. Will you do as I say?"

Sayr locked eyes with the queen standing over her. She would always do her duty to the queen, just as she had always done before. She would do anything to strengthen her claim as a member of the Eastern Court and prove that she was more than just a girl with unpredictable, and even more uncontrollable, gifts.

"Of course, Your Majesty." The words slipped effortlessly from Sayr. "I am forever at your command."

Sayr entered one of the many rooms of the queen's private hall, alone. Small groups of people were scattered around the dark room, while a larger group, including Her Majesty, huddled around a grand table.

The room, surprisingly, had no windows. Sayr had never seen a single room in the palace without windows to showcase the beautiful ocean views or the City Center. Candles were placed on every table and desk in the room to offer enough lighting to see. A few Fire Elementals in the room cast small flames around their heads and arms to create more light around them. Water Elementals stood next to the rows of bookshelves, casting worried glances between the delicate books and the flickering flames.

Sayr silently made her way over to the large table. King Mylan stood farthest from her across the table. Two Creobian guards stood to his left. A Visarian guard separated him from standing next to Queen Cheralin, who wore an oil-colored gown that climbed up to her throat. Marenda stood next to the queen, followed by two more Visarian officials who stood closest to Sayr.

"Sayr, thank you for joining us." Her Majesty greeted her. "First and foremost, you all need to be aware of the truth about why the Western Court has come to Visaran."

The queen turned her attention to King Mylan and the rest of them followed. The king looked only at Sayr, his gaze no longer humorous or feline as it was yesterday.

"I have recently received alerts in Creobe that some sectors of the country have detected attacks on various cities," the king explained. "These threats have been small so far, more injuries than fatalities, but it concerns me that they have occurred so close to Athar."

Sayr's brows creased in confusion. She knew the history of the continent, including Athar, well, having been taught by the royal tutors since she was nine.

Before the continent was divided east and west, six colonies took over the large landscape. Elementals of every kind lived in the colonies, though it was known that some Elementals lived more peacefully than others. Some colonies fought with those closest to them for land or power, causing constant unrest between their people.

Most of the colonies were peaceful, though, until three leaders came together centuries ago with talk of combining the colonies into one kingdom with one ruler to govern them all. Most colony leaders hated the idea, wanting to keep their land and their freedom, but there were some that whispered of wanting to rule the entire continent, having the land and the power for themselves. The leaders fought for days before returning to their colonies, angrier and more paranoid over their land.

The leaders who wanted to rule the entire continent began to attack right away, ridding the colonies of those who did not want to combine. The people fought alongside their leaders, killing anyone who would go against their cause to unite into one kingdom.

War began to break out over the entire continent, the battles took place mostly in the north. Elementals of every kind fought against each other with such brutality that the northern lands were destroyed beyond repair. The earth had been consumed by so many wildfires, earthquakes, and floods that hundreds of miles of land was deemed uninhabitable.

Only two colony leaders survived the war. They created a treaty that one leader would rule over the eastern territory, now known as Visaran, and the other would take over the west, now known as Creobe. The territories were divided naturally by the Silia River that ran from the south all the way up to the abandoned lands in the north. The time of war and bloodshed had been named the Dividing War, the bloodiest and most brutal war known in history.

From what Sayr remembered from her tutoring, the land where the war had taken place remained untouched, considered undesirable land by both leaders. Neither were willing to claim and clean up the territory where so much death and destruction had taken place. The thick forest land in the north became its own barren wasteland and was named Athar, unclaimed by anyone to the day.

Sayr was unconvinced by the king's story. No threat could come from Athar besides maybe a few mild earthquakes from the dead and shifting terrain.

"Her Majesty and I have been arranging a battalion of both our troops to assess these threats and be ready if they continue through my kingdom. My Court and I will leave for Creobe along with five hundred Visarian soldiers and a small group of Her Majesty's high officials, including all of you."

"My officials will act as overseers for these troops, nothing more," Her Majesty added. "My troops have been ordered to continue their training in Creobe just as they would here. Until further threat is revealed, they have no loyalty to the Western Kingdom. And in return, all of Visaran's past conflicts and disputes with Creobe will be forgotten and *not* used against us in political extortion."

The king's eyes narrowed in the smallest glare. Sayr eyed the queen as well. What sort of conflicts did Creobe have against Visaran that they could use as extortion against their kingdom?

She peered down at the table where a map was sprawled over it. Small wooden statues were arranged throughout both countries on the large map. A small cluster of figures were placed on the path to the Silia River across the border into Creobe.

"My Court and Visaran's overseers will travel by carriage over the Silia River to the Western Palace," King Mylan explained. "The troops will travel on foot and horseback."

"You will leave in three days," the queen said to Sayr. "I have scheduled a Council meeting for two days from now, which you will attend."

"How long will we be gone for?" Sayr asked the queen.

Her Majesty looked hard at Sayr before answering. "For as long as you are needed. I will be in communication with my officials. If no new threat is detected after three months, you all will be brought safely back to Visaran."

Sayr glanced at the abandoned lands at the top of the map. "And what if a threat is detected during that time?"

"Then we will do our part in the agreement and assist the Western Kingdom in stopping these attacks," the queen answered. "We do not want this to spread through the continent and into Visaran."

Her Majesty looked over at King Mylan for confirmation, who simply nodded his agreement. Sayr nodded as well, her mind racing as the royals continued planning for their departure in just three days.

9

$\mathcal{S}$ayr let out a groan of boredom as she watched Everett perfect another move, watering the white and blue hydrangea bushes with water from the fountain, which she was sure the royal gardeners would not appreciate.

Since the announcement of the Queen's Army leaving in two days, Everett had opted to spend as much time with Sayr as possible before she was to leave. He'd called on her this morning to have breakfast with him in the tea gardens. They spent the late morning hours sipping tea and coffee and nibbling on different breads topped with pickled onions and thinly sliced salmon.

The air was tense between them at first, neither had forgotten how he'd reacted in the City Center after she'd told him about her run-in with Lilith and the girls. Neither of them had spoken on it, though, and they seemed to silently agree to put it behind them. The tension melted away quickly when they eventually wandered into the royal gardens, though Sayr suspected her upcoming departure had much to do with it.

"Wonderful job," she said sarcastically. "If ruling the country doesn't work out for you, you'd make a great royal gardener. At least, once you figure out how to not overwater the hydrangeas."

Everett laughed and influenced the water back into the fountain.

"Alright fine." He walked back over to where she sat perched in the grass and kneeled down so his face was level with hers. "What would you like to do?"

She rolled her neck and peered down one of the cobblestone paths to her left. She liked watching Everett and Marenda and most of the other Elementals use their gifts. She had to admit that jealousy often tugged at her when she watched them using their influences out in public. While everyone else threw their gifts around freely and was celebrating them, she was looked down on and kept a secret for her own.

Her eyes landed on the shimmering water in the distance. Her lips formed into a devious smile, and she looked back at Everett. "What if we played with a bigger body of water?"

His brow creased. His gaze followed where hers had just been and he shot back up, shaking his head. "Absolutely not."

"Oh, come on!" She threw her arms up in exasperation, but he only stood above her, arms crossed and head still shaking.

She rose from her spot in the grass and stepped closer to him, fully prepared to beg for him to take her down to the beachy shores. She clasped her hands tightly together and looked up at him.

"Please, Ev," she begged. "We'll still technically be on palace grounds. How many chances will I have to be near the ocean in Creobe?"

They stared each other down, Everett's face hard as stone and Sayr's soft and pleading. She knew bringing up her departure was a low blow, but it was also her biggest gambling chip to get him to agree. After an exceedingly long stare down, Everett let out a tired sigh and ran a hand over his face.

"Fine," he muttered again from behind his hand. "But don't wander off the beach without me, the waves can get very rough."

"Yes!" Sayr jumped in the air and gave a loud whoop before grabbing Everett's arm to lead him down the path towards the rocky cliffs.

An old, soggy staircase had been carved from the rocks all the way down to the beaches. Once they had safely made it down the slippery stairs, Sayr kicked off her sandals and dug her toes into the warm sand that surrounded them, letting out a happy sigh. The waves seemed calm enough, gently rolling over the beach. She closed her eyes and breathed in a gulp of salty sea air and smiled. She loved the beach, the sound of the waves crashing onto the sand was like music to her ears.

She sensed Everett behind her and opened her eyes to look at him. He gently pulled off his own shoes and rolled up his sleeves. With a deep breath, he turned towards the water.

"I'll show you something better than a fountain trick."

Everett focused on the crashing waves before him. He lifted both hands in front, palms facing down. Sayr watched as he inhaled deeply and began lightly pushing his arms up and down, in tune with the waves pushing and pulling.

He swung his arms high above his head. A large wave rose almost to Sayr's height and… stopped.

Beads of sweat gleamed on his forehead as he concentrated, gritting his teeth. His arms trembled from the exertion it took to manipulate the wave. With a grunt, he swung both arms down and the water once again followed his command. The massive wave shot out and crashed hard into the sandy beach, the water rolling all the way up to the wall of rocky cliff where Everett stood.

Sayr caught herself as the water stirred up to her knees, soaking her pants, and then gently rolled back into the ocean. Her sandals floated past her, and she quickly plucked them out of the water.

Her jaw was still slack with astonishment when the remaining water lulled off the beach. She turned to Everett, who was huffing from the force of manipulating the wave.

"You have the ability to control the ocean," she said slowly, "and you've been spending all this time manipulating a *fountain*?"

Everett laughed heartily at that and Sayr joined him, laughter taking over them both. She was truly astonished. Everett was never one to show off his abilities in front of others, but she'd had no idea what he was truly capable of before. It all made sense, she realized. He *was* a member of the royal Water Elementals after all, and she wondered just how strong Everett really was.

"I'm a gifted Water Elemental, it's not something that all Water Elementals can do," Everett noted.

"You say that, but every Elemental I've met seems to have strong gifts. They can all manipulate or create the elements," Sayr countered.

"That's because you live in the Eastern Palace where all the strongest Elementals reside," Everett explained. "If you were to visit one of the cities farther north like Northow, you'd see an abundance of Elementals that are barely gifted at all. I've seen Earth Elementals that can barely move a pebble or Fire Elementals that can barely light the wick of a single candle; it all depends on how blessed we are at birth. Even as a strong Elemental, my gifts are limited. I can control a wave, but only briefly and it takes tremendous effort. The stronger we are, the quicker our abilities can experience burn out, leaving our gifts useless for sometimes days at a time."

Sayr rolled her eyes. "At least you're modest," she muttered.

She had no idea how blessed she was at birth, as she had no one else gifted like her to base her abilities on. But with the limited control she had over her visions and when they came to her, she guessed she couldn't be nearly as gifted as Everett or Marenda.

"Now you can tell those Creobians what the Visarian royal family can really do. You'll be just as much of a threat once they see what you can do on the training grounds." Everett's voice thickened with emotion and Sayr walked up the beach towards him.

Worry was etched all over his face, and something else that she couldn't quite place. Maybe sadness? Her own sadness made her throat tighten.

She pivoted her weight through the soaked sand and reached up to gently wrap her arms around his neck. He buried his face against her shoulder and held her tightly. They stayed embraced for a long time, neither of them wanting to let go.

A thought briefly crossed her mind that he might talk to his mother for her and try to get her out of all this. Part of her wanted to believe that he would, but she remembered his rage in the throne room and how quickly his mother had shut him down when he tried to go against the king's request. No, even the crown prince would not be able to keep her here.

Even a prince must bow to a queen.

She was the first to break them apart, looking up at him and offering an encouraging smile. "Come on," she said softly and took his hand. "Show me that move again."

They spent hours down on the beach. Everett continued manipulating the waves, pulling them up the beach and pushing them far back. Each time, Sayr would run towards the waves and grab as many seashells as she could before he released the waves, and they came rushing towards her again. She squealed while she ran from the waves creeping towards her, covering her feet with water and foam.

At the last wave, she lost her restraint and ran into the water, jumping into the waves and submerging her entire body in the ocean. The salty water was cold and refreshing on her skin. Her head emerged from the water, and she swam further into the ocean before looking back towards the beach, searching for Everett.

She laughed loudly as he came racing after her and dove into the waves himself. His head popped out of the water, and he swam towards her while she continued laughing and splashing at him. The two of them paddled through the waves, their hair plastered all over their faces.

"I should have known you wouldn't listen when I said not to stray off the beach." He sent a small wave in her direction.

"What can I say?" Sayr joked. "I'm impulsive."

They continued swimming through the lulling waves until the sun was high in the sky, sparkling the water like the hundreds of jewels in the queen's crown. They swam back towards shore and trudged up the sand. Their drenched clothes weighed them down and Sayr felt as if she was a drunkard trying to walk while she made her way up the beach.

With a wave of his hand over his body, Everett collected all the water from his soaked clothing and threw it back into the ocean before doing the same for her. She instantly felt lighter, and her hair, clothes, and skin were completely dry though the scent and itch of the salt still clung to her. She gave him a grateful smile as he put a hand on her shoulder.

"I have to go." His voice was soft, and he looked up at the sun shining high above. "One of Her Majesty's officials needs to speak with me this afternoon."

Sayr nodded and glanced back at the water. "I think I'm going to stay down here a little bit longer."

Everett gave a disapproving grunt, his face twisted with concern.

"I won't go back in the water alone," she insisted. "I just want to stay on the beach a little longer."

Everett didn't try to argue with her. Instead, he pulled her into a quick hug before heading back up the rocky stairs.

Sayr waved him goodbye before turning back to the waves. She would keep her promise and not stay too long, but she wanted to savor a few more moments of the sand between her toes and salty air in her nose. She sat down on the sand. The water inched around her toes as she stared out into the distance.

Sayr stood in the center of the courtyard of the Eastern Palace. A tall stone pillar was placed before her. Lilith kneeled before the pillar, her exposed back towards Sayr. Sayr gripped the long, sharp-tipped whip in her hands and looked around the courtyard. The entire Court, it appeared, had come to watch Lilith's punishment.

The Western Court stood near the steps into the palace to Sayr's right. The two girls that were usually seen with Lilith held each other tightly. The blond man stood behind the girl with short, coiled hair, Willa. He kept one hand rested on her shoulder in a comforting hold. Dimitri stood next to him, but he did not look at Lilith. He glared at Sayr, his hazel eyes piercing her, and she quickly looked from him to the king.

King Mylan also looked at Sayr. He nodded at her when her eyes met his, as if he could see the battle within herself. She only gripped the long whip tighter, trying to keep her hands from shaking.

"Let this be a reminder to those who dare defy a royal's orders." Queen Cheralin's voice echoed throughout the courtyard. Everyone watching remained deathly silent. "Those who defy their king or queen in my palace, in my country, will face severe punishment."

Sayr did not need to look behind her to know that the queen's eyes were on her. "When you are ready, Sayr."

Sayr flinched at her name and looked down at the whip, then at Lilith's exposed back. Lilith's body was tense. Sayr took a few steps closer to Lilith and raised the whip. Every soul in the courtyard held their breath. Sayr would always obey the queen's orders. She would show her strength and loyalty to the Eastern Queen. She would prove that she belonged in the Eastern Court.

But she would also show mercy.

Sayr brought the whip down on Lilith, light enough to not break skin, aiming for the girl's shoulder. A faint crack sounded as the whip met Lilith's back and the girl jumped. She turned her head slowly towards Sayr, and the expression on her face looked something like surprise and confusion mixed before she turned back to face the pillar.

"Harder." The queen's voice was strained. Sayr turned to look at Her Majesty. Her jaw was clenched against her teeth and her eyes were like chips of ice as she looked through Sayr at Lilith. Sayr knew what the order meant. Lilith needed to pay for embarrassing the queen in front of her own Court.

Sayr slowly turned back around. She did not look at anyone else, only at Lilith. Lilith tensed again in anticipation, waiting for the next lash. Sayr lifted the whip again and swung down. She flicked her wrist, and the whip cracked a second before it met Lilith's skin. The loud crack echoed throughout the courtyard. Sayr willed Lilith to understand, to lurch forward or cry out. She silently pleaded for the girl to make the lashing seem worse than Sayr knew it was. Sayr was loyal to her queen, but she didn't know if she'd be able to truly wound the girl.

Lilith jumped when the leather struck her shoulder again and a small whimper escaped her, but Sayr knew it wasn't enough. Her reaction was not enough to satisfy the queen's bloodthirst.

A hand shoved Sayr away and she stumbled, dropping the whip to the ground. Queen Cheralin picked up the whip, turned towards Lilith, and raised it high above her head. In one swift movement, the queen used all her strength and struck the whip at Lilith's exposed skin. The crack that sounded was not like Sayr's attempts, this time thunderous and cruel.

A pained scream erupted from Lilith, and she curled into herself. Gasps and murmurs floated from the watching crowd. No one dared to move while Queen Cheralin turned from Lilith to look at Sayr. Her eyes were ignited with fury. She shoved the whip back into Sayr's arms as she passed, leaving the courtyard.

Lilith's strained cries rang through the courtyard. The watching crowd began to disperse. Sayr held the whip in her shaking hands. She did not move while Her Majesty entered the palace, and the Eastern Court followed their queen up the steps and inside.

King Mylan rushed over to Lilith. He covered her back with a cloth. A deep red slit had opened across her back where the queen's lash had broken skin. Blood leaked from the wound and down her back, soaking into the cloth. Lilith's entire body shook as she tried to contain her sobs. The rest of the King's Court ran to their king's side. Some stood behind their king, others crouched down and blocked Lilith from view.

Sayr's body was numb. She couldn't look at the girl's wound or hear Lilith's muffled cries ring through the courtyard. She abandoned the whip and moved towards the steps of the palace. The whispers and stares surrounding her weighed heavily on her as she walked to the East Wing. She kept her hands clenched and jaw set while she walked. Only when she closed the door to her suite and was completely alone did she crumple to the floor and let the sobs rake through her body.

The Council members differed from the last meeting Sayr had attended. She sat back in the Council room, this time without Marenda, and listened to Her Majesty tell the Council about the plans for tomorrow's departure. Danil was also at this meeting—as he had to attend every meeting Sayr attended to keep up their ruse—and sat across from Sayr.

He, along with the rest of the Council, listened intently while Her Majesty spoke. "We have arranged for our troops to leave at sunrise. Mylan's Court and our group of officials will depart in the afternoon, taking the carriages that the Western Court arrived in."

Every statement that the queen made was followed by a series of questions from the Council.

"Why has this specific group been permitted to leave for Creobe?"

"How do we plan to keep in contact with these members while they are in the Western Kingdom?"

"It's very convenient that His Majesty has enough room in his carriages for his Court and members of our own, don't you think?"

Sayr's head was completely muddled by the time Her Majesty had finished, and she hadn't even had to speak. Once again, no one asked her opinion on the matter or even looked her way when the queen announced that she was on the list of Court members who would be leaving.

Once the meeting was called to an end, she made to get up with the rest of the Council to prepare for her departure. Before she could exit the room, Queen Cheralin's voice called after her.

"Just a moment, Sayr."

Sayr clasped her hands behind her back and turned to face Her Majesty.

Queen Cheralin strode towards her so that they were barely a foot apart from each other. When she spoke, her voice was strained and rough. "I want to apologize again for the position you are in. I know this is not easy for you."

Her Majesty paced closely around Sayr, wringing her hands as she spoke. "I want you to know that I would not be going through with King Mylan's request if I had any other choice. There are so many things about the world that you do not know yet. And for your sake, I hope it remains that way."

She stopped once again in front of Sayr. "I do care for you, Sayr. You have been a wonderful friend to my son, and I see how much he cares for you, too. I have plans for you, plans that will make you great in this Court."

Sayr nodded while the queen spoke. She wanted to put all of her faith in the queen, but she couldn't squash the growing doubt that gnawed at her.

"Why did you agree to it?" she asked.

Her Majesty stopped wringing her hands, suddenly unnervingly still. "You have not seen much of Visaran outside of this palace and the City Center, and I doubt you remember much of Talluh." Sayr shied away at the mention of the city where she was born. "We are strong here, so close to the palace and the water. But the Western Kingdom is also strong, in many different ways. I fear that, if Mylan were rejected, his request would become a demand with many more requirements. Our countries may be at peace at the moment, but our relationships are strained and fragile. I cannot imagine what he may do when he is already within our palace walls."

"I still don't understand how this involves me," Sayr said, shaking her head.

"This does not just involve you. You are exactly what I need for this plan to succeed," Her Majesty answered. She gripped Sayr's arms tightly and closed in on her. "Mylan takes great interest in you because he believes there may be something deeper about you that he cannot see, which there is, of course. He and I have agreed that you will go with him to Creobe, but you have no duties that you are required to fulfill for him. I am well aware that he will try to get close to you, either by himself or through the members of his Court."

The queen's grip tightened, pinching Sayr's arms. "What he does not know is that you will have separate orders from me while you are in his Court."

"And what will my orders be, exactly?" Sayr asked.

Her Majesty's response sent icy shivers down Sayr's spine. "You will help me destroy the Western Kingdom."

ayr sat on her small bed inside the Creobian royal carriage. The Western Court and members of the Eastern Court had left the Eastern Palace only a few hours before and already Sayr missed the walls of the Eastern Palace, and the ocean, and Everett.

Her thoughts raced over the secret mission Queen Cheralin had planned specifically for Sayr. The queen had spilled so much information that Sayr's head was still reeling as she thought back to their conversation.

"The king will tell you all kinds of stories to try and convince you to remain in Creobe with him. Do not believe anything he tells you, everything that comes from his mouth is a lie," the queen had told Sayr. "We cannot let Mylan suspect that you are what you truly are, and we need him to underestimate you in order for him to let you close to his Court. The more he and his Court underestimate you, the more resources they will offer you and the greater opportunities you will have to take his Court down."

"What exactly are you asking of me?" Sayr asked.

Cheralin's stare was unyielding. "You will kill the king's mercenary."

"The king's what?" Sayr's voice pitched higher.

"Your sleuthing has paid off," the queen explained. "Mylan indeed holds an inner Court he calls the King's Court, made up of his strongest Elementals, including his own mercenary. The king's mercenary is the closest position to the king within this Court. They are considered his second in command, holding the highest position in the King's Court. However, their identity is kept completely secret from anyone outside the King's Court."

"Mylan will not want to let you go when the time comes for you to return to Visaran," Her Majesty continued. "Before this happens, you will find the king's mercenary and kill them. You will make it appear that Mylan's own Court betrayed him, killing his mercenary for their own power. It will be easily believable, an inner Court means struggles for higher rank and power, another Court member could easily kill one of their own to advance their rank. We will ruin the king's strongest unit from the inside. Once your mission is complete, you will go to Marenda and convince her the two of you must leave. She will not question your word and lead you safely out of the palace."

Sayr had opened her mouth to speak but the queen cut her off. "I do not know which members the king will keep you closest to, so you must familiarize yourself with every name before you leave. Then, when you have found who the king's mercenary is, you will kill them. One of my officials will be stationed on the outskirts of the palace every night. When the time comes for you to escape, you and

Marenda will go to them, and they will lead you on horseback back to Visaran."

Sayr shook the memory from her mind and looked down at the small piece of paper in her fist. Seven names were scrawled across the paper.

Ryon Petrov

Willa Simon

Adelaide Hill

Tomas Lambert

Dimitri Lim

Lilith Blanche

Mina Navarro

Sayr's ears rang as she read the names for the hundredth time. She could not imagine killing someone; watching as the life faded from their eyes, their body going limp, all by her hands. Even the thought of it brought bile to her throat and her head began to spin.

The queen had ordered her to continue her training in Creobe, to get stronger and learn the Creobian army's techniques. And when the time came, she was to do as she was ordered.

"Why?" Sayr had asked the queen. "I understand the Western Court isn't our most ideal ally, but this would make us very clear enemies. Why would you want that?"

"Mylan made an enemy of me the moment he forced me to agree to this arrangement in front of my entire Court." The queen's tone had become cold. "War would have eventually broken out between our countries when he refused to let you, and my armies return to Visaran. His Court is strong, and if he had you in his Court and the numbers of my army, he may become unstoppable. I believe that by dismantling it, we will take apart his strongest force and put our kingdom back on top."

Her steel gaze softened, and she reached back for Sayr. "You are my secret weapon," she cooed. "When you succeed, you will return home a hero, and I will reward you greatly. You will no longer live your life under scrutiny. No one will question you or your position in this Court any longer. You will live the life you have always wanted."

Sayr's entire world could have stopped right then and there. Her breathing hitched and every nerve in her body stilled.

"If I do this," she said slowly, "I'll be accepted in Court? I can be myself? No more hiding?"

The queen smiled widely, *proudly*, at Sayr. "No more hiding," she said. "With the position I'll give you, no one will dare question your gifts or undermine you any longer. When you return, we will tell the entire Court—the entire kingdom—of your gifts and your new position in the Eastern Palace. Everyone will find you worthy, Sayr."

Sayr's mind had felt murky while she took in her queen's words. She could be accepted in Court as she truly was once all this was over, but she still had to dismantle the King's Court to achieve that life.

"And if I fail?" Sayr asked. No matter how badly she wanted the life Her Majesty was offering her, she was not a killer; she could never be a killer. The queen was setting her up for failure, for death.

Her Majesty pushed a strand of hair behind Sayr's ear. "You will not fail."

"You must swear to secrecy on this, Sayr. My officials have been briefed and will be watching you, but only one of them knows what is to happen. Only you can do what needs to be done."

"Remember, Sayr. There is strength in duty."

Sayr repeated the words. "There is strength in duty."

The door to the cramped bedroom swung open and Sayr came back to reality. Cordia, one of the Visarian officials ordered to accompany the king back to Creobe, poked her head in. "We're stopping for a short break," she said to Sayr.

Sayr nodded, keeping the crumpled paper hidden in her fist, and rose from her bed. She walked through the bedroom to the main room of the carriage where Cordia and Marenda were waiting for her. Sayr looked at her best friend and the queen's words rang through her all over again.

Marenda knows that she is duty-bound to protect you at all costs, though she does not know the full extent of your orders. You are to be the only one to know about my given orders.

Marenda offered Sayr a small grin as she walked over to her friend, linking their arms as the carriage came to a stop. Cordia exited the carriage first, Marenda and Sayr followed close behind and onto solid ground. The night air smelled sweet and Sayr inhaled the fresh air deeply. The carriages remained in a line at the side of the road. A small group rode on horses past the carriages into the distance.

"Where are they going?" Sayr asked Cordia.

"There's a village about a mile from here, they're going to collect supplies," Cordia answered.

She walked down the road, past the two carriages at the end of the line of carts.

"Don't stay out here too long," Cordia called behind her. "The guards will continue their rounds all night, but it's still safer to remain inside."

The girls remained close to the carriage, walking towards the back so no one else could see them. Once they were hidden, Sayr opened her hand to reveal the crumpled paper.

"I need you to burn this," Sayr said. "Don't look at it, just burn it. Please, Mar."

Marenda glanced at the paper and plucked it from Sayr's hand. Her eyes left the paper, and she looked only at Sayr as the paper ignited into small flames in her hand. Within seconds, the paper was nothing more than ash. Marenda wiped her hands together to clean the ash from her fingers.

"Thank you," Sayr said and let out a small breath.

Marenda smiled at her. "We're in this together, Sayr. I'm here for you no matter what."

Sayr smiled back at her friend, but she knew the smile didn't reach her eyes. Not when the queen's mission for her and the names on that paper were still fresh in her mind.

They'd traveled through Visaran for ten full days. Sayr had never seen so much of the country before, even if it was flying by quickly.

She spent most of the time in the front room of the carriage with Mar, bringing in meals and eating or drinking while they watched the carriage fly past the golden croplands around them.

"I've never seen so much of the country before," Sayr said to Mar in awe. "It's amazing how much of Visaran is covered in fields. What kind of crops are those?" She pointed a finger out the window to rows and rows of golden-brown crops that stood about half the height of the carriage.

"I don't know, wheat maybe?" Mar guessed. She spared a quick glance out the window. "Maybe corn?"

"I'm pretty sure corn is green," Sayr said.

"Dead corn, then." Marenda smirked.

Sayr shuffled a deck of cards in her hand and spread them out on the small table. She flipped every other card over and slid half the deck to Marenda's side of the table.

"So, what's the plan?" Marenda asked.

Marenda didn't need to say anything more for Sayr to know what she meant. "They're going to try and separate us the first chance they get," Sayr said. "We're going to let them."

She saw the determination in Marenda's eyes. "I'm staying by your side no matter what, Sayr. I'm not letting them separate us."

"Not permanently," Sayr assured her friend. "Just long enough for them to give themselves away. If they think they have us separated, they'll let their guard down and hopefully give some much need information about what they want from me. I know you don't like the idea, but I need to get close to the Western Court somehow and being alone with them is a start."

"No," Marenda protested. "I am here to protect you, and I can't do that if I'm separated from you."

"King Mylan requested me to join his Court for a reason," Sayr started. "I cannot find out what that reason is if I have you keeping me guarded from them every minute. The king and his Court think I'm naïve, that they know more about my strange gifts than I do. I'm going to play into that a bit. They'll be more open and willing to slide information my way if I keep up the act as a naïve girl imprisoned within the Eastern Court."

"What am I supposed to do if they separate us?" Marenda asked.

"First, I want you to find somewhere safe to lie low. I have no idea how they plan to separate us, but I can bet they will try within the first few days of us arriving at the palace. When they do, do not struggle too much. If we are still separated for more than forty-eight hours, I will come looking for you." Sayr's gaze strayed away from Marenda.

"The queen said you're already familiar with the layout of the palace, is that true?"

"Most of the palace, anyway," Mar answered. "Many of the levels look the same but the higher levels are tougher to access and therefore there isn't much information on what's up there."

"Pick a location for us to meet," Sayr ordered. "If we are separated any longer than planned, we will meet there."

Marenda lowered her eyes, but she nodded. "Just for a short while, though. I will not let you be alone with them for too long."

Sayr grimaced. "Trust me, I'm not looking forward to it, either."

They sat in the front room all day, playing different card games and running through brief exercises that the small space would allow. Though they enjoyed the luxury of rest that the trip offered, the two were getting restless. Neither of them was used to sitting around for so long and while they completed small exercise routines, the carriage offered no room to spar or truly train.

"Sayr, look!" Marenda exclaimed and stared out the window. Sayr followed her stare and gasped at the sight outside.

The golden fields were gone and replaced by rushing water. The carriages slowed when they approached the Silia River. The water raged down an incredibly wide bed, creating heaps of white water that sloshed over the banks.

Sayr stood from her seat to get a better look through the window and Marenda did the same. She pulled the locks on the window free and pushed it open, popping her head out to see the front of the carriage line. With a better view of the water before them, Sayr realized that the road ended right at the edge of the river.

Her eyes widened as she took in the rushing water before them. This road was the main road that connected both countries, so where was the road over the river?

"Sayr."

Mar sounded breathless and Sayr swung her head back into the carriage to see her friend looking out the opposite window. Sayr ran over to the other side of the carriage to find what she had seen. A small group of people were standing only a few feet from the river.

"They're not going to try to swim across, are they?" she asked.

Marenda shook her head. "That's suicide. The river is too violent and too wide for anyone to successfully swim across without drowning."

The two of them watched as the group spread across the bank of the river, positioning themselves in a line. As one, half of the group lifted their arms and began swaying through a series of fluid motions.

"Oh, wow." Sayr watched the wet, earthy floor of the river emerge from beneath the water. The group shifted motions, and the earth curved up at the center to form a soggy bridge over the wide river just high enough for the river to continue raging below.

The other half of the group began different motions, and the girls watched from the carriage while the new dirt bridge began to dispel water out the bottom like a wrung-out sponge, leaving a dry, earthy bridge over the river.

"They can't be Visarian officials, right?" Marenda asked. "What would they be doing so far from the palace?"

"They're not officials." Cordia stood behind the two girls. "They are citizens of Visaran. They live in Talluh and travel to the village closest to the Silia River to aid the royal families in crossing the river."

"Talluh?" Sayr quickly surveyed the landscape around them, looking for any outline of buildings in the distance where the city could be. Mar grabbed her hand and pulled the two of them back down in the seats, shaking her head.

"The city is still a far distance from here," Cordia said. "We pay these citizens to come down to construct the makeshift bridge over the river. I must say these past few weeks have been the busiest for them in quite some time."

"There can't be much business in that," Marenda thought aloud.

"There certainly isn't," Cordia confirmed. "I'm sure they have other occupations back home, but we pay them very well to keep their job a secret and ensure they do their job up to standard when necessary."

The carriages began to move again, much slower, and they crossed over the bridge. The rushing waters below made Sayr's stomach flip as they passed a few dozen feet above. The river was astonishingly wide and unforgivably rough. Without the Elementals from Talluh, she doubted anyone could successfully cross the river by swimming or taking a rowboat. Finally, they made the trek over the river to the other side of the bank. The same tall, golden crops continued to cover the land around them.

"Welcome to Creobe, ladies," Cordia announced.

"Doesn't look much different from Visaran," Marenda muttered. She leaned back in her seat and closed her eyes.

Cordia turned towards the door to their beds but paused. "Just wait," she said with a sly smirk. "You'll find out just how different it is soon enough."

11

$\mathcal{S}$ayr soon realized how true Cordia's words were. Within half a day of travel, the flat croplands of Creobe had turned into thick green forests. The late morning sunlight had dimmed between the trees as the carriages continued down the barren road. A guard had taken the place of the second footman on the front seat of each carriage for extra security.

The extra guard set Sayr's nerves tingling anxiously. Creobe must truly be as dangerous as she'd been told if an extra guard was needed throughout the rest of the trip.

Sayr wondered how much of Creobe was covered in forests. She was used to the flat grasslands of the Eastern Palace and City Center with the sun always on her face and salty ocean breeze in her nostrils, not sheltered from the sun underneath looming trees for miles. The landscape began to rise into hills and mountains. The carriages climbed up and down over rocky terrain, making Sayr feel sick when she looked down at the jagged drop below.

She stopped spending so much time in the front room and opted to spend the remaining days working out or meditating in the bedroom. She hadn't been expecting to see anything new while meditating, but the meditation helped calm her nerves. They'd been in Creobian territory for six and a half days; they would arrive at the Western Palace sometime tomorrow.

The carriages stopped earlier than usual, around dinner time. Sayr expected Cordia to announce their plan for the night, but one of the footmen swung open the door to the carriage and popped his head in.

"His Majesty has requested to stop and dine here for dinner before moving on," his nasally voice called through the carriage and the three riders emerged into the first room.

Sayr and Marenda exchanged looks. Neither of them felt comfortable dining in a foreign village, but they'd grown tired of the dried beef and cheese dinners that were provided by the riders going in and out of the towns for resources. The thought of a hot meal made Sayr's stomach rumble.

"I'll certainly take up that opportunity," Cordia said. She stepped out of the carriage with the footman. Sayr followed her out of the carriage and Mar exited last.

The landscape surrounding them was so full of color and different sounds and scents that Sayr's eyes and ears didn't fully register everything around her for several minutes. Once her vision and hearing finally adjusted, she spun in slow circles, taking in the high mountains surrounding them. The mountains looked constructed completely from chiseled rock, as if giant boulders had cut through the earth to form the terrain.

Vibrant green trees covered the mountains, filling the air with a sharp, sweet scent that made Sayr think of winter nights in Talluh when she was a child. The scent of tree bark and crisp, chilled air filled her nose.

People began to file out of the carriages, some to stretch and chat. The riders in the first two carriages exited and huddled together, looking back at the end carriages patiently. Sayr spotted the king and his guards and turned away towards the forestry. Cordia crept close to her, pretending to take in the scenery alongside her.

"I understand that you don't want to do this," she whispered so only Sayr could hear her. "But remember, you need to convince them that you want to be a part of His Majesty's Court. When we find a tavern to dine at, you need to appear as if you are in awe of everything you are given. The king will likely have someone watching you. We need him to think he has a chance at keeping you here."

Sayr gave a small nod of understanding. So, Cordia knew about Her Majesty's plan for Sayr.

Sayr took a deep breath. This was the first step to a real life, a life of belonging and acceptance. She could do this, take this first step, and the rest would come as it may. Boots crushed twigs on the ground as Cordia walked away and Mar took her place.

"I hate this idea," she admitted, "but I'd rather see an early grave than refuse a hot meal."

She smirked at Sayr, and they turned towards the king's entourage. The riders of the last two carriages began to file out and join them. There were maybe a dozen Visarians riding in the carriages. The King's Court turned down a vacant street and the Visarian group followed.

A short way down the road, houses began to appear on either side. Chimney smoke rose from many of the houses and firelights loomed through the windows. The further they walked, the more buildings lined both sides of the road. Some were homes that had been built side by side with one another, others were little shops with signs posted outside their doors listing the goods or services offered inside.

Sayr made sure to take in everything around her, eyes wide and a smile plastered on her face. Marenda shot her several annoyed looks before giving up and grumbling to herself about the chilly air and vacant streets.

The smell of cooked meat hit Sayr before she spotted the tavern, and her mouth instantly began to water. She could smell roasted meats and spices. Cordia led their group as they followed the King's Court into the tavern. Sayr doubted anyone in the town knew that they were Visarian, and Sayr wondered if any of the villagers were aware that their own king walked their streets.

By the time Sayr entered the tavern, the King's Court had disappeared into a private room. The Visarian group all stood waiting in the entrance of the tavern.

"Welcome!" A short, stocky woman welcomed them into the tavern, arms open wide.

Cordia shook the woman's hand and spoke in a muffled voice that Sayr couldn't hear. She must have said something kind though, and about the group, because the short woman smiled brightly and craned her neck to peer at every face in their group.

"I have the perfect table for you all," she said. She tugged Cordia with her and walked deeper into the tavern. The rest of the group followed the woman to a long table and sat down. She gave a satisfied look to the group before rushing back into the kitchen.

"She sure is welcoming," Marenda muttered, and though Sayr knew she was trying to sound sarcastic, the suspicion in Mar's eyes was beginning to fade just slightly, giving way to hunger and anticipation for food to come through the kitchen doors.

Servers rushed through the kitchen doors towards the table offering water, wine, coffee, and all sorts of drinks to each guest. Sayr opted for water, knowing if she accepted any coffee, she wouldn't sleep a wink tonight and that would not bode well when they arrived at the palace tomorrow. Marenda accepted a glass of water but eyed the liquid for quite some time before taking a final sip. She demanded Sayr's glass, too, before Sayr could take a sip of her own.

"I am not about to go home to the queen and tell her you were poisoned before we even made it to the Western Palace," she explained.

Another round of people came through, offering samples of food. Most of the food looked nothing like the dishes in Visaran, Sayr noticed there was no seafood offered. The food looked delicious despite the fact, and Sayr reluctantly wanted to try everything offered to her. Marenda, however, still demanded to eat anything that Sayr looked interested in first to make sure it hadn't been compromised in any way. She even tried going as far as taking the first bite of Sayr's sample before her, but Sayr quickly shut the idea down.

Soon, full dishes of the food they had just sampled were being placed in the middle of the table, with plates in front of each guest so they could pick from the multiple dishes in front of them. The food was like nothing she'd ever tasted before. The different meats were spicier, with deeper hints of herbs that Sayr could have eaten every day for the rest of her life. Every dish was sided with vegetables, though she'd never seen such vibrant vegetables of red and orange and green. Some had been sliced and cooked while others were left raw and shaped into little balls.

The group ate heartily as the food continued to come swiftly from the kitchen. Sayr didn't need to try and pretend to be in awe of the food or atmosphere around her. It was all so delicious and new and filling that she caught herself smiling throughout most of the meal.

The mood seemed to change while the group filled their bellies and began talking louder and friendlier with one another. One of the men at the end of the table continuously cracked jokes that had Sayr almost choking on her food from laughter.

Sayr had lost track of just how long they were at the tavern, but all too quickly the food was finished, and empty plates were being carried off back into the kitchen. The short woman came back with a satisfied grin and spoke quietly with one of the officials farther down the table. She carried a pile of steaming containers full of food and handed them to Cordia when they all rose to leave.

Sayr grabbed onto Marenda's arm while they walked out of the tavern. The sun had fully set over the mountains, leaving the night air even colder than before. Sayr wrapped her free arm tight around her body and pulled herself closer to Marenda to feed off her unnatural heat. She still wore her usual clothing and, come to think of it, she hadn't packed anything that would suit this climate.

Her whole body shivered, and she ached for the warmth and the sea in the Eastern Palace. A familiar voice in the distance stopped her in her tracks. The voice itself wasn't familiar, but the accent sure was.

She turned to the side of the road where a mother pulled two children—a boy and a girl—along in each hand. They all swung their arms while they walked, holding hands, and it sounded as if the mother was telling her children a funny nursery rhyme while they walked.

Sayr had never heard the nursery rhyme before but the mother's accent, or the lack thereof, was as familiar to Sayr as Mar's close warmth against her skin. The woman didn't connect her words or soften the harsh vowels like the Creobian accent did. The woman's words were more separated by breath, and she hardened her vowels. The Visarian accent sounded almost muted, as if it were being worn away by the woman, but Sayr could still make the connection.

She sounded Visarian.

Without a second thought, Sayr released Marenda's arm and wandered closer to the family.

"Sayr?" Marenda called after her. Gravel crunched beneath her feet as she followed behind Sayr.

Sayr was a dozen steps away when she called to the family. "Visarian?"

The mother's face paled. She froze mid-stride and stared at Sayr. Her two children smiled, and the daughter waved at Sayr, but the mother looked fear stricken.

"You're from Visaran, correct?" Sayr asked. "I can tell by your accent."

"I don't know what you're talking about," the woman said. Her voice was strained as she suddenly took on a thick Creobian accent. "We are Creobian."

Sayr opened her mouth to speak again but a hand grasped her by the shoulder and quickly swung her around. She expected to slam into Marenda, who had been following her a moment ago, but Cordia stood only inches away and held her tight.

"My apologies," Cordia said in a clear Creobian accent. "My daughter is learning accents in school and becomes all too excited when she thinks she recognizes one."

A bit of color returned to the mother's rosy cheeks and nose, and she gave a small, shaky smile before turning again and hurrying off faster down the road, tugging her children close to her.

Cordia waited until the mother was out of sight before casting her heated glare down at Sayr. "You cannot go around asking people if they are Visarian like that, especially in this country!"

She kept her voice low, but Sayr caught the severity in it. She took a step back and Cordia released her grip on her shoulder.

"That woman sounded Visarian," she explained. "She was telling some sort of nursery rhyme to her children, but she didn't have the Creobian accent."

"And that suddenly makes her Visarian?" Cordia's tone grew more frustrated, as if Sayr's explanation only made her sound more foolish. "There are other countries outside of this continent, Sayr, she could be from any one of them. Or she could just have a strange accent!"

She yelled the last part and quickly turned around to make sure no one had heard. Sayr peeked over her shoulder to see the rest of their group had left them behind to head to the carriages. Only Marenda stood on the opposite side of the road, her eyes locked on the two of them.

"But her accent changed clearly to Creobian when I said something," Sayr argued. "Why would she try to hide her real accent if she was Visarian? Wouldn't she be pleased to know that we're Visarian, too?"

Cordia pinched the bridge of her nose, clearly at the end of her patience with Sayr.

"She is not Visarian," she concluded. "Maybe her family migrated to Creobe sometime in her life or maybe she just has a strange accent that you have never heard of. There are countless numbers of people in Creobe with different accents or no accent at all, just like in Visaran. But she is not Visarian. Immigration between our two countries is illegal. You are accusing this woman of illegally leaving Visaran."

"And that is not the point," Cordia continued. "You are not under the queen's protection anymore, Sayr. You are hundreds of miles away from the Eastern Palace. Visarians are not welcome here. You cannot go around asking people if they are Visarian, likely giving yourself away in the process. If anyone were to find out what is happening between our two Courts, you could be taken away or killed. All of us could. Do you understand?"

Sayr glanced in the direction the mother had gone with her children. She had looked so afraid when Sayr had called out to her, as if Sayr had just blurted out a dark secret of hers. The encounter still didn't make sense to her, but she had to admit she'd been foolish just walking up to the woman and asking if she was Visarian. She was here because of the queen's mission, and she wasn't going to be found out so easily.

"I understand." She nodded at the official.

Cordia gave a final huff and walked her back to Mar. As a trio, they silently made their way back to the carriages. Mar's eyes flicked to Sayr several times in question and Sayr returned her gaze with a look that she hoped said *I'll tell you everything later.*

However, later never came as Cordia never left them alone together for the rest of the night. Eventually, Sayr gave up on trying to communicate with Marenda, deciding to tell her everything tomorrow, and settled into bed.

The carriages rounded into the courtyard of the Western Palace as Sayr entered the main room of their carriage. Cordia had pulled down the shades of the windows in the main room, blocking the view of the Creobian Palace.

She heard the rumbling of voices and cheers as the carriages slowly came to a final stop. They waited for several minutes before the door to their carriage finally opened and bright sunlight streamed inside.

The light was blinding at first and a chilly breeze swept in, leaving goosebumps all over Sayr's exposed arms. She had put on her warmest clothing but even the thin material of her flowing pants didn't shelter her from the cold.

The group stepped out of the carriages one by one and onto the gravel. Sayr took a moment to assess her surroundings. A crowd of people stood all along the outer walls of the palace, smiling and waving and cheering with excitement.

Sayr's instinct to hide from the crowd immediately took over and she stepped back behind Marenda, who seemed to stand at her full height to try and better hide Sayr. Her eyes took in the greenery around them. The ivory palace stuck out against the green forest. Pillar walls trapped her inside the palace grounds. She could only see above them, white-tipped mountains poking up from every direction.

Another carriage door opened, and they all turned their attention to King Mylan standing on the top step of his carriage and beaming out towards the crowd. The crowd erupted in cheers. The citizens waved and blew kisses to their king, and he waved and smiled back at them all, thanking them for welcoming them all home.

After he received enough praise, he stepped down from the carriage and walked towards the carriages filled with Visarians. His demeanor had shifted from his time in the Eastern Palace. He walked more confidently, almost strutting, and even his tone seemed lighter when he addressed the crowd around them.

He beamed at the groups from the carriages, threw his arms wide open and announced, "Ladies and gentlemen, welcome to the Creobian Palace!"

The rest of the carriages emptied out into the green and white courtyard, filling the stone walls with echoing voices and laughter. Sayr took a step closer to Marenda and linked their arms. They watched the Western Court all smiling and hugging one another, happy to be home.

The Visarian Court officials joined the three of them. Cordia immediately turned and began whispering urgently to the others. A few of King Mylan's entourage came to stand behind him.

"Allow my ladies to show you to your chambers," he said. "I'm sure we are all exhausted from the trip."

The king looked anything but exhausted, he looked ecstatic to be back in his palace. His *ladies* stood behind him, looking newly refreshed and electric with energy.

Willa strode forward. "Your rooms have already been prepared for you," she said. "You will be staying in the same hall. After dinner, I would be more than happy to give you a tour of the palace."

"How thoughtful," Marenda deadpanned.

The change in atmosphere chilled Sayr. In Visaran, the Western King and his Court were much more reserved. But now, they seemed electrified and confident and… happy. The tables had now turned, and they had not turned in a favorable direction for Sayr.

King Mylan clasped his hands together, catching Sayr's attention once again. "Shall we make our way inside?"

The crowd quickly followed His Majesty up the white stone stairs into the palace. Guards opened the tall, stone doors into the palace for them and Sayr's breath hitched when she took in the scene before her.

The tallest section of the Eastern Palace was three stories high, and the glass halls that led towards the outskirts of the palace were all one level. The Western Palace, though, not only soared dozens of levels above their heads, but also dropped far below them all. Sayr expected the main entrance of the palace to be on the first floor, but when she looked down from the railing in front of them, she counted at least seven floors beneath where they now stood. Looking back up, she couldn't count the number of levels above before they began shrinking and blending together.

The empty space beyond the black iron railing opened up to a cylinder-shaped hole in its floor so that the halls of each level could be seen. To their left and right were two staircases, one that led up and one that led down. The levels were filled with people bunched around the black wrought iron railings, staring up and down at the new arrivals. Just like the crowd outside, many clapped and cheered at the sight of their own Court back in their palace.

Mylan took a step towards the staircase leading down and most of his Court followed closely behind him. "Willa will show you to your chambers," he repeated. "I will see you all in the dining hall for dinner!"

The king rounded down the staircase, circled past the cylindrical hall, and disappeared out of sight.

Willa cleared her throat, and the Eastern Court all shifted in her direction. She smiled softly and waved a graceful hand towards the staircase going up. "This way, please."

Willa led them up at least a dozen staircases by the time they arrived at their private hall. She seemed unaffected by the trek, but the rest of the group was winded, breathing heavily with exertion while Willa began assigning rooms.

She took her time appointing each member of the Eastern Court to their own chambers, giving each of them time to scout out their room before moving on down the hall to the next chamber.

Eventually, Mar and Sayr were the only two left waiting to be assigned a room, and only two doors remained side by side at the end of the hall.

"Here you are." Willa stopped and faced them. Her fingers brushed the handle of one door. She lightly pushed it open, and they all walked in together.

Just like the center of the palace, this room was cylindrical. The ceiling towered high above with a beautiful glass chandelier ignited brightly by firelight. A large wooden desk sat next to the wardrobe in the bedroom and exquisite furniture was placed around a long center table next to the fireplace. A large mirror was placed next to the wardrobe, along with wrought iron sconces high above on the wall around the room. Across from the fireplace was a large, canopied bed, and next to the bed were two more doors.

Marenda looked over every inch of the chamber, no doubt taking note of every exit within the room. "Why so many doors?" she asked.

Willa walked to the center of the room and faced the two girls. "The door to your right leads to your washroom, Lady Sayr."

"So, this is my room?" Sayr interrupted.

Willa nodded and continued. "You will find your vanities, bathtub, and closet in there."

She walked towards the double doors and threw them both open. "These doors lead to your balcony."

Sayr followed Willa out onto the balcony with Marenda in tow. As soon as they crossed the threshold onto the balcony, the rushing winds hit Sayr and tossed Marenda's red and black braids over her face. Marenda sputtered as she tamed her hair, tying it back into a bun and took a few steps back into the bedroom.

"What's with the wind?" she asked accusingly. "There's no breeze coming into the bedroom."

Willa turned to face Marenda, her coiled hair bobbing in the wind. "The palace is enchanted to keep out the cold. The weather here is not as warm as where you are from, but we like to keep our windows open still to enjoy the beautiful views."

Sayr pivoted to look out past the balcony railing, and it took all her control not to gasp at the sight. Being on ground level in the mountains was one sight but being high above all the mountains was like drifting above another world.

Mountains peaked from the earth in every direction, coated in deep evergreen trees and topped with what Sayr assumed had to be snow. Snow never reached the Eastern Palace, but she remembered maybe a handful of snowfalls during her childhood in Talluh and recognized the sparkling white layer glinting in the sunlight at the tips of the mountains in the distance.

Looking down, Sayr's legs began to shake. The palace looked to be constructed at the top of one of the highest mountains in the region, casting the uncountable levels of the tall palace high above the mountains. At the bottom of this mountain was what looked to be a large lake, the water was so still from up here that it looked like glass reflecting the greenery of the mountains and the cloudless blue sky above.

"What do you mean by enchanted?" Marenda asked, still standing in the doorway.

"Our Air Elementals found a way to keep the cold air out of the palace a long time ago," Willa explained. "We have a few keeping up the enchantment at all times so that we can enjoy the palace without feeling so closed inside."

"That's amazing," Sayr admitted, still staring far down below.

Marenda backed farther into the room and pointed to the last door they hadn't opened yet. "Where does that door lead?" she asked.

"Ah, that one," Willa remarked. She and Sayr entered the chambers once again. "That door leads to the next chamber."

"Your queen demanded that you two be together at all times," Willa explained. She pushed open the door to reveal a chamber exactly like the one that they currently stood in. "This is the best arrangement we could provide for you two without assigning both of you to one chamber."

Sayr walked into the room to look around. "Both of these rooms are ours?"

Willa nodded. "You each have your own chamber. You can stay in both or just one, it is up to you. Now, I will let you get settled before dinner. We will be eating in the dining hall tonight; I will return to escort you all there."

Before Willa left, Marenda shot around. "Are we supposed to just sit here until you escort us everywhere?"

"You are free to roam the palace as much as you like, you are not forced to remain in your rooms. Some parts of the palace require access which you will likely not have, but you are treated as guests during your stay and may do and see whatever you like as any guest would." With a final nod, Willa exited the chambers and left Marenda and Sayr alone.

The girls spent the first hour alone investigating each room; checking for spying holes in the walls and crevices, testing Marenda's abilities to ensure the rooms were not Elemental-proof, and setting up small traps by each door, especially the balconies and entrances to each room. Once they'd deemed the chambers safe enough, they each began unpacking their bags the servants had brought up for them.

Sayr sat on the canopied bed, surveying the bedroom for the hundredth time. She felt foreign in this room, though she suspected she was going to feel foreign in every room of this palace. Marenda burst in from the door adjoining their rooms, a new and much more exciting air to her.

"Can you believe this?" she asked a little breathlessly. "I mean your suite in the East Wing is impressive but *this*..." She didn't bother to finish her sentence and ran for the bed, jumping onto the mattress beside Sayr.

Sayr let out a huff of a laugh. It always amazed her how differently Mar acted around those she trusted and those she didn't. Those who didn't know her well rarely, if ever, got to see the devoted, loving girl behind the armor and fire.

"It certainly is something," Sayr said and fell against the soft mattress next to Marenda.

The two girls laid on their backs, staring at the intricate design on the canopy above the bed. Sayr looked over at her best friend. "What are we going to do, Mar?"

Marenda met her gaze, any sign of humor gone. "We're going to do as we've been ordered. We will continue our drills and play guest in King Mylan's Court, and once our time is up, we'll head back to Visaran and hope these trips don't become a habit."

Sayr sighed. "I don't think it's going to be that easy."

I have to find the king's mercenary, Sayr thought. *I just need to become a murderer, and then I'll get the life I've always wanted.*

Mar nodded next to her. "I think you're right. But if we don't keep the easy plan in our minds, we let the difficult stuff take over."

She twisted onto her stomach and smiled at Sayr. "Right now, though, we're going to get ready for dinner. I hope the food's as good here as it was at the tavern. I'm starving."

Too soon, Willa knocked on Sayr's door to escort her to dinner. Peering in, she found Marenda in the room as well and the two girls followed her out into the hall. The rest of the Eastern Court followed behind Willa while they walked to the dining hall, chatting about their views of the mountains and the bellowing wind that never entered their rooms or blew out the candles in the chandeliers. One of the officials murmured about a large catlike animal she'd seen prowling through the mountains not too far from the castle.

The group walked and talked while Willa silently led on, not partaking in any of the conversation. Sayr couldn't help but to be in awe of the Western Palace, and she hated the feeling. While the others all talked in excitement and curiosity, she barely uttered more than a few words.

The two palaces truly couldn't have been any more different. Where the Eastern Palace was constructed of glass and rock, the Western Palace was made almost entirely of stone and iron. Instead of windowpanes like the Eastern Palace, the Western Palace had cut out large chunks of stone just above Sayr's eye level as windows. Black iron lanterns lined the walls, their orange candlelight flickering across the white and black mosaic floors they walked on.

Sayr expected the halls to be filled with Court guests, but the halls were almost completely empty on this level. Only a few guards stood at attention as they passed.

Willa approached two guards stationed at a single door. Soft chatter and the clanking of dishes floated through the cracks of the door and Sayr's nerves softened just a touch at the sound of life. The guards caught sight of Willa approaching and bowed low. One pushed the door open, continuing his bow while they all entered the dining hall.

Sayr was starting to get annoyed at all the breathtaking views this palace offered. The dining hall was unnecessarily large to only hold an incredibly long stone table placed in the middle of the room, three fireplaces along the right wall, and a set of velvet chaise in front of each fireplace.

The wall opposite the fireplaces was missing entirely, leading out onto a balcony with stone pillars holding the roof above. Less than half of the two dozen chairs were filled at the dining table; Sayr recognized Lilith seated at one end of the table and the red-haired girl sitting next to her, as well as Dimitri and the blond boy from the throne room. Three other people that she did not recognize sat at the table, and King Mylan sat at the head. He stood when the group filed in.

"Welcome!" he bellowed, and they started making their way to the table, selecting seats and sitting down.

Sayr snagged a seat in the middle of the table next to Mar. Her mouth watered when she looked down at the array of dishes before her. Pots of steamed stew and meats were at the center of the table. Bowls were piled high with red and green round fruits and small brown loaves of bread that were topped with little seeds. The table held at least ten different dishes that all looked delicious. Her fingers twitched and she urged to reach out and grab a plate-full of everything on the table. The king cleared his throat loudly and called a servant over.

"I have had only the best delicacies prepared that Creobe has to offer," he boasted and gestured over the display on the dining table. "Including the best wine ever tasted on the continent."

As he spoke, servants began pouring deep red wine into the crystal glasses placed in front of each guest.

"Please enjoy," King Mylan said and reached for his own glass. He lifted it in a small toast and took a long drink.

Servants began filling up bowls and plates for each guest. One filled Sayr's dish with beef stew, bread, and a tasty looking pastry stuffed with cheese. She noticed that there was no fish on the table. Seafood was regularly eaten for at least one meal a day in the Eastern Palace.

Sayr's hand clutched her spoon tightly, unwilling to bring it to her mouth. What if the food had been poisoned? What if this was King Mylan's way of ridding Queen Cheralin of her Court just as she intended to do to him? It would be the perfect plan to get rid of the Eastern Court before she could rid the king of his Court.

He had to know that nothing good could come from belittling Her Majesty the way he did in her own palace. He had to be expecting some sort of revenge from her. And why wouldn't he strike first when he had the chance?

She glanced around the table at everyone eating, scooping stew into their mouths and ripping off hunks of bread with their teeth. Her eyes followed the hands of the servant serving the king, watching every dish that they piled neatly onto his plate.

Mar grabbed the plate that the servant had made for Sayr and began eating, switching out her still empty plate with Sayr's. Sayr shot a worried look at Mar, remembering what she'd said and done at the tavern, that she wouldn't go back to tell Her Majesty that Sayr had been poisoned and volunteered to take the first bite of all her food.

Yet no one looked ill as they all ate from the same dishes on the table.

"Could I have some of that, please?" Sayr asked as she pointed to the thick orange stew that the king's servant had set in front of him.

"And a piece of that." She pointed to the bread the king had taken a bite of.

"And a couple of those, please." She pointed at the cheese stuffed puff pastries that were also piled onto the king's plate.

The servant's eyes followed every dish she pointed to and nodded. "Of course, milady."

The chatter in the dining hall quieted while everyone ate. Sayr's hand landed just above her dinner knife on the table, her fingers gently pushing the knife into her sleeve. She eyed every person at the table, Visarian and Creobian, waiting to see if someone would fall. When no one did, she assumed the food had indeed not been poisoned. If the king were to poison the Eastern Court, she guessed he would not do so in front of his own people and risk poisoning them as well. Still, better to be safe than sorry.

Sayr tried a little of everything, especially the desserts displayed before her, except for the wine. She pushed the glass closer to Marenda who happily took it for herself.

Once everyone had cleared the last of their many plates and dessert had been cleared from the table, King Mylan rose from his seat.

"I would like to discuss our arrangements with our guests." His eyes passed around the table and landed on Cordia.

"I have been told by Her Majesty that Cordia will oversee the Visarian troops that will be arriving in about a week. I expect you will divide these troops amongst your officials." He nodded to the other officials that had come to Creobe. "Each of you will observe different troops, as well as attend routine meetings with my war officials about the attacks on my country."

Cordia nodded while the king discussed the roles that Her Majesty had assigned before they had left the Eastern Palace. After some back and forth between the king and one official who had tried to bargain the role he'd been given as an overseer of one of the more brutal combat troops, King Mylan settled his gaze on Sayr and Marenda.

"You two," he practically purred, "will be specially trained, at Her Majesty's request, of course. My ladies are skilled swordswomen, archers, and can lethally wield just about any weapon."

Lilith, Willa, and the red-haired girl sat up straighter in their seats, swelling with pride.

"Lady Sayr, it would be my pleasure to offer you one-on-one training with my most skilled warriors in the armory," he smiled.

Before Sayr could open her mouth, Marenda slammed her empty wine glass onto the table.

"Absolutely not," she refuted. "Sayr and I have been ordered to stick together during our stay here and we will do just that. If you want to train Sayr specifically then I'll be more than happy to watch from the side, but she will not be going alone."

Sayr put a hand on Marenda's arm to settle her. She agreed with her best friend, but if she was going to complete her mission, she would have to get close to the king's inner Court. These trainings just may be her ticket in.

She turned back to the king and gave him her sweetest smile. "Thank you for the offer, Your Majesty. I will think about these private trainings, but for now I'd feel more comfortable training with Mar and everyone else."

King Mylan finished his own glass of wine before returning her smile. "Of course, I will have the arrangements made just in case."

Lilith swung open the door to the king's quarters with Addy and Willa in tow behind her. Tonight's dinner had worn her out beyond exhaustion, and she wanted nothing more than to have her servants fill a hot bath and bring her a personal bottle of wine.

Addy surged forward and sprawled onto one of the chaise chairs closest to the fireplace. "Oh, it feels sooo good to be home!" she squealed and turned closer to the fire.

"It is nice to be back in my chambers," Willa agreed and took a seat for herself.

Lilith scoffed and shot both girls annoyed looks. How could they both be in good spirits after the day they'd all had? Their arrival home had been just as exhausting as it was exciting, and the king's dinner with their guests had her practically swaying on her feet from exhaustion.

Neither of them had to manipulate their element during the entire dinner like she had. Influencing a single person was stressful enough, influencing the entire Eastern Court to feel happy and excited about everything they'd seen and tasted since they arrived in the Western Palace took a heavy toll on her, physically and mentally. A headache pulsed against her skull, and she massaged her temple.

And yet the king had instructed her not to use her influence on the Visarian girl and the guard with the red and black braids. She had no doubt he gave her the orders because she had violated the king's terms in Visaran.

She felt a soft pressure on her shoulder and turned to see dark shoulder-length hair and large biceps.

"Hello, Ryon," she greeted.

"How was your time in Visaran?" Ryon asked.

"Brutal," Lilith admitted. "You missed absolutely nothing of interest, trust me."

Ryon smiled at her. "I would have loved to see the ocean. Tell me you saw the ocean for yourself."

"I did," she admitted. "It looks just like the ocean from our shores."

"I've never seen then ocean." Ryon's gaze drilled into Lilith, and he lowered his voice so only she could hear. "Does it still hurt?"

Lilith stiffened. "Heard about it already, have you?"

"The entirety of the King's Court heard about it," Ryon said. "I'm sorry Lilith. The queen had no right having you publicly whipped."

"That girl had no right to go squealing when my influence didn't even touch her," Lilith corrected. "She will pay for it while she's here, though, believe me."

"Of course, Lilith," Ryon soothed.

Lilith kept her tone friendly enough, though her blood sizzled at the sight of Ryon. If he had finally arrived, then perhaps every member of the King's Court was here, too. She looked around the room, mentally taking count of each person. The slight glow of hope in her chest fell again. Six people sat in the king's quarters, only one specific member was missing. The door to the king's quarters opened again and His Majesty and his personal guards stepped into the room.

Each member of the King's Court bowed low while His Majesty took his time snagging a drink off the liquor table and settled into one of the lavish velvet seats displayed around the fireplace. He took a long swig and shimmied further into his seat before looking around at the six members of his personal Court.

"Your Majesty." Ryon took a step around Lilith. "What do we do now? We hadn't anticipated their refusal."

"You mean *you* had not anticipated it," Willa noted. "Those of us who kept eyes on the two of them back in Visaran highly anticipated the Royal Guard would refuse the two of them being separated."

"And how could you have anticipated that?" Ryon argued.

"They are very close," Willa countered. "The guard feels protective over her friend, and they are both aware of our plan to keep them separated as much as possible in order to sway Sayr to our side."

"So how do we sway her to our side?" Tomas spoke up from his seat closest to the balcony on the far side of the room.

"If they will not choose to separate themselves during their stay," the king said slowly, his eyes trailing over to Addy, "then we will just have to force some separation between them."

Addy met the king's gaze and smiled impishly. "As always, I am at your service, my king."

Mina stood from her seat next to Willa. "We promised that no harm would come to any member of the Eastern Court," she reminded the group. "We cannot just kill the guard and throw her body over a balcony. Besides, she is the queen's personal guard. She may be useful in information if we can get them separated in a more civilized way."

Many members of the group nodded thoughtfully but Lilith rolled her eyes. Leave it to Mina to be compassionate over the Eastern Court, while the rest of them wouldn't give a second thought if their Court started dropping like flies.

"And how do you plan to separate them in a *civilized* manner?" Tomas asked, putting mock emphasis on the word.

"Leave it all to me," Addy spoke up as she snuggled deeper into the chaise. "I'll get them separated. And keep them separated."

"Excellent." The king twined his fingers together, elbows propped on the armchairs. "We start tomorrow. I have a public training lesson for you to attend, Adelaide."

Lilith turned her gaze onto Addy. She kept her eyes on the fire that she laid in front of. Her body tensed, as if she knew Lilith was staring at her but didn't want to meet her gaze.

Lilith kept her gaze locked on the girl until finally Addy looked her way, and Lilith threw her a sinister grin full of unspoken words of what was to come for the two Visarian girls.

Addy grinned back, but there was much less malice behind it, irritating Lilith even more. She walked out of the room, head pounding and ready for a long night's sleep.

13

$\mathcal{A}$ bright beam of sunlight shone through the cut-out windows into Sayr's chambers, hitting her square in the eyes. She squinted through the brightness, tossed the thick comforter off her, and stretched out her limbs.

And immediately froze.

The doors to her wardrobe were opened and someone was sifting through the drawers. Sayr's heart raced, her eyes darted to the small traps set by each door to her chamber. The bells on each should have made enough noise to alert her, but they'd been moved to one corner of the room, still set to go off.

She fumbled around the bed for the knife she'd stolen from dinner last night and raised it between her and the stranger.

"What are you doing?" Sayr shouted and they jumped back in surprise.

A girl stood before her. Her big brown eyes met Sayr's and they stared at each other in surprise. Her long black hair was tied back into a braid, and she looked young, younger than Sayr. A stack of clothing was tucked underneath one arm.

"Y-your clothes are too thin for our climate," she stuttered. "I've brought you some thicker clothing. A gift from His Majesty."

Sayr stared at the girl while she turned back towards the dresser and placed more clothes inside its drawers. She didn't look like a threat, but Sayr knew looks could be incredibly deceiving.

"Who are you?" she asked.

"My name is Dema, I am your lady's maid."

"Lady's maid?" Sayr repeated.

Dema closed the wardrobe doors with a final thud and walked to the sofa where another stack of clothing sat. She placed the stack in the bottom drawers and closed them She peeked one eye past the wardrobe and over at Sayr, who still held the knife between them, then slid her gaze away again.

"Thanks for the clothes, but I don't think I'll be needing a lady's maid." Sayr lowered her arm but kept the knife tight in her grip.

Dema tiptoed towards the bed and laid out a small stack of clothing onto the corner of the mattress before stepping back. "You'll want these for the training grounds."

Fur-lined leggings, a brown knitted top, and a shawl with some type of animal fur lining the hood rested on the bed. Sayr reached out to rub the fur lining between her fingers and glanced back up at the girl.

"Are my boots acceptable?" she asked. Embarrassment reddened her cheeks for being so unprepared and so willing to accept the warmer clothing.

Dema studied the worn boots at the foot of the bed, failing to hide the pitiful smile playing on her lips. "I suggest you double up on socks, but they will do."

She headed for the door, with no more explanation other than, "Lady Willa will be here shortly to take you to the training grounds. You should get dressed."

As soon as the door shut behind Dema, a second door to her room opened and Mar slinked in. She was clothed head to toe in fur, wool, and a thick coat. Her outfit was so unlike the uniform she usually sported that Sayr let out a surprised laugh.

Mar shrugged the laughter off. "I don't do well in the cold."

Sayr couldn't hide her smile. Not even a full day in the Western Palace and Marenda looked as if she'd been forced to spend a month chipping ice. Her smile vanished as she remembered waking up to a stranger in her room.

"Did you see that girl?" she asked and pointed to the door. "She walked right in while I was sleeping."

Sayr took in Mar's new outfit, and she gaped at her. "Did you know she was in here?"

Mar shrugged again. "Of course, I knew she was in here. She came into my room first although she was smart enough to knock so I didn't accidentally kill her. I let her in your room but told her not to wake you. Clearly, she didn't listen."

A small wave of relief rushed over Sayr. She dropped the knife and grabbed one of her pillows, flinging it at Mar. At least the girl hadn't snuck in while Mar was sleeping, although she thought it might still be a good idea to swipe a real weapon or two from training to sleep with.

By the time Marenda and Sayr arrived at the training grounds at the base of the mountain that the palace had been built on, Sayr was silently thanking Dema for the warmer clothing.

The outside air made her shiver even with the fur-lined clothing and she tugged the hood of her shawl over her head. A few clouds floated lazily up above, but the sky was otherwise a perfect shade of deep blue.

Sayr scanned the training grounds around them while Mar shot questions at Willa about the status of the Visarian troops arrival. The grounds didn't look too different from those back in the Eastern Palace. Short cut grass covered most of the grounds in front of her. Perhaps a dozen large pits dug about half a dozen feet into the earth. Some of the pits had soldiers occupying them, practicing defensive strategies, or already facing off against one another.

Behind the pits were tall pillars that other soldiers were climbing high up. Sayr watched as soldiers each took turns climbing one pole and jumping from platform to platform, then barreling back to the ground and finishing with a sprint to a long course of obstacles fit for different Elementals.

"This way." Willa led them away from the course and towards the pits where an impressive group was already assembling.

While Sayr and Marenda seemed to fit right in with their fur-lined training clothes, Willa stuck out like a sore thumb in her flowing baby blue gown that cuffed at each wrist.

"Someone will receive you once your training is over," she said. She looked only at Sayr before making her way back up towards the towering palace. Mar flashed a raised eyebrow at Sayr before standing in to blend with the crowd where a general spoke.

"Today you will be fighting one-on-one using only your element," the man explained. "Each of you were chosen for this group because of your Elemental abilities and will be paired with other Elementals of different abilities in order to strengthen your offense and defense skills."

He scanned through the crowd. "We will start by analyzing fights against the different Elementals. Once I think you're ready, I'll split you into pairs and you'll continue your one-on-one's in each pit."

Sayr smirked and peeked a look over at Mar, whose eyes were glittering with excitement. She could hardly contain her own excitement, fighting one-on-one was their specialty and she was itching to get to face off against a Creobian soldier. Just put a dagger in her hand and she'd be good to—

Wait, the general's words finally caught up with her racing thoughts, *fight using* only *our element?!*

Her excitement quickly melted into panic as she pieced the words together. No weapons. Just the elements. And even with her gift, she still wasn't an Elemental.

I'm screwed. I'm screwed. I am so screwed!

The Western Court had no clue what Sayr truly was. King Mylan suspected that she could fend off other's abilities, or at least fend off whatever abilities Lilith possessed, but if she were to face off against another soldier and not use any Elemental gifts, the king would certainly know that she was not a typical Elemental.

Panic rose in her throat and her hands began to shake when the general called two names to the edge of the pit. Two men emerged from the crowd, walked over to the general, and faced each other. Sayr watched the men, glad that her name hadn't been called. She took a deep breath, steadying her shaky breaths as the two soldiers jumped down into the pit.

As soon as the soldier's feet hit the ground, the fight began. Sayr watched in silent amazement as the two soldiers strategically maneuvered around each other, anticipating their opponent's strike.

With a warrior's shout, one of the men ran towards his opponent and swung up one arm. A current of water lifted from the floor below his feet and gathered around his body. His opponent ignited both hands in flames of fire and began tossing fireballs at the Water Elemental, who blocked each one with his stream of water.

They went back and forth; each man manipulating their element strategically to try and advance over the other. Sayr's nerves vibrated along her body while she watched.

Shouts erupted around her, and soldiers cheered for the men, both now panting hard from the fight. The Water Elemental kept trying to get close to the Fire Elemental. Sayr quickly analyzed his strategy; to get the water close enough to cover his opponent's mouth and nose and, hopefully, knock him out or get him to surrender before taking water into his lungs.

Every time he got an inch closer, the Fire Elemental's flames would rage bigger and brighter, and the water was quickly turning to steam. The Water Elemental tried summoning more water from the earth, but it was evaporating too quickly in the heat of the pit to keep up.

The Fire Elemental swooped low to the ground and a line of fire shot from the ground towards his opponent. The Water Elemental struggled to keep some of the water in his grasp while he used the rest to extinguish the flames near him. Sayr could barely see either man as the thick waves of steam rolled up from the pit. The men appeared to be getting closer to one another, the Fire Elemental circling his opponent like a thresher shark circling its prey.

A cry of fury bounced up the walls of the pit and a cool gust of wind blew the steam away, giving the crowd a clear view of the men. The Fire Elemental had his opponent backed into a corner. The stream of water that had been wrapped around the Water Elemental was now gone and his right arm looked red and enflamed. Small holes had been burned through his thick jacket.

Cheers rang out from the soldiers above and the Fire Elemental jumped, grabbed the edge of the pit, and pulled himself out.

"Well done," the general said and faced the crowd. "We have a Fire Elemental who has bested a Water Elemental, why is that?"

A soldier behind Marenda raised his hand. "The Water Elemental didn't create any water; he just used the water from the earth around him."

"Excellent." The general nodded his approval. "As Elementals, we often forget our gifts are for creating as well as influencing. We prefer manipulating the already existing elements around us as it is easier and quicker than creating the elements ourselves. However, when you are in the middle of a fight and you've run out of resources, you may have no choice but to start creating them yourself. Remember to focus on creating your element during these trainings, it'll become easier the more you practice."

The general pivoted to address each soldier in the crowd. "Only the most gifted Elementals are able to create and manipulate their element. It is your job to find your strengths, whether that be creating or manipulating, and stick with that. Some of you will be stronger than others. You must learn how to fight against Elementals stronger than you and spin the fight to your advantage. What else?"

Sayr stared at the Water Elemental while the general spoke, assessing his reddened arm and burnt clothing. She couldn't take her eyes away from the panting soldier when another hand raised in the crowd.

"The Fire Elemental had the advantage of the sun," another soldier answered plainly.

Sayr watched the soldier clutch his burnt and twitching arm.

"Correct!" the general shouted. "Elementals are stronger when we are around our element and know how to control it. Fire is not so easily found, but the energy of fire is all around us, in the rays of the sun. Fire Elementals should take advantage of that, as it not only allows you to create, but also manipulate fire better than most Elementals can manipulate their element."

Sayr watched the burnt soldier fall to his knees, his head hanging low.

The general finally looked over at the Water Elemental. He jumped into the pit, assessing the soldier for any serious injuries before ordering him to be taken to the medic's level. Sayr had seen worse burns in training, in fact she'd had worse burns herself, but never during group trainings. No doubt the soldier would be out for at least the rest of the day. Two more soldiers jumped into the pit and helped pull him out before taking him to the medic's level.

Was this how all Creobian soldiers trained? Burning or drowning one another into submission and being taken to the medic's level for assessment? It didn't seem like the most practical way to train. Though, this type of training would create fierce soldiers with experience in full combat with their element. The queen would certainly want to know about this.

The general paced around the dirt circle, inspecting the soldiers gathered once again. "Let's go again," he ordered. He paced in front of the soldiers across the circle from Sayr. "Can I find a volunteer this time?"

A few soldiers around Sayr shuffled and hollered in glee. She turned around at the noise, only to see Mar's hand raised high in the air. The general turned in their direction and stared, as if pondering her for a moment, taking in her height and build before gesturing for her to approach. More people hollered and hooted when she strode forward, each step filled with confidence. Others gave her high fives and encouraging pats on the back, and she stepped around the pit.

Marenda made a show of stretching her arms and rolling her neck, ready for a fight. The general stared at her for another moment. "Name, soldier?"

"Marenda Caster," Mar announced more to the crowd than to the general. "Fire Elemental."

The general looked back into the crowd of soldiers. His eyes landed on another hand in the crowd, and he pointed, calling out another name. "Adelaide Hill, join us in the clearing."

The crowd dispersed to let a small girl through, and she stepped into the clearing while the general stepped out. Sayr recognized her the moment she spotted her fire-red hair. Her gaze turned on Mar, who also recognized the girl with clear distaste. The girl from Lilith's trio, *Adelaide*, now stood by the pit next to Mar. Sayr could've laughed aloud at how ridiculous the pairing was. Mar had about eight inches on the girl and where she was strong and muscular, Adelaide looked slender and fragile. Soldiers around her laughed at the sight of them, too. Clearly everyone knew the outcome of this fight.

"Oh, this is going to be good," one girl behind Sayr whispered. Sayr turned her head in the girl's direction and threw her a challenging grin.

The two girls jumped down into the pit and faced each other. Everyone hunched over the pit again, anticipation building for the fight. The two took their fighting stances. Small flames danced around Mar's fingers, and she sent a handful of flame darts at Adelaide. The girl dodged the fire darts one by one, barely avoiding a flame near her left shoulder.

Sayr knew this would be a quick fight. Mar loved being on the offensive side of a fight and giving her the offense right away was Adelaide's mistake. She continued to duck out of Mar's reach and dodged each string of fire darts. Her footwork was clean and precise as she twirled and spun out of reach, as if she were rehearsing a dance around the pit.

"Come on, Mar!" Sayr cheered along with the others watching from above. Many were cheering for Adelaide, but more began switching sides and cheering for the new Fire Elemental.

Mar was growing frustrated with each failed attempt to strike Adelaide. She began throwing bigger missiles of fire, two or three fireballs the size of her hand in opposite directions to try and trap Adelaide. Adelaide was beginning to panic as well. She tried to switch positions and take the offense, but Mar's fireballs kept her on the defense long enough to grow ever so closer. Her eyes grew wide and frantic as each dodge came closer and closer to getting hit by a fireball. She twisted and ducked as a fireball came directly at her, singeing the end of one of her braids.

Adelaide stopped in her tracks suddenly, unsure of which way to run before Mar threw more flames her way. Mar threw out her hands and flames licked the walls of the pit. The flames crawled up and up until they were peeking just over the side of the pit. The soldiers nearest the gaping hole staggered back, their arms and hands sheltering their faces from the heat of the flames.

Adelaide doubled over, choking on the rising smoke. Black smoke rippled all through the pit and up into the cloudless sky. Sayr could barely see Mar or her opponent. Both figures were distorted by the rippling heat and dark smoke. Adelaide coughed into her arm, keeping her sleeve over her nose and mouth.

Still doubled over, Adelaide lifted one arm high above her. The flames that ignited the walls of the pit and danced around Mar's hand all flickered and died. The pit filled with smoke from the dying flames, crawling up and up until the smoke hit a non-existent ceiling at the top of the hole. The smoke floated to the invisible barrier and rested there, unable to escape.

Sayr looked back down into the pit. Mar was now on her knees, clutching at her throat. Her mouth gaped open and shut and her wide-eyed gaze was stuck on Adelaide. The small girl rose to her full height once again. All the flames that had just consumed the pit were gone. Mar looked like she was choking, as if she could not get any air within her lungs.

Sayr took in the invisible barrier still containing the smoke, Mar's gasping mouth and hand clutching her throat, and Adelaide standing tall. Sayr's jaw dropped in disbelief as she loomed over the pit. The roaring cheers around her sounded miles away in her ears.

An Air Elemental.

She couldn't believe what was happening before her eyes. Sayr had never seen an Air Elemental in action before. Willa had mentioned Air Elementals in the Western Palace, but she hadn't expected to see one in action so soon.

She pushed her way towards the lip of the pit again. She needed to get to Mar, she needed to help her friend. Before she made it through the crowd, the invisible barrier dropped, releasing the climbing smoke high into the air. Mar's gasping breath was loud enough for the entire crowd to hear. She was on all fours on the ground, clutching her throat and coughing viciously.

Adelaide heaved an arm just above the ground and up at Mar, whose eyes were wide in shock and disbelief. The strong wind followed, slamming into Mar and knocking her into the wall behind her. Mar yelped and gritted her teeth in pain. One hand was held firmly against her ribs as if she could block the pain.

Mar peeled herself off the dirt wall. She quickly tried to reposition her feet to gain her balance when another gust threw her back against the wall. She let out a pain-filled roar that rang through the pit. Adelaide let out a cry of her own and sent another gust at Mar's feet, lifting her off the ground.

Mar's arms flailed in the air. Her feet swung below her as she tried to get out of the wind's grip and back onto solid ground. Adelaide granted her wish and released the wind, casting it above Mar, and sent her plummeting to the ground. Mar gave a final grunt of pain as she laid crumpled on the dirt floor, panting in exhaustion and rage. The girl stood over her with both hands outstretched to bring more wind down upon her, daring her to get back up. When she didn't, another round of cheers erupted from the crowd above.

Adelaide climbed out of the pit. A soldier jumped into the pit and helped Mar up and out of the gaping earth. Adelaide proudly stood on one side of the pit while Mar was slumped over on her knees, cradling one arm. She stood up on both feet and tried to hide just how much pain she was really in. Mar glared daggers down at the red-haired girl, though she didn't seem to notice Mar's glares as she made a show of bowing to the crowd, accepting their cheers and applause.

"Excellent work." The general stepped back into the clearing. "We have an Air Elemental who has bested a Fire Elemental, why is that?"

A series of hands shot up in the air to answer. The general pointed to one soldier, and he answered, "The Fire Elemental was too cocky coming into the fight. She didn't properly size up her opponent's strengths and weaknesses right away."

"Correct," the general nodded. "Anything else?"

Soldiers began shouting their answers all at once.

"The Fire Elemental didn't expect to fight such a strong Air Elemental, or it looked like she didn't know how to fight against her."

The general simply nodded and ordered the girls back into the crowd. Adelaide bounced back into the crowd with cheers and high fives. Mar took a moment to step away, stumbling when the leg of her injured side almost gave out under her weight.

"Wait a second." The general caught her by the arm. "Let's have you taken to the medic's level for examining."

He waved over two more soldiers who attempted to take each of Mar's arms over their shoulders and lead her away, but she angrily shook them off, muttering something about being able to walk on her own. They resulted in keeping a hand on each of her shoulders to steer her in the right direction. Before she made it too far, she looked back into the crowd and motioned for Sayr to follow.

"Come on, let's get out of here," she muttered.

Sayr took about a dozen steps forward before the general stopped her. "Not so fast," he said. "You're up next."

"Oh, no sir. I'm supposed to stay with the girl being taken to the medic's level. I can't leave her." She spoke quickly before the soldiers took Mar too far away.

"The girl will be fine on her own," the general said, already pointing at someone else for Sayr to face off against.

Sayr looked towards Mar being led to the medic's level, yelling at the soldiers the entire way. Her heart beat out of her chest as a boy emerged from the crowd and stepped towards the edge of the pit. This was it, the moment they would be separated. Sayr didn't have to guess if this was the king's doing; she had mentioned wanting to train with the other soldiers at dinner last night and Adelaide had been the one to separate Mar from her. She racked her brain for a way out of this fight.

I'll lose quickly, she thought as she put one shaking foot into the ring. *I'll tap out after his first hit, so I won't have to throw any hits myself.*

As she stopped at the edge of the pit, she decided she would explain her lack of Elemental influence later. She would tell them that she was more skilled with daggers than any Elemental was with their abilities, that was how she earned a position in the Queen's Army. She prepared for the general to shove the two of them down into the pit. Her heart climbed up her throat in anticipation and fear.

"General!" A voice called out from the crowd. The soldiers all parted to let a lanky boy through, holding a small envelope.

"General," the boy wheezed as he approached. "A letter from His Majesty."

The general snatched the letter from the boy and yanked it open. His eyes quickly scanned over the writing, and he looked back at the boy. "You're dismissed," he said, and the boy quickly dissolved back through the crowd.

He pivoted around the pit, scanning the crowd for someone. "Lady Sayr Rieve!" he shouted, and the crowd shuffled, looking for whoever that might be.

Sayr slowly raised her hand. "That's me, sir."

He turned back to look at her. For a moment he said nothing, looking down at the letter in confusion and back at her, clearly hung up on the fact that a soldier was being addressed as a "Lady" in the letter. He stuffed the letter in his pocket and said, "You're being summoned to meet with His Majesty."

"His Majesty?" she repeated and looked back towards the direction that Marenda had just gone.

"Do you know the way?" the general asked.

She looked back at him. His words sounded almost jumbled. "The way to where?"

"The king's quarters," he said impatiently and yelled out for another soldier to show her the way.

The soldier gave her a shallow bow before heading up the mountain towards the palace.

Sayr paused a moment. This was exactly what the king had planned for her and Mar. This was how he was going to separate them. Sayr thought about the location Mar had given them to join back up. Forty-eight hours. That was all they'd be separated for and then she would go looking for her friend.

14

$\mathcal{L}$ilith swung open the door to the king's quarters. The sour look on her face made even the Royal Guards shrink away from her.

His Majesty was on the balcony at the far end of the room, seated in a large velvet chair with his back towards her. She stalked past shelves of war books, maps of the continent, and tables with wooden soldiers replicating the layout of where the king's armies were stationed around all of Creobe, searching for those recklessly attacking their country. She stormed towards the king. Her anger was brimming over when she reached him.

"I won't do it," she said through gritted teeth. "I don't want to be anywhere near that Visarian wretch."

The king slowly turned towards Lilith as if just noticing she was there; despite the commotion she had made in her entrance. "Ah, Lilith. Why don't you have a seat and join us?"

King Mylan gestured to an empty seat across from him on the balcony and Lilith's eyes bounced around at the other chairs, finding who 'us' might be. Her eyes landed on

Dimitri leaning against the pillar near the railing of the balcony, and she straightened her posture to look up at him through her lashes.

"Good morning, Dimitri." Her voice was suddenly thick and sultry.

His gaze flicked over at her and back out towards the mountains around them. "Hello, Lilith."

"It's nice to see you in the palace," she said and walked over to sit on the balcony close to him. "You spend far too much time in Therod instead of here."

Without looking at her again, Dimitri said, "I have business in Therod."

"Well, His Majesty will have to give you more business in the palace and away from that disgusting city." She glanced towards His Majesty, who remained seated in his velvet chair.

"You're in luck, then, Lilith," His Majesty chimed in. "Dimitri will be in on this business with you."

"What?!" She whirled around towards the king. "What kind of business could he possibly have with that girl?"

Dimitri turned towards the king as well. A small smirk played at his lips while His Majesty told Lilith his plan. "You will train Lady Sayr in sparring. You are an expert in all weapons, and I need her strong, or stronger than she is now if she is to be of any help to me."

Lilith seethed as she spoke. "I thought she was supposed to be assigned to Addy, she's just as skilled at weaponry."

"Adelaide is needed on the medic's level for the time being. And since we suspect Lady Sayr is like you and me, Adelaide cannot train her to use all sorts of weapons without the advantage of a seen element. You, however, can do just that." The king's feline smile returned as he stared up at Lilith from his seat.

"And what do you plan to do with this girl?" Lilith pushed. "If she is what you think she is, how could she be of any use to you when you already have a strong Spirit Elemental in your Court?"

Mylan clasped his hands together, his elbows propped on the armrests. "If one Spirit Elemental can strengthen my Court, imagine what two Spirit Elementals can do. I want to know what her true gifts are. If they are what I believe they are, then I want to keep her in my Court where she can be of use to me rather than used against me. There is a reason she has been hiding in the Eastern Palace, and I intend to find what that is."

Lilith stared hard at the king, waiting for the genuine answer to her question.

Mylan sighed. "Do not worry, Lilith, your position in my Court is still safe." The king's wicked smile grew. "For now."

"Then why is Dimitri here? If she really is a Spirit Elemental like we think she is, how can she benefit from him?" she asked.

"I have other plans for Dimitri." The king's eyes bounced towards the door and his smile widened as he said, "I'd explain more, but it appears our guest has arrived."

The soldier slowly creaked a door open and let Sayr through first. The king's quarters were exceptionally large, but not at all what she'd expected. The room looked more like a giant meeting room instead of quarters fit for a king. Shelves of books, tables and desks, and velvety chairs were scattered around the room. The high ceiling pointed into a crest at the top and the far wall of the quarters was missing, just like in the dining hall. The missing wall instead extended out onto a balcony. Sayr was beginning to wonder if there was any room in this palace that didn't have a balcony that she could possibly throw herself off. Or, given the company that awaited her, be thrown from.

Voices sounded from the balcony, and she looked at the soldier, who motioned for her to go on without him. She walked out onto the balcony where only three people sat or stood: the king, Lilith, and Dimitri. Two names from her list were already within ten feet of her.

"Welcome, Lady Sayr." King Mylan stood from his plush seat and turned towards her. "How are you enjoying the Western Palace so far?"

Sayr's eyes quickly swept over the two Court members. Lilith wrinkled her nose at Sayr, and Dimitri pretended to be distracted, polishing his sword with his sleeve.

She looked back to the king. "It's colder than I expected. And I don't just mean the weather."

King Mylan chuckled. "It's not always so cold." He gestured for her to take a seat. "I'm sure it will become much warmer during your stay."

The king's eyes glinted with mischief. "And I don't just mean the weather, either."

Three seats were before her. Two of the seats left at least one person behind her, which she did not like. She selected the seat to the king's right, leaving Lilith directly in front of her and Dimitri slightly to her right near the railing.

"We're only here for a short while," she said and looked out towards the green mountains. "I suspect it will only get colder by the time we're gone, and autumn sets in." She made sure to include herself in the number.

The deal between the two royals was that the queen's soldiers and officials would remain here in Creobe until the queen called for their return or a real threat was seen. Sayr knew Queen Cheralin would not see any threat as a real threat when the time came to decide if her troops would stay in Creobe any longer.

She also knew exactly what His Majesty was trying to do, she just didn't expect him to try so quickly.

The king's eyes bored into hers, and his voice was low when he spoke. "I believe we all know that your stay here will be much longer. I suspect there is more to you than what I see on the surface, and I am very intrigued to find what it is that makes you so valuable to Cheralin Lemay, and how you may be valuable to me."

Sayr lifted her chin in slight defiance. "I am an apprentice to one of Her Majesty's Councilmen and have been for nearly two years. My position in the Eastern Court goes only as far as that."

The king motioned for Lilith, and she moved to sit on the king's armchair. "That is the part that I am least interested in, what I am most interested in is your element. No non-Elemental would be seen in Queen Cheralin's Court if she could help it. And since you were able to fend off Lilith's manipulations, I suspect that maybe you, too, possess an unseen ability."

Sayr almost laughed aloud. She clenched her teeth together to keep from smiling. The Western King was a… unique man, but Sayr never thought him to be a ridiculous man.

Until now.

This must be exactly what Queen Cheralin had warned her about. King Mylan truly would say anything to keep her here, and Sayr wasn't buying any of it.

"An unseen ability." Sayr's voice was mocking while she repeated the king's words. She leaned back into the velvet seat. "I've heard hundreds of excuses from non-Elementals on why they don't possess any gifts, but I admit this is the first time I've ever heard the excuse of an unseen ability."

King Mylan leaned forward in his chair. "And yet you sit here amongst two unseen Elementals."

Sayr forced herself to remain still and not whirl on the three of them. Was this meant to be some kind of joke, or a threat? She fixed her eyes solely on the king, but she didn't disregard the two others on the balcony.

The king chuckled. "I'm getting ahead of myself. This is Dimitri's domain, after all."

The light shining on the balcony dimmed as Dimitri came into view, no longer the flirtatious man she'd spoken with under the willow tree. His face was all sharp disdain and sternness when he looked down at her. He stared at her with such a bored expression that she threw him a hateful glare just to give him something to look at.

"Dimitri will teach you about the politics and history of this kingdom," the king said while they continued their stare down. "You will learn our traditions and the ways of the Western Kingdom until it becomes first nature."

"Why?" Sayr asked. She broke her stare from Dimitri and back to the king. "Why teach me your ways when I'll just return to Visaran afterwards?"

At least the king had the decency to look almost sincere when he spoke. "Oh, Lady Sayr. After all this time in Creobe has passed, I doubt you will have very little choice to return to Visaran at all."

Sayr made a show of looking shocked and confused. Her wide eyes bounced back and forth between the three of them, as if she were looking for some sort of answer on their faces and finally landed in her lap where she wrung her hands nervously.

"Her Majesty won't allow it, she'll come for me if I don't return to Visaran." Sayr kept her voice soft and small.

King Mylan shook his head slowly. "She will not," he answered. "And I think you know that just as much as I do. You may be valuable to her in her Court, but she has abandoned those like you before, and I do not doubt that she will do so again."

The king looked at her with so much solemnity and pity that Sayr strained to keep up her helpless façade and not grab Dimitri's sword to prove she was anything but helpless.

"She has manipulated you, Lady Sayr," the king went on. "She has made you think that you are different, that there is no one else like you, because she is afraid of what you could truly be capable of if you knew what you were."

"And what am I?" Sayr asked. Her tone was suddenly hard and challenging.

"That is what I'm hoping you will learn for yourself." King Mylan stalled. "It seems I am getting ahead of myself once again. Like I said before, this is Dimitri's domain to teach you. Lilith, on the other hand, will teach you all about weaponry and fighting."

"I already train with weaponry with Mar," she countered.

"Yes, Lady Marenda is a skilled fighter, but she is only skilled with spears and swords, as you are only skilled in daggers. You need a trainer who is skilled in all sorts of weaponry to teach you, and Lilith is just the one for you."

Lilith glowed with pride as the king continued to boast about her and glared down at Sayr again. Sayr met her stare, then Dimitri's, and finally looked back at the king.

"And you're sure about me training with her? I think we all know that one of us will just end up killing the other." She clamped her mouth shut, hoping her words hadn't sounded like a threat, but she didn't cool the fire in her eyes.

The king shifted to rise from his seat. "I believe Lilith likes the idea even less than you do. However, orders are orders for her. I cannot force you to do anything, Lady Sayr, and I will not do so. But I can offer you so much more in this Court than Cheralin can offer in hers. I can offer you freedom, the chance to find out who you truly are. And since you haven't denied the idea of being an unseen Elemental, I believe that you may be interested in finding who you truly are as well."

Sayr took her time pretending to mull things over while they all watched her closely. After several long minutes, she looked up at the Western King.

"You're right," she said. "I don't know who I am. But I don't know if I can find who I am by staying here, either. As far as I can tell, your Court is just as sadistic and secretive as the Court I come from."

She stood to face the king head on. "But I will do as you say. I'll train and learn about your kingdom. And if I decide that I can find a better life for me here in Creobe, I will stay."

King Mylan smiled at her. Lilith looked as if she'd swallowed sour milk, but it was Dimitri that closed in on her.

"What makes you so willing to join this Court?" he asked. "We watched you in Visaran, there's no more reason to lie to you, and we know your close relationship with the Eastern Prince. Why would you give all of that up so easily?"

Sayr slowly turned from the king's direction toward Dimitri. Though he hovered over her, she took a step forward so that they were mere inches apart.

"First, don't ever speak about the Eastern Prince to me. You know nothing about the Visarian royal family, whereas I know everything. And I will do anything to keep you, and your people, out of Visaran for good. You will not speak of the prince when you are near me."

She spoke so low that she was almost whispering, her voice filled with unspoken threats. Dimitri's eyes narrowed into what might have been a glare if he still hadn't looked so bored with her.

"Second," she continued, "my position as a Councilman's apprentice is the only thing keeping me in Her Majesty's Court. She has already threatened to throw me out before. If I can truly learn more about these abilities that you think I have, then I have nothing to lose back in Visaran simply by staying here."

A small glint of surprise ignited in her chest at how much the lie sounded like the truth.

She firmly held Dimitri's stare while he scrutinized her, likely pondering whether any part of what she'd said was true. His lips quirked upward in the most unwelcoming smile. "If that's what you want us to believe. But if you even attempt to betray His Majesty, I will kill you and throw your corpse over this balcony myself."

Sayr gave him a challenging grin. "I would love to see you try."

Dimitri's threat oozed with violence; violence a king's mercenary would certainly be able to commit. She eyed the sword sheathed at Dimitri's side. Dimitri stepped back and put a hand on his sword just as the king intervened.

"You are safe here, Lady Sayr," King Mylan interrupted. "And unlike in Visaran, unseen Elementals are always welcome in my Court, and my country."

He smiled at her, no longer wicked or feline. This smile was different. Softer.

Sayr gave him the smallest smile back, even as her heart sank. She preferred his usual approach—pretending he was the cat, and she was the mouse—to this. If he were to start treating her with kindness, it would only make it that much harder to destroy his Court.

"You will begin by learning our continent's history," the king continued, "spending this afternoon with Dimitri. He will debrief me after dinner on your lessons. As I am told, you already started regular drills this morning. You can begin your training with Lilith at a later date."

Lilith gave a displeased grunt before rising from the armchair of the king's seat and leaving the king's quarters without another word. The king's cat-like grin returned, and he watched her go, clearly amused by her exit. "I will send someone to bring you to the armory in the next few days. Lilith will meet you there."

"Dimitri is more well-mannered and will escort you to the libraries." His Majesty stepped close to her. "You are always welcome in the royal quarters," he said. "If you need anything at all, do not be afraid to come find me."

He stepped closer still, close enough to whisper in her ear, "I do hope you find what I believe we're both looking for. For the sake of both our countries."

Before Sayr had any time to react, the king pulled away and nodded at Dimitri. Dimitri released his grip on the sword and walked off the balcony. She eyed him warily as he made his way through the quarters. He didn't bother to glance behind him to see if she followed as he called back to her.

"Come with me, little imposter."

15

ayr rubbed her temples and let out a slow, frustrated breath. She'd been in the palace library for two hours while Dimitri assessed her knowledge of the history of the continent, including the Dividing War. A stack of books was piled on the table along with a map of the palace that Sayr constantly flicked her gaze over.

"I was educated in the Eastern Palace," she huffed. "I am aware of the events of the Dividing War. Can we move on?"

Dimitri's only response was the thump of a heavy book landing on the table in front of her. Sayr picked up the book and inspected the title.

The Elemental's History of Magic

She stared blankly at the book for a moment, then up at Dimitri hovering over her. "Magic?" she asked.

"Yes. Magic," Dimitri responded.

"Are you going to tell me what that is, exactly?" she asked.

"If you don't already know, then you haven't been *properly* educated," he retorted. "This book will tell you everything there is to know about Elementals on this continent from the beginning. You will read it from cover to cover."

"I thought *you* were going to teach me about the history of the continent," she said through her teeth and dropped the book back onto the table. "This is a huge waste of my time."

"If you do not know the connection between Elementals and the Dividing War, then I assume you know very little about the truth of our continent's history." He crossed around the table in a few strides and sat down across from her.

Sayr sat up straighter in her own chair. "Are you questioning my education?" she asked. "I was taught by the Visarian royal tutors. I have a proper education."

Her small amount of patience for this man was quickly beginning to dwindle.

Dimitri didn't bother to look at her when he spoke. "I have no doubt that the crown prince and princess are highly educated. What I'm questioning is whether your tutors gave you the same education as Prince Everett and Princess Elanor."

"I told you not to speak of them in front of me," Sayr shot back.

That only seemed to amuse Dimitri. "How do you expect me to educate you on the entire continent's history when you forbid me to speak of the rulers of half the continent? Are you that ignorant?"

"Insult me one more time," Sayr said all too calmly and leaned forward, "and I will shove the blade of that pretty sword of yours through your throat."

Sayr stared at Dimitri, the deadly challenge clear in her eyes. Who did this man think he was? Who did he think *she* was to speak to her so rudely? She was a member of the Eastern Court, an apprentice to the queen's Councilman, or so he believed. No matter, she could have been a lady's maid to the most unimportant aristocrat of the country, and he still wouldn't have the right to speak to her this way.

Dimitri sighed and leaned back in his chair. Sayr's threat hadn't seemed to bother him in the slightest, and she clenched her fists in anger. "His Majesty believes that the Eastern Queen deliberately did not fully educate you on specific pieces of history in order to keep you and your abilities at bay. He also believes that she kept you from certain information to ensure that you and many others in Visaran would remain unquestionably loyal to her."

Dimitri propped his elbows on the table and pressed his hands together. "Tell me what you know of the War."

Sayr retold the story that she'd heard hundreds of times in as much detail as she could to ensure that Dimitri wouldn't think her education was subpar. Once she'd finished, she leaned back and crossed her arms over herself, satisfied.

"Just as I suspected," Dimitri retorted. "You've only been taught the pieces of history that Her Majesty wants you to know."

Sayr threw her hands up in the air and jumped from her seat. "Fine!" she yelled. "Are you happy now? My memory of history is inaccurate, but that does *not* mean that I am uneducated. And either way, your king still wants me in his Court. Why does it matter?"

"It matters because this is exactly what your queen does to those in her Court!" Dimitri exploded and leaped out of his own chair, stalking closer to Sayr. "She feeds you lies to make you, and the rest of her people think that the royal family is still strong, and that we are the enemy! You Visarians have no idea what our country is like, what the entire world is like outside of your own lands!"

His voice echoed throughout the library before falling silent. Dimitri had stalked around the table so close to Sayr that his peppermint and clove scent consumed her. The two of them stared each other down, his face fueled with anger and hers with shock. Neither of them moved a muscle as he spoke in a much lower voice.

"The Eastern Kingdom is so shut off from the rest of the world. Your queen does not allow any of her citizens to leave the country or citizens from any other country to enter because she does not want her people to see what is out there in the world, and how weak your country really is. She tells you that your country is the strongest so that you will never want to leave, believing you are under the protection of the strongest royal family in the world when in fact, it is the opposite."

"The Visarian royal family *is* strong," Sayr argued. Her voice shook with anger and a touch of fear. Visarians couldn't cross the Silia River without help from Earth and Water Elementals, and the Visarian royal family hindered travel outside of the kingdom for their people's safety.

"You say that because it has been drilled into your mind since you were a child," Dimitri argued back. "But there is so much in this world that your queen fears and therefore shelters her people from. You are dictated by your own monarchy, keeping you prisoner in Visaran. Nothing your queen does is of any benefit to anyone except herself and her family."

"Do you know why Visaran's motto is 'There is strength in duty?'" Dimitri asked, though he didn't bother waiting for Sayr's answer. "It is because Visarians are brainwashed into believing that the more dutiful they are to the Visarian Crown, the stronger they will become. Whether that means strength in their abilities, in themselves, or possibly in their positions within the Court." He cocked his head to one side when he finished speaking, his eyes drilling into Sayr.

"How could you possibly be so sure about all of this?" Sayr asked. "It's true that no one can leave or enter Visaran without Her Majesty's consent, but that is for our protection. And how could you have any of this information if you and this Court had never visited Visaran before the last month?"

Dimitri backed barely an inch away from her. "We have Creobian spies in the Eastern Court. One of the king's ladies, Willa, oversees these spies and reports information back to His Majesty."

"What?!" Sayr roared. Her eyes strayed away from his face and down to his throat. She'd never wished for a weapon more than she did at this moment.

Dimitri did not react to her explosion or the deadly rage in her eyes. "If you're going to remain in Creobe, you shouldn't be so upset over a couple spies in the Eastern Court."

Sayr stopped cold. She'd forgotten the role she was supposed to be playing for a moment. She pushed her anger down and cleared her throat.

"I'm not angry about the Court," she lied. "I'm angry that there might have been spies watching me bathe in the public barracks. Though I doubt you would have minded those details, seeing as how you so pathetically sought me out in the Eastern Palace."

Dimitri's brows lowered as he glared at her. Finally, she'd gotten under his skin. He stooped towards Sayr, so low that their noses almost touched, and her breath hitched. He paused a moment, then quickly rose again, fanning the book he had grabbed off the table in front of her face.

"If that's what you want me to believe, little imposter."

Dimitri rolled up the map of the palace and tucked it under one arm. He shoved the book into her arms. "If what you told His Majesty in the king's quarters is true, and you genuinely want to find out more about your gift, then you will read this book in full. This will tell you the true history of the continent and Elementals alike. You will speak of this book to me, and only me."

He turned and walked towards the many aisles in the library, no doubt returning the books and the map. He didn't turn back to look at her as he ended with, "Once you're done reading, try telling me that the Eastern Kingdom is truly what you believe it is."

Marenda gritted her teeth together while the healer tended to her immobile arm and bruised ribs. The pain had dulled since the fight, but the throbbing in her ribs and immobility of her arm hadn't gone away.

The healer examined her from head to toe, looking for any hidden injuries, which only angered Marenda more. She wanted to get out of the medic's level, find the small red-headed girl, and demand a rematch against her. She hadn't known the girl was an Air Elemental until she'd faced off against her. The girl had an advantage against Marenda, one she would not have again.

"Ouch!" she roared when the healer lifted her stiff arm and bent it at the elbow.

"My apologies," the healer said, though she looked anything but sorry. "I need to examine the damage to your arm."

The healers in the medic's level all wore the same white collared shirts and loose pants. The men and women alike kept their hair incredibly long; some braided the long strands back into loose braids or in low ponytails to keep it out of their faces while they assessed patients on the many beds lining the medic's level. Grey curtains separated each bed from the others to give the patients and healers privacy when needed.

The healer in front of Marenda wore her golden blonde hair in one long braid. She repeatedly bent and straightened Marenda's arm, humming thoughtfully each time she straightened the arm out again.

Marenda flinched at the pain that erupted every time her arm straightened. "Do that one more time," she said through gritted teeth and nodded to the syringe on the table next to her bed, "and I will shove that needle deep into your neck."

The healer ignored her threat. "You have a hairline fracture in the ulna," she explained and looked up at Marenda. "One of the bones in your elbow has chipped, that is why you cannot move it without immense pain."

"Then maybe you should stop moving it so much," Marenda fumed. The healer ignored her once again and continued examining her elbow.

"How long will it take to heal?" Marenda asked. She'd broken plenty of bones in fights before, but as the personal guard of Queen Cheralin, broken bones had to be mended quickly. Even with the best healers in the Eastern Palace, she usually resumed her duty rotation with a cast or sling until the injury was fully healed. "I'm supposed to be in training, I won't be much use with just one arm."

"Not to worry," the healer assured her. "This will only take a few minutes; you should be fully healed by dawn tomorrow."

Marenda's brow furrowed when the healer put both hands around her arm, covering her elbow. A tingling sensation slowly started to grow from where the healer touched her arm. She gripped Marenda's elbow tightly with both arms, and pain shot through her arm. She yelped and tried to yank her arm out of the healer's grasp, but she held on. The tingling sensation crawled up Marenda's entire arm She felt the healer's grip release her arm and she looked down. Marenda lifted her arm, the tingling had disappeared completely, along with the pain. She stretched out her arm, bent it and straightened it again.

She looked slowly up at the healer. "What in the elements are you?"

The library was surprisingly busy during the late afternoon hours. Sayr's lesson with Dimitri had ended hours ago, and she hoped she'd waited long enough to ensure he had left the library, too.

Dema had been in her chambers when she'd returned from her lesson, and while Sayr hadn't initially wanted anyone in her rooms, she had to admit the girl was becoming useful. Sayr noticed how the girl reacted to Sayr naming any member of the King's Court. She jumped and avoided eye contact every time Sayr mentioned Lilith, Willa, or Tomas. Sayr's questions were innocent enough at first, but she would need to start pressing Dema a bit harder for information.

She walked towards one of the large desks where a library scholar sat, hastily scribbling on a piece of parchment.

"Hello," Sayr greeted the scholar warmly. "I was in here this morning, but I forgot one of the books my instructor had given me, and I believe he put it away after I'd left. Do you mind if I look for it?"

The scholar peered up at Sayr, looking her up and down before turning back to his parchment. "You are the girl with Dimitri, correct?" the scholar asked.

"That's correct." Sayr kept her tone sickeningly sweet. "Dimitri assigned a book for me to read but I believe I left it here."

"Of course," the scholar drawled. "Let me summon Dimitri, he will be able to find the book you are looking for."

"No need," Sayr called behind her. She was already making her way towards the aisles of books. "I know where it is."

She made her way towards the row of shelves Dimitri had gone through when she'd first seen him put the map of the palace away. If she was going to successfully kill the king's mercenary and get away unharmed, she needed to know the layout of the palace perfectly and find an escape route before she made any further moves.

Before she entered the row of shelves, she looked back towards the scholar. He looked stunned while he watched her walk towards the aisles, eyes wide and mouth open. She smiled at him before walking down the aisle. She needed to be quick, to not raise any attention or suspicion her way. She hurried through the aisle, looking for the roll of parchment.

"Miss?" The scholar's voice floated through the bookshelves towards Sayr. "What did you say your name was, again?"

Sayr's eyes scanned the shelf behind her. Only books filled the shelves, she quickly looked over each shelf for a single roll of parchment.

Nothing.

She could hear the scholar's footsteps getting closer through the aisles. She turned back around and looked further up the shelves of the row in front of her. She was running out of time.

"You do not have access to these books, not without Dimitri's permission." The scholar was only a few aisles away.

"He gave me permission when he assigned the book to me," Sayr called back sweetly.

Her eyes landed on a rolled piece of parchment on a high shelf between two unruly stacks of books.

"Why don't I get Dimitri to find the book for you if he assigned it to you?" The scholar was rounding the corner to her aisle.

Sayr jumped up and snagged the parchment. She immediately folded the paper and shoved it under her shirt, snug between her stomach and the waistband of her pants, just as the scholar poked his head down her aisle.

"It doesn't seem to be here." Sayr stood with her hands behind her back and swayed slightly, feigning innocence.

The scholar grunted softly and walked further through the aisle towards Sayr. She backed away just slightly as he turned to scan the row where she had taken the map from.

"Which book were you looking for, again?" The scholar asked without taking his eyes off the shelf.

"*The Elemental's History of Magic*," Sayr lied and backed further away from the scholar. She moved as little as possible, fearing too much movement would wrinkle the parchment and the scholar would hear the shifting of paper underneath her shirt.

"It doesn't seem to be here." The scholar peeked a look at her. "You're certain Dimitri put it away?"

Sayr shrugged. "I must have looked over it in my chambers. I'll look again, it must be there."

She turned in the opposite direction and stalked out of the aisle towards the exit of the library. "I apologize for the inconvenience. Thanks again for your help!" she called back to the scholar, who followed her closely to the door.

She quickly shut the door and hurried to the guest's level of the palace. Once she'd entered her chambers, she lifted her shirt and took out the parchment.

Her heart raced as she unfolded the parchment. She hadn't had time to look at the contents of the parchment and if she'd taken the wrong one, she doubted the scholars would let her back through the aisles without Dimitri accompanying her.

Her eyes roamed over the parchment and the layout of the palace. The map showed the layout of the levels of the palace from the king's quarters down to the main entrance. Finally, she let a smile creep over her lips.

16

The halls of the Western Palace were unusually quiet while Sayr walked next to Tomas through one of the upper levels. Sayr had asked him to show her around the palace after breakfast that morning, and he was all too eager to agree.

She had asked about his regular duties within the palace and what he liked to do with his days. Tomas was an avid hunter and spent much of his time out in the mountains near the palace hunting with the king's officials.

Cordia had come to see her yesterday to speak about the mission. She was highly disappointed to hear that Marenda was stuck in the medic's level. She asked about Sayr's cover and if anyone suspected there was more to her than being a non-Elemental.

"The king still thinks there's something unique about me, but he can't pinpoint what that may be," Sayr had answered. "He was sorely disappointed when he couldn't pull any information about me or my gifts."

Sayr knew if Cordia found out about *The Elemental's History of Magic*, she would likely take it from her. And the king had mentioned unseen Elementals, something neither the queen nor Cordia had ever mentioned to her before. Sayr wanted to know more, and she knew deep down that Cordia would end all of her lessons if Sayr told her what the king intended for her to learn. Cordia was not just there to help Sayr, she was there to monitor her every move.

Tomas pulled her arm around his and Sayr pulled herself out of her thoughts.

"And how do you enjoy spending your days?" Tomas asked as they rounded a corner to another hall.

Small balconies lined the outer wall of the palace, scattered with chairs and a few tables for guests to sit and enjoy the views.

"I enjoy training," Sayr admitted. "And the Eastern Palace has beautiful gardens that I enjoyed spending my time in. The City Center is a wonderful place, too; my favorite shops are all within the City Center."

Tomas chuckled. "So, you enjoy shopping?"

His voice was softer than Dimitri's, and his eyes were much kinder. Thin creases lined his mouth and the corners of his eyes from constantly smiling and laughing.

"Not particularly," Sayr admitted. "My two favorite shops in the Center are the coffee shop and chocolatier. I don't have much interest in shopping if it doesn't have to do with something tasty."

Tomas smiled wider. "Do you enjoy hunting?"

"I've never hunted before," Sayr said. "I think I would enjoy it, though. I like a good chase."

"I like to meditate, too," Sayr continued. "It helps me calm my mind, keeps me feeling in control at times when I feel like I'm not."

Tomas nodded along while Sayr spoke. He stopped walking and turned towards one of the open balconies, looking out towards the mountains. Sayr watched him while he took in the view. His eyes sparkled when he again met her gaze.

"It's beautiful, is it not?" he asked, grinning down at her.

"Absolutely." Sayr let a soft smile play across her lips. "I've never seen any other place that compares to this palace."

Sayr spotted a delicate gold chain around Tomas's neck and her smile grew even wider.

Tomas turned to pull Sayr past the threshold of the palace walls, where the wind would meet them. Just before she crossed the threshold, Sayr tripped and tumbled towards the ground. Tomas caught her in his arms before she could hit the ground, both arms holding tightly to her waist. Sayr held one arm over his shoulder and the other at his neck while she looked wondrously up at him.

"Thank you," she said a little too breathlessly. "I apologize, I'm not usually so clumsy."

Tomas smiled, his eyes trailing over her face. Sayr's fingers brushed over the clasp of the chain.

"Don't apologize," Tomas said, though he didn't pull Sayr upright just yet. "I'm here to catch you whenever you fall."

Sayr fought hard not to roll her eyes as her fingers played with the clasp. She let out a small laugh and Tomas began to lift her upright. Her thumb lifted the clasp of the chain, and the jewelry dropped from Tomas's neck. Sayr clamped the chain in her fist and swiftly pulled the hand away as she stood to her full height once again.

"What time is it?" she asked. "I should be getting to the library soon for my lesson with Dimitri."

"Ah, yes. How are your lessons going?" Tomas asked.

"They are excruciatingly long and even more boring," Sayr admitted. "I've never been one to follow history or customs much. I have no doubt they would be much more entertaining if you were my instructor."

Tomas leaned towards Sayr. She let him lean close enough that his nose briefly touched hers before she pulled away.

"But I shouldn't be late." She took another step back. "Dimitri will be furious if I'm not on time."

Tomas hesitated for a moment before straightening. "Shall I escort you to the library?"

"There's no need," Sayr insisted. "I know the way and I wouldn't want to take up any more of your time. I'm sure this won't be our last meeting, though."

Tomas flashed a smile and gently grabbed Sayr's hand. Sayr flinched when his fingers met hers. Her other hand was tight behind her back, gripping onto the chain. His lips brushed her fingers, and he glanced up to meet her gaze.

"If you'd ever like a tour of any other parts of the palace, I am at your beck and call."

Sayr kept the smile on her face while Tomas turned to leave. Once he was gone, she let the smile turn sinister and looked down at the gold chain in her hand.

One member down, six more to go.

She stuffed the chain into her boot and walked towards the balcony. She needed evidence to frame the King's Court for the death of the king's mercenary. But she couldn't frame only Tomas, especially if he turned out to be the mercenary. She needed possessions from each of the King's Court.

She stood near the balcony for a while. Her thoughts whirled over the mission, the clasp in her boot, the map hidden in her chambers, and Mar.

Was Mar still safe? Was she alright? They had agreed to meet after forty-eight hours, but Sayr wasn't so sure she could wait that long before going to search for her friend.

A hand lightly touched her shoulder. In a flash, Sayr's hand grabbed the dinner knife at her belt and whirled around, pointing the sharp edge up at the intruder.

Dimitri held both hands in the air and took a step back. A smirk grew on his face when she straightened to look up at him. He wore a long dark cloak that looked to be made of thick animal fur over his wool shirt and thick pants. A glint of morning sunlight streamed across his face, making his hazel eyes shine and teeth glint while he grinned humorlessly at Sayr.

"So skittish." He grinned harder. "All those years training in the Eastern Court and you're startled by someone approaching you from behind."

"Why are you following me?" Sayr asked, not moving the knife.

"Who says I was following you?" Dimitri pushed. "You're in the public halls, I could have just happened to run into you by accident."

"Cut the act," Sayr spat. "You have this entire palace to go terrorizing people, and you just happen to find me? Why are you following me and what do you want?"

Dimitri's lifted a brow. As quick as lightning, he reached up and grabbed Sayr's wrist. He twisted her arm hard until the knife fell from her hand. With his other arm, he spun Sayr around until her back was against him, her twisted arm between them.

Dimitri leaned down and *tsked* in her ear. "You're not much of a soldier, are you? You're so easy to take down."

Sayr kicked Dimitri's knee as hard as she could. He grunted as his knee gave out. His grip loosened on her arm, and she shook free of him, elbowing him in the gut before taking several steps back.

Dimitri leaned over and grabbed his stomach. Sayr put the knife away, smirking down at Dimitri.

She pouted tauntingly down at him. "So easy to take down, huh?"

Sayr rolled her eyes at him and backed away towards the balcony. She hadn't crossed the threshold where the frigid air would reach her, staying just far enough inside to savor the warmth of the palace.

"What do you really want, Dimitri?" she asked.

Dimitri grinned at her, an amused gleam in his eyes, and stood again. He stepped towards the threshold of the balcony and stood in front of her. "I came looking for you with good news and bad news. Which would you like to hear first?"

Sayr slanted her eyes at him. "Good news first."

"The good news is that I have business outside of the palace, so our lessons will be canceled for the next two days," he started.

Sayr smiled up at him. "That is great news, indeed."

Dimitri smiled back, but there was something dark beneath it. "Don't look so happy just yet, I haven't given you the bad news."

"I don't think anything could damper the joy of not having to spend two miserable hours with you for the next two days." Sayr cooed harshly. "What's the bad news?"

"Your lessons with me have been canceled," he repeated. "But your first training with Lilith begins today."

Sayr's smile dropped into a scowl. "You have to be joking."

"I assure you, I'm not," he said. His grin was no longer menacing, he was truly enjoying seeing Sayr miserable.

Sayr crossed her arms and glared up at him. "You certainly do enjoy other people's misery far too much. When is the training?"

"Now. I'd be happy to escort you to the armory." He gave a mocking bow low enough that Sayr could've kneed him in the nose, which she had to fight hard not to do.

When he straightened again, she said, "Lead the way, then. And don't get too cocky, or I just might bring some special gifts from the armory to our next lesson."

Dimitri led them down, down, down to the deepest part of the palace. The stone walls down here didn't sparkle like they did in the main halls of the palace and some even looked partially rotted through. The air was musty, and the halls seemed practically abandoned, as if no one had dared come down this deep into the palace in years, if not decades.

"*This* is where the Western Court keeps their armory?" Sayr asked and hurried to keep pace with Dimitri's long strides.

"Of course," he answered. "This part of the palace appears run down for a reason. None of our enemies would suspect the amount of weaponry that is hidden down here."

Thanks for the tip, Sayr thought and smiled to herself. She'd have to make a note of that on the map resting under her pillow in her chambers.

They kept walking until they reached the end of a hall at an old door that looked as if it would break from its hinges if Sayr gave it one hard kick.

"Ladies first," Dimitri said and pulled the ancient door open for her.

As soon as she stepped through the door, she was immediately transported out of the ancient halls into a completely new, sleek area. A series of smaller rooms lined the walls and opened into a hallway. Each room held distinct types of weaponry that were displayed from floor to ceiling.

While they walked, Sayr took note of the guards stationed in each room, heavily armed and on edge. She couldn't help but think of the amount of damage someone could inflict if they were to find this place and all its weaponry.

Each guard nodded in respect to Dimitri when they passed. Sayr side-eyed him while they walked. What sort of position did he have to earn the Royal Guards respect?

She pushed the thought to the back of her mind. When she reached Visaran again, she'd tell Everett all about the royal armory as soon as she saw him. She couldn't trust Queen Cheralin with that kind of information right away, especially when the queen was already planning a surprise attack on Creobe. But she could trust Everett. He would know what to do.

Her thoughts quickly dispersed as she and Dimitri walked past the weaponry. The end of the hall opened into a large, dome-shaped room built completely from glass.

When Sayr looked up, she could see the deep blue sky high above them through the large glass panels. She looked out through the side panels and the view made her knees shake.

The dome had been constructed off the side of the mountain where the castle stood high at the top. Sayr thought back to the dozens of flights of stairs that led down to the armory, they had to have been in the center of the mountain by the time they reached the door that led into here. As she scanned every panel of the room, she realized the only thing that separated them from the thousand-foot drop to the base of the mountain was glass.

Sayr was transported back to the Eastern Palace when she stood in this room. The glass dome was just like the domed ceilings of the halls that she always strolled through with Mar and Ev, usually heading to the training grounds or the royal gardens.

"What is this place?" she asked. Her voice was barely above a whisper, and she continued to look out towards the surrounding mountains.

"This is the royal training center," Dimitri answered, not far behind her. "The Creobian Royal Guards are all trained here in this room. Each one specializes in a certain type of weaponry. Once a Royal Guard is initiated, they choose a room at random before knowing what weapons are within that room. Once they choose, they spend a full year training with only those weapons before they can be put on duty in the castle above."

"And I'm supposed to train down here?" Sayr assumed. She didn't like the idea of being so far down in the mountain, but she couldn't deny her excitement at getting to train with so many types of weapons.

"Precisely."

A familiar female voice approached them and Sayr and Dimitri both turned as Lilith made her way into the center of the dome. She was dressed in a deep grey body suit, boots, and gloves, leaving only her head exposed. Her brown hair was tied into a high ponytail and her slender brown eyes remained on Sayr. A large hunting knife twirled between her fingers while she walked.

"Sayr, you remember Lilith," Dimitri droned.

Sayr could've sworn his demeanor shifted as soon as he noticed Lilith. The smallest hint of playfulness he'd had when he first approached her on the balcony was long gone and replaced by his usual, stone-faced expression.

"Good morning, Dimitri," Lilith crooned, still twirling the knife. "Will you be staying to watch the show?"

"This isn't a show. Your orders are to train Sayr just as you train the Royal Guard initiates." Dimitri's voice was heavy as lead as he spoke.

Sayr's gut twisted at Dimitri's words, and she gaped at Lilith. *She* trained every Creobian Royal Guard down here in the armory? She barely looked any older than Sayr herself, and many of the guards she'd seen in the halls looked to be in their mid-twenties and thirties, few even looked as if they were pushing fifty.

She looked back at Dimitri who was already staring down at her instead of Lilith.

"Your training attire is in the dressing room; I'll take you there and then you're all Lilith's." His eyes darted towards the brunette girl when he said her name before bouncing back to Sayr. The two of them walked towards a small door that she assumed was the dressing room.

"Willa will escort you to your rooms after your training, and then the king will be waiting for a training report at dinner," he said while they walked. "I'll be back by tomorrow night; I assume you know how to find the library by now."

When they reached the door to the dressing room, Dimitri's mouth quirked up, the sinister playfulness returning in his eyes. "Don't get too comfortable without lessons for the next two days. I just might extend our next lesson by a few hours to make up for lost time."

Sayr frowned and hit him on the shoulder before they turned separate ways. Sayr opened the door to the dressing room while Dimitri walked back through the heavily armed halls and through the ancient door back to the palace.

Marenda sat on the edge of her bed on the medic's level, staring at the grey curtains around her. Two hushed voices came from the other side of the curtain, and she closed her eyes in concentration to listen.

"The king would have our heads if he knew what you're planning."

"He'll never know," another voice whispered back. "And what other choice do we have? She's already seen you heal her. If you'd just used my remedies, we wouldn't be in this situation."

"I didn't know about her background when I'd healed her. And her arm would've been completely immobile for several months if I hadn't done so," the first voice answered. "She's a soldier, I gave her the chance to fight again."

Marenda glanced down at her newly healed arm. It was true, she'd been able to use her arm again only minutes after the healer had touched her and was completely healed only a couple hours after. She was still in shock from the experience. Had her injury truly been that severe that she should've been unable to use the arm for the rest of her stay in Creobe?

The grey curtain flung open, and Marenda looked back up. The fiery-haired girl stood in front of the curtain, smiling. "Hello," the girl said, her voice floating towards Marenda like music. "How are you feeling?"

Marenda glared at her. "Where's the healer?"

As if on cue, the healer appeared from behind the curtain and stood next to the red-haired girl. Without looking away from Marenda, the girl continued, "My name is Adelaide Hill. I understand you have some questions for me."

"I have nothing to ask you," Marenda said. "I only want to speak to the healer."

Adelaide walked further into the small space, closer to Marenda. "I'm afraid that's not possible," she explained. "The healers are not permitted to speak about their craft."

"What is happening here?" Marenda practically shouted.

The healer flinched at her tone, but Marenda didn't care. Something strange was going on here and she was going to find out what it was.

Adelaide simply closed her eyes for the briefest moment before opening them again and flashing her same smile at Marenda. "I am the head remedy healer here in the medic's level. If you have questions, as I know you do, I am the one to ask. So, ask away."

Marenda studied the girl in front of her. "I thought you were an Air Elemental," she said.

Adelaide nodded. "I am an Air Elemental, but that gift was given to me at birth. Being a remedy healer is a passion of mine besides my ability. I can be an Air Elemental and a remedy healer, just like you can be a Fire Elemental and a soldier."

"And what is she?" Marenda asked and nodded towards the healer.

"She is a healer," Adelaide answered.

Marenda waited for more, but as the silence stretched on it was clear that was all Adelaide was going to say. "What did she do to me?"

"She healed you," Adelaide said. "And you should be grateful that she did, or your arm would be completely useless right now."

"I suppose I have you to thank for that," Marenda hissed.

This time, Adelaide did look away from her. "I apologize for that, I got carried away. Your reputation in the Eastern Palace seems to have followed you here and I suppose I wanted to prove myself."

"I didn't know you were an Air Elemental." Marenda glared at the girl. "I told myself the next time I saw you I'd show you what a real fight with me is like."

Adelaide giggled, the sound like popping bubbles, and walked over to the side of Marenda's bed. She hopped up on the small table that held an empty food tray, a dry sink, and a few empty vials.

Marenda kept her eyes on Adelaide. "If you're the head remedy healer here, then tell me what the healer did to my arm. The...tingling I mean, what was that?"

Adelaide and the healer exchanged looks. The healer slightly shook her head, but Adelaide just looked back at Marenda. "It is a kind of practice that is not performed in Visaran. It is a quicker and more precise form of healing the body, our healers focus on a more... physical form of healing."

"Can you do what she did, too?" Marenda asked.

"No." Adelaide shook her head. Her fiery braids swayed over each shoulder. "I tend to stick to remedies; herbs, medicines, and such. That is my area of expertise."

Marenda looked between Adelaide and the healer several times. None of them spoke as the gears in her head turned. She thoughtlessly bent and twisted her arm while she pondered. After a long pause of silence, she looked back at Adelaide.

"I want you to show me this new practice."

"I can only show you so much," Adelaide offered. "Like I said, the healers cannot speak about their practices, but I can show you remedy healing. I can teach you how to heal, just in a unique way."

Marenda lifted her chin. "Fine. Show me everything you know."

Sayr took her time passing through each of the small rooms filled with all types of weaponry. Many of the weapons she had seen on the training grounds in Visaran, others she had never seen before and had no idea what their use was or how anyone could possibly wield the ones that were bigger than her.

She spent quite some time in the room filled with various daggers of all shapes and sizes. A few caught her eye; one double-edged dagger, another with an intricate steel handle, and a third with a blade so long it could've been considered a small sword.

"Hurry up," Lilith called from the training dome. "You're wasting enough of my time down here already."

Sayr ignored her. Lilith's first order in training after she'd appeared from the dressing room in her training suit was "pick a weapon," which Sayr was happy to do. She remained in the room of daggers, deciding between her three favorites before settling on the double-edged dagger and the other with the single, long blade.

She walked back into the dome, weighing the two daggers in her hands. Lilith examined her choices and rolled her eyes. "I said pick *a* weapon. One. Singular."

Sayr flipped the daggers in her hands. "I favor a dagger in each hand. A sword takes both hands to wield, a dagger only takes one. Why not have a dagger in each?"

Lilith shook her head in annoyance before stalking to the middle of the dome, Sayr followed close behind. "Your suit is made of a special material, like flexible armor," Lilith said. "These weapons down here won't cut you with that suit on, unless enough pressure is added behind the blow like a direct stabbing, which is prohibited in training."

"And if someone is accidentally stabbed?" Sayr asked, putting just a hint of emphasis on *accidentally*.

"Then our healers would take care of the wounded and the other soldier would be dishonorably stripped of their title and prohibited from entering the palace grounds again."

Sayr nodded. No stabbing, then. She wouldn't be much use to Visaran if she was kicked out of the palace for stabbing Lilith.

"The soles of your boots are rubber," Lilith continued. "You will not slip against the floor in these shoes and your gloves are similar, so you won't lose grip on your weapons."

Sayr flipped the double-edged dagger in her hand while Lilith went over the rules of training. After listing rule after rule of what was and was not permitted in the training dome, Lilith faced Sayr.

"Today is a test in your training. I need to assess your abilities and advancements in a one-on-one fight." She gripped the hunting knife tightly and took a defensive stance. "Ready?"

Sayr bent into her own defensive stance. "Ready."

The two were a blur of steel as they dodged and struck. Lilith swung her hunting knife at Sayr, who swiped it down with the elongated dagger and lunged the double-edged blade to slice Lilith's thigh. Lilith angled her body away, just missing the dagger.

"Your training in Visaran clearly wasn't as rewarding as you think," Lilith barked. "You're weak and clumsy."

Sayr tried hard to ignore Lilith's words. She had been trained to become a skilled fighter for the last eight years; she was trained by the best warrior Visaran ever had.

The girls took turns dodging and striking. Sayr panted from the exertion of continuously fighting back and forth with Lilith. She lunged at Lilith, aiming for her shoulder with the elongated dagger. Lilith twirled out of the way just inches from where the dagger would have hit her. In the same movement, she swiped the hunting knife into Sayr's leg, just behind the knee.

Sayr grunted in pain from the hit and retreated backwards. Her armor threaded suit took most of the damage, but she still felt the pain as if her knee had indeed been slit. If not for the suit, Lilith would have easily severed the tendons in the back of her knee, leaving her leg paralyzed.

Lilith paced back and forth a dozen feet away, waiting for the next attack. "Your mentor has only put you at a disadvantage. Has she ever fought against you with real weapons? Those dulled weapons that you use in Visaran are useless, all those years of training have taught you nothing."

Sayr tried to block her out. She sprinted towards Lilith again. Lilith was ready for the attack and ran to meet her, but Sayr crouched low before Lilith could reach her. Lilith's face contorted in confusion as she tried to dodge out of the way, but it was too late. Sayr slid onto the ground and shot up from behind her. As she turned in her direction, Sayr flung her elbow backwards, connecting hard with her jaw.

Lilith yelped in anguish and fell to her knees. Sayr grinned in satisfaction at landing the hit. She twirled to Lilith's side and pointed the tip of the elongated dagger at the nape of Lilith's neck.

Her knee still throbbed with pain, but her chest bloomed with pride. She'd bested Lilith in their very first training. She waited for Lilith to drop the hunting knife in surrender, and once she did, Sayr would make her admit that Mar was the better trainer.

Lilith bent forward slightly so Sayr's dagger was no longer against her neck and turned swiftly towards Sayr.

Her elbow hit Sayr at the wrist, knocking the dagger from her hand and Lilith swung her leg at Sayr's legs.

Sayr lost her balance and hit the ground hard. Her ears rang from the impact and her vision blurred. She quickly got up onto one knee in time to see Lilith throw the large hunting knife directly at her.

She let out a shocked scream when the knife nicked her face, right below her ear. She felt blood dribble down her face and neck and onto the suit.

With her free hand, she covered the wound and looked behind her where the hunting knife laid on the floor, just a few feet from where a small group of soldiers had left the closest rooms of weapons to watch. Some of them gaped at her and the blood dripping down the side of her face. Others stared behind her in disbelief at Lilith, and Sayr turned to look at her as well.

Lilith breathed heavily and her nostrils flared in anger. She looked down at the hunting knife lying on the other side of the dome and walked to pick it up, refusing to look at Sayr or the amount of blood as she passed.

"We're done for today," she ordered. She retrieved the knife and stalked past the soldiers still watching. "Clean yourself up before dinner."

17

Sayr slammed the door to her chambers shut before letting out an enraged scream. She hadn't bothered changing out of her training suit or waiting for Willa before leaving the armory and getting to her chambers as quickly as possible to assess the damage Lilith had done to her.

A cut on her face would likely bleed a lot, but she doubted it was very deep and knew it wasn't near anything vital to need to visit the medic's level. She wasn't about to have them examine an injury she could likely patch up herself.

She couldn't believe she'd been so stupid to think Lilith would surrender to her. She'd trained every Creobian soldier for years, of course she wasn't going to give up in front of all the soldiers in the armory. She'd been foolish to let her guard down before Lilith had dropped her weapons.

A small head of long black hair popped out from the open doorway to the washroom. A squeal escaped Dema's lips, and she rushed towards Sayr, reaching out for her.

"Your face!" she cried once she'd reached Sayr and lifted a hand to examine the cut. Sayr let Dema turn her face over in her hands to get a better look at the damage.

"It's just a scratch," Sayr said.

"It's quite deep for a scratch," Dema noted and dropped her hands from Sayr's face. "What happened?"

"Lilith happened," Sayr muttered and walked with Dema further into the bedroom. "I've been assigned to train with her every day after my lessons with Dimitri. Clearly, she went a little too far on the first day."

"Dimitri? Dimitri Lim?" Dema asked.

Sayr swiveled back towards Dema. "You know him?" she asked.

Dema's eyes were wide, but she blinked repeatedly and shook her head, gently grabbing Sayr's hand and leading her towards the washroom. "Never mind, let me help you. I'm no medic, but I can at least help you wash up and clean your wound."

Sayr looked Dema over for a moment. Dema was one of the few people in this palace that Sayr was beginning to like. Whatever Dema knew about Dimitri set her on edge, and she vowed not to let Dimitri get within ten feet of the young, innocent girl holding tight to her hand.

"Thank you, Dema," Sayr said with a smile. "I could really use a bath, actually."

Sayr slowly lowered herself into the tub, hissing at the heat of the water. Dema had cleaned the blood from her face and neck and rubbed a salve over the cut before bandaging the side of her face and calling on the Elemental servants to draw a bath for her. She'd found fresh lavender somewhere and added it to the water. The smell made Sayr's eyelids grow heavy, and she leaned back against the side of the tub.

A hand lightly tugged at her hair, and she flinched away from the touch, looking up at Dema sitting next to the tub.

"I'm sorry," she said and lifted her hands up from Sayr's head, one hand holding a brush. "Your hair's a bit tangled."

"It's alright." Sayr rested her head back down as Dema slowly grabbed her hair again and began brushing. For a while, they sat in complete silence while Dema brushed through the waves of her hair and began styling them at the top of her head to keep the strands out of the water.

"How old are you, Dema?" Sayr asked. She didn't know why she asked, but she found herself wanting to know more about the young girl. If Sayr was going to keep the lady's maid around, she may as well get to know her.

Dema's hands stilled, Sayr's hair only half styled. "Fourteen," she answered softly.

Sayr whirled around to look at her. "Only fourteen?" she asked in disbelief. "What in the elements are you doing here in the palace?"

Dema gently grabbed Sayr's shoulders and turned her back around. She grabbed a length of Sayr's hair and continued brushing.

"My brother has worked in this palace since he was fifteen," she explained. "He left home when I was only ten but would come back to our village every few months to visit our parents and me. My father has a decent job in our village back home, but with his job in the palace, my brother quickly became the stability in our family. Last winter, he came home with an offer for me as a lady's maid in the palace. There have been younger girls than me who work as lady's maids here and my brother had provided so much for our family that I couldn't refuse. I accepted and traveled back with him that same trip. I've been here ever since."

Sayr listened intently while Dema told her story. She'd come to the palace last winter, almost a full year ago. She looked young, yes, but hearing Dema say it aloud felt... different. She was too young and too kind to be working in such a horrible place.

"Your parents must be very proud," Sayr muttered and sunk deeper into the sweet-scented water.

Dema laughed softly at the icy tone in Sayr's words. "They are. It is an honor to work for a king or queen, don't you think?"

"Of course." Sayr's reply was automatic.

"How old are you, Lady Sayr?" Dema asked.

Sayr inhaled deeply, the calming lavender easing her wariness. "Just Sayr, no need to call me Lady. And I'm seventeen."

"Of course… Sayr," Dema nodded. "And how old were you when you became a member of the Eastern Court?"

Sayr didn't respond at first. She remembered exactly how old she was when her father had brought her to live in the Eastern Palace, and she remembered the day that her father left the palace for the last time and never returned for his daughter as if it had been just yesterday. But did she want to share a part of her that was so personal with Dema? Would speaking about those days reopen old wounds?

"I was nine…when I first came to the Eastern Palace." Sayr's voice was barely above a whisper.

Dema stalled her work on her hair again. "That is very young."

"It is," Sayr agreed. "But my position was different from yours. I needed to be trained young in order to be of use to the Visarian royal family."

"Of course." Dema styled another strand of Sayr's hair on top of her head. "Your queen would not have sent just anyone from her Court to help our country. Your position must be very important."

Sayr didn't know what to say to that. Was her position important? She thought back to what Lanni had said about how alike she and Sayr were.

We're dispensable, she'd said. Was this Her Majesty's way of starting a war and getting rid of Sayr? If Sayr failed, would she be rid of so easily?

Sayr shook the thoughts from her head. She had a duty to fulfill. Her queen would never throw her out once Sayr completed her mission.

Dema finished styling Sayr's hair and wrapped a warm robe around her. She had ordered one of the servants who was emptying the tub of the now cold bathwater to bring a message to His Majesty that Sayr would not be attending dinner tonight and therefore would not be able to give him her training report.

The streets of Therod were slick with rain. The few people still out tonight were running into taverns and homes to get out of the downpour. None of them spared a glance at the hooded figure passively walking through the streets. A thick hood cloaked Dimitri's features, rendering him unrecognizable to anyone. The slanting rain did not hinder him as he slowly made his way down the street, occasionally glancing left and right at each building.

Finally, Dimitri stopped at the door of a closed jeweler shop. No light shown through the windows and no noise could be heard from behind the door. Dimitri knocked three times, paused, knocked once, paused, and knocked once more. No one answered the door for several moments, until the soft pattering of feet came from inside. The sound of keys jingled and finally the door opened just slightly.

"Who is there?" a voice whispered from behind the door.

"A friend of the king's," Dimitri answered, shoving the door open and stepping into the shop.

Dimitri barged through the shop and a stout middle-aged man stumbled back. The man took note of the soaked cloak and the king's emblem on the large bronze clasp that secured the cloak around Dimitri's shoulders.

"Wh-what do you want?" the man stammered. "You have no business here."

"Oh, but I think I do," Dimitri said and pulled his hood down around his shoulders. He took his time walking slowly through the shop, eyeing dazzling necklaces, crystal goblets, and bejeweled candelabras.

The stout man looked Dimitri over. His eyes widened when he spotted the sword sheathed at Dimitri's hip. Dimitri stopped in front of a dagger on display. The handle of the dagger had been carved in an intricate twisted design and had been studded with amethysts. Dyed purple leather was wrapped around the hilt for a secure grip.

"It has come to the Crown's attention that you have been refuging rebels against His Majesty, Mr. Coburn," Dimitri said smoothly. He picked up the dagger and held it up into the lamplight shining in through the windows, inspecting closely. He glanced back at the sweating shop owner.

"I-I don't know what you're talking about." Mr. Coburn stumbled back against the counter, propping himself up against the glass with both hands. He looked around for something, anything to defend himself with that was in reach, but there was nothing. He looked helplessly back at Dimitri. "You have the wrong man, surely."

A low chuckle rumbled from Dimitri's throat. "You and I both know that I have the right man, Mr. Coburn, and that man is you."

Dimitri lowered the dagger from the light and looped it through the belt at his hip. "You visited your family in Abelforth not too long ago, correct? Your neighbors say you were gone for days. You made it to Abelforth just two days before the attack on the town."

In a few steps, Dimitri was within arm's reach of Mr. Coburn, but he did not attack. He simply reached into a pocket within his cloak and pulled out a small envelope, holding it out to Mr. Coburn without a word.

With a shaky hand, Mr. Coburn took the letter and opened it. His jaw dropped in horror when he read the familiar handwriting, his own. He pleadingly looked up into Dimitri's hazel eyes.

"Please," Mr. Coburn begged. "These Elementals deserve justice; I am only trying to help them after the king failed to do so himself."

In a flash, Dimitri's hand was around Mr. Coburn's throat, pinning him against the glass counter.

"Do not insult His Majesty in my presence," he said through gritted teeth.

He let go of the man and took a single step back, unsheathing his sword from his belt. "By aiding these rebels, you have committed treason against the Crown and will pay the penalty with your life."

Tears streamed down Mr. Coburn's face, and he fell to his knees.

"Please," he begged. "Please."

But Dimitri had already lifted his sword high over his head. Mr. Coburn closed his eyes just as Dimitri swung down the sword.

Sayr jolted up in her bed and quickly scanned her room. Her gasping breaths filled her ears, and she realized she was panting. Hard.

Had she had a nightmare? She could still see the dying forest and the ash-covered earth. Her limbs tingled with the remnants of the dream. Or was it a vision? Were her visions now occurring in her dreams? She put her head against her knees and covered her eyes with her hands.

She breathed in, and out, in, and out, until her breathing was once again steady. She touched each of her fingertips together, one by one, a habit she found comforting every time she came out of a vision.

She must have been dreaming about the vision that continued to haunt her. That had to be it. She could not be losing control of her visions so much, not now while she was in enemy territory.

But the vision had still felt so real, just as it had every time she'd had it. Sayr inhaled shakily. If she could not control her abilities, she feared they would slowly drive her insane.

She stilled for a moment, listening to the soft patter of feet approaching her.

Sayr quickly reached for her dinner knife just as a hand clamped tightly over her mouth. She kicked and flailed to try and free herself from the invader's grasp.

She caught a glimpse of the invader, and all movement in her body stilled. Marenda looked down at her, eyes wide and lips pursed as if she were making a silent shushing sound.

The tension in Sayr's body melted away and Mar released her hand from Sayr's mouth. As soon as she was free, Sayr leaped from the bed and into her best friend's arms.

"Where in the elements have you been?" Sayr whispered harshly. "What happened to you?"

Mar hugged Sayr back but quickly pulled away. "Sayr, the healers, the people here, they are not what they seem." Her voice was barely a whisper. "They are not what we believed they were."

"What do you mean?" Sayr asked. "What are they, then?"

Mar looked at Sayr, but her eyes were distant and glassy. "The healers in the medic's level, they possess gifts outside of the natural elements, or so I believe. The way they healed my arm…the things I've seen them do…it's like nothing I've ever seen before."

"You think they may be like me?" Sayr asked. A mix of fear and hope bloomed in her chest.

"No," Mar answered. "At least not completely like you, but it's a start. If we can just get more information, I think we could find out what they really are."

Her eyes darted all over Sayr's face, narrowing when she took in the bandage just above her cheek. She lifted one hand to Sayr's cheek and ripped the bandage off her face.

"Ow!" Sayr tried to keep her voice quiet as she shrieked. Her face stung where the bandage had just been ripped and Mar took Sayr's face in her own hands.

"What was this?" she asked.

"A cut," Sayr explained. "From training. It's nothing serious, it'll heal soon."

"It's already healed," Mar noted and tugged Sayr into her washroom.

She ignited the candles around them for light and Sayr took in their reflections in the mirror. Mar was right, the cut was almost completely healed. Only a thin red line marked her cheek.

"How is that possible?" she asked aloud. Even Dema had noted that the cut was rather deep earlier that day.

"This is what I'm talking about," Mar said. "Something is going on here that they're not telling us. I've seen it in the medic's level most, that's where all the healers are. And they don't hide their practices from anyone there."

"You've seen this for yourself?" Sayr repeated.

"Yes," Mar answered. "They use these gifts on all kinds of injuries in the medic's level. And their remedy healer cures the sick almost instantly with her remedies."

Sayr could hardly believe what Mar was saying. There were people in this palace with gifts outside of the natural elements. Was that why His Majesty had brought her here? Did he truly know what she was? And there may be people like her, people that understood what it was like to possess gifts outside of the elements. She had to know more about them, but she couldn't get into the medic's level herself. Not without Dimitri or another Court member following her everywhere.

"Do you think you could visit the medic's level occasionally? Find out more about these people without building suspicion?" Sayr asked.

Mar nodded. "I already have the remedy healer showing me some of her remedies. I can use that excuse to continue entering the medic's level if necessary."

"Perfect." Sayr began pacing while she plotted. "Don't let them know you're trying to uncover information about the healers and their gifts, not until we can possibly get one of them alone and out of the medic's level. Are you going back there tonight?"

Mar shook her head. "I've been away from you for too long already. I'm staying by your side. When you go to your trainings, I'll keep investigating, but other than that I am by your side."

"Thank you, Mar," Sayr said and hugged her friend close. "I think this is a good time for a conversation with His Majesty."

Sayr's thoughts raced with the information from Mar. Mar had been admitted only recently and had uncovered more than Sayr could have ever imagined. What had Sayr accomplished so far?

She'd met five of the seven members of the Western Court on her list: Adelaide Hill, Lilith Blanche, Willa Simon, Tomas Lambert, and Dimitri Lim. Unfortunately for the king, he had aided her by assigning her daily lessons with Lilith and Dimitri. She had only seen Adelaide a few times in the palace and during dinners with King Mylan, but it was enough.

She still had a long way to go before she could go through with her mission and far more work to accomplish. She needed to get close to all members of the King's Court, learn their schedules, their behaviors, and their weaknesses. She needed to find out which of them was the king's mercenary. She needed to find out which of them she was going to kill.

Mar settled into a couch by the fireplace, determined to wait in Sayr's room while Sayr went to speak with the king. She hurried from her spot near the bed and stalked to her wardrobe, quickly changing from her nightgown into a warm sweater and pants.

She noiselessly made her way down the halls, hoping she could remember the way to the royal quarters on her own. King Mylan had said if she ever needed anything, she was always welcome in the king's quarters. And now she was going to see how true his words really were.

She reached the cylindrical clearing that revealed the palace entrance far below. The upper levels of the palace loomed high above. She looked up past the railing at numerous levels, trying to remember which one the guard had escorted her to. She thought back to the map hiding in her chambers, the layout of the palace fresh in her mind.

She ascended level after level until she was breathing heavily from the climb. Two guards stood at the top of the next level, eyeing her as she approached.

"You cannot be on this level, milady. You need to descend these stairs and go back to your guest level," one of the guards said as soon as Sayr reached the top of the stairs.

Sayr assessed each guard for a second. Both looked older than the members of the King's Court and were heavily armed. Their expressions were cold as stone as they stared at her.

"I am here to see the king." Sayr tried to put as much confidence into her voice, not wavering as one of the guards stepped closer.

"It's quite late to be requesting to see the king," the guard said. "And you have no jurisdiction on this level to request His Majesty."

Sayr didn't falter or step back from the guard. "His Majesty told me that I could visit his quarters any time I wished."

The guard's expression didn't change, but he finally looked at her as if noticing her standing before him for the first time of him. "What is your name?"

"Lady Sayr Rieve," she answered.

The other guard's eyes widened and the guard in front of her shifted to move back. The king must have mentioned her to his Royal Guards and had kept his word of letting her visit these quarters whenever she needed. Both sets of eyes swept over her, looking for weapons.

"This way, Lady Sayr," one guard said, and he began to climb towards the second level of the king's quarters. Sayr glanced at the remaining guard on the first level before following the other up the stairs.

Sayr was starting to believe the halls of every level of the palace looked exactly the same for a reason. It would be very difficult for enemies of the king to enter this palace without getting lost or confused.

The guard silently led her down the hall, nodding to the several Royal Guards that they passed. This level was much more heavily guarded than the levels below. Quickly, the guard stopped at a single door that looked just like the doors that led to her own chambers. He silently opened the door and stepped halfway into the room, murmuring to someone behind the door. He glanced back at Sayr and turned to murmur again.

Sayr eyed the different weapons strapped all along the guard's uniform, wondering which room he had chosen in the armory to train, and which weapon could be the easiest to steal from him without him noticing. He quickly turned back to her and Sayr instinctively took a step away from him, feigning innocence, while he pulled the door wide open and gestured for her to enter.

The room she entered was much smaller than she had expected. A few bookshelves, multiple small tables stacked with papers, a few chairs, and a large desk full of clutter where the king now stood hunched over with his back to her. This was not the room she had been taken to the first time she'd entered the king's quarters.

The guard cleared his throat loudly and announced, "Lady Sayr Rieve, Your Majesty."

King Mylan turned to face them. He wore loose trousers and a very ruffled shirt. Strands of hair stuck up in all directions as if he had been running his hands through his hair repeatedly and his eyes were bleak and tired. He clearly had not been to bed tonight, but his usual smile appeared when he saw Sayr.

"Please, come in." He waved her over to the table and nodded at the guard to return to his post. Sayr silently made her way over to the king and the table he stood in front of.

"I have to admit, when I offered the invitation for you to visit at any time, I hadn't expected your visit to be in this room." Though the king looked tired, his voice still held its usual amusement.

Sayr ignored the comment and peered over the king's shoulder at the candlelit table. Her brows furrowed together as she took in a map of Creobe just like the one Dimitri had shown her in their lessons, only this one had been heavily marked in black charcoal all over the map.

"What is this?" she asked the king.

He ran a hand through his hair, ruffling it even more, and sighed. "This is a map of all the attacks on my country. Every charcoal marking is a town, city, or village that has either been burned to the ground or robbed of almost everything."

Sayr moved closer to the table. Her eyes roved over the map, noting the black dotted line encircling the palace and the land around it, and the other four lines separating the rest of the country into four sections. "What are these lines?"

"These lines divide my country into sectors," King Mylan explained and traced one of the lines with his finger. "Creobe is divided into five different sectors; the Northern, Eastern, Southern, Western, and Royal Sector." He jabbed his finger at the circle encompassing the palace to emphasize the last sector.

Sayr wanted to ask more about these sectors, but the charcoal markings all across the map grappled for her attention and she turned back to them. She'd ask Dimitri about the sectors of the country another time.

The king pointed to a small black blotch near the top of the Western Sector. "This was the first attack, six months ago. The village was burned and completely destroyed. All of its citizens were forced to flee, leaving everything they had behind. Many lost more than just their homes or belongings; they lost children, parents, and loved ones in the destruction."

"That's horrible," Sayr whispered and looked at the king. "You said there hadn't been many casualties when you explained your situation in the Eastern Court."

"I lied," Mylan admitted. "I couldn't completely explain our situation in the Eastern Court. I don't trust

Cheralin not to take advantage of just how much my kingdom is struggling."

Sayr lowered her eyes at that. With her daily lessons and training and her worry for Mar consuming her, she had all but forgotten the reason she and the Queen's Army were sent here in the first place. This country truly did need their help.

"Do you have any idea who is behind these attacks? Or where they are coming from?" she asked.

King Mylan sighed again. "The only solid lead that we have is that they must be located in the Western or Northern Sector. The majority of the attacks are in those two sectors, they are not straying too far from familiar territory."

"How many attacks have occurred since we arrived in Creobe?" Sayr asked.

"Two," Mylan said. "The most recent attack was in Abelforth, in the Eastern Sector. Their attacks seem less severe since I've returned. My people have reported that these rebels are looking for something now instead of simply burning everything to the ground."

"They're getting closer to Visaran," Sayr muttered. "Her Majesty will not be happy about this."

"I am hoping Her Majesty will now see this as a real threat since they are moving closer to her territory and will be willing to extend the time her troops are here," King Mylan said.

A thought suddenly hit Sayr, and she turned her eyes from the map towards the king. "When you came to the Eastern Palace, Queen Cheralin said that she would give you her troops and, in exchange, you and your people would end the political extortion against Visaran. What sort of extortion do you have against the queen?"

King Mylan straightened and turned away from the map to face Sayr. "There is so much you do not know about the world, Lady Sayr. Then again, I believe there is much you have to learn that you will not accept. You have lived under Her Majesty's lies for too long."

Sayr straightened from the table to face the king. "Since your Court came to Visaran, everyone has told me that there is so much that I do not know or understand, and that I still have so much to learn. Yet not one person has offered to teach me whatever it is that I don't know. I am consistently left in the dark." Sayr took a step closer to the king. "What is it that I need to learn?"

One corner of His Majesty's lips quirked upwards. "I tried pushing pieces of information at you in the Eastern Palace, though it was much harder than I anticipated under Queen Cheralin's eye. You have heard Lilith and I refer to ourselves as unseen Elementals many times, yet you never questioned what an unseen Elemental is or what we may be capable of. Why is that?"

"We do not have unseen Elementals in Visaran," Sayr answered. "With all due respect, Your Majesty, I haven't questioned any of it because it all sounds like lies to me."

"You have been indoctrinated by the queen not to question or accept things your people find unnatural," King Mylan said. "The unseen elements are not spoken of in

Visaran because they are not accepted in Visaran, only the seen elements remain in the Eastern Kingdom; water, earth, fire, and maybe even air, though it is rare. Or that is what we all believed until we found you in the Eastern Court."

Sayr shifted, uncomfortable with the change in topics coming back around to her. "What does this have to do with the attacks?" she asked.

"The divide between the different elements has been a struggle for centuries, since the Dividing War," King Mylan explained. "Each Elemental believes they are stronger than the rest. I am afraid that what is happening in these sectors has to do with this divide. The villages that are being burned to the ground are likely being overtaken by seen Elementals while the ones being ransacked are being taken over by unseen Elementals."

"They are ruining these locations to rebuild them solely for people of their abilities," Sayr whispered. "What about non-Elementals? Who is protecting them?"

"That is another presumption that you Visarians have wrong," the king corrected. "Non-Elementals are not weak. Many of my own inner Court and Royal Guards are non-Elementals. You do not need an Elemental ability to be powerful, though Her Majesty believes otherwise."

"Many non-Elementals within my own Court have gone to help the nearest city after the attacks to aid survivors as much as possible," King Mylan continued. "Other non-Elementals have been out searching for these perpetrators or anyone who sympathizes with them. I am sure you have noticed Dimitri's absence."

Sayr nodded. She had indeed noticed his absence, but how did that connect—

Sayr almost gasped aloud when she made the connection.

Dimitri, an esteemed member of the King's Court, who held the respect of the Creobian Royal Guards to bow their heads when he entered a room, was a non-Elemental?

Sayr had never seen him manipulate any element, she realized. But she had never done so in front of him, either, and he had never questioned it. She had assumed that they had an understanding when it came to showing off their abilities, there was no need to do so in front of each other. She hadn't even considered that he was a non-Elemental.

Valuable information, indeed.

"How do we stop all of this?" Sayr asked, trying to turn the topic once again to the matter at hand.

"I have sent Her Majesty's troops to each village and city to stop the unrest and ensure word does not spread to the rest of the sectors," the king answered. "I suppose I will need to send members of my own Court to the locations that are at risk of being attacked next."

The gears in Sayr's head began to turn and she blurted, "I can go. Send Mar and me with the troops to deal with the unrest. Or I could be of help in the sectors that could be at risk."

The king looked at her as if sizing her up. "You have not had enough combat training with Lilith, I'm afraid."

"I've had plenty of training in the Eastern Court," Sayr countered. "If the time comes when another town is attacked… there are people in your Court that you can trust to keep me with them if you let me go be of help. If you allow me to go with your Court to the next attack, I promise that I will not run, I will help in any way I can, and then I will return with the Court back to this palace."

The king did not respond for a long while. He stared at the map in front of them, his eyes bouncing between the locations of previous attacks. When he finally did look back at Sayr, his eyes were clear and resolute.

"Her Majesty will surely come after me if I let you go and these rebels kill you," he said gloomily. "Let me see how much you advance after you have had further training with Lilith, and maybe I will let you go with Dimitri and my Court. Then we will see what you can do."

Sayr expected to hate the king's last words, but they ignited a new excitement within her. This was her chance. Not only to stop these rebels, but this may be the opportunity she needed to find and kill the king's mercenary. If he was willing to deploy Sayr to the attacks, surely, he would deploy his own mercenary, too.

Yes, they would all see what she could truly do.

Three weeks. It had been over three weeks since Marenda was taken to the medic's level, over three weeks since she had revealed the healer's secrets to Sayr. Since then, Mar had remained at Sayr's side, besides attending her lessons and training when she would head to the medic's level or train with the Creobian soldiers. She told Sayr about the healer's abilities to mend bones within minutes and the strength of many Elementals in the Creobian army. King Mylan's army was strong but spread all throughout the country and were focused on the rebel attacks.

Sayr's thoughts raced while she sat in her usual chair at the farthest table in the back corner of the library. She was gaining information, but it wasn't enough. It wouldn't be enough to satisfy Cordia or Her Majesty. The only thing that would satisfy them would be the death of the king's mercenary and the fall of the King's Court.

"No spunk this morning, I see," Dimitri said from across the table. Sayr didn't know what he did with his mornings, but he was always first to the library, already sitting at their usual table by the time she arrived.

Sayr barely lifted her eyes in acknowledgement as she shook her head, her thoughts spinning. Dimitri frowned at her. He crossed his arms and leaned back in his chair, watching her.

Finally, Sayr spoke. "What can you tell me about the Creobian army?"

Dimitri's frown deepened in what almost looked like concern. "What do you want to know about the Creobian army?"

Sayr shrugged and finally looked up at Dimitri. "Hundreds of soldiers from the Queen's Army are staying here near the palace. I'm curious as to how and where they're housed, how the king could have room for five hundred more soldiers, and the size of his own army since he still needed aid from Her Majesty's troops."

"I see," Dimitri thought aloud.

"You see," Sayr repeated. "I'm glad you *see;* now can you *speak?*"

Dimitri shot her a withering glare. "I don't typically deal with the Creobian troops. I know that many of the king's armies are spread around Creobe, leaving room in the barracks at the base of the mountain for troops from the Queen's Army. If you want to know more about the troops, talk to Ryon. He deals more with soldiers than I do."

Ryon. Was his position in the King's Court one that brought him closer to the Creobian army? Would a king's mercenary hold a position like that?

"Anything else before we get started?" he asked. "That aren't smart mouth comments, I mean."

Sayr ignored his ridicule and thought back to her encounter with His Majesty. "What can you tell me about the sectors of Creobe?" she asked.

"How did you learn about the Creobian sectors?" he asked. He kept his face neutral, but his voice was etched with interest.

Sayr explained her conversation with the king in the royal quarters, leaving out the specific hour of the visit.

"His Majesty told you all of this?" he asked.

"Yes," Sayr answered. She wanted to ask about the seen and unseen elements, but every time she came close to bringing it up her stomach tied into knots. Something about Dimitri being a non-Elemental still made her uneasy about asking him about the elements. She would save it for another lesson.

Dimitri stood and walked to the closest aisle of books. He walked further through the aisle until Sayr could no longer see him. Just when Sayr was beginning to think he'd left the library completely, he returned through the aisles with another stack of books and a large roll of parchment.

He laid the books onto the floor near his seat and unrolled the parchment across the table. Another map laid in front of Sayr, but this one was a map of the entire continent, not just Creobe.

A thick blue line divided Creobe and Visaran, representing the Silia River that ran directly between the two countries. The map showed every city in Visaran; Talluh, Northow, Pastole, and the City Center, as well as smaller villages that went unnamed on the map. In Creobe, there were black dotted lines separating the country into four outer sections, and one smaller section directly around the lands surrounding the palace.

The five sectors.

"These here," Dimitri said and pointed to each divided land, "are the five sectors of Creobe. The Northern, Eastern, Southern, Western, and Royal Sector. All of Creobe is ruled by His Majesty, but each sector is overseen by a Lord or Lady, or both. The citizens within each sector answer to their Lord or Lady who in return look over the sector, dealing with the smaller issues within the land and bringing any key issues to the king."

"Why would the king divide up his power like that?" Sayr asked. Queen Cheralin would die on her throne before passing any ounce of power to another person in her Court, let alone multiple people, whether they answered to her or not.

"This is how Creobe has always operated," Dimitri explained. "Kings and queens long before King Mylan choose Lords and Ladies to oversee the sectors on their coronation day. Kings and queens ruled over the Royal Sector and all of Creobe, but it helps to have the Lords and Ladies to oversee the other sectors. Think of it as another set of hands in each part of the country, they handle the legal dealings within the sectors and bring bigger issues to the palace for His Majesty."

"If the king oversees the Royal Sector, then there are four Lords and Ladies within the other sectors, right?" Sayr asked. She gripped the arms of her chair in concentration.

"Not exactly," Dimitri said and nodded back to the map displayed on the library table. "There are four other domains for Lords and Ladies to oversee, but some sectors are overseen by both a Lord and Lady while others are only overseen by one of them. Often times, a chosen man and woman will oversee a sector together as Lord and Lady. Otherwise, there is only one."

Dimitri pointed towards the top of the map. "The Northern Sector is overseen by Lord Darmoth, the Eastern by Lord and Lady Sutten, the Southern by Lord Poleen and Lady Koln, and the Western by Lady Dunqer."

"Can I ask a different question?" Sayr asked.

"Of course." Dimitri leaned forward from across the table and rested his chin in his hand.

"Why is His Majesty not married?" Dimitri's brow furrowed at Sayr's question, so she continued. "Queen Cheralin gained the throne by marrying King Luzan. After his death, she became the sole ruler of the country by Visarian law. They've secured their lineage to the throne through Prince Everett, ensuring that their bloodline will remain on the throne through the next generation. Why hasn't King Mylan done the same?"

Something sparked in Dimitri's eyes. "The Creobian throne is not secured through bloodline."

"What do you mean?" Sayr sat up straighter in her seat.

"A Creobian king or queen is decided by the people," Dimitri explained. "When a king or queen dies, their spouse or children do not remain on the throne, assuming that they have any at all. The throne remains vacant for one year. The Lords and Ladies of each sector rule, in fact, and during that year a new king or queen is voted onto the throne."

"You're kidding." Sayr's mouth hung open a moment. She had never learned of Creobe's royal history. She, along with every other Visarian, assumed the royal lineage worked the same as Visaran's royal lineage.

"I'm quite serious." Dimitri's lips quirked up again. "Have I ruined your plans of taking the Creobian throne by marrying King Mylan?"

Sayr threw the closest book at Dimitri, which he caught easily. He turned the book over in his hands and looked back over the table at her. "How far are you in *The Elemental's History of Magic*?"

"I'm… getting through it," Sayr said.

"Have you at least gotten to double digits in page numbers?" Dimitri lifted his other hand when Sayr reached for the second closest book to throw. "Alright, alright. Have you learned anything new in your reading?"

"Not exactly," Sayr huffed. "Any information that is new to me is about the layout of the continent or Creobe. I haven't found anything new that pertains to Creobe and Elementals."

Dimitri nodded thoughtfully. "You have much reading to do, then."

"To be fair, you instructed that I finish the book before the queen tries to take me back. You didn't specify how much I should be reading each day; I'm still technically following your orders."

Dimitri huffed out a laugh. Sayr almost fell out of her chair as she leaned forward. "Did you, Dimitri Lim, truly just laugh?"

Dimitri's smile faded quickly.

"Don't trip over yourself on the way out," he said, the bored façade taking over him once again. "You should be getting to the armory soon."

Sayr rose from her chair and headed for the library doors but turned back towards Dimitri. "You don't need to hide, Dimitri. Not from me."

He remained perfectly still, not looking at Sayr as she walked out of the library.

Marenda lined the vials up into a neat line. She filled each one halfway with distilled liquor before opening the drawers of her worktable and retrieving various ingredients.

She plucked a deep blue plant that smelled of sweet lemon and placed it into a small bowl. Marenda picked up the rounded pestle and began grinding the plant down into a fine powder before sifting the blue powder into one of the vials. She fumbled through the bottles scattered around the table and selected one filled with a milky white substance, poured a few drops into the vial, and sealed it shut. She shook the vial to mix the ingredients, then watched as the medicine finalized into a milky blue color.

"Too much Tearoot." Addy's voice chimed from behind her, causing Marenda to roll her eyes.

Addy swung back and forth on a cloth-made hammock high up in the corner of the herbalist room. One eye peaked open to investigate Marenda's remedy.

"Tearoot is a strong sedative herb," she explained. "You only need one small stem to calm even the most frantic patient. Grinding three stems into the remedy, like you did, could relax a patient's body to the point of stopping their heart."

"You couldn't have said something before I added it into the vial?" Marenda grumbled under her breath. She disposed of the vial and began the process again, this time with one stem of Tearoot.

Callum, Addy's apprentice, slunk into the herbalist's room, a bushel of grassy-looking herbs in his arms. He set the herbs onto his worktable and peeked over Marenda's shoulder, silently watching her work.

"Having you closer doesn't make it easier, you know," Marenda protested as she grinded the Tearoot into a fine powder.

"You're doing well." Callum's soft voice was barely audible, even with him so close to Marenda.

Marenda glanced behind her, almost annoyed at the compliment. "Why don't the two of you leave the room, and I'll call for you when I'm finished? I concentrate better when I'm alone."

Addy grinned, one arm dangling over the hammock. "No can do," she said. "If you want to become a remedy healer, I need to approve your skills throughout the entire process. You could bring me a vial and say that it's a Tearoot sedative when really you made a Plyweed stimulant and overdrive my senses, leaving me in a comatose state if I were to ingest it the same way as I would a Tearoot sedative."

Addy sighed dreamily, as if the thought was a fantasy to her. Marenda side-eyed the small girl, taking in the dreamy expression on her face. "You're strange, you know that?"

Addy's smile widened. "Of course, I do. It's one of my more intriguing qualities, and part of the reason I make such a great remedy healer. I don't fear the consequences of combining such risky ingredients."

Marenda rolled her eyes again, this time so Addy could see.

Callum crossed his arms and tilted his head as he watched Marenda work. "Why are you so concerned with remedy healing? The healers in the Eastern Palace are proficient enough to heal any nonfatal wound you'd see in battle."

"You have too much faith in other's healing abilities," Marenda noted and mixed the ground Tearoot into the vial again.

She'd seen what the healers in the Eastern Palace could do and, while their abilities were impressive, they didn't shine a light on the gifts of the healers here in the Western Palace.

"I want to be able to heal myself if the situation were to come up. I don't want to have to rely on others to do the job for me," Marenda explained.

Callum studied Marenda for a long moment, still close behind her. Too close. "I think it's more than just that."

Marenda gripped her vial tightly. He was right. It was much more than that.

Marenda had seen what the healer had done to her fractured arm within just a few minutes. The healer's gifts were not elemental like the gifts given to Elementals for centuries, and there was only one other person that she knew of that had been blessed, or maybe cursed, with gifts outside of the elements.

She couldn't tell Addy or Callum any of this, though, or anyone else for that matter. She would never give up her best friend's secrets, but she supposed she could offer a secret of her own instead.

"I want to learn remedy healing because I am a Fire Elemental," she answered.

Addy's expression twisted, clearly disappointed in Marenda's answer. "Yes, I'm aware of that."

"I am a Fire Elemental, and a warrior, and the personal guard to the Queen of Visaran. All of these…

titles… are fierce and honorable, but they are also destructive."

Addy leaned forward. "You are a fierce woman." Her tone was almost mocking, as if she were almost jealous.

"That's just it!" Marenda slammed the vial onto the table, her voice growing as her words intensified. "I'm only seen as a fierce woman, a fierce warrior. The kind that kills and destroys. The kind that is angry and savage. Never the kind that fixes or heals or helps. I've always enjoyed being feared, I'll admit that, but I never wanted fear to be my only identity. I want to learn remedy healing so that I can show others that I'm not a destroyer, that I can be a Fire Elemental and a warrior and a healer just the same."

The room was filled with silence. Marenda stared at the vial gripped tight in her hand, not willing to meet Addy or Callum's surprised stares. Her breathing had quickened as she'd given her confession away, and she exhaled slowly.

Sayr had been one of the few people to know how she'd truly felt. Many of the elements were capable of destruction, but none as much as fire. It warped its burning flames through everything; fields, buildings, homes… people. Being a Fire Elemental automatically marked her as a raging and vicious person, and she was beginning to accept that that was all she would be.

She thought becoming the queen's personal guard would change that narrative, but it only made her appear more savage as the rumors spread of what Marenda must have had to do to make her way to the top. No one saw her kindness or her worth beyond that. No one except for Sayr.

"Well, that was a much more complicated answer than I expected… or wanted for that matter." Addy broke the silence.

Callum's shoulder brushed against Marenda's, and she looked over at him as he picked through the ingredients on her table and began dumping them into his own vial.

He met her gaze, his lips quirking upward in a small smile.

"You should learn not to take what others say so personally," he advised. "You know who you are, and I hope the ones closest to you do, too. What others say about you can certainly affect your reputation for other people, but it should never affect your self-worth."

Marenda let out a mocking laugh. "You don't get it."

Callum shook the vial in his hands as he turned and leaned against the worktable, his full attention on Marenda. "You're right, I don't understand your situation because I'm not a Fire Elemental. But every Elemental has preconceived ideas made against them. Those in Court, like us, have other assumptions made of them, too."

Callum glanced up at Addy, and Marenda's gaze followed.

Addy stopped swinging in the hammock, watching Callum and Marenda closely. "I do know what it's like to be completely different from what everyone thinks you are, though. According to the rumors in this palace, I am the king's whore. Lilith, Willa, and I all are. That's why they call us the 'king's mistresses'".

Heat rushed up Marenda's neck and cheeks and she turned away from Addy. When the Western Court had first come to Visaran, she and Sayr had both assumed that was the case simply because of their closeness to the king.

"Are you not?" Marenda asked.

Addy let out a bubbly laugh, as if the idea were hilarious. "Of course not. His Majesty doesn't bother with intimate relationships. If he did, I'm sure he would have been married long ago."

"What about heirs?" Marenda asked. "Won't he need a first-born to secure his throne for the next generation?"

Addy gave Marenda a look that suggested the questions she was asking were similar to those of a child. "Creobe's rulers are not secured through heirs. After the death of a king or queen, a new ruler is voted onto the throne by the citizens within the sectors. King Mylan was voted to become King of Creobe not even a full decade ago. He completely reconstructed the Western Court, assigning new positions in his Court and removing most of the past Court members, replacing them with the people you see in his Court now."

"Why?" Marenda's brain was reeling with this information. She hadn't lived in the Eastern Palace a decade ago, but she hadn't heard any rumors about a new king rising to the Creobian throne back in her village, either. "Why not just continue the royal line so that no one has to vote, and a king or queen is always secured for the country's throne?"

"Because what you're suggesting sounds like imprisonment to us," Addy answered. "A child is handed a future title and throne simply because of who they are born to? What kind of life would that be not to experience the hardships and labors of their country's citizens, yet make decisions that would affect their people's lives forever? If it were me in that position, why would I work at all to understand my people if I were already secured the title of king or queen?"

Marenda thought hard for an argument against Addy, but she had to admit that the girl made a good point. Prince Everett was a good man and would make a great king. He joined war meetings and even a few Council meetings with Her Majesty, talked with the people of Visaran when they came to the palace to discuss their grievances, and was beginning to command his own armies.

But he had never left the palace to work the way the people of Visaran worked, and he'd had everything handed to him since he was an infant. Chefs cooked for him, tasters risked their lives to ensure his food wasn't poisoned, maids ran his baths, cleaned for him, and even clothed him. Everything that took basic human skills was done for him. Marenda didn't think Visaran needed to change the royal family line by any means, but maybe when Prince Everett became king, she would mention the idea of labor opportunities for future royal children and children of the Court, or at least some basic training skills in the barracks.

"If Visaran was to ever change its ways, I believe your friend would make a good queen," Addy stated. Her words knocked the breath from Marenda's lungs.

"Don't talk about her," Marenda snapped, causing Addy to laugh again.

"Why not?" Addy asked. "She's spending quite a lot of time with the King's Court, you know. She trains personally with Lilith and takes lessons from Dimitri. Does that worry you?"

"You ask too many questions," Marenda seethed.

Addy waited for a different answer, but she didn't receive one. Sayr told Marenda about the king's intentions for her, that he would try and keep her in the palace rather than let her return to Visaran. Marenda would never let that happen.

The silence continued. Marenda's hands roamed over the ingredients on the table. She made a point of looking preoccupied by the remedy she was mixing. After a few minutes of silence, Callum shuffled back to his worktable and Addy huffed an annoyed sigh, giving up on the conversation.

No, Marenda wouldn't speak a word about Sayr.

Marenda wanted to learn remedy healing for herself, but she also needed to learn more about the healers here. The people in this palace were all aware of their healer's abilities, including the king. If Creobe had been keeping people with gifts outside of the elements a secret, what else could this country be hiding?

And what did those secrets mean for Sayr?

Cordia paced back and forth in Sayr's suite. The girl hadn't returned from that morning's lesson yet, and Cordia was beginning to worry.

What were they telling Sayr in those lessons? What could they possibly know that the queen did not want Sayr to know? Did Sayr already know too much? Was she keeping information from Cordia?

The door to the suite opened and the girl stepped in. Her eyes rose from the ground, and she froze in place when she spotted Cordia.

"What are you doing in here?" she asked accusingly.

"We haven't spoken in some time," Cordia said. "I'm here for an update. How are your lessons going?"

"I'm getting beaten to a pulp by Lilith." Sayr nodded casually, mockingly. "And my brain is melting through my ears during my time with Dimitri."

Cordia frowned. "Be serious. Have you learned *anything* new?"

Sayr glared at Cordia but sighed heavily and walked towards the canopied bed.

"I know that there have been attacks in Creobe since we arrived," the girl said and plopped onto her bed. "The king thinks that the threats are originating from the Northern or Western sectors."

"All of that we already knew," Cordia said impatiently.

"Well, I didn't!" Sayr's voice was once again accusatory. "Maybe you should be giving me information when you come visit instead of the other way around."

"Remember your place, Sayr," Cordia warned. "I am here for your benefit, to help you complete your mission. I am just here to see what progress you've made and what you've learned."

Sayr seemed to settle as she sat on her bed. "I've learned about the sectors of Creobe," she repeated. "I've met each member of the King's Court and learned their positions. Ryon deals with the Creobian armies, Tomas is a hunter, Addy is the head remedy healer, Mina deals with the Court's aristocrats and officials, Willa is head of the king's spies, Dimitri seems to be in charge of the guard—or he has something to do with the guard since they all respect him—and Lilith trains the Creobian Royal Guards. I've been studying Dimitri and Lilith's movements throughout the palace and learning their daily schedules. I know Tomas's morning and night routines and where each of them spends the most time in the palace. I believe they all interact with one another quite often; I just need to get closer to them and find out which of them is truly the king's mercenary."

"And your abilities?" Cordia spoke low. "The king still seems to hold hope that you have some sort of ability. Why is that?"

"I have to get close to him and his Court somehow!" Sayr threw her arms up in exasperation. "I haven't admitted to anything, but I haven't shot down any hope that he may have of something more, either. That hope is one of the few reasons that he is keeping me so close and allowing me to train with Lilith and meet with Dimitri. He hasn't uncovered anything, none of them have."

Cordia nodded. "That's good, that's a start. But we need to begin moving quicker, learning more."

"I know, I know," Sayr said, and her face dropped into her hands.

Cordia made her way to the doors, leaving Sayr alone. "Your time is running out, Sayr."

Cordia opened the door but did not leave. A Royal Guard stood outside the girl's doorway. Worry and fear was etched all across his face and he looked past Cordia to Sayr.

"His Majesty is requesting you, Lady Sayr." The guard's voice matched the urgency in his eyes. "There has been an attack within the Royal Sector."

19

ayr followed close behind Dimitri as they sprinted up the multiple staircases to the king's quarters, taking two and three steps at a time. Dimitri had found her running through the halls and taken her with him through the levels and up towards the quarters. He reached the doors to the king's quarters and threw them open before any guard could do so for him. The two of them darted through the doors.

Willa, Ryon, and Tomas all stood behind their king. King Mylan was hunched over a table, accompanied by several Royal Guards, the drill instructor from Sayr's first day of training, and a few soldiers.

"Thank the elements." King Mylan turned from the map towards Sayr and Dimitri. "There has been another attack. The village is just inside the Royal Sector, only a few miles from the borders of the Royal and Northern Sectors."

"They're getting closer," Tomas murmured. The group approached the table. "That's only a few hours ride from here."

"A few hours by carriage," Mylan corrected. "You will travel faster on horseback."

Addy and Mar appeared through the doorway, both breathing heavily. Mar quickly walked to Sayr's side when she spotted her, gripping her hand.

Addy gasped when she took in the map.

There were at least three times as many charcoal marks on the map as there had been when Sayr had met with the king weeks ago.

"Why are there so many more?" Sayr asked.

"We have been able to identify some of the rebels," His Majesty explained. "The marks with an X are where these rebels have been spotted."

Sayr looked at the X's, they were marked in every sector of the country. These few rebels had travelled through every sector of Creobe.

"They're all over the map." Her voice rose with panic. "These people have been identified in every single sector?"

"Yes." His Majesty's calm voice was beginning to unravel. "We have identified them, but we have not captured a single rebel. They are moving far too quickly for us to track them. It seems they disappear almost immediately after the attacks, not a trace of them left."

King Mylan pointed to a charcoal mark in the northern-most portion of the Royal Sector. "We have received notice that the attacks here began this morning.

Three of the known rebels have been identified, we need to send reinforcements as soon as possible."

Mylan turned towards the members of his Court. "I will be sending you with a group of soldiers to apprehend and identify these rebels and bring them back to the palace for questioning. Reinforcements will be brought in to help ease as much of the damage as possible."

"You leave at the top of the hour," King Mylan ordered his Court. "Go, prepare yourselves."

The Creobian guards and soldiers all saluted the king before quickly leaving the room. The King's Court quickly ushered out of the room as well. Dimitri kept close to Mar and Sayr, leading them to the armory to arm themselves before their departure.

The ride to the village had been rough and fast. By the time Sayr had touched solid ground once again, the sun was high above the looming mountains. Smoke rose from buildings all around them and Sayr could hear the screams and wails coming through the scattered debris of the village. This was no small rebel group.

From the damage already done to the village, there had to be dozens of rebels that had attacked. Their numbers had to be strong in Earth and Fire Elementals. Sayr could tell simply from the damage to the landscape and the fires still burning around them. What other Elementals did they possess in numbers?

The King's Court immediately began to split up into two groups. Addy, Lilith, Tomas, and Willa bounded over the debris to the far side of the village while Dimitri, Marenda, Ryon, Mina, and Sayr sprinted for the village square where the damage was worst.

"We need people on every street!" Dimitri shouted. "We can capture anyone who tries to run if we trap them in the square!"

The group split into pairs. Mar and Sayr banked to the right and took a street for themselves. "We need to get to that fire," Mar said and jutted her chin towards a burning building a few blocks away. "Anyone that we find on the way we can usher towards the square."

The two sprinted faster, faster towards the fire. Citizens were running through the streets and out of buildings and Sayr had to shove a few out of her way to keep up with Mar.

She had just crossed an alleyway when a shadow jumped for her and tumbled with her to the ground. Her face slammed against the cobblestone, and she instantly tasted blood as her lower lip split open.

"Mar!" Sayr shouted and reached for one of the daggers sheathed at her hip.

Mar was on top of the rebel, pulling them off Sayr. Her sword was unsheathed in one hand, and she forced the rebel onto their stomach with the other. Her fingers trailed into the rebel's hair, and she yanked hard, lifting his head, and brought the sword to his throat.

"Bind him," Mar said to Sayr and nodded to the rope around her belt. Sayr tied one rope around the rebel's wrists behind his back and another around his feet.

"We'll leave him here for now and bring him back to the palace for questioning," Sayr said.

Mar nodded and they were off again towards the square. Sayr looked up to where black smoke streamed out of the flaming building and her jaw went slack.

The rebels were everywhere; on the roofs of buildings, climbing through the trees, running through the jagged streets of the village. They all looked to be heading towards the fire, too, and Sayr willed herself to run faster. Shouting reached her ears, and she could no longer tell if it came from civilians or rebels. The shouts and the sound of her ragged breathing consumed her as she ran, her hand gripping her daggers.

The village square was consumed by fire, bodies, blood, and steel. Sayr could hardly tell rebels from citizens or soldiers. Mar and Sayr stayed close as they swung and struck, weaving through the mass of bodies and blades. A rebel swung their sword at Mar and she blocked the hit while Sayr jabbed her dagger into the rebel's thigh. Sayr tugged her dagger out of the rebel's flesh and a scream ripped through her as she fell to the ground.

The girl's dodged, and struck, dodged, and struck. Sayr could see a tall mass with raven-black hair and her heart lurched. Relief surged through her veins when she spotted Dimitri alive and fighting.

An arrow struck the shoulder of a rebel nearing Mar. They looked up to find Addy firing arrows into the square from a building window. Willa poked her head through the open window, her hands twitching to guide her own iron-tipped arrows at her target.

Another rebel reached out to grab Sayr. She tilted her blade and sliced through his palm. She jabbed the hilt of a second dagger into his temple, rendering the rebel unconscious. The king had said to capture rebels and bring them back for questioning. She needed them unconscious, not dead.

Mar and Sayr were an unmoving force together. Mar wasn't as quick with her sword as she was with a spear, but her strikes were still deadly. Sayr twisted the daggers in her hands. Another soldier swung their blade at Sayr, and she deflected it, spinning out of the way just as Mar struck them down.

A single scream pierced through the noise of the battle and Sayr twisted to find its source. Mina was on the ground, clutching her leg. An arrow protruded from her right knee and blood leaked from the wound and onto the ground around her. Rebels were advancing on her, but she only slumped over herself, defenseless.

Sayr did not hesitate before she bolted for the girl. Mar continued to swing her sword while she followed Sayr to where Mina remained crumbled against the cobblestone. Her long black hair was soaked with her own blood that continued to spill over the stones. A rebel advanced on Mina, but an arrow from above struck him in the back and he fell just as Sayr reached her.

"Keep our cover," Sayr ordered Mar and landed hard on the cobblestone.

She barely registered the pain in her knees as she pulled Mina into her arms and assessed the injury. The arrow hadn't pierced completely through her knee, but the wound was bleeding too much for Sayr's comfort. Sayr wiped the strands of hair away from her face. Her usually tan skin was sickly pale, and her eyes were squeezed shut. A slow moan came from Mina, and she slumped against Sayr, no longer able to keep herself up.

"She needs a healer!" Sayr screamed to someone, anyone. She needed a healer now. Sayr couldn't tell if Mina's artery in her knee had been cut, but if a healer didn't tend to the injury soon, Sayr feared Mina might still lose her leg…or her life. She couldn't carry Mina herself, and Mar was too busy fending off any rebels that dared to approach them. They were stuck, rooted to the spot while Mina's blood continued to cover the ground.

Sayr could only think of untying a rope from her belt and looping it above Mina's knee. She pulled it tight into a tourniquet, using her second dagger as a rod to tighten the rope. Mina cried out in pain as Sayr twisted the dagger, tightening the tourniquet against Mina's lower thigh. Tears stung Sayr's eyes, but she blinked them away while she worked.

The sound of boots against stone grew louder and Sayr pivoted her body to shield Mina. Mar pivoted with her sword and Sayr held one dagger up between her and the threat. Tomas came running, his jaw slacked with terror at the sight of Mina slumped against Sayr and all the blood around them. Tomas cut down three rebels before he made it past Mar and to Sayr's side.

"She needs a healer," Sayr repeated. She didn't know what else to do or say. She'd done all she knew how to do to help Mina, and she scooted aside while Tomas effortlessly picked Mina up in his arms. He paused for the briefest second to study the tourniquet around Mina's leg, then at Sayr's belt where one of her daggers was missing, before he sprinted off without a word.

Sayr didn't have time to watch Tomas as he took Mina away. As soon as they were gone, Sayr turned back to the village square. The fighting had continued, but the masses were dwindling. Sayr realized the rebels were running.

"They're retreating," she said to Mar. "We need to bind these rebels and prepare to take them back to the palace."

Mar took care of the remaining rebels that dared lunge for her or Sayr while Sayr bound two more unconscious rebels and sat them together. By the time she finished, the sounds of battle had faded, and the square was almost completely empty of any sign of life beside the King's troops.

She turned to survey the damage. Bodies littered the square, but Sayr couldn't recognize any of them. She thanked each of the elements while she continued her search through the square for the rest of the King's Court. Addy and Willa came bursting through the building they had been firing arrows from and into the square. Lilith stood next to a fallen rebel, counting the blades at her belt. Ryon and Dimitri were wiping their bloodied blades and sheathing their weapons. A breath of relief left Sayr, and she rushed to meet the Court all gathering near Ryon and Dimitri.

"Do we know how many civilian casualties there are?" Ryon was asking Dimitri.

Dimitri shook his head. "It's too early to know for sure. We'll need a few soldiers to stay back and assess the count of civilian and rebel deaths."

"Where are Tomas and Mina?" Willa asked. Worry etched through her voice while she looked at each member of the group, then around the village square for the missing members of the King's Court.

"Mina was badly wounded," Sayr explained. "Tomas took her somewhere. I don't know where he took her."

Sayr's voice shook when she spoke, and she clamped her mouth shut. She looked down at her blood-soaked hands, only to find that her hands, too, were shaking. Her whole body shook as she stood in front of the remainder of the King's Court and Mar.

Dimitri came close to her and put a hand against her back to turn her around. "Let's go."

Dimitri led Sayr towards the edge of the square before he turned her around again to face him.

"Take a deep breath," Dimitri instructed and Sayr obeyed. She took a shaky breath, then another, and another.

"Tell me what happened." Dimitri spoke low and slow.

Sayr took her time while she explained what had happened to Mina and what she had done to try and help before Tomas had reached them and took Mina away.

Dimitri nodded. His eyes narrowed as he scanned her face. He lifted a hand and gently wiped the blood from her mouth. "Are you hurt?"

"I'm fine," she answered, though her voice still shook.

She looked back towards the rest of the Court not far from them. Addy had a burn on her neck and Ryon and Willa had minor wounds, but none of them had been seriously injured like Mina had.

Dimitri gave Sayr another once over and lifted a brow. He breathed in heavily through his nose and out through his mouth. Sayr followed Dimitri's actions until her body was no longer shaking. She nodded, not willing to trust her voice, and the two of them returned to the group. Dimitri explained to the group what had happened to Mina and Tomas and turned to Ryon before anyone could ask Sayr any questions.

"How many rebels were captured?" Dimitri asked.

Ryon nodded to Mar and Sayr. "I saw you two binding at least two rebels."

Mar grinned. "There's another rebel bound back in one of the streets."

"I bound two more," Lilith added. "That's at least five we can take back for questioning."

"I'll speak with the king's soldiers." Ryon began to back away and Willa turned with him. "Some of them can stay behind to deal with the damages and assess body counts. If they find any survivors, they can bring them back to the palace as well. The rest of you get back to the horses and make your way to the palace. His Majesty will want a report as soon as you arrive."

"With that, Ryon walked off and Willa followed close behind. She looked nothing like her usual picture of grace. She wore no billowing dress and blood covered her hands and clothing. She looked like a princess of death. Looking at every member of the King's Court, Sayr realized they all looked terrifying, like death's own Court instead of the king's.

The ride to the palace had been much slower than before. Exhaustion seeped into Sayr's bones as their horses finally climbed the steep mountain up to the palace and she willed her eyes to remain open just a while longer.

The Court entered the palace and immediately made their way up to the king's quarters. Royal Guards and Court members gawked at them as they walked by, exhausted, and still splattered in blood, but no one screamed or ran away from them, almost as if they were in awe of the bloody and brutal Court.

The king was waiting for them in his quarters. A wide smile broke across his face when they entered the quarters together. His eyes roamed to each member of the Court, silently counting for every single one of them, including Mar and Sayr. Addy plopped onto one of the chaises and closed her eyes. The king just smiled wider at her, not seeming to care about the dirt and blood that was no doubt going to stain that chair.

The king's smile dropped when he counted four less members of his Court and Dimitri quickly explained that Ryon and Willa had remained behind temporarily.

"Mina was injured," Dimitri explained to the king. Sayr stiffened and she turned towards the two to listen in on the conversation.

"I found Tomas before we departed. He is uninjured. Mina was severely wounded in her right leg, and she lost a lot of blood." Dimitri's eyes left the king's and found Sayr's, as if he were speaking directly to her. "But she will live. The tourniquet saved her life, and she will not lose her leg."

Sayr let out a shuttered breath. Her throat tightened and she squeezed her eyes shut so the tears would not spill over. Mar grabbed her hand and Sayr squeezed it. When she opened her eyes again, the king now looked at her, too.

"I am so glad to see all of you again." The king's voice was heavy with emotion. "I know how exhausted you all are, and I will let you rest soon, but first I would like your report and for each of you to see a healer before you take some much-deserved rest."

Lilith and Dimitri gave the king their report. The other members of the King's Court spoke up to fill in certain details of what had happened to them in the village or what information they'd brought back to their king when necessary. The king had brought up three healers to assess each person.

"We were able to capture five rebels," Lilith said. "Pending whether or not the soldiers find more to bring back, they will all be taken to the cells and questioned."

"Thank you," King Mylan said to each member of his Court. "Thank you all. Believe me when I say that I know the risks you take in these matters, and I do not take those risks lightly. I am honored to have each of you in my Court."

The remainder of the King's Court began filing out of the quarters to their separate chambers where they would all no doubt pass out for the night and likely most of the next day. Sayr grabbed Mar's arm, and they began leaving the quarters together when the king stopped them.

"I have the two of you to thank most of all," he said and turned his eyes to Sayr. "You asked me to send you to help if there was ever another attack closer to the palace, and I was not sure if you could be completely trusted. You both could have easily betrayed my Court or run, but you stayed and fought. You both helped my kingdom more than you could ever know, and you saved the life of a member of my inner Court. I thank you both immensely for it."

Sayr's eyes shone with unshed tears, and she smiled at the king. Marenda gave the king a low nod. "This is what we're here for," Sayr said. "No matter Her Majesty's intentions, if there are innocent lives are at stake, we will always fight."

Sayr's back muscles screamed in protest as she held a sword in both hands. The training lessons filled with lunges and crunches and pushups were definitely over, replaced once again with combat training. Lilith ordered Sayr to forget the daggers, as she clearly already knew how to wield them, and pick up a sword instead.

"We'll be practicing with a different weapon each week," Lilith had said. "By the time your queen wants you back, you'll be able to fight with an assortment of weapons."

"I'm not going back," Sayr taunted. "Your king wants me here, so I'm staying."

Lilith only smiled fiendishly. "We'll see about that."

The first portion of this week's lessons consisted of Lilith teaching Sayr how to wield a sword correctly. They went through the offensive and defensive stances, raising and lowering a sword, and sheathing it, being able to walk correctly with a sword strapped to one side, before Lilith even considered fighting with them.

Once Sayr had mastered handling a sword correctly, Lilith had ordered her to change into her training uniform. The two stood in the training dome once again, facing off with their swords.

"I will show you a series of moves with the sword, which you will have to dodge," Lilith said and tied her hair back. "I'll go slow at first then speed up, so be prepared."

Sayr nodded and took her defensive stance with the sword lifted in front of her. Lilith moved forward, swinging the sword down from her left shoulder. Sayr lowered her sword slightly and twisted it to the right to block Lilith.

"Angle the sword more," Lilith ordered. "If I were to use my full force, my sword would slide right off yours and cut through your arm. You need to angle the sword fully to block my attack and my sword's momentum."

Sayr gritted her teeth as she angled the sword. The weight of the sword was beginning to make her arms shake. She really missed her daggers.

Lilith turned and brought her sword around with her. She lifted it up from the ground directly towards Sayr's middle.

If Sayr didn't block the hit—and wasn't wearing the suit—the sword would cut her completely in half from the bottom up. She wasn't looking forward to the pain that would cause even with the suit. She quickly swung her own sword down, grunting at the exertion it took her to do so, and swiped Lilith's own sword back down with hers.

"Let's speed things up," Lilith ordered.

She twirled around to hit Sayr's right side with her sword. Sayr lifted the hilt of her sword upwards to block the low hit with her blade. Her blade moved closer to her body from the impact of Lilith's sword, and she had to push harder to keep her own blade from touching her.

"You need to be in control of both swords," Lilith barked. "Just because you block my hit doesn't mean you've stopped the momentum to stop your own sword from hitting you."

Lilith moved faster and faster until Sayr could hardly keep up. She thrusted the sword to the left, hitting Sayr's left side, and she yelped.

The pain sliced through her ribs and her shoulders ignited in pain as she moved the sword to block the remainder of the hit. She swiped Lilith's sword away and returned to her defensive stance.

Lilith got a few more hits at Sayr in the next hour. By the time, the lesson was over, Sayr was panting hard and slick with sweat, but still in one piece. She swiped at the hairs plastered to her forehead and slumped against the wall between the training dome and the armory. Lilith made a show of swinging the sword behind her back and over her shoulder.

"Pathetic," she spat. She walked towards the armory to put up the sword, only to stop dead in her tracks.

Her eyes widened and a shocked smile spread across her face. Sayr looked up towards the armory to see what had caused such a change in Lilith.

Dimitri stood near the entrance of the armory, arms crossed and glowering at Lilith.

"Dimitri," Lilith called in a sing-song voice. "Always a pleasure for you to join us, but I'm afraid the lesson's already over."

"I'm aware." Dimitri's tone was again stone cold. "You haven't taught her anything besides how to block your hits for the past half hour."

Lilith went incredibly still, but her smile remained. "We're working on defense techniques."

Dimitri walked through the armory and into the training dome, not bothering to look at Sayr on the ground as he plucked the discarded sword next to her. Every guard in the armory stood at attention while they watched Dimitri walk into the center of the training dome where Lilith still stood.

"Most learn best through demonstration," Dimitri droned. "You want to teach her defenses; then why don't you show her some defense moves of your own?"

In a flash, Dimitri swung Sayr's sword down on Lilith. Lilith's sword barely shot up quick enough to defend herself. Her boots gripped the floor as the swords collided with one another.

"Dimitri—" Lilith tried to speak, but Dimitri swung again.

Lilith angled the sword completely perpendicular to the ground as Dimitri swung his sword at her side.

His motions were as fluid as water while he gracefully handled the sword. His movements were slowed, as if he didn't intend to hurt Lilith, but there was enough fire in his eyes to let her know he was furious with her.

She lifted her sword up in front of her in a defensive stance, but Dimitri didn't swing. He reached out and leveled his sword at her so that his blade was behind hers, closest to Lilith.

And then he pulled.

Lilith's sword tipped forward with the momentum of Dimitri's pull and she stumbled forward from the change in weight.

Dimitri caught her by the shoulder and pointed his sword directly at her throat. If Dimitri hadn't stopped her fall, and she hadn't been wearing the suit, the tip of his sword would have pierced clean through her neck.

"You train her properly," he whispered the threat, "or I will humiliate you after each and every lesson. And then I'll train her myself."

He lowered the sword, releasing Lilith, and she stumbled forward. She was panting hard when she looked back up at him. Dimitri walked over to Sayr and dropped her sword next to her. He did not say a word to her as he walked back out the door of the armory.

20

$\mathcal{S}$ayr laid sprawled across the loveseat in her chambers with her feet propped against the sofa back. *The Elemental's History of Magic* was held open above her and over her eyes as she laid on her back on the couch. Dema sat on one of the chairs nearest the fireplace, admiring the new vase of roses she'd brought into Sayr's room.

"I mean, he just popped right in, bested Lilith with *my* sword, and now he ignores me?" Sayr dropped the book onto the couch with a soft *thud*.

She looked over at Dema, seated across from her. "He's canceled our lessons twice now," she said. "And the other two mornings that he held our lessons, he barely spoke to me at all. He didn't even bother looking at me, ordering me to read silently from this ridiculous book."

She flicked her hand over *The Elemental's History of Magic*.

Mar sat in a chair next to Sayr. She'd kept her eyes on Dema most of the night, watching the young girl arrange the flowers into a vase. Mar hadn't liked the idea of letting the girl stay and sit with them after she finished her duties, but Dema was quickly growing on Sayr and Sayr enjoyed the girl's company.

"He is a member of the King's Court," Dema thought aloud. "It's possible he's been busy tending to the king's orders."

"But why the change in demeanor?" Sayr asked. "We were actually starting to get along before all of this. Why does the whole interaction with Lilith change things?"

Dema smiled softly as she eyed Sayr. "If I didn't know any better, I'd say that you miss him."

She dodged the pillow that Sayr chucked at her and laughed.

"I do *not* miss him," Sayr retorted. She pulled herself upright onto the cushions of the sofa. "But he's supposed to be teaching me about the history of Creobe, and our lessons just started to get interesting."

Sayr huffed, hoping Dema and Mar believed her. This was getting far too complicated, she wasn't supposed to be forming any sort of bond with anyone in the Western Palace, let alone in the King's Court. She shouldn't care that Dimitri was ignoring her. It didn't matter to her; it couldn't matter to her.

You cannot like these people, Sayr reminded herself. *Not if you're going to destroy them.*

Sayr had a duty to fulfill. She was Visarian and she would protect the Visarian Crown no matter what, especially if that meant she would gain a position as a known Seer in the Eastern Court in return. Her duty lied far beyond her personal feelings.

She picked up the book again and opened to the page she had been reading when Dema spoke.

"Give him time," she said. "This could be new to him as well. Dimitri is not the type to open up to any sort of… friendships."

Sayr snorted. "I don't think we're even friends. We shouldn't be friends."

She angled her head towards Dema again. "It's frightening how you all speak about one another like you're all friends, but I never see any of you around one another."

"What do you mean?" Dema asked.

"I mean you and the servants and the members of the King's Court," Sayr clarified. "I hear you all mention each other like you know each other well, but your positions are completely different in the palace, and I barely see any of you actually speaking to one another."

"We see each other around," Dema explained. "We work under King Mylan, there's nothing more to it. Just because some of us work closer with His Majesty than others does not make them better than the rest of us. We are all serving our king in different ways, and we have a mutual understanding that our separate roles are just as important as the others."

Sayr frowned. She and Mar both exchanged a look. That sounded nothing like how the Eastern Palace was run. Those closest to the queen were treated the best, except for her. Everyone believed she was just an apprentice to a Councilman, there was no sort of special treatment in a role like that.

Dema hummed a rhythmic tune while she opened the rose petals. *To help them bloom better,* she'd told Sayr.

Marenda shivered. She turned around towards the fire. One hand ignited in flame, and she threw the flame into the fire. The logs of the fireplace quickly blazed bright, and Mar snuggled deeper into the cushions.

Sayr continued reading *The Elemental's History of Magic,* losing herself in the pages and the warmth of the fire and Dema's humming.

The Dividing War had taken the lives of four leaders of the six elements, and the connection between the elements had been severed. The remaining leaders, a Water and an Air Elemental, were the only two to survive, and rather than aiding the other Elementals, their focus remained on strengthening their own colonies and gaining as much territory within the continent in order to rebuild their kingdoms. The colonies of the Earth, Fire, Space, and Spirit Elementals were abandoned by their people and overtaken by the remaining colony leaders—

"Wait." Sayr sat up on the couch. She reread the paragraph once more. Then a third time.

"What is it?" Dema asked but Sayr was already flipping through the book, eyes rapidly scanning through each page before flipping to the next one.

Mar leaned over her armchair towards Sayr. "Sayr, what's wrong?"

Sayr stopped flipping through the book and blinked at one page. She stared at the page before her, turning it over so that Dema and Mar could see.

"Do you know what this is?" she asked frantically.

A diagram laid across the two pages of the book. Six symbols formed an elaborate circle, three on each page, and each a distinct color, all surrounded by swirling designs that connected them one by one. The six symbols looked to form a circular rainbow: red, green, blue, white, pink, and purple.

Mar stood and crouched onto Sayr's couch to better examine the diagram. Dema leaned forward, too, but shook her head.

"I have no idea," Dema whispered. "I've never seen a diagram like this."

The girls all stared at the pages before them. "The leaders of the six elements," Sayr whispered aloud and looked to Mar. "There are six elements, not four or even five like the king was hinting at. There are *six elements.*"

Mar just stared at the diagram, her eyes wide and unmoving. A shiver crawled down Sayr's spine and she met Dema's eyes. "We may not know what this is," she said. "But I believe I know who would."

Dimitri walked through the halls of the Western Palace. The morning sunlight was just beginning to shine through the open balconies and glassless windows of the palace. Servants rushed through the halls to serve breakfast and assist guests of the Court to prepare for the day.

He took a sip of his coffee, nodding to a pair of lady's maids as they passed. The knot in his stomach tightened as he approached the library. He'd arrived an hour early to prepare himself for this morning's lesson. He couldn't stall facing her head on any longer. With a steeling breath, he pushed the stirring emotions deep down, opened the library door and stepped inside.

"Good morning, Lenora." He greeted one of the scholars with a raise of his coffee cup.

She greeted him with a smile before glancing over at his usual table. He followed her stare and immediately froze, almost tripping over himself and spilling his morning coffee.

Sayr sat at their table, seated in his chair in the corner. Her feet were propped up on the table and she stared smugly at him when he entered the library.

He cleared his throat and shot a look at Lenora, whose shoulders jumped up and down in a quiet laugh, before trudging the rest of the way to the table.

"You're early," he said as soon as she was within ear shot. "Our lesson doesn't start for another hour, and I have other things to do before dealing with you."

Sayr ignored him. She opened *The Elemental's History of Magic* and pushed it across the table at him.

"What do you know about the six elements?" she asked.

He looked down at the open book. A diagram of the six elements connected into a circular pattern faced up at him. He glanced from the book up at Sayr. She looked tired, as if she'd been up all night either reading more of the book or pondering over this diagram.

"Finally, you're figuring it all out." An approving grin etched across his face, and he asked her, "What would you like to know?"

Dimitri sat next to Sayr at the table while they stared at the diagram.

"The six elements are made up of the three seen elements, and the three unseen elements," Dimitri explained.

"But why are they called the seen and the unseen elements?" Sayr asked. "What separates them?"

"They are called the unseen elements because you can't see them being manipulated," Dimitri started. "Air, spirit, and space make up the unseen elements; you cannot see any of these Elementals physically manipulating their element. The seen elements are earth, fire, and water because you can see these Elementals manipulating their element."

"You saw an Air Elemental in action during your first day of training when Addy sparred against your friend. Are you aware that Lilith and His Majesty are Spirit Elementals?"

"What is a Spirit Elemental?" Sayr asked.

"A Spirit Elemental is one of the unseen elements," Dimitri explained. "Along with air and space. Have you ever heard of a Space Elemental?"

Sayr narrowed her eyes at him. "A Space Elemental? No."

"I figured as much," Dimitri nodded and leaned closer, pulling the diagram towards him. "Each of these symbols represents one of the six elements. Each element is represented by a color and an emblem."

Sayr's finger lightly touched the first, deep red symbol with jagged lines and curves throughout its emblem.

"The element of fire." Dimitri nodded. "Fire Elementals can manipulate and create fire through the energy in their bodies and, while they cannot be harmed by fire that they create themselves, another Fire Elemental's fire can burn them."

Sayr trailed a finger clockwise to the next forest green symbol. Dimitri explained each element while she followed the circular diagram.

"The element of earth. Some Earth Elementals can manipulate the deep earth around them while others can only manipulate simple greenery and wildflowers."

The next symbol was royal blue.

"The element of water. Also, the element of the Visarian royal family, as you already know. Water Elementals can manipulate water near them, from small pools to ocean waves. They can also create water to a certain capacity."

Sayr slowly touched a finger against the next element with a spiraling white symbol.

"The element of air. Air Elementals can manipulate the air around them, from a simple breeze to the air that we breathe."

Sayr trailed a finger over the light pink symbol.

"The element of spirit. Spirit Elementals can sense and influence another being's emotions and feelings. While they cannot completely control a person's emotions, they can sway a person to feel or even act a certain way."

Sayr immediately thought back to her first encounter with Lilith. Lilith had told her that she was anxious and angry. And she had been at the time. She had also told Sayr to beg for forgiveness. Was this the influence they all talked about that Sayr had been able to fend off? Did her incoming vision have something to do with Lilith not being able to manipulate Sayr?

Sayr moved to the final, deep purple symbol.

"The element of space. Space Elementals can read the stars and envision events of the past, just as they played out in history. They are also the rarest Elementals on the continent."

Sayr's attention remained on the purple symbol. "You mean Space Elementals have visions of the past?"

"In other words, yes," Dimitri answered. "They read the stars, and the stars show them pieces of the past that they wish for the Space Elemental to see."

Sayr's head buzzed with excitement. Space Elementals had visions. She had visions. Sure, hers were visions of the future and Space Elementals envisioned the past, but it was a start to finding out just who or what she was.

"Do you know of any Space Elementals here in the palace?" she asked.

Dimitri shook his head. "Like I said, Space Elementals are the rarest of all the Elementals…but I do know one."

Sayr perked up and leaned closer to Dimitri, her anticipation growing. She remained silent, not daring to say anything that would steer Dimitri off this path.

Dimitri's eyes narrowed at her eagerness, but he continued. "She lives in Therod, the city a few miles from the palace."

"Can we go there?" Sayr blurted.

Dimitri couldn't hide the smallest chuckle that escaped his lips. He stood from the table and held his hand out to Sayr.

"Come with me, little imposter."

Sayr's mare followed close behind Dimitri on a horse of his own down the steep trail through the mountain and towards Therod. She had little practice riding horses and, though Dimitri kept a tempered pace, the steep cut off the mountain trail and hundred-foot drop below made her stomach drop every time she glanced to her right. She took a deep breath and steadied herself in her saddle before looking ahead at Dimitri.

"How far is Therod from the palace?" she asked, trying to focus on anything but the steep drop below.

"Ten miles, about a two hour's ride at this pace."

Sayr looked around at the forest surrounding them. Autumn had begun to set in during her time in the Western

Palace. The never-ending greenery of the mountains had turned slight shades of red, orange, and yellow. Her cheeks were already rosy from the chilly morning air.

Dimitri had given her time to change into something warmer before their departure. Dema was already in Sayr's chambers when she arrived with a stack of warm clothing. She wore a thick wool sweater, and her pants were lined with soft animal fur. Dema had also given her wool socks to keep her feet warm in her worn boots and a thick, hooded fur cloak similar to Dimitri's.

She looked like any other Creobian citizen.

Sayr wrote a brief note for Mar, telling her where she would be the rest of the day, and gave it to Dema. Mar would be furious at Sayr for leaving the palace without her, but Sayr couldn't miss the opportunity Dimitri was offering her by waiting for Mar to leave the medic's level or training grounds to come with her.

"You're certain Lilith won't gut me for missing training today?" she called ahead to Dimitri.

Dimitri chuckled. "I'm sure she's more than happy to have your lesson canceled."

Sayr huffed a laugh at that. Lilith was probably upset that she couldn't use Sayr as her personal cutting rack today.

Dimitri had sent a message letting her know that he was taking Sayr on a personal trip today, stating he was taking her to experience more of the Royal Sector. From the way Lilith crooned every time she was in the same room as Dimitri, Sayr doubted she argued much.

"How long have you worked in the palace?" Sayr asked. A two-hour ride gave Sayr plenty of time to get some information out of Dimitri. Or at the very least they could try to get to know one another now that he was speaking to her again.

"Almost five years," he answered. "I left my village and started a life here where I was needed."

"How did you come to be in the King's Court?"

Dimitri's lips quirked up as he looked back at her. "I told you; I don't consider myself to be a member of the King's Court. But before I came to the palace, I was an initiate in training as a guard for my village. Every sector of Creobe has a program for young boys and girls to train to become guards of the cities and towns within that sector. It's nothing like being a Royal Guard here in the palace, but it is still an honor to serve the Crown in any way. I was twelve years old when I began the program, one of the youngest initiates to enter. I lived at what we called The Cell for the first two years until I was assigned as a guard in Dristol, the main city of the Western Sector."

"I wasn't a very good guard, though," Dimitri admitted. "I didn't like to listen to my upper ranks. Being a guard meant doing the honorable thing in challenging situations, even if it wasn't what I thought was right. I never understood that mindset and I couldn't handle it. I got myself into trouble quite often for doing the opposite of what my upper ranks expected of me."

"My first year as a guard, there was a break in at one of the warehouses in the city. By the time we reached the building, the group inside had started taking hostages. We were ordered to block all exits of the building and wait for them to surrender, knowing we were outside and there was no chance of escape, until we started hearing the screams from inside. I found out later that they had been killing off hostages while we just waited outside for them to surrender. Once the screams began, I abandoned my post and snuck into the warehouse."

Sayr inched her mare further up the path so that she was almost riding next to Dimitri. He looked lost in thought as he relayed the memory. His eyes stared off into the distance, but Sayr knew he wasn't seeing the path ahead of them, he was seeing the warehouse all over again.

"By the time I'd broken in, half of the hostages were dead. Our plan wasn't going to work, they didn't care about killing innocent people and they weren't going to surrender. I stayed hidden in the shadows while I got closer. Luckily, they'd spread out throughout the warehouse so I could take one or two down at a time without alerting the others. I'd killed all eight of them by the time anyone had realized I'd left my post. My lieutenant was furious when I'd walked out of the warehouse with the remaining hostages."

Dimitri looked over at Sayr and shrugged. "The lieutenant wanted me out of the guard after that, said I couldn't be trusted to take orders or defend my brothers and sisters in the guard when I went wandering off alone like that. He was right. I was discharged from the guard and sent home after that."

"I don't know who saw what had happened or how they got word to the king, but a month later I received a letter at my home from the king himself asking me to join

303

him at the palace. I thought it was just for a visit, or even to reprimand me for my actions, but he'd offered me a position that would require me to live in the palace on that visit. At the time, I had nothing else to lose so I left my old life in Dristol and began my life here."

"But you're not in the Royal Guard," Sayr noted. "I've never seen you in any of the rotations or on duty and you leave the palace whenever you wish."

"All Royal Guards can leave the palace when they are off duty," Dimitri stated. "As long as they return in time for their rotations, they can live their lives as they wish."

Sayr didn't know what to say. She thought of Marenda, who could only leave the palace when Her Majesty needed to leave the palace grounds.

"But you're right, I'm not in the Royal Guard," Dimitri said.

The two continued down the mountain path silently for a few moments. Sayr took in the trees surrounding them, jutting high above and piercing the bright blue sky.

She didn't want to bring the conversation back to their first encounter, back to when Dimitri had asked about her position in Court, back to when he had asked for any information about her, and she had lied to him.

She didn't want to relive that memory that had stained their impressions of each other from the start, but she needed to know more about him.

She wanted to know more about him.

"Then what is your position?" Sayr asked.

"I don't consider myself to have any real position in the King's Court," Dimitri retorted.

"Why not?" Sayr pushed. "You seem to meet with the King's Court and take on the king's tasks just as much as any other member. What makes you different from the rest?"

Dimitri sighed. "There are many other members of the King's Court whose roles are more important than mine. My role is to fill in whenever the king actually needs me in his Court, otherwise I'm usually put on duties overseeing the Royal Guard or out on business in the Royal Sector."

Sayr nodded. "Who do you consider to be closest to the king, then?"

If Sayr could find who was closest to the king, she would likely be closer to finding who the king's mercenary was.

Dimitri's brow creased as he thought. "Maybe Ryon? He doesn't leave the palace much to be in service of His Majesty. Or Addy? They each have specific duties in the King's Court, but His Majesty often uses them both for separate duties, as well."

Sayr's nerves ignited at the mention of Addy's name. If Addy was the king's mercenary and she was spending quite a bit of time with Marenda in the medic's level... would Mar be safe with her? Mar was a strong fighter and could defend herself, but could she protect herself against the king's mercenary?

Dimitri turned around to face her before she had the chance to ask any more questions. "When was the last time you'd left the Eastern Palace on your own?"

"Never," Sayr answered. "I've been to the City Center many times, but I'd always gone with Ev, and we'd always had guards with us."

"The crown prince?" Dimitri asked. "You two were very close."

"We were," Sayr admitted, though she knew he hadn't meant it as a question. "Ev and Mar were the only people I trusted in the Eastern Palace; they were like my family."

"Do you still see him as your family?" Dimitri asked.

Sayr remembered the role she was supposed to be playing, silently cursing herself for crossing a line talking about the Eastern Prince.

"How can I?" she asked. "I'll never see him again and even if I could, his mother gave me up to King Mylan. I guess I never realized how much Ev was like his mother, and no matter how close we were he would never disobey her. He would never put me over his queen."

Sayr's voice hitched at the end, her throat tightening with sadness. The lies and the truths were all blurring together. Everything she was saying was meant to be a façade, but the words felt too true to ignore.

Dimitri nodded when she finished. "From what I've seen in the Eastern Court, the crown prince will rule just as his mother does now. He will continue to keep his people trapped and have them believe that Creobe is full of dangerous people to keep us away."

Sayr wanted to speak up for Everett, but she kept her mouth shut. She believed Everett would be a good ruler, but she knew the truth that he always tried so hard to follow in his mother's footsteps, as a child and even now.

"Why does Her Majesty keep the unseen elements a secret from her people?" she asked.

Dimitri glanced sideways at her. "If I tell you the truth, will you believe me?"

Sayr opened her mouth to answer, then closed it. Would she? Could she believe him? So much had been revealed to her in a month and a half, about both Courts. She still wasn't sure how much of it was the truth, and how much was a lie to keep her where either royal wanted her.

"I don't know," Sayr answered honestly. "There's so much that I didn't know before coming here, but you have to understand you're battling against eight years of living in the Eastern Palace, speaking with the queen and hearing her lies for that long. It's hard to erase all of that in less than two months. But so much of what you and the king have said makes enough sense that I can't continue to ignore it. I don't have much time before Her Majesty will try to take me back, I need as much of the truth as possible before then."

Dimitri nodded in understanding. "Your queen has kept the unseen elements a secret because the unseen elements are strong. Her Majesty wants her people to believe that the royal family is the strongest Elemental family in Visaran, and therefore deserves to remain on the throne."

"When unseen Elementals began to rise up throughout Visaran, she became afraid that her people would want Air, Space, or Spirit Elementals on the throne, like in Creobe, so she had all unseen Elementals and their families exiled from Visaran. She wouldn't risk losing her throne to any family. Her people fled to Creobe through the Silia River, but since no one knew what was happening, there were no Water or Earth Elementals on either side of the river to construct a bridge for them to flee. Many drowned in the river. She had guards scavenge through every village and city for unseen Elementals, any still remaining after exile were taken to the palace and executed privately."

Sayr gasped, letting go of the reigns to cover her mouth in disbelief. "How could we not know of this? How was all of this kept secret?"

"This was over two decades ago," Dimitri said. "The Eastern King made sure the exile happened under a low profile. Most families fled because of the rumors, before any action had taken place. The royal family made certain that any executions happened behind closed doors within the palace so there wouldn't be any means for a riot. Most Visarians do not know why their neighbors and friends disappeared in the night and those that were aware… well, you'd be surprised how quickly humans forget the past."

Sayr almost couldn't believe what she was hearing, but a piece of her could believe it. She hated the fact that she could believe it so easily. After years of watching Her Majesty and being by her side for so long, she knew Queen

Cheralin would take any action she deemed necessary to protect her family and her throne.

"What happened to those that were able to cross the river?" she asked.

"Very few succeeded in crossing the river," Dimitri answered. "But those who did fled into Creobe. The queen before King Mylan still ruled and accepted any fleeing Visarians into the country to live the remainder of their lives peacefully in Creobe. She knew that there was nothing she could do against the Visarian royal family without starting a war, so she remained silent while the executions continued. The only way she could help was by offering aid to those who made it into her country."

A memory flashed in Sayr's mind; the woman in the village when she had first entered Creobe, singing a lullaby to her children. Sayr had mistaken her for a Visarian, she'd still had the accent. She must have been one of the Visarians who'd successfully fled to Creobe, and now had a life as a Creobian. It made so much sense now, why she'd feared Sayr so much when she'd approached the family.

"That's why you hate Visarians so much," Sayr realized.

"I don't hate all Visarians," Dimitri corrected. "But I will admit I hate the Eastern Court. They sat by and did nothing while their royal family murdered their own people."

"Then why would she keep me in the palace?" Sayr asked. "If she was afraid of those with unseen gifts, and the king believes I could be an unseen Elemental, why wouldn't she kill me right away?"

"I believe that is exactly why she kept you so close," Dimitri said. "She knows that some of the exiled families had escaped into Creobe, which strengthens our country even more. I think she finally realized the mistake she had made and that she needed unseen Elementals in her Court to keep up with the Western Kingdom and the rest of the world."

Sayr's mind raced with everything Dimitri had said, and deep down she knew it had to be true.

The Eastern Kingdom was falling apart.

Was that why Cheralin was so eager to start a war with Creobe? Did she need to strike at them before they struck at her first?

"My turn to ask a question," Dimitri said, snapping her out of her thoughts. "Are you truly content to live in the Western Palace?"

"That is quite a loaded question," Sayr said.

"It is, but it's also something you need to think about. You've been in Creobe for nearly two months now, it must have crossed your mind at some point. I know you don't have much say in the matter, but if you were given the chance to return to Visaran, would you?"

Sayr took her time coming up with an answer. After everything she'd learned during her time here, would she be able to return to Visaran as the Queen's Seer? She couldn't stomach the idea of returning to a life of ignorance, letting innocent people continue to be killed just so the queen could feel safe on her throne.

And what would become of Everett? Would he truly be a different ruler?

"I don't know," she answered. "I'd never left the Eastern Palace until now and I never had the freedom to imagine a life outside of the palace. I know you say I have no choice here, but I had no choice in Visaran, either."

She met Dimitri's stare. "Why do you ask?"

Dimitri shrugged and looked away, focusing again on the path ahead. They had completely descended the mountain, Sayr realized, and were now on even ground.

"You've mentioned your life in Visaran before; growing up there, your routines, your friends… but you've never once called the Eastern Palace your home."

Sayr pulled on the reins and the mare stopped. Dimitri quickly pulled his reins to stop next to her. The light in Sayr's eyes was gone when she spoke.

"The Eastern Palace is not my home." Her voice was thin and angry. "I was abandoned there when I was a child with nowhere else to go. I have had nowhere else to go for the last eight years. I lived in that palace, but it has *never* been my home."

With a light kick in the side, her mare continued down the path. She kept her gaze on the path ahead the rest of the way to Therod.

21

The tops of buildings poked above the tree line as Sayr and Dimitri approached the outskirts of the city. The jumbled sound of voices grew louder the closer they came to the buildings.

"I almost forgot," Dimitri said. He pulled his stallion up next to Sayr and reached over to his belt.

"The only way I'm letting you into this city and out of the palace is if I know you're protected." Dimitri pulled out a dagger from his belt and offered it to Sayr. "Even if I'm not around."

The dagger looked to be made of steel and was thin and sharp, glinting in the sunlight. The steel handle twisted all the way down to the tip and was studded with purple amethyst. Purple leather was wrapped around the hilt for a firm grip.

"It's beautiful." Sayr carefully picked up the dagger, admiring the clean steel and glittering amethysts.

Electricity surged through her veins as she held the dagger. This wasn't a weapon she had seen in the armory, and she had inspected all the daggers there. "Where did you get this?"

"I got it on one of my missions a couple weeks back," Dimitri admitted. "It's yours, as long as it's not used on me."

Sayr smiled, a bit wickedly, and spun the dagger easily between her fingers. The dagger was light in her hand, like an extension of her wrist.

"Thank you," she said as she carefully placed the dagger into her belt. "I will keep it with me, always."

Dimitri nodded in return. "Let's get going. Your time in Therod is dwindling."

The streets of Therod were packed with people by the time Sayr and Dimitri made it into the city. They'd left their horses with a stable hand and continued through the streets on foot.

Sayr's eyes bounced back and forth as she craned her neck to look inside every shop they passed. There seemed to be a shop for everything a person could ever need or want. They passed markets where local farmers were selling fresh produce underneath canopied carts and boutiques where ladies were waiting patiently to put in orders for custom dresses. Tavern owners were beginning to open their doors for early customers, a chocolatier was handing small pieces of chocolate to children outside, and restaurants were overflowing with guests enjoying an early lunch.

Her mouth watered as she inhaled deeply, breathing in the sweet and savory scents that floated out of each restaurant. Everyone looked to be shopping through the streets of the city. The only shop that didn't look open to the public was a small jeweler's shop snugged between a busy boutique and a tavern. Her senses were overloaded with all of the different sights, laughter and voices, and the amazing smells.

"Where are we heading?" Sayr asked, disappointment thick in her voice as they passed by the restaurants and vendors.

"To the square," Dimitri answered.

"What's in the square?" Sayr asked but quickly shut her mouth as they approached.

The multiple streets of the city all led to the square. The shops all ended to make a circular clearing in the center where the square opened up.

Sayr shifted her body to look around. The area was made up of mostly grass and one large, circular road that connected all the streets of the city to the square. In the center of the square was a massive fountain that sputtered water into a large basin. Children chased each other around the fountain while parents rested on the lip of the basin.

Entertainers of all sorts were gathered in the clearing, mesmerizing children and bystanders with card tricks, instruments, and elaborate dances. Music and laughter filled the square and Sayr couldn't help but laugh, herself, as she watched a child try to follow the intricate dance of one entertainer and trip over himself, tumbling into the grass.

Dimitri led them closer to the fountain, stopping near the basin to watch another entertainer sitting on the ground next to the fountain.

An impressive group of children surrounded her. The children watched her with wide eyes as she crawled slowly on all fours to the middle of the circle of children. She turned her head, her long black hair cascading over her shoulders, and Sayr could see that she was speaking, but couldn't make out what she was saying from a distance.

The entertainer slowly surveyed each child as she spoke, turning in circular motions. In a flash, she pounced in front of one child, consuming her within the folds of her thick cape.

The other children all screamed and ran. The entertainer threw her head back and laughed, uncovering the small child from the folds of her cape. A wide smile was plastered on the child's face, and she laughed, too, while the other children all crept back into the circle, giggling themselves.

"What is she doing?" Sayr asked Dimitri.

"She is telling a story," Dimitri answered. "The children come to her to hear her stories of faraway lands and the creatures that dwell in the forest at night."

The entertainer turned again and looked up, catching Dimitri's stare. She smiled and stood. She spoke again to the children, and they went running back to their parents, smiling and playfully pushing one another as they went. The girl watched closely as Sayr and Dimitri approached her.

"Hello, Tri," she greeted Dimitri. "I am surprised to see you again so soon."

She embraced Dimitri, kissing both of his cheeks. Sayr eyed the two of them closely as they greeted each other.

"I've returned for personal reasons this time," he said and turned towards Sayr. "Sayr, this is Hoshi. She's a good friend of mine."

Hoshi turned towards Sayr and immediately took Sayr's breath away. She had been pretty from far away, but up close she was devastatingly beautiful. Her skin was an ivory cream, and her long, dark hair swayed in the breeze, catching on the beads embroidered along her cape.

She wore an intricately beaded emerald top, the straps hanging to rest on her biceps. Her floor-length skirt matched the top perfectly, though it lacked the beaded designs, and had a long slit that revealed her leg all the way up to her upper thigh. A long black cape sheltered her from the autumn weather.

She stood taller than Sayr, almost Dimitri's height, with long and slender limbs. Her face was flawless with a narrow chin, pouty lips, and straight black eyebrows.

Her most striking feature was her eyes. One a deep brown, the other a pale blue, narrowing as she also inspected Sayr.

"You are the first girl that Tri has brought to me in a long time." The corners of her pouty lips turned upwards in a sly smile.

"I've brought her here because she has some questions for you," Dimitri crossed his arms over his chest, but Sayr could have sworn his face turned the slightest shade of red, "about being a Space Elemental."

"I see." Hoshi's eyes again turned to Sayr. "What would you like to know?"

"Anything you can tell me," Sayr answered. "Dimitri's taught me the basics of the elements, but I'm curious to hear how your gifts work as a Space Elemental."

Hoshi nodded and turned away from them. She motioned for Sayr to follow her. Sayr moved to follow when Dimitri gently grabbed her arm to pull her back.

"I have business elsewhere, so I won't be coming with you. Go ahead, I shouldn't be long but if you finish your business before mine…" His eyes flicked to Hoshi. "Could you bring her to the Department of Records for me?"

Hoshi dipped her chin in a single nod and continued walking.

Dimitri took one final look at Sayr before letting her go and turning away, too. Sayr watched him for a moment before jogging to catch up with Hoshi.

Hoshi swiped the curtain of the large tent aside and entered, Sayr following close behind. The tent was quite cozy with colorful rugs and pillows decorating the floor. A few tall candelabras were lit around the tent to give the faintest source of light in the room. Feathers and stones were tied with string and thread along the walls of the tent, and a single, short table sat in the center of the room.

She led Sayr to the table. It was low enough to the ground that chairs were not necessary, only a few small cushions padded the ground around the table. Hoshi gestured to Sayr to sit, and she did.

"Is this where you live?" Sayr asked.

"No," Hoshi said as she walked to the opposite side of the table. "This is where I do my business, though my home does reside in Therod."

The Space Elemental removed the cape from her shoulders and let it fall to the floor by the table, revealing her back and shoulders and the heavy tattoos that covered her.

A black arc swooped across her shoulder blades, dipping lowest right at her spine like a half sun. Beneath the black arc, a series of symbols were arranged around the arc like spokes blooming from it. The spokes of symbols ran from one side of the arc to the next, reaching all the way to Hoshi's lower back. More symbols ran from her shoulders down the back of each arm, ending at her elbows where a crisscrossed design of lines and dots completed the tattoo.

Sayr hadn't realized she had been staring until Hoshi spoke up. "Most people are quite surprised when they see them for the first time."

"What are the symbols?" Sayr couldn't help but ask.

"An old, forgotten language," Hoshi answered. "These symbols tell the names of every constellation in the sky."

Sayr's eyes traced over the symbols. They all just looked like jumbled markings to her. How many people saw these tattoos as Hoshi passed by and thought they were simply arcs and swoops, not knowing they told stories in another language entirely?

"If it's a forgotten language, how do you know what the symbols say?"

Hoshi smirked. "I asked the stars themselves. This is the oldest language known in history, the stars are the only ones that still speak it. I asked the stars to tell me the name of the constellations in their language. This is what they gave me."

Hoshi finished by rolling her arms and shoulders to fully display the many symbols decorating her back and arms.

"They gave you the tattoos?" Sayr asked incredulously.

"No," Hoshi laughed. "When I had come back from asking the stars, back into my body, these were written on paper in front of me. This design had been perfectly constructed by the stars, and then I had them tattooed on me afterwards."

"What do you mean, when you came back into your body?" Sayr's body was tingling with a mix of fear and anticipation.

"You will soon see for yourself," Hoshi said as she sat across the table from Sayr.

"Now before we begin, have you ever seen a Space Elemental use their gifts before?" Hoshi asked as she took a match to one candelabra and began to light the candles sitting on the table.

"No," Sayr answered.

Hoshi clicked her tongue thoughtfully. "It is much different than the other elements. We belong to the unseen elements because, like spirit and air, our gifts cannot be seen when we are using them. Only I will be able to see what the stars want us to see, but you will see changes as well when I begin."

"How exactly do you get a message from the stars?" Sayr couldn't help but feel ridiculous asking such a question.

"I simply clear my mind and breathing and wait for the star's entity to enter my own mind, I give them limited control. Our bodies are vessels and Space and Spirit Elementals have been gifted with limited powers of the body. Spirit Elementals are gifted in influencing control over other's emotions, as well as their own. Space Elementals have been gifted with the power to let other entities control the vessel that is our body if we will it. When I am telling my stories, it is my voice that you will hear, but it will not be me that you are speaking to."

"Do you remember the interactions afterwards?" Sayr asked.

"Yes. I give the entity control willingly. They can see through my eyes, speak with my tongue, and hear through my ears, but I am still there. They cannot move me from the spot where I give control, which is why I prefer to be seated when I open myself to them."

"And it doesn't need to be night for you to read the stars?"

Hoshi looked at Sayr almost ridiculously. "The stars are always out; we just see them better in the dark when they burn the brightest."

Hoshi finished lighting the candles on the table. "Tell me something from the past that you wish to see. I will take that question with me when I open myself to the entities."

"How far in the past can I go?" Sayr asked.

"That depends, you ask the questions, and I will search the stars for an answer. Usually, the stars show a piece of the past that has to do with the questions I bring them, then you decipher the answer for yourself. Sometimes the stars show me a moment in time from centuries ago and other times it is an entire story from just yesterday. Now, what is your question?"

Sayr thought hard for several minutes. Hoshi waited patiently as she racked her mind for something important that Hoshi could find the answer for.

There was only one piece of history that could resolve the conflict within her, one piece of history that decided whether she would be destroying an entire kingdom or helping to save it.

"What can you tell me about the exile of the unseen elements from Visaran?"

Hoshi raised an eyebrow at her. "Why would you want to know about such a tragic event?"

Sayr thought back to what Dimitri had told her on their way to Therod. "I've recently just learned about the exile of unseen Elementals, but I still don't know much about what really happened or if what I've been told is completely true. I'm hoping you'll be able to tell me more."

Hoshi must have approved of her reasoning because she nodded hesitantly, shifted into a more comfortable position on the cushions, and closed her eyes.

Sayr could've sworn the light within the tent dimmed, the candlelight burning low, as Hoshi began to hum softly to herself. A breeze swept through the curtains of the tent, sweeping Sayr's hair forward. She stared at Hoshi as the girl continued humming, her eyes still closed.

When she did reopen them, her brown and blue irises had vanished. The entirety of her eyes was an iridescent white like shimmering opals. When she spoke, the same voice that had greeted her and Dimitri spoke, but the voice held something ancient, something wise that was not there before.

"The unseen elements; air, spirit, and space, thrived among the entirety of the continent for centuries. Citizens gifted with these elements dwelled all throughout Creobe and Visaran, until Luzan Lemay rose to the Visarian throne. For years, King Luzan was known as a kind and just ruler, but he had all too quickly been blinded by love. For Lady Cheralin Ivanov had captured the young king's heart, and within the king's first year of reign, the two were married."

"This upset many Visarians, for the new queen's family was known for holding prejudice against unseen Elementals and non-Elementals alike. The new queen's family held all Water Elementals to a higher prestige and tolerated Fire and Earth Elementals. The rest of the elements practically did not exist to the new queen. Many did not want their king marrying this prejudiced woman, for she would then have equal rule over all people of Visaran. Many rioted before her coronation and the Crown's favor began to dwindle."

"Soon after the marriage, power began to shift underneath the royal's feet. The new queen could feel the shift between the seen and unseen elements as the unseen Elementals' anger over their rulers grew increasingly."

"The ultimate action for the people of Visaran was Queen Cheralin's removal of all unseen Elementals within the Eastern Court. She tried to go as far as giving the unseen elements only the most mundane and laborious means of employment, hoping to keep them low in rank to ensure they had no resources or means to prosper. Many Visarians had neighbors and friends who were gifted in the unseen elements and grew angry as well for their suffering friends and family. The unseen elements began gaining support. The royal family's power was quickly slipping between their fingers, but Her Majesty was quicker. She devised her plan to rid the country of her problem, town by town and city by city. She whispered her plan into her husband's ear and within months, the exile had begun."

"Friends and neighbors began to disappear overnight. The royal family's plan took years to complete as they made certain that each town was eradicated from unseen Elementals before moving on to the next. Once the people of Visaran began to notice and flee, it was too late. Her Majesty's control had taken over most of the country.

Many citizens close to the Silia River tried to flee; others close to the ocean managed passage to other countries by boat. But many failed, thousands of Visarians died during the years of exile."

"After twenty years, the idea of the unseen elements had been erased from Visaran. Any who remained had hidden their gifts and lived their lives as non-Elementals. The only unseen element that was spared was air, and even their population was fleeting. The elements of earth, fire, air, and water became the only elements recognized in the country and the royal family had regained control over their kingdom."

Hoshi, or the entity within her, finished speaking and did not wait for any questions before closing Hoshi's eyes. Her body shook severely, and her head slumped forward. Sayr was frozen in fear as she watched Hoshi breathe heavily, head still slumped against her chest. After several long minutes, her head lifted, and her eyes squinted open.

"That doesn't exactly seem like a pleasant experience," Sayr noted warily.

"It certainly is not, but it is necessary for the information received." Hoshi rubbed her temples as she spoke. "The stars gave you much information, more than they have given most in my experience. Did you find the answers you were looking for?"

"Some," Sayr answered. "But now I have even more questions."

"Any questions that I may be able to answer for you?" Hoshi asked.

Sayr thought for a moment as a million questions jumbled in her head. She thought about everything she had just heard, but one piece of information stuck out that still didn't make sense.

"There is one," Sayr said slowly, trying to piece her words carefully to not reveal herself too much. "You said–"

"The stars said," Hoshi corrected.

"Right, the stars said that the unseen elements were eliminated from Visaran, yet many Visarians still know about Air Elementals but not Space and Spirit, or so I've heard from Dimitri. Why would Air Elementals still be known by Visarians and not Space or Spirit?"

Hoshi's mouth quirked to one side as she thought, and she gave Sayr a knowing look. "I am not Visarian, so I cannot speak directly for your people, but I do know that Air Elementals are considered to be lesser than Space and Spirit Elementals since the two have to do with manipulating the body where the other elements do not. I assume the Visarian royals found no threat against air like they did with space and spirit, and when talk of the unseen elements sprang up after the exile, the royals did not squander the knowledge of the element as they did with the other unseen elements. Many later generations still have some recollection of the unseen elements but refuse to speak of it. Only our generation and the generations after us have forgotten them in the east."

Sayr sat still. "How'd you figure it out?" she asked. Neither she nor Dimitri had mentioned that Sayr was from Visaran, but somehow Hoshi had known.

Hoshi's lips spread into a proud smile. "Your accent, though I did not want to assume. Many Creobians still have Visarian accents even years after they fled. Your burning questions proved that you, too, are from Visaran."

Sayr nodded, and thankfully, Hoshi did not push the topic any further. Sayr thought about Hoshi's story, or the star's story, she still wasn't sure. She knew so little about the country that she had spent seventeen years in. Hoshi had never visited Visaran but still knew more about the country than Sayr did. And everything Dimitri had told her on their way to Therod was true.

"I believe I still have a lot to learn about the past," Sayr thought aloud.

"One piece of advice," Hoshi said. "Reflect on the past, but do not divulge yourself. You will drown in the events of the past if you think on it for too long, especially since they are events that you cannot change or solve."

Sayr nodded and looked at the entrance of the tent. "Dimitri must not be finished yet."

"I will take you to him." Hoshi shakily stood from the table.

"Are you sure you're all right?" Sayr asked, stretching out a hand to help her.

"Yes. It only lasts a short while."

Sayr helped Hoshi out through the curtain and into the sunlight. Hoshi shielded her eyes as they walked.

"Does this happen to every Space Elemental when they use their gifts?" she asked.

Her visions always left her senses feeling numb, but Hoshi was visibly shaken and rubbing her temples as if she were experiencing a pounding headache.

"Not always," she admitted. "It depends on how strong our gift is and how much we let go of our body to let an entity take hold. Letting go can certainly cause some stress on the body, but the more I let go, the more the stars let me see. I determine that the consequences afterwards are worth the risk."

They passed the fountain in the town square once again. A small group of children began to follow behind them as they continued through the dwindling crowds of the townspeople.

"You mean other Space Elementals could be even stronger than you?" Sayr asked. The question came out almost harsh, but Hoshi gave an astonished laugh.

"You truly know so little about the elements?" she asked. "Not all Elemental gifts are equal. Take the seen elements, for example. Some Water Elementals can manipulate the waves of the oceans while others can barely control a puddle of water. It all depends on how blessed an Elemental is from birth."

"I've been shielded from the truth for much of my life," Sayr muttered. "It's hard to understand what's true and what's false when so many people are throwing different stories at me."

In truth, she knew very little about the elements other than what she saw other Elementals do in training. She never had the same experiences that a true Elemental possessed when gifted in manipulating the elements, her gift simply appeared by force, and she had very little control over her gift.

Sayr was so distracted by her own thoughts that she barely registered Hoshi as she whipped around. Sayr stumbled in surprise as Hoshi crouched low to the ground, bared her teeth, and roared.

She looked around for the threat that Hoshi must have seen, but all that registered was the sound of children's screams and laughter. The group of children that had been quietly following them bolted from the two girls in all directions, still screaming and laughing as they ran. Hoshi laughed as she rose again and looked over at Sayr's startled expression.

"What was that?" Sayr asked.

She looked around the square. The children waited close by, hidden behind food carts or tables and chairs with big grins on their faces.

"Not to worry," Hoshi eased as she continued leading Sayr through the square. "Children love thrills. They do not have the fears that adults have from experiencing life just yet. That is why they love my stories so much."

"What sorts of stories do you tell?"

"All sorts. Though, the children prefer the scarier ones about ancient creatures that used to roam these lands before man conquered the continent, or battles fought long ago and the ferocious warriors that fought in them."

Hoshi looked sideways at Sayr. "Space Elementals used to be feared, you know. All the unseen elements were, but none more than Space Elementals. Our visions of the past were believed to be bad omens. People thought the stories we told of the past were likely to happen again if we spoke of them enough. Our gifts are more accepted now, but I like to continue the tradition of telling the darker tales of the past. The children like those tales most, too."

The two girls arrived at the base of a set of stairs as Hoshi finished, leading up to what looked to be a very old building.

"Here we are," Hoshi said and climbed the steps. "The Department of Records."

The two of them entered the building, the inside looked just as ancient as the outside. The entrance led into a large room where old wooden desks were placed in rows, stretching from one wall to another. Two more levels stretched above them, about half the size of this room.

The levels above were shielded from the open space by glass windows so Hoshi and Sayr could see above and the people on those levels could see below. Unlike the main level, the two levels were filled with bookshelves instead of desks. The shelves overflowed with books, rolled parchment, ink and quills. People hurried up and down the rows, arms filled with books. Others sat at the desks on the main level, scribbling quills onto parchment. A rickety spiral staircase connected the levels to the main floor. Hoshi walked straight to it.

"I have a feeling I know exactly what business Tri has here," Hoshi said, and she walked down the spiraling stairs.

One look down told Sayr that the stairs went even lower down multiple levels below them. Hoshi was quickly making her way down the stairs when Sayr landed on the first step. She followed Hoshi down the spiraling staircase as they descended down one, two, then three levels deeper.

The natural sunlight that had illuminated the levels above was slim down here. Lanterns were strung on every wall and on top of every desk, giving an eerie look as the shadows of the shelves and desks and books all jumped and danced in the flamelight. Sayr had thought the level was completely empty of people, until she heard the laughter coming from deeper inside.

The two followed the voices, growing louder as they approached. On the far side of the level, behind a few abandoned bookshelves, stood Dimitri and another man.

The man stood just as tall as Dimitri but lacked Dimitri's muscular build and heavy stance. He was dressed in deep brown trousers held up by suspenders and a ruffled white button down. Ink stains blotched the sleeves that were rolled up to his elbows. His sandy brown hair hung in his eyes and the man kept having to sweep the strands out of his face and away from the wide-rimmed glasses on his nose.

Sayr wasn't interested in assessing the man any further. What caught her attention was Dimitri's expression, she had never seen that expression on his face before.

A wide grin was plastered on his face, and he threw his head back in a laugh so deep that his shoulders shook. He clasped the other man on the back and the two smiled at each other. The man's gaze darted to the side, and he caught sight of Hoshi and her quickly approaching.

"Company," the man said, and Dimitri turned his head towards the two girls.

They turned in the girl's direction as they approached. Dimitri's grin didn't leave his face, but it was now much smaller than before, and he stood stiffer than he had before he'd spotted Sayr and Hoshi.

"I didn't expect you to be finished so quickly," Dimitri said to Sayr.

"I think I've gathered enough information for one day," Sayr answered.

The air between the group shifted uncomfortably, as if she and Hoshi had interrupted something, and she looked from Dimitri to the stranger. The man's eyes darted from Sayr to Hoshi, then landed and remained on Dimitri like he was the only source of comfort in this room.

"Sayr, this is Julen; my best friend from back home." Dimitri clasped Julen on the back. The stranger winced slightly but smiled shyly at Dimitri. "Julen, this is Sayr. She is the lady that I'm training as an initiate into the King's Court."

Julen's eyes bounced to Sayr, he avoided looking her in the eye and focused more on her nose and mouth as he greeted her.

"Nice to meet you, Sayr." His eyes bounced to Dimitri. "Tri has told me quite a bit about you."

A slight blush crawled up Dimitri's cheeks and he lightly elbowed Julen, causing the young man to jump slightly before huffing a small laugh.

Sayr couldn't help but laugh a little herself. "It's nice to meet you, too. So, you said you two know each other from home?"

"Y-yes," Julen stammered, choosing his words a bit carefully. "We were both raised in the Western Sector. We lived just three doors down from each other growing up."

Dimitri's stiffness began to melt away while Julen continued talking of the two of them as children. "We were inseparable when we were young, just like brothers."

Sayr smiled. "Did the two of you come to the Royal Sector together?"

Julen's lopsided grin fell just slightly. "Actually, no. Tri was brought here about eleven months before me. I remained in…the Western Sector until I was offered an internship here in the Department of Records the following summer."

"Julen is now the head of the History Department here." Dimitri elbowed Julen again. "Quite the bigshot here in Therod."

Julen rubbed the back of his neck with his hand. His cheeks turned pink from embarrassment.

"It's nothing much," he retorted. "I just copy old parchments that need restored and keep the history books of the continent in order."

"You do much more than that," Dimitri boasted. He turned back to look between Hoshi and Sayr. "This man is a genius; he can find anything and anyone just from the Department's records of the continent."

Sayr's gaze snapped back to Julen.

"You keep documentation of the entire continent's history?" she asked. "People, too?"

"Of course," Julen answered. "It's important to know the history of all families and people on the continent. If we don't remember our history, we will inevitably repeat it; the good and the bad."

Julen glanced again at Dimitri almost as if he were looking for approval before looking back at Sayr, or rather her nose. "Would you like me to show you around?"

"I would love that." Sayr smiled up at Julen and walked with him towards the many rows of bookshelves. As she glanced behind her, she watched Dimitri step closer to Hoshi, the two whispering harshly to one another.

She turned back in Julen's direction. Let Hoshi tell him everything she had asked or seen in that tent, it would keep them busy and away from her and Julen. She had more valuable information that she was dying to get out of the head of the History Department, anyway.

"Does your department keep records of only the continent?" she asked.

"Oh— uh, no," Julen stammered. "I mean our records consist mostly of information of the continent, but we also have records from the Magdallian Islands and other countries not too far from our coast."

"What sort of records do you keep from other countries?" she asked. She pretended to marvel over an old magnifying glass of his.

"All sorts," he answered more confidently. "We keep the records of agriculture trends, important people such as royals, generals, and the unordinary, maps of the countries with changing populations every few years, trade routes, almost anything you could think of."

"What do you mean, the unordinary?" she gave him a pointed look.

Julen looked from her back down at the magnifying glass. "After the unseen elements were exiled from Visaran, we began to keep records of what we called 'the unordinary.' Any Visarian refugees that made it to Creobe were counted for, for population records, of course. Now, we keep records of any unseen Elementals that are discovered in Visaran, or any new refugees that make it over the river into Creobe."

"You mean Visarian citizens are still trying to escape into Creobe?" she asked.

Julen nodded. "Yes. Some may not see it so close to the palace, but the towns further from the capital are struggling increasingly. Many believe they can find a better life here in Creobe."

"So, you have records of all Visarian refugees that come here to live? Even if they were to arrive recently?" she repeated.

"Well... yes." Julen's eyes darted around the room, as if he were unsure if he was giving too much information.

He certainly was. Lucky for him, though, Sayr wasn't looking for this information to bring back to Her Majesty. This was information that she needed for herself.

She drew herself upright and leaned over the table, closer to Julen. "If I were to give you a name, would you be able to check the records to see if they were here in Creobe?"

Julen hesitated, a bit too long. After some coaxing and a promise of a tour of the Western Palace's libraries, he yielded. "I'm not sure… it could be possible, but…why would you need that information?"

Sayr sighed. There were too many lies that she'd told since entering this country, she wasn't sure if she could spin another lie to Julen. "If I tell you why I need this information, will you promise not to tell Dimitri? Or anyone else for that matter? And you won't ask questions?"

Julen took a step back, but said, "Yes, I promise you."

Sayr looked back down at the magnifier standing on the table. "My father disappeared six years ago. I just recently learned the truth about Visaran's exile of unseen Elementals, and possibly being an unseen Elemental myself, I can't help but think that my father may be living somewhere in Creobe, either by choice or by force."

"You think your father was from Visaran?" Julen's voice was thick with shock.

"I said no questions," Sayr snapped. Her gaze remained on the magnifier.

Sayr didn't look up at Julen, but she could feel his presence next to her as he shifted on his feet. She didn't want to meet his eyes now that he knew a secret that she had kept even from Dimitri.

Julen didn't speak a word. Instead, he silently walked to the spiral staircase, leaving Sayr no choice but to follow, and climbed two levels just beneath the main floor.

They walked through aisle after aisle of unorganized shelves full of different items. Suddenly, Julen stopped in front of a stack of books scattered on a shelf, labeled alphabetically and by number.

"I would need a full name and an approximate year that your father fled from Visaran. Can you give me that much?"

Yes, she could.

Without hesitation, Sayr gave Julen the name of her father, Jespon Rieve, and the approximate date that he had stopped coming to see her in the palace six years ago.

22

$\mathcal{D}$imitri and Sayr said goodbye to Hoshi and Julen at the Department of Records early that afternoon, heading from Therod back to the Western Palace.

The two-hour trek left Sayr feeling exhausted. By the time they had made it back through the halls of the palace, the King's Court was assembling for dinner in the dining hall.

They walked in silence, until Sayr side-eyed Dimitri and smirked. "Tri?"

She didn't have to say anything else as the blush returned to Dimitri's cheeks and he grinned almost sheepishly. He looked so unlike his usual bored expression of stone that she laughed aloud.

"It's a nickname I'd acquired over the years," he explained. Sayr expected him to say more, but he remained silent again.

"I sense there's more of a story here than you're telling me," Sayr teased.

The grin faded a bit. "It's a story for another time, perhaps."

Sayr nodded, not wanting to push Dimitri any further on something he clearly wasn't ready to share with her. She understood. There was much information that she wasn't ready to share with him yet, either.

She realized only her footsteps were clacking against the floor and she turned to see Dimitri had stopped walking. He looked at her in a way he'd never looked at her before.

"Why Aryn?" he asked.

"What?" Sayr retraced her steps, so she was standing in front of Dimitri.

"Why did you tell me your name was Aryn when we first met?" His hair fell into his eyes as he looked down at her, shadowing his features.

"I— uh," Sayr stammered.

She had no true reason why she had given him her mother's name instead of hers the first time they had met. She just knew she needed to hide her identity as much as possible.

"I don't know," she admitted. "When you and the rest of the Western Court arrived, all I knew was what I had been told; that you were all manipulative monsters. When you met me underneath the tree that day, you were the first Creobian I'd ever willingly spoken to. I'll admit I was a bit frightened, and you kept asking me so many questions. I was afraid that you would find out who I was and why I was in the Eastern Palace, which you ended up finding out anyway. I guess I wanted to prolong anyone knowing of my existence in the palace for as long as I could. I figured that if I gave you a false name, you would forget about me and move on to another member of the Court."

Dimitri inhaled slowly as they stared at each other. "You are not that easy to forget, Sayr."

Dimitri continued walking without waiting for Sayr's response. She was too stunned to follow for a moment, watching as he walked further down the hall. Had Dimitri Lim really just complimented her? Or was that even supposed to be a compliment?

She hurried her feet to catch up with him. She now had a thousand more questions to ask but bit her tongue as they reached the doors to the dining hall.

Dinner was in full swing as they entered the hall. Clinking dishes and happy chatter filled their ears. The two of them quietly made their way to the end of the table to snag empty seats and whatever food was left when His Majesty stood from his seat.

"Dimitri, Lady Sayr. Welcome!" Everyone at the table turned in their direction as the king spoke. "I apologize, we were not expecting you to join us tonight, so we did not wait, but there is still plenty of food. Please, dig in."

Dimitri bowed before sitting down. "Thank you, Your Majesty."

Sayr copied his movements and made to sit down next to Dimitri.

"Lady Sayr, please come sit next to me. I insist," His Majesty called from the opposite end of the table.

Sayr froze mid squat into her seat. Her mouth opened but she said nothing, instead she looked over to Dimitri who nodded and scooted her in the king's direction.

She walked over to the king's end of the table just as a servant pulled out the empty chair next to the king for her. She murmured a "thank you" to the servant before taking her seat next to King Mylan.

"How have you been enjoying your lessons these past weeks?" the king asked. He cut a knife through the roast on his plate while he and Sayr spoke.

"Some have been more pleasant than others," Sayr admitted. A servant stacked meat, potatoes, and steamed vegetables onto her plate. "But I'm learning a lot from my lessons with Dimitri, and I *think* my lessons with Lilith are making me stronger."

Sayr didn't want to explain her lessons with either Dimitri or Lilith any further. She didn't know how much King Mylan knew about Lilith's extensive methods in training, and she didn't want him knowing about her and Dimitri slowly growing closer to one another.

She didn't need the king holding anything, or anyone, over her head to keep her there.

"What have you learned thus far?" King Mylan continued.

Sayr scooped up a fork full of potatoes and roast, and stuffed it into her mouth, chewing as she thought. As usual, the meal was mouthwateringly delicious, and though she wanted to immediately take another bite after swallowing, she instead looked at the king.

"If I'm being honest, a lot of this new information has been circling around my head. It's hard to make sense of it all when it contradicts everything that I've been taught all my life. That being said, I have learned the efforts that Creobe made in trying to help those Visarians that fled during the years of exile, and though you were not king during those years, I do have to thank the Creobian Crown for those efforts. And I have you to thank for continuing those efforts."

King Mylan smiled approvingly at Sayr and leaned back in his seat. "I don't mean to question you, in fact I'm quite proud of your change in mindset in just two months, but why are you so quick to trust everything that Dimitri has taught you when you were so against me and my people when you arrived?"

I don't trust anyone, Sayr thought to herself.

She needed the king to believe she did, though. He needed to believe that she fully trusted everything Dimitri and His Majesty and everyone had told her since she arrived in the palace.

Sayr thought hard for a moment. She thought back to the first night that she'd stepped out of the carriage and onto Creobian soil, in the small town where they'd eaten dinner in the tavern. One moment she truly could not forget or understand.

"The night that we left the carriages to eat dinner in one of the villages here in Creobe, I spotted a mother and her children walking through the streets. When she spoke, she had a Visarian accent. I thought I was losing my mind at first and I approached the woman, asking her if she was from Visaran. Cordia had corrected me after I'd approached the woman, saying that there was no way that she could be Visarian. But she had looked so terrified when I'd asked her, and she left so quickly with her children. It makes sense that she would be so afraid of me if she thought I had identified her as a Visarian who had fled to Creobe during the exile."

Mylan nodded thoughtfully as he looked at her. His eyes quickly passed from her to the others at the table as Addy had tossed a roll at Willa from across the table.

"Tell me, how was your trip to Therod?" the king asked, and he took a sip from his wine glass.

"It was… very educational," Sayr answered. "I learned a lot about the terrain of the Royal Sector and the people living near the palace."

"And did you find any new information about yourself?" King Mylan's voice lowered so only Sayr could hear him as the rest of the dinner guests began talking to one another again.

Sayr thought about Hoshi and her vision, and Julen's promise to try and find information on her father. Her lips helplessly stretched into a smile, and she answered, "I did, Your Majesty. Thank you."

King Mylan smiled and patted her hand. His eyes drifted to the Visarian officials at the table, to Cordia, who watched Sayr and the king all too closely.

The king kept his voice low and even as he spoke. "I am very happy to hear that, Lady Sayr. I suspect I will need to make room for a new Spirit Elemental in my Court soon?"

Sayr's smile widened. Her plan was all coming together. The lie fell from her tongue all too easily.

"Yes, Your Majesty. I believe you will."

The king did not need to know about her suspicions of her gifts being closely related to those of a Space Elemental. She was getting closer and closer into the King's Court, and closer to the members within.

23

Sayr opened the small drawer of her desk and dropped a hair clip inside. She had taken the hair clip from Willa during one of their after-dinner gatherings with Mina and Addy. The girls got together almost every night, and ever since the attack on the village in the Royal Sector, Mina kept inviting Sayr and Mar to join them.

"I can never thank you enough," Mina had told Sayr the first time they were together after the attack. "I admit I never expected that you would be my savior. But you were. You saved me. I want to thank you for that and apologize for my misconceptions about you and your intentions here."

Mina had grabbed Sayr and Mar and linked her arms with both of theirs. "I think we will all make great friends," she told them.

Sayr had smiled at Mina, but her throat tightened with emotion. Her mission was not to make friends, her mission was to gather as much information from the girls as possible.

Willa had taken the clip out of her hair before stepping out onto the balcony and leaned against the railing. Sayr, Addy, Mar and Mina all sat in the chairs around a small table inside the threshold of the palace, safe from the wind.

Almost everyone had been drinking at dinner, and the wine seemed to be getting to many of them as Addy and Mina laughed and hollered while Willa's dress billowed around her. Mina moved to help Willa fight to keep the skirts of her dress down, giggling the entire time. A tall man with buzzed hair appeared, pulling Addy off the balcony and into the hall. Sayr had snatched the clip while they were all distracted. Even Mar hadn't seen her thievery, her eyes glued to the man's back as he hovered over Addy.

She peered into the small drawer; Tomas's chain, Willa's hair clip, and a small ring Sayr had been able to take from the dressing room during one of her training sessions with Lilith all laid in the drawer.

She was getting close, but she still had much to accomplish. And she still had no idea who the king's mercenary could be. Tomas seemed too frivolous with his duties and Mina was out of the palace so often that she didn't think it could be either of them. Dimitri also left the palace rather often and Addy spent so much time in the medic's level instead of with the king. That left Willa, Lilith, or Ryon. Any three of them could be the king's mercenary, the one that she would have to kill.

For the first time since she'd arrived at the Western Palace, a surge of guilt tugged at her core as her eyes flitted over each object from members of the King's Court. She was a thief, and soon she would become a murderer. The queen's mission was turning her into something dark and ugly, something she did not want to become.

With a huffing breath, Sayr slammed the drawer shut.

Sayr spit out blood and ran her tongue over her teeth, checking that none had broken or fallen out from Lilith's punch. They were supposed to be working on defense strategies; Lilith had told her so when she walked into the armory this morning. The two girls discarded their weapons and focused on hand-to-hand combat today. Sayr hated to put the weapons back in their holsters on the walls, but the feel of getting a hit at Lilith with her own hands felt thrilling.

The two girls shuffled back and forth.

Sayr was supposed to be on the defense throughout the entire session today, but she had already broken that rule when she landed a punch to Lilith's jaw and a kick to her knee, and Lilith was beginning to take her own defensive stance against Sayr.

Lilith retracted her arm from where she'd thrown the punch at Sayr. She kicked out and landed a kick to her stomach. Sayr fell to the ground and toppled over. She gasped hard, searching for air.

"Pathetic." Lilith paced back and forth, waiting for Sayr to get back on two feet. "You can't even defend yourself against a forward attack."

Lilith was much angrier this morning. She had been practically seething when Sayr entered the armory. She barely spoke to Sayr, shooting only a few words of instruction at Sayr before they faced off.

Sayr wheezed as she rose to her feet. She quickly crouched back into her defensive stance. Her vision blurred and she stumbled back a step. She quickly crouched forward to regain her balance.

She was so dizzy.

Lilith took advantage of the extra seconds and kneed Sayr straight in the face.

Blood sprayed from Sayr's nose. She yelled as pain burst through her face. Her legs wobbled and she fell to her knees, doubled over as her blood splattered the training floor.

"Come on!" Lilith screamed at Sayr. "Get up!"

Sayr rose to her feet once again. Her mouth filled with the metallic taste of blood and her nose still gushed. She held a hand over her nose and mouth to try and stifle some of the bleeding. She took her defensive stance and watched closely as Lilith advanced.

Lilith sprinted towards her. Sayr took note of each movement she made. The slight bend in her knees told Sayr that she'd be dropping low to the ground to try and knock her off balance.

Lilith dropped low, kicking one leg out. Sayr stumbled to the right. She was out of Lilith's range of motion. Lilith would have to turn her body completely to reach Sayr in the position she was now in.

Sayr advanced on Lilith. She rolled her hand into a fist and threw another punch to the other side of Lilith's jaw. Lilith yelped in pain and rolled to the far side, out of Sayr's reach.

The fast motion made Sayr dizzy again. She unlocked her knees to keep from passing out. Her head thundered with pain, and she choked on the blood that continued spilling from her nose. Her lungs were raw from the air being knocked out of her again and again.

"Enough," she huffed out, panting from exhaustion. "That's enough. We're done."

Lilith rose from the ground. The hateful glare she threw at Sayr screamed of murder.

"You don't get to say when we're done!" she screamed and hopped off the training floor.

Sayr was too dizzy to defend herself. Stars peeked in the corners of her vision. Her heart was beating so fast, too fast.

She blocked Lilith's hit with one arm, only to be knocked away and hit on the opposite side of her body. She stumbled back, but Lilith advanced.

"It's about time I repaid you for those lashings," Lilith taunted.

Sayr blocked as many advances as she could, but her strength was fading, and her vision grew darker and darker.

"I told them all that you would pay for what you did to me!" Lilith screamed. Her face contorted with fury and her eyes were wide and crazed. She breathed heavily as she watched Sayr stumble and try to regain her footing.

"I didn't want to," Sayr tried to tell Lilith, but her words were coming out in gasping breaths.

Sayr could faintly hear shouts coming from the rooms of the armory. Feet hit the floor hard as someone ran towards them.

Still, Lilith didn't back down. She grabbed Sayr by the shoulders.

"Your payment for those lashings will be your life," she murmured in Sayr's ear. "You won't be of any use to the king when you're dead."

She kicked the back of Sayr's leg, forcing her down on one knee and kicked.

And punched.

And kicked Sayr.

Something inside her cracked and her chest exploded in pain.

She could not speak, she could barely breathe without blinding pain radiating through her body, as hit after hit kept coming at her.

Sayr tried to suck in air, but no air filled her lungs.

She was suffocating.

Her vision had blurred completely, the black stars almost taking over her vision. She couldn't defend herself anymore. She fell to the ground, bleeding and wheezing while Lilith remained over her.

An orange light ignited throughout the room. Sayr could faintly make out the flames that surrounded her. Lilith backed away, outside the ring of flames. A figure stepped in front of Sayr, their hands ignited in brilliant fire.

The glint of something slick and wet spilled across the floor, catching Sayr's eye for a moment. She could just make out the red blood spilling from her body. She looked back up at the figure prowling towards Lilith. Lilith's mouth opened and closed as the person walked through the flames untouched, closer to her. Her hands trembled and she stepped back until her body pressed against the glass of the dome.

The stars consumed Sayr's vision, and she fell into darkness.

Sayr's body jostled up and down, darkness surrounding her. She felt so heavy, like she was sinking deeper, and her entire body throbbed with dull pain. Her eyelids felt too heavy to open.

Faint voices came through the darkness around her, whoever was speaking sounded frantic. Sayr strained to listen to the voices, but she was sinking further and further away. The voices grew more distant as her body sunk deeper and deeper into the darkness.

An acidic smell filled her nose, and she began drifting higher and higher, closer to the growing voices.

"Should we give her another one?" one voice asked.

"Wait until we reach His Majesty," another voice answered. "We don't want to do anything too drastic without his orders."

The dark pool Sayr floated in was beginning to melt away, a dim white light obscured her vision. The dull pain grew more intense with every moment that she floated away from the darkness.

Sayr finally opened her eyes, her vision was blurred and foggy from the bright lights around her. Her body continued to jostle up and down and she craned her neck slightly to look up. A young woman with black and red braids carried Sayr in her arms up the stairs of the palace. Her face was consumed by anger and worry, and she was panting from the exertion of climbing the stairs with Sayr's dead weight.

How had she gotten out of the armory? Had Mar carried her the entire way?

She breathed in and nearly fainted again. The blinding pain in her chest and abdomen made her head spin. She wanted to gasp but her body wouldn't let enough air in. Her face ignited in pain, too. White hot pain ignited in her head and made her throat burn with bile.

Another face popped into her blurred vision, a female with fiery red hair and big brown eyes.

"Oh good, you're awake!" Addy said. She stuffed a small parcel back into the pocket of the apron wrapped around her dress. "I was worried I'd have to give you another smelling salt to bring you back."

"What happened? Where are we going?" Sayr tried to ask but her words came out slurred and thick like syrup.

Addy must have caught some of her words, though, and she answered, "The king's quarters. His Majesty will want to assess your injuries for himself."

Addy took another look at Sayr's beaten body. "Or maybe he should wait until you're healed enough."

Sayr closed her eyes again. Her body felt heavy and exhausted and painful, she wanted to drift back into the dark waters of unconsciousness.

"Sorry, hun," Addy lightly pinched the skin under Sayr's bicep. "We need to keep you awake. We don't want you slipping into a coma right before the ball."

Mar carried Sayr three more flights with Addy in tow before they reached the king's quarters, bursting through the doors in the king's main room.

King Mylan was pacing back and forth in front of his large desk when they entered. When he saw them, he rushed to the plush chairs near the fireplace, knocking pillows off the chaise lounge to make more room.

"Bring her here!" His voice sounded as panicked as Mar's.

Mar gently laid Sayr onto the chaise lounge. Immediately, Addy began unzipping and removing Sayr's training uniform, ripping the blood-soaked fabric that stuck to her skin with a pair of shears. Sayr fought to stay awake, barely registering anything but the exhaustion and pain. She could only grunt in pain when Addy's hands got too close to her ribs.

Mar was on her knees by the chaise. Her eyes bounced between Sayr's wounds and Addy's quick hands working to stop the bleeding.

"Three of her ribs are broken and she's lost a lot of blood," Addy noted while she inspected the bleeding wounds and nasty bruises already appearing.

She brought one hand up to Sayr's face. "The cartilage in her nose is shattered. Her right cheekbone is broken, too. She's lucky they weren't training with weapons, or I'd have to worry about stab wounds, though I'm still not sure that she doesn't have any internal bleeding."

"Put her under," the king ordered, and Addy quickly obeyed.

She fumbled in her apron pocket and brought out a tiny vial of dark liquid. Popping the cork off, she brought the vial to Sayr's lips and tipped the contents into Sayr's mouth. The liquid tasted slightly bitter, but the moment Sayr swallowed, the pain coursing through her body began to ease and her senses started to fade.

She let out a moan of relief and let her eyelids close as her senses dulled again, leaving her more exhausted.

A door flung open, so hard it crashed against the wall, and heavy footsteps quickly ran into the room. Sayr could feel another presence next to her, grabbing her hand and holding tight. Someone was yelling something, but Sayr was already too deep in the darkness to understand them.

The strong hand holding hers let go, leaving the space where it had been cold and empty, before Sayr succumbed to the darkness once again.

A fire blazed brightly in the fireplace of the king's quarters. It was far past midnight, and the moonlight shone through the open balcony. Sayr laid on the chaise closest to the flames, wrapped in blankets to keep her body temperature up.

Addy had tended to as many of her injuries as she could before the healer had come. And even then, His Majesty only let them heal her enough to repair any broken bones and the bleeding inside of her abdomen. His Majesty ordered the healer to leave the bruises, even the nastiest of them, so Sayr would not suspect the healer's higher gifts just yet.

Dimitri could have killed the king for it.

He had wanted to kill someone, anyone, when he'd burst into the king's quarters and seen her lying on the chaise; clothes tattered, and body broken. Her broken ribs had come so close to puncturing her lung, she'd been so closely beaten to death by Lilith.

Dimitri had wanted to stay by her side while Addy worked on her injuries, but he had been in such a rage that the king had ordered his guards to take Dimitri out of the room at least until Addy and the healer were finished.

"She needs to be stripped of her position," Dimitri growled. "She needs to leave this palace before I find her and kill her."

"Easy, Lim," Mylan muttered and raised his glass to his mouth.

The king looked about as awful as Dimitri felt, his polished appearance gone. His shirt was untucked from his pants, the wrinkled sleeves rolled lazily up to his elbows. His pantlegs were unfolded at the bottom and his shoes had been abandoned and tossed near a bookshelf.

"I agree with him," Marenda chimed in from the couch closest to Sayr. She had refused to leave Sayr's side—even when Dimitri had been ordered out of the room—and had nearly set the room on fire when anyone suggested she do so. "If I see that girl, inside or outside these walls, I will kill her myself for this."

"I believe you've punished her enough," Mylan said to Marenda.

"Not hardly," Marenda shot back. "She'll recover all too quickly from those burns. I should've given her a more permanent punishment."

"She has already been given a more permanent punishment by your queen," Mylan shot back. "Lilith will be temporarily suspended, at least until I can determine what to do with her." King Mylan tried to ease the two warriors. "Her father will be livid with her when he hears about her suspension."

"None of that is Sayr's fault," Marenda argued. "I was in that courtyard with the rest of you. I saw exactly what you saw. Sayr tried to show Lilith mercy that day. She did not want to harm the girl, but she had no other choice than to give those lashings. The first two never broke skin.

Only the lashing from the queen harmed Lilith. I am not saying it's right, but none of that should fall on Sayr."

Dimitri shook his head angrily. "Sayr was supposed to be protected here, not almost beaten to death. And for what? Because she missed a single training lesson to come to Therod with me?"

Mylan shot Dimitri a knowing look, then glanced towards Marenda. "Could you give us a minute alone, Lady Marenda?"

"Absolutely not." Marenda crossed her arms and leaned back on the couch. "I'm not leaving her alone here with any of you, especially after what just happened to her by a member of your Court."

King Mylan sighed and stood, gesturing for Dimitri to walk with him out to the balcony. Once they were on the balcony, out of earshot, the king turned towards Dimitri.

"You know that this is over much more than a missed training lesson. I do not condone Lilith's actions whatsoever, but I believe she has been pushed over the edge these last few months. She has been wanting revenge against Lady Sayr since the girl was forced to whip Lilith in the Eastern Palace. She has been using her abilities more than ever since we left for Visaran. And when I brought Lady Sayr to my palace, I admit I practically offered her Lilith's position as a Spirit Elemental in my Court. Lady Sayr has been spending several hours every day with you, and the other members of my Court are beginning to appreciate her quite a lot. Everything that Lilith has worked and yearned for since she arrived in this palace, Lady Sayr was able to take for herself in two months."

"So, Sayr deserves this because she is better at making people like her?" Dimitri spat.

"That is not at all what I'm saying. I think revenge was Lilith's biggest motive, but it is likely that she also saw her position in my Court beginning to crumble, as Sayr likely would have taken the position as the Spirit Elemental in my Court away from her. Don't give me that look, Lim, she was also able to make you like her quite easily."

Dimitri looked away from the king. "I don't know what you're talking about."

Mylan just shrugged. "All I'm saying is that your mind seemed more occupied than usual once we had entered the Eastern Palace. I noticed your absences during our stay with the Eastern Court. Every time I called for someone to find you, you were not far from where she was, watching her as she went about her daily routine. It seems nothing has changed since then, though I know how seriously you take orders."

The king chuckled into his glass as he took another long sip.

Dimitri ignored the king. "She was supposed to be protected," he repeated. "What will you tell the Eastern Queen when she arrives? You can't let the Visarian royal family see her like this and expect them not to immediately take her back to Visaran. Especially not the prince."

The king's eyes were almost black under the night sky. "I will think of something before then."

Marenda's voice rose from the quarters and Dimitri and Mylan swiftly turned.

Marenda was kneeling behind the chaise, her eyes focused on Sayr. Sayr's eyes were open, and she was saying something to Marenda, too quietly for them to hear on the balcony.

Dimitri strode into the king's quarters and dropped to his knees next to the chaise. Sayr turned from Marenda when Dimitri came close and stared only at him. Her eyes were still clouded with sleep, but they widened just slightly as she took in his face.

He couldn't help the grin that stretched over his face and every muscle in his body relaxed ever so slightly.

She was awake.

"Hello, little imposter."

A smile of her own began to form but then she grimaced and reached a hand towards her face. Her fingers lightly touched her cheekbone. Her whole face throbbed in pain, but her cheek and nose felt like they had been broken and reset.

"You shouldn't move." Dimitri reached for her hand, bringing it back down to her side. "You were badly injured; you need to stay still and rest."

Marenda remained kneeling behind Sayr, but now she looked at Dimitri, her face filled with warning.

"How are you feeling?" Dimitri asked. His eyes scanned over her face and body.

"Like I've been almost beaten to death," Sayr answered. She looked between Dimitri and the king.

"Anything you'd like to say now that your Court's target practice is awake?" Mar nodded to Sayr lying on the chaise, her voice simmering with malice.

King Mylan leaned over the back of a chair. "While I'm sure you meant that as mostly sarcasm, there is something you both need to be aware of. The Visarian royal family is coming to Creobe to celebrate the Harvest Festival here in my palace. It was Her Majesty's idea, of course, as a show of union between both our countries. Though I have no doubts that she simply wants to check in on the troops that she sent us." His eyes met Sayr's. "And on you."

Sayr's brain still felt muddy as she tried to understand the king. "The royal family... Ev and Lanni will be here, too?"

"Indeed," the king answered. "We will be hosting this year's Harvest Ball. The royal family and part of their Court are permitted to stay here for one week only. Queen Cheralin and I will discuss the extension of her troops in Creobe, and then they will be on their way back to the Eastern Palace."

Sayr could barely believe what she was hearing. She had come to the conclusion that she'd likely never see Everett again. Even if she did complete her mission, she would likely be found out and killed if the king didn't decide to keep her as his own personal Seer. Now she would get to see him again, and at the Harvest Ball!

She looked from the king back to Dimitri, and all the excitement coursing through her quickly diminished. The happiness in his eyes when she'd first woken up was gone. He looked defeated as he stared down at her. Sayr remembered his stories of the queen's exile of unseen Elementals.

Everett's mother had exiled and murdered her own people. Sayr would never say so aloud, but her time in Creobe had changed her so much. Her views on the world, on Creobe, had completely changed. She had never considered the Eastern Palace her home, but now the royal family was coming here to try and bring her back. What would be waiting for her when she returned? A life sentence as the queen's lapdog Seer?

What would happen when Everett rose to the throne? He was her longest friend, and they cared for each other, but she knew deep down that he would deny any request of hers to leave the palace if he thought that he could still use her gifts to benefit Visaran.

He would never set her free.

King Mylan cleared his throat and backed away from his chair. "Lady Marenda, I would like to discuss our upcoming situation with you, as you are Queen Cheralin's personal guard. Would you mind speaking out on the balcony for a moment?"

Mar exchanged a look with Sayr. Sayr nodded her approval and Mar looked back at the king. "Only for a moment. And we stay where I can see her."

"Of course," Mylan agreed and looked at Sayr, again. "I am so glad you are awake, Lady Sayr, and I will leave Dimitri to watch over you."

The king and Mar walked to the balcony, already speaking low with one another.

Sayr watched Dimitri. His face looked pained as he stared at the fire behind her. She wanted to reach out and touch him, but the pain coursing through her and her own pride kept her still.

"I'm so sorry," he whispered, still not looking at her. "I never should have let this happen."

Sayr wheezed out a small laugh that sounded more like a painful cough. "I don't think anyone could've stopped her. Mar got there right at the end, thank the elements, or I don't know how far she would have gone."

The memories came rushing back to her. Lilith had looked so hateful when she'd first arrived for training that morning. The two of them had made it very clear that they didn't like each other, so Sayr thought nothing of Lilith's mood. Why had Lilith gone into such a blinding rage to go so far?

"I wish I had been there to stop it," Dimitri admitted. "I should've started attending every lesson with you after seeing how she trained you with those swords."

Sayr ignored the twisting in her stomach at the emotion in Dimitri's voice. "I highly doubt the Royal Guards get beaten this badly in their training with her, and I understand her anger for what…what I did to her in the

Eastern Palace. I never even apologized to her. But why would she do this now? Why would she go this far?"

Dimitri's expression turned almost sad. "It's partially my fault, but I think the other part is because she's afraid of you."

Sayr would've snorted if the effort hadn't hurt so bad. Instead, she rolled her eyes, and even that caused pain to shoot through her face.

"It's true," Dimitri said, though his tone was a touch lighter. "Ever since she encountered you in the halls of the Eastern Palace, she's been afraid of the potential that you hold. If you truly are a Spirit Elemental, the fact that you were unaffected by her gifts could only mean that you are stronger than her, strong enough to fend off her own manipulation. And after the queen made you…hurt her, she's thought of nothing but revenge. She never should have taken it out on you, though, that sort of punishment was not your doing."

Sayr thought over Dimitri's words. "I never should have done that to her," Sayr admitted. "Whether a queen ordered me to or not, I should have been brave enough to refuse."

"From what you've told me and what I've seen from the Eastern Queen, I know now that you didn't have any choice then," Dimitri admitted. "You were doing as your queen had ordered. And you had shown mercy to Lilith. Even though the queen saw it as weakness, we all saw it as strength. We saw that you were capable of defying the queen, even if in just the slightest way."

Sayr blinked rapidly to keep tears from spilling over. "I still don't see how any of that is your fault."

Dimitri's eyes finally found hers, his hazel irises glowing bright in the firelight. "I was too careless in spending my time with you outside of our lessons. I became too attached to you, finding interests in you besides the ability that you might possess. It's foolish, but Lilith's had this hope that the two of us would be spoken for each other. It gives no reason for her actions whatsoever, but I doubt she appreciated the amount of time we spent together outside of lessons."

Sayr's gut twisted. Dimitri was her instructor, and may had even grown to become her friend, but nothing more. There could be nothing more. He was a part of the King's Court, and she was a member of the queen's. She would be forced to return to Visaran in a matter of weeks and they would never see each other again. Still, something about Dimitri's words made her stomach flip.

"And are you? Spoken for, I mean."

The look in Dimitri's gaze intensified. "No," he answered. "I'm not."

An odd wave of relief rushed over her. He was not spoken for, but that didn't stop her nerves from igniting.

"And are you spoken for?" he asked her. "With the crown prince?"

Sayr squinted at him for a moment, confused. Suddenly, her eyes widened with realization. "You mean with Ev?"

Dimitri nodded, causing a laugh to burst out of Sayr. She hunched over, grasping her abdomen in pain. Dimitri leaned towards her and placed a hand on her back as she coughed.

"I'm fine," she said as the pain ceased, and she laid back on the chaise. "No, I'm not spoken for by the crown prince."

Saying it aloud almost made her laugh again. "He is my oldest friend, and I love him dearly, or I did, but not in that way," she clarified.

Dimitri nodded again, but the shadows in his eyes did not disappear. "Does he know that?"

"It's not as if we ever talked about romantic feelings with each other," Sayr countered, though she knew what Dimitri truly meant.

She knew Everett's feelings for her went deeper than her feelings for him. And though she never felt the same way, she also couldn't stomach the idea of losing her oldest friend. She never brought it up in fear that he would walk away from her if she refused him, and she thanked each one of the elements that he never mentioned it, himself.

"Then you're not spoken for at all?" Dimitri pressed. "Not by a Royal Guard or Court official back in the Eastern Palace?"

Sayr's grin turned slightly mischievous. "Why? Thinking about putting in a word for me?"

She expected a sarcastic retort from him, but Dimitri just leaned back on his knees. "I'm surprised, is all."

"Right," Sayr teased, though she could feel the heat of a blush blooming across her cheeks.

Dimitri turned from Sayr to look behind him at Marenda and King Mylan, who were deep in conversation. Marenda kept her eyes on the two of them as she and Mylan spoke. Dimitri stood from the ground and took the love seat across from Sayr. The musky mint scent of him lingered over her and she almost ached for him to be close again.

"You should get some rest," he said as he grabbed a blanket off one of the loveseats and settled into the cushions of the chair. "I'll stick around tonight. I'd prefer not to leave you or His Majesty alone just yet. I'm sure Marenda won't be leaving your side all night, either. You'll be under the utmost care."

Sayr nodded and shut her eyes. As much as she wanted to stay awake and talk to Dimitri more, she couldn't help but let sleep overtake her as the exhaustion set in once again. Within minutes, she had drifted off to sleep.

Sayr remained in the king's quarters for three days before she felt well enough to move around. The pain in every muscle of her body had dulled to an aching soreness now, enough that she could at least walk around the quarters without help. The king's healers visited her twice each day, giving her some sort of drug to knock her out while they examined her injuries. Every time she woke up afterwards, her pain and discomfort grew less severe.

She spent most of the days on the king's balcony, even eating the meals brought in by servants in the fresh air, looking out over the mountains.

Creobe was beautiful in autumn, the trees that coated each mountain varied in shades of orange, red, and yellow. The mountains themselves looked as if they had been ignited by flames of wildfire when the wind sifted through the branches.

Dimitri and Mar stayed with her, refusing to let anyone else tend to her. Dimitri occasionally left to speak with His Majesty, only to return right after. He'd practically moved himself into the king's quarters; having his meals with Sayr, completing paperwork or holding meetings with officials inside the quarters, and sleeping in the quarters near the fireplace each night.

After much coaxing, Sayr convinced Mar to leave occasionally to snoop around the medic's level or question the Creobian soldiers she had been training with.

"I can't go investigate on my own and I need to find more about the healers, especially now that the queen is coming here so soon," she'd told Mar. "I need you to be my eyes and ears while I'm stuck in here."

Though Mar had agreed, Sayr couldn't fight her hesitation to give Mar the orders. She swallowed down the doubt she kept feeling over completing the queen's mission. For the first time since she'd arrived in Creobe, she began thinking seriously about King Mylan's offer to remain in Creobe for good.

While Mar was gone, Sayr and Dimitri would sit out on the balconies and talk. Dimitri told Sayr about his life growing up outside of the palace and getting into trouble with Julen back in his home village. He told her of his family. He had a younger sister that he loved dearly, and he described his parents as kind, loving people.

When he asked her about her family, she felt almost embarrassed by the lack of information she had to offer.

"There's not much to say about my family," she offered. "My mother died when I was an infant, and I haven't seen my father since I was a child. I'm an only child so I have no siblings."

Dimitri listened patiently, as if understanding the difficulty that it took for her to talk about her family. "What was your father like, if you remember him well enough?"

"Of course, I remember him," Sayr said, looking off into the mountains again. "He was a great man, is a great man. I don't even know if he's still alive or not."

"Why haven't you seen him in so long, if he may still be alive?"

Sayr told Dimitri the story of arriving at the palace, though she made certain to leave the parts of her visions out. As far as Dimitri knew, she had been brought to the palace in search of work. She had been put into training sessions in the barracks to see if she would make a good soldier. After a few years in the palace, her knack for politics earned her a position as the apprentice of a Councilman in the Eastern Court while continuing her training as a soldier.

"My father would visit often when I first arrived at the palace, but his visits became less frequent after a few years. The last time I ever saw him was right before my eleventh birthday. He had promised to take me to the City Center for the first time for my birthday, but he never showed up. I haven't seen him since."

Dimitri nodded his understanding. "Was he an Elemental?" he asked.

Sayr shook her head. "He was a non-Elemental. He worked as a tailor in our city, the best there was. Everyone came to him for his skills, even people outside of our city would travel to have him custom tailor suits and dresses."

Sayr smiled at the memory of her father. He'd loved his job, and she used to love sitting at the desk of his shop, watching as his hands worked intricately with pins and needles and beautiful silks all day.

"What about your mother?" Dimitri continued. "Was she an Elemental?"

Sayr shook her head again. "I don't know. My father never really talked about her and when he did, he never mentioned any gifts that she may have possessed."

Sayr thought for a moment before perking up. "What is your position in the Western Palace, really?"

Dimitri's lips quirked up in a small smile. "Why are you so curious about my position in this palace?"

Sayr glowered at him. "You can't answer a question with another question."

He didn't answer her, and she blushed at the confession she was about to make. "The night His Majesty told me about the Creobian sectors, he let slip that you were a non-Elemental."

Sayr paused, looking for any sort of change in Dimitri's face; a twitch of an eyebrow or narrowing of his eyes, but he remained perfectly still.

"I admit I was prejudiced at first. I thought non-Elementals couldn't be nearly as strong as Elementals, but you've proven me wrong. You're a highly skilled warrior and even the Royal Guards bow their heads when you pass. I don't doubt that you deserve your title by any means, but I am curious as to what exactly that title is."

Dimitri looked away from her, his expression still unreadable.

"I am a mercenary. The king's mercenary."

24

Sayr's body felt like ice as Dimitri's words repeated in her head.

"You are the king's mercenary?" she asked slowly.

"Yes." Dimitri's tone held no emotion. "Mainly, I kill the king's enemies for him. I don't consider myself a member of the King's Court because I complete violent deeds for others besides the king, but His Majesty pays me well to keep him my first priority, and to make sure I don't cross him by accepting tasks that go against the Crown."

Sayr watched him. He remained motionless, unreadable.

This couldn't be possible. He'd said he wasn't a part of the King's Court. His position was different. Dimitri couldn't be the king's mercenary. He couldn't be the one she was looking for, the one she needed to kill to earn the life she'd always wanted.

"Does the king have any other mercenaries?" Sayr asked. Maybe the queen had been mistaken. Maybe King Mylan had more than one mercenary, or there was another mercenary besides Dimitri that she was supposed to kill. Anyone besides Dimitri.

He shook his head slowly. "The king only keeps one mercenary. He only needs one to do his most bloody deeds for him."

She looked around the king's quarters to make sure they were alone. No one else could know that he was the king's mercenary, and no one could know that she knew. There would be no getting out if Cordia found out that Sayr had identified the king's mercenary.

Sayr shifted in her seat. She could not lose her composure now. She would find a way out. She would find a way to earn a true position in the Eastern Court without killing Dimitri. She had to find another way.

"I won't push you any further about your position," she said slowly so that he understood every word. "I understand. The Courts, our positions, all of us have been tainted by our duties in some way."

"I have to ask, as your position is close to the king, what do you think of the attacks on Creobe? Do you really believe these rebels are Creobian Elementals?" Sayr asked.

Dimitri inhaled deeply. "The king believes that is the most likely conclusion, but I don't believe it. Creobians are proud, tightly knit people. We pride ourselves on community and self-expression. Creobians would not partake in senseless destruction like this."

"His Majesty believes it's another example of the divide between the seen and unseen elements," Sayr countered. "That they are taking these cities for themselves."

Dimitri shook his head. "I don't believe that. The seen and unseen elements are all accepted in Creobe. There is no separation or prejudice against any of them. There is no reason for any Elemental in Creobe to act out in such a manner."

"Then what do you believe is happening?" Sayr asked.

"I believe these threats are coming from Athar." Dimitri's voice was final. "Just as the king initially believed."

"Why did His Majesty change his mind?"

"Not many people believe there are people living in Athar, so the king was forced to come to another conclusion," he explained. "But neither kingdom has sent anyone into Athar in years, if not decades. And the land across Athar is vast, much bigger than most know. How can we be so sure that there is absolutely no threat, no people coming from there without our knowledge?"

Sayr looked down at her hands, touching her fingers together. "It just doesn't seem possible for anyone to exist in such a place and survive."

Sayr fought against Dimitri's words, and the feeling in the pit of her stomach tugged at her, telling her that he may just be right.

Marenda opened the door to the king's quarters and walked out onto the balcony. She set a breakfast tray down on the table and lowered herself into a seat across from Sayr and Dimitri. Sayr's eyes were twinkling with emotion, and Mar shot a withering glare at Dimitri.

"Can you give us some space?" she asked, her voice cool but sharp.

Dimitri looked over at Sayr, who nodded her approval, and he rose from his seat next to her. He leaned over to whisper in her ear, loud enough to let Marenda hear that he would be right outside the king's quarters if Sayr needed him, before heading for the door. Fury burned Marenda's skin as she watched him leave, overplaying the role of Sayr's glorious protector.

She looked down at the tray of pastries, a cup of fruit, a bowl of oatmeal with browned sugar, a large cup of coffee, and several vials full of different liquids. "I brought you some breakfast, and Callum recommended the medications."

"Thanks, Mar." Her friend smiled at her and reached for the coffee with one hand and a pastry with the other. Her body was stiff, and she grimaced as she leaned back in her seat again.

"You're stiff this morning," Marenda noted. "Have the healers not seen you today?"

Sayr bit into the pastry. "They've been in and out." Crumbs fell onto her lap as she talked with her mouth full. "Every time they come to monitor me, they put me under with some sort of drug. I'm feeling better, though, after every visit. I'm still having some trouble taking full breaths, but most of the pain and discomfort has gone away."

"They should have been able to get rid of these bruises by now," Marenda said. "Why haven't they healed you completely?"

Sayr didn't have an answer. She believed what Marenda had said about the healers and their unusual gifts in healing. After all, she'd mostly recovered in a matter of days when it should have taken her weeks, if not months, to recover to the extent that she had now.

"The king is keeping secrets from us," Marenda said. "I don't trust him."

"Can you fully trust any royal?" Sayr asked, causing Marenda to look away. Things had indeed changed since their arrival in Creobe. Sayr never would have questioned a king or queen before, neither of them had the authority to do so.

"No matter," Marenda shrugged. "We need to get one of these healers alone for questioning. If their abilities could somehow be connected to your own gifts, we need to know everything."

Sayr didn't speak for a long time. She stared at the vials on the table between them, her eyes flickering back and forth in thought. When she did look back at Marenda, there was a new emotion in her eyes.

"I think I may be a Space Elemental." Sayr whispered.

An odd sense of relief washed over Sayr after saying the words aloud. For the first time in her life, she had a lead to what she may be, where her gifts may have come from.

Marenda's brows shot up. "A what?"

Sayr explained what Hoshi had done in Therod, the way she was able to use her gifts. The only parts she deliberately left out were what they spoke about in Dimitri's lesson and Hoshi's vision of Queen Cheralin's exile of the unseen elements in Visaran.

Marenda may have been her best friend, but she was still the Eastern Queen's personal guard, and she wasn't sure where her loyalty lay between the queen and Sayr. She would keep the information to herself until she was certain that Marenda was loyal to her and only her.

"You think you may be… a backwards Space Elemental?" Marenda asked in disbelief.

Sayr picked up another pastry and bit into the flaky bread. "It's the closest tie I've found to my own abilities," she said between bites. "Space Elementals can read the stars and have visions of the past; I have visions of the future. It's not that far of a stretch."

Marenda nodded slowly as if she could see the possible connection, though it was small. The two tried to find some sort of connection to the healer's gifts and one of the elements, but they couldn't think of any element that would cause a person to be able to heal such drastic injuries within minutes.

"How do we find out if that's what you truly are? We need a new plan." Marenda concluded.

Sayr looked away from Marenda and back through the king's quarters, at the door that Dimitri stood outside of, patiently waiting for her to call him back in. This was not supposed to happen. She wasn't supposed to form a bond with anyone in the Western Court, especially not him. She could not fall for the one person she needed to kill. But she couldn't help the pull that brought her closer to him. He had taught her the truth about the continent and about Visaran, and he had been there for her when no one else was.

Was the life that Sayr fought for truly what she wanted? Would the queen really give her a position in Court, revealing what she truly was to the entire kingdom? If everything Dimitri had taught her was true, Her Majesty was more likely to kill Sayr after she had done the queen's bloody deed for her rather than reveal Sayr as an unseen Elemental.

Marenda was right, they needed a new plan. One devised by them; not any royal, official, or member of either Court.

"Alright," Sayr said, resignedly. "But we do this my way. It's not just you and me anymore. Tri has been there for me these past weeks; I want him to be a part of this."

"You want him to know everything?" Marenda's tone was still icy, but there was a hint of worry mixed in.

"Not everything," Sayr answered. "Not yet. Soon. And I will be the one to tell him. If there is anyone in this palace that could give us the information that we want, it's him."

"You've been spending a lot of time with him. And the way he looked at you before he left…" Marenda didn't need to finish her sentence to get her point across.

"And *you've* been spending a lot of time with Callum." Sayr picked at another pastry. "I've seen him following you around the palace like a lovesick puppy."

Marenda immediately went into defense, and she opened her mouth to give any excuse possible, but Sayr stopped her.

"I'm happy for you," she said. "But I'm also worried. Healer or not, he's a part of the Western Court."

"I know," Marenda said. "But I trust him, just as you trust Dimitri. And he's not like the other healers. I would like to visit the herbalist room in the mornings to continue learning remedy healing, but if you need me, I will stay be your side instead—"

"No," Sayr cut her off. "I'm happy to see you doing something for yourself for once. You deserve to have something that is your own."

The door to the king's quarters opened again and the two of them turned to see Willa standing in the doorway. She was her usual picture of grace; coiled hair laid perfectly above her shoulders and a flowing lavender gown floated around her ankles. Behind her, Dimitri remained in the hall, looking in.

"His Majesty is requesting a meeting with his Court. He has asked that the two of you be present, assuming you feel well enough to attend, Lady Sayr."

Sayr slowly pushed herself up from her chair. "I'm all right, we'll follow you."

Marenda rose with her and out of the quarters. Sayr walked up to Dimitri who offered her his arm. She rested a hand on his arm. Marenda remained on her other side, and they followed Willa through the halls.

The royal ballroom was already being prepared for the Harvest Ball. Ribbons swung from chandelier to chandelier in varying shades of red and green to represent the transition of summer to autumn. Tables were being placed around the dance floor with beautiful white lace linens.

Sayr's eyes immediately caught onto the numerous banners strung along the walls of the ballroom. Even the glass wall that led out to the balconies and the stunning mountain view beyond was decorated with alternating banners of the Visarian royal insignia and Creobian royal crest.

"A show of good faith," King Mylan said as he approached the group, observing the banners himself. "My people have been told that we are hosting the Harvest Ball in this palace as a show of a strong alliance forming between our countries. Only those of us within these walls know the true reasons for all of this."

King Mylan addressed his entire Court. "The Visarian royal family has asked that the Harvest Ball be hosted here in Creobe this year, as a show of good faith between our countries since she has offered many troops to aid in our fight against the rebels."

"This isn't as a show of good faith," Marenda spoke before the King's Court. "Her Majesty wants to see the troops for herself in hopes that she can bring us all back to Visaran."

"Precisely," the king admitted. "She and I will discuss the extension of her troops in Creobe, though I doubt she will accept my terms and will likely attempt to take you all back with her during this visit."

"It won't happen," Marenda stated. "Her Majesty struggled to let her troops and the rest of us out of the palace in the first place. She would never have that time extended…for any of us."

Sayr nodded her agreement as she continued to stare at the royal blue Visarian banners. Dimitri had told her everything about the queen's plans to come to Creobe in celebration of the Harvest Ball.

Queen Cheralin would be here in the Western Palace in less than two weeks. So much had changed in so little time; the truth of Visaran that Sayr had uncovered, her knowledge of the six elements and where her own gifts may have come from. It changed everything.

And Dimitri…

She would not follow through with the queen's mission. Sayr's worth was not determined by a single royal. Not when she'd finally seen Dimitri in a new light, and Marenda had uncovered so much information in the medic's level for her, and Everett would understand. Maybe he could bargain for Sayr if she were taken back to Visaran. No matter how much he bent to his mother's will, he would never let the queen actually kill Sayr.

She had become too close with Dimitri, and Marenda too close with Callum, to be able to willingly go through with her mission. When the queen came to the Western Palace, she would face the repercussions of her failure then, but she would never kill Dimitri. She would let him go, let him continue his life here. She would forget about the King's Court; about Dema, and Willa, and Ryon, and thankfully even Lilith—

Lilith.

Sayr looked around, realizing for the first time that the girl was not with the rest of the Court.

"Where is Lilith?" Sayr asked, her tone flat.

Dimitri's arm that Sayr's hand rested on tightened at the mention of her name.

"She has been suspended from her position, pending a trial," the king answered. "I am so very sorry for what happened to you. I admit, I have always known there was a vicious side to her, but her gifts are strong, and she is ambitious. I believed that was where her viciousness came from. She is a…complicated individual, and though it does not make her actions any more acceptable, do understand that she is struggling. I believe bringing you here and putting you in the spotlight made her crumble more than I realized."

"I never wanted the spotlight," Sayr snapped. "I never wanted to come here at all, in fact."

"And it is unfortunate that all of the blame was directed at you for Lilith's shortcomings." His Majesty leaned in closer and whispered ever so quietly, "I will have guards stationed outside your doors from now on until the queen leaves, for your safety. I hope you still remember our arrangement and what I can offer you here in my palace."

Sayr nodded once again but did not speak. Mylan turned from her to stand in the center of the ballroom. "The Harvest Ball will take place on the eve of the half-moon, twelve nights from now. We are rather strung up on time, but I have no doubt that this ball will exceed all of our expectations, and I hope you will all enjoy yourselves as we celebrate a successful Harvest season."

"I will have roles for each of you on the night of the ball, but I will speak with you all individually on the roles I have assigned between now and the night of." Mylan smiled at his Court. "Let us show the Visarian royal family just how well their people have been treated in our kingdom."

Sayr almost laughed aloud. Had the king so quickly forgotten that she had been almost beaten to death not so long ago?

The servants continued preparations for the Harvest Ball, draping curtains of assorted colors to represent the Harvest around windows and balconies and arranging candles in just the right places to reflect against the many chandeliers hanging above.

Willa and Addy met with the orchestra to arrange music, while others left for the kitchens to discuss food. One servant had asked for Marenda's help with Visarian cuisines but skittered off with one withering glare from Mar. It seemed she was intent on staying beside Sayr's side, no matter how many times Sayr said she was all right.

Sayr had been specifically ordered by the king to not help at all. She was to rest and heal as much as possible over the next week and a half before the Visarian royal family arrived. His Majesty was preparing new training lessons for her with Addy, but she was ordered not to partake in any sort of physical activity until the healers permitted her to.

Still, she remained in the ballroom for some time, watching servants and Court members running back and forth as the preparations continued. She had always loved the Harvest Ball.

All guests within the Eastern Palace were always invited to attend. The food and drinks, dresses and suits, and decorations were provided by the people within the City Center. A mass of wealthy officials always attended with their families from farther across the country, but most guests resided either within the palace or the City Center.

A new crowd attending the ball with a twist on Creobian traditions excited her, but she couldn't settle the nervous pit in her stomach. So soon, too soon, she would be forced to face the Eastern Queen once again.

The days before the ball flew by quicker than Sayr would have liked. She was finally able to return to her chambers in the guest hall and Mar returned to her chamber next door.

Sayr would awaken to the sound of Mar's door closing each morning as she returned from the herbalist rooms. Mar would leave at an unreasonable hour in the morning to practice her remedy healing in order to return just before Sayr woke up for the day. When Mar returned, the two would sit on her balcony, wrapped in blankets as she pushed through *The Elemental's History of Magic.*

That morning, she sat on her balcony alone as she read. Mar hadn't returned from the herbalist room at her usual time and Sayr decided to read only one chapter of the book before going to search for her.

She had found an original map of the continent before the Dividing War within the pages of the book. The continent was much bigger before Athar had separated the dead and burned country land in the north from Visaran and Creobe.

Sayr had almost reached the end of the chapter on the first generation of Elementals and the original gifts when Mar burst into her room and hurried out onto the balcony.

"Take this," she ordered as she shoved a vial of liquid into Sayr's palm.

"What is it?" Sayr asked and rolled the vial over in her hand.

The liquid inside was the color of dirt after a rainstorm. Mar had been practicing hard on her remedies, but Sayr wasn't certain that each remedy was accurate, and the color of this vial looked anything but appetizing.

"It's supposed to help with your bruising," Mar answered excitedly. "I made it myself. Go on, make sure you drink it all."

Sayr eyed her suspiciously, but Mar just nodded her encouragement. She popped off the cork and sniffed the liquid inside. It smelled like aged ginger and something earthy. She tried not to think too hard about the ingredients inside the vial as she quickly tipped her head back and drank.

She coughed as the liquid went down her throat, it was surprisingly spicy.

Mar grabbed her face when she swallowed and stared hard at her. Her eyes grew wide as teacup saucers, and she grinned almost madly. She rushed inside Sayr's room and came back out holding a small mirror, bringing it up to Sayr's face.

Sayr gasped and touched her cheek that had been an ugly shade of green just minutes ago. Her complexion wasn't completely back to normal, but the green bruising on her face had vanished almost completely, and her cheek and nose no longer felt sore.

"Your ribs took the brunt of the damage so they won't heal as quickly, but at least your face should be completely healed in time for the Harvest Ball." Mar struggled to contain her excitement over her successful remedy.

"This is amazing," Sayr swooned as she continued running her fingers over her cheek and nose. "Thank you, Mar."

Mar sat with Sayr for the remainder of the morning, ordering a light breakfast of fruit, cheese, and thin slices of meat with crackers. She brought a blanket out from Sayr's room and wrapped it around her body while they ate. Sayr needed to meet with Dimitri in the library in less than an hour for their first lesson since the incident with Lilith, so she ate quickly.

A small twinge of excitement sparked through her at the thought. Dimitri had shown a completely new side of him since she'd been injured. He had stayed by her side for days, catering to her every need and want while she was recovering. Even after she had recovered enough to return to her chambers, he took every opportunity to come check on her. He had become almost protective of her as if ensuring no harm would come to her again.

She had already decided she could never kill him, but every time she thought of how furious Queen Cheralin would be when Sayr refused her, fear coursed through her body, making her veins tighten.

"Mar." Sayr looked over at her best friend, the sudden excitement now gone and replaced with dread. "Have you ever killed anyone before?"

Mar's hand stilled, a cube of cheese halfway to her mouth. She looked at Sayr warily before dropping the cheese.

"I never told you?" Her voice was filled with hesitation.

"Told me what?" Sayr asked.

Mar drew the blanket tighter around her body and drew her knees to her chest. "The first time I had ever killed someone, I had just been assigned as Her Majesty's personal guard. I was assigned the position for not even two full weeks, so another guard and I rotated shifts until Her Majesty decided that I was ready to take on the role by myself."

"One night, a group of Elementals had broken into the palace. I don't know how they got in; some guards believed they climbed the cliffs near the gardens. I was off duty that night but came running as quickly as I could when the bells rang in the barracks. I had been taken through the secret passageways in my training as a personal guard, so I arrived quicker than all the others in the barracks. By the time I reached the Royal Wing, one of them was trying to pick the lock to the library. I think they thought it was one of the royal bedrooms."

Mar dropped her face into her hands as she continued.

"I was so scared that they would reach Her Majesty, or Everett, or Lanni that I didn't think before I burned the man. I'll never forget his screams as he ignited into flames. There was barely anything left of him by the time the flames were extinguished, and I'd torched three of the royal portraits in the process. The halls smelled of burning flesh for days afterwards. The other traitors were caught and executed, but Her Majesty was most furious with me for stinking up the Royal Wing and ruining heirlooms of the royal family."

Mar lifted her face from her hands, a new heaviness in her eyes.

"I've had to kill plenty after that. Her Majesty has a lengthy line of enemies, believe it or not, and she sends me to take care of her unwanted business when those enemies come to the palace. I wish I didn't have to, but I suppose I knew what I was getting myself into as her personal guard. You do whatever it takes to protect the queen."

"Why did you accept the position?" Sayr asked.

She remembered when Mar had been promoted, and she had seemed so happy to be the queen's new personal guard. Neither of them discussed the requirements of the position and they had grown so busy in their own duties that they rarely ever discussed such topics like death.

"I wanted so badly to prove myself as a warrior," Mar explained. "I was the top trainee in my class, but it never felt like enough. I knew I was meant for something better, a bigger challenge. When Her Majesty came to me to request me as a personal guard, I never entertained the thought of refusing the position."

Sayr nodded. She understood how influential the queen could be. After all, she had agreed to pose as an apprentice and hide her abilities for years just to please Her Majesty and remain in the palace. She had even agreed to come to Creobe under Her Majesty's orders and stain her own hands with blood for the queen. She could never put blame on Mar for doing the same.

She thought of Dimitri's position as a mercenary. His position was so much like Mar's, though he was not a personal guard of the king, and he could come and go as he pleased without worrying about returning to the palace in time for his shift. Mar had been given the roles of personal guard and murderer in one, without ever realizing it.

Sayr stood to sit closer to her friend for comfort but stopped before she could take a step.

The familiar pull against her core began to grow, until her ribs felt like they were going to snap again. Her heart raced in her chest, a cold sweat sliding down her back.

Her knees became weak, and she stumbled into the small table. She looked up at Mar, but stars blocked her vision.

Then everything went dark.

Sayr squeezed her eyes shut as nausea rolled over her in waves. She felt as if she were being strung in all different directions. A new sort of pain coursed through her body, and she screamed aloud, though she heard nothing.

There was no sound. Everything was black. Only pain and nausea as she was flung into oblivion.

Then everything stopped all at once. Sayr tumbled onto the ground on all fours, vomit burning her throat. Her hands pressed into the cold, hard ground and she looked at the blurry environment around her.

Her vision began to clear as she looked around her. She was no longer sitting on her balcony with Marenda.

She was crouched on all fours, kneeling in front of stairs made of cracked stone. Looking further up, she spotted an old stone throne placed on the crumbling dais at the top of the stairs.

A young man sat on the throne, hiding in the shadows.

Sayr looked up at the sky, or the parts of the sky that she could see through the large chunks of the ceiling that were missing above her. Sunlight shone through the open ceiling, radiating the dust that floated through the crumbling building surrounding her.

Sayr quickly looked back at the man on the throne.

"There she is," the man on the throne cooed. "I was starting to think you wouldn't be coming back."

Sayr stared at him while he stood from the old throne, its stones cracked and dull.

The pain and nausea had vanished. Sayr felt nothing. No pain, no emotion, no nausea, only the cold stone against her palms. This did not feel like one of her visions, it was as if she were part of a dream.

Sayr watched him closely as he stepped down the dais towards her. He had fire-red hair, similar to Addy's, but darker. He tilted his head and studied Sayr kneeling on the floor before him.

"A traveler, indeed," the man said from the shadows.

"Who are you?" Sayr's voice sounded strange, echoing as if she was speaking from far away. "Where am I?"

The young man lifted a hand to stop her.

"All in good time, dearest. You will learn all you need to know soon." A small grin grew on his lips as he looked down at her.

He continued descending the dais slowly, step by step, as he spoke.

"Where are you now?" he asked. "Physically, I mean. When I send you back, where will you end up?"

"I'm sorry?" Sayr asked.

She looked back through the broken ceiling at the sky. Red, yellow, and brown leaves swayed above, covering the sky.

"Is this still Creobe?" she asked, more to herself than the man. "Am I still in Creobe?"

"Creobe," the man noted. "Indeed. Then I suspect you're still in the Royal Sector. In the Western Palace."

Sayr lowered her head to glare at the boy as he finally descended the stairs. "How do you know where I am?" Sayr asked. "How do you know about me?"

The boy's lips stretched into a proud smile. He walked ever so closer to her.

"You've been chasing us for quite some time," he mused. "But what happens when you finally catch us? When you can touch us? When you can touch me?"

He bent low so the two of them were face to face. Sayr could finally see his features, pale grey eyes, white eyelashes, high cheekbones. He looked maybe a few years older than her, but he spoke with a tone of aged authority.

He lifted a hand and Sayr caught sight of the black leather gloves on each hand. He removed a black glove from one hand. His fingers stretched out to touch Sayr's face, and she flinched away.

"Wait—" She didn't want this stranger touching her, but he ignored her protests.

"I will see you again soon, dearest," he murmured, and his fingers met her cheek.

The moment the boy's hand grazed her cheek, the nausea and pain returned. Everything went black again as the nausea and pain overtook her. Sayr's body felt foreign as her limbs stretched in every direction and her heartbeat raced. She tried to take a sharp breath, but she couldn't breathe. She reeled in pain as she tumbled into nothingness.

All at once the pain and nausea ended. Sayr's senses came back to her slowly. She could feel the tingling sensation of her limbs, the ringing in her ears, and the heaviness of her tongue.

As the pain and nausea finally ceased, she opened her eyes. She was back on her balcony. Mar's face took up most of her sight, a bit of blue sky behind her. Sayr looked to her side, she was lying on the balcony floor.

"Are you all right?" Mar's tone was thick with worry.

"What happened?" Sayr's senses were all coming back in phases, her tongue still couldn't form words properly.

"I'm not entirely sure." Mar scooped Sayr and lifted her upright, placing her back in her chair. "You must have fainted and fallen out of your chair. You were only out for a few minutes."

"I think I just had another vision," she said, trying to recall what she'd just seen.

Mar's face flooded with concern, and a touch of fear.

"Your visions are coming to you unannounced more often?" she asked. "I thought you were gaining control over them."

"I don't know what's happening." Sayr touched the place on her cheek where the man's touch had grazed her skin.

He had looked eerily familiar, but Sayr couldn't place where she'd ever seen him before. And as soon as he'd touched her, the vision had ended, and she'd been sent back to reality.

Was it all part of her own gifts wanting her to see what she had seen, or had he been able to force her out of her own vision? And who was he? Where was he?

When was he?

Did he exist now or had Sayr had a vision of the future?

Sayr's throat began to tighten as panic took over her. Her breathing quickened and every part of her body shook violently. She could not start having visions out of nowhere. The Western Court was still unaware of her true gifts, passing out from a vision in front of them would set their suspicions on her. For now, she could likely blame it on her injuries, but what if this continued even after she returned to Visaran?

"I think I'm losing my mind," Sayr said between panicked breaths. She couldn't catch enough air in her lungs and her brain felt foggy, as if reality was slipping away from her.

Warmth spread through her palms, and she looked down at her hands that were clutched tightly in Mar's.

"It's alright," Mar soothed, trying to calm the hysteria that was rising in Sayr. "Everything is all right. We will deal with this. We will control it. I'm here."

Sayr nodded, though she was still hyperventilating. Mar made a show of breathing deeply and slowly and Sayr followed Mar's breathing. The shaking ceased and her heart rate began to slow again as she breathed in and out.

Mar was right. It had happened only this once. She would worry further if it happened again, but for now she had more important tasks to worry about. She would control it if it ever happened again. She had to.

She wouldn't forget the vision, though. She couldn't recall any memory or encounter with the man. The way he had spoken about her and her whereabouts made her look out into the mountains surrounding the palace, as if he were out there behind the trees, watching her.

25

$\mathcal{S}$ayr sat on her bed, waiting for the healer to arrive. She had called a healer to check over her injuries, claiming she'd woken up with excruciating pain in her neck and back.

A knock sounded at her door and Sayr straightened. "Come in!" she shouted.

The doors to her room opened and a healer stepped in. "Good morning, Lady Sayr," he called to her and entered the room, leaving the door open. "How are you feeling this morning?"

"I'm hoping to feel much better once we're done with you." Sayr's smile turned wicked, and her eyes flicked back to the door.

The door shut with a thud and the healer jumped. He turned back towards the door, where Marenda had hidden behind it. She smiled at him, too. Her left hand ignited in flames and her right held one of Sayr's daggers.

"We have some questions for you," Sayr told the healer and rose from the bed.

"W-what do you want from me?" The healer's voice shook almost as much as his hands.

Sayr walked over toward the fireplace. "Why don't you have a seat?" she said and claimed a chair for herself.

The healer looked from Sayr to Marenda. Marenda stepped closer, no longer smiling, and twirled the dagger between her fingers. The healer quickly went to the loveseat and sat down.

"What's your name?" Sayr asked the healer.

"Antoine," he answered. Sayr sprawled across the couch across from Antoine and Marenda stood behind her, the two a menacing force.

"We want to know about the healers, Antoine," Sayr said. She kept her voice calm and soothing. "We want to know how they are able to heal the way they do."

Antoine was already shaking his head before Sayr finished. "We are not permitted to speak about our abilities."

"And why is that?" Marenda asked. She focused on the flames dancing over her hand as she spoke.

"Our gifts are not common practice on the continent," Antoine whispered. "We are not welcome in Visaran at all, we are lucky to be welcome here."

"Do you consider yourself an unseen Elemental, then?" Sayr asked.

"No, we are different. Something else entirely." Antoine's breathing quickened and he shook his head harder. "I should not be speaking of this. They could kill me if they knew what I was saying."

"Who would kill you?" Marenda pushed.

"The other healers," Antoine admitted. "Our gifts are allowed here as long as we keep them secret. Only the Western Court knows about us, and our king forces us to keep quiet as not to start a war between the kingdoms."

"Why would he be worried about starting a war with Visaran?" Sayr leaned forward on the couch. "He personally went to Visaran looking for aid. The queen's own troops and Court members are here in his palace. Why would he allow all that if he thought war could be coming?"

Antoine just shook his head again. "Not war between Visaran and Creobe. The king hopes that his secrecy on these gifts will persuade Her Majesty into an alliance. He fears war from the north."

Sayr almost stopped breathing. Her knees became weak, and she thanked the elements that she was already sitting. "The king still believes there is a threat in Athar," she whispered and turned to Marenda. "His Majesty is preparing for a war against those in Athar."

"How is that possible?" Marenda's gaze turned from Sayr to Antoine. "Athar is in ruins. No one could survive living up there for long."

"I do not know," Antoine said. "I just know what I have been told, what reason I have been given to keep my healing abilities secret from anyone outside of this palace."

Sayr's head raced with possibilities. Dimitri had warned that the threat may be coming from Athar. The raids had begun in the northern section of Creobe.

"But His Majesty had told me he thought these threats were coming from his own people," Sayr said more to Marenda than Antoine. "He thought they were dividing between the seen and unseen elements once again."

Marenda looked down at Sayr. "Don't we know by now how good royals are at lying?"

Marenda looked back up at Antoine. "You have told us nothing about your gifts. The information you gave us is only about the king and the supposed threat in the north, which is why we are here. You have not given anything away to us that you are prohibited from saying, and we will keep it that way. For now. If you tell anyone what we have asked of you or that you came here for anything more than a check up on Sayr, we will tell the king what we know and exactly who told us. Do you understand?"

Antoine nodded. He hadn't stopped shaking since he spotted Sayr's dagger and Marenda's flames. "I understand."

"Good." Marenda smiled much more pleasantly. "You may go now."

The two girls watched the healer scurry to the door. Once he was gone, they looked at each other with a million unspoken words.

"It seems there really are gifts outside the natural elements," Marenda said and studied Sayr. "There are even more gifts besides your own."

Autumn had quickly set in throughout the mountains in the Royal Sector. Leaves floated through the air, zipping past the cut-out windows of the palace.

Sayr and Marenda walked back to their chambers from the armory. The healers had permitted Sayr to continue light training, and Addy had replaced Lilith as Sayr's trainer. While she was nowhere near as ferocious as Lilith, Addy didn't let Sayr cut any corners in her training. And now that Marenda insisted on going to training with her, Sayr practically had two instructors as they both commented on her stamina and skill.

"Your legs aren't tight when you take your stance." Marenda elbowed Sayr lightly as they walked. "And your core needs to be tight when you strike."

"I'm, sorry, I've been more focused on trying to stay *alive* during my trainings," Sayr refuted. "Give me a break."

Marenda chuckled as they climbed the steps to their guest level. Sayr kept her head up as she climbed, lifting her foot to the next step.

Her foot went completely through the staircase, and she fell straight down into darkness. Sayr tried to scream but no noise came out. She squeezed her eyes shut, trying to shield herself from the blinding light of a vision.

When she opened her eyes, she was already back in her chamber, standing in the middle of her bedroom.

A pounding knock came from the bedroom door, and she jolted around to the door.

"I have authority to enter these chambers." Cordia's muffled voice came from the hallway. "You must let us in!"

"She is not here, milady." Another voice—a guard, Sayr presumed—answered Cordia. "There is no need to enter these empty chambers."

"We will enter these chambers. Whether the girl is in there or not, we shall see for ourselves."

That voice.

That voice turned Sayr to ice. She did not breathe, did not even blink, as she listened to Queen Cheralin argue with the guard right outside her door.

"I order you as the Queen of Visaran." The Eastern Queen's voice vibrated through the room. "Open this door at once."

There was a pause of silence before the jingling of keys came from the door.

Sayr thawed from her spot in the middle of the room and dashed for the balcony doors. She swung them open and dashed over the threshold, the wind whipping her hair around her face. She slammed the doors shut behind her and leaned against the thick wood.

Get me out of here, her thoughts screamed in her head. *Get me out of here, get me out of here!*

Sayr stumbled forward, gripping the stone railing until her knuckles turned white. The slamming of a door came from inside her room. Her Majesty was in Sayr's room.

"Sayr!" The queen's scream raged through her chambers and out to the balcony. "Sayr!"

Sayr fell to the ground, her eyes squeezed shut. The queen's voice rang through her body, through her soul. She curled her arms and legs inwards, close to her body.

"Sayr." A faint voice this time. "Sayr!"

Sayr gasped as her eyes flung open. No breeze swept through her hair. She was no longer in her chambers. She stood on the stairs again. Marenda stood inches away from her, clutching Sayr by the shoulders.

"What in the elements?" Marenda started.

Sayr's legs and arms tingled numbly, and her head still felt foggy, but she grabbed Marenda by the arm and tugged her back down a step.

"The queen is in the palace." The words shot out of Sayr in a rushed whisper. "She is in my chambers. We need to go; we need to hide."

"Her Majesty is here?" Marenda's eyes widened and she looked up towards their guest level.

"Yes." Sayr's voice was frantic, her hysteria began taking over her dulled senses. "I can't let her find me, not yet. Please, Mar."

Marenda's brows tightened and her jaw twitched. Sayr could see the internal struggle within Marenda; protect her best friend or go to her queen.

The flame in Marenda's eyes settled as she looked at her best friend.

"Let's go," she said quietly, and they descended back down the stairs, away from their queen.

Sayr stood at the foot of her bed with her eyes pinned to the large box laid on top of it, the lid abandoned on the floor. Inside the box, laid neatly in deep purple paper, was the most beautiful dress she had ever seen. She gently lifted the gown out of the box and held it up to examine it fully.

The gown was blush pink with long sheer sleeves. The sheer fabric of the sleeves fell all the way to the floor at the wrists. Small white flowers and pearls rimmed the heart-shaped neckline and decorated the bodice all the way down to the pink tule of the skirt.

Turning it over, Sayr saw the dress had barely any material covering her back, it would reveal all the way down to her hips. Pearls lined the back from the hipline all the way down to the flowing train of the dress.

"Pretty," Marenda commented as she closed the door to her chambers and walked closer to inspect the dress. "Though I'd say it looks more like a gown to celebrate spring, not autumn."

"Who is it from?" Marenda asked, feeling the soft fabric between her fingers.

"The king," Sayr answered and gestured to the box. "He left a note inside."

Marenda reached into the box and pulled out a small, handwritten note laying at the bottom.

Lady Sayr,

I hope the gown is to your liking. I feel it is the least I can do after the events of the last few weeks. I spoke with Dema on your measurements and had it specially tailored for you, and I would much appreciate you wearing this beautiful gown to tomorrow night's Harvest Ball. From your lessons with Dimitri, I have no doubt that you are aware that this shade of pink represents the element of spirit. I look forward to seeing you in the gown tomorrow night.

Mylan

"The element of spirit?" Marenda repeated, aghast. "He wants you to wear the color of Spirit Elementals in front of Queen Cheralin. What is he thinking?"

"He's going to tell her," Sayr whispered. "The king is going to tell Queen Cheralin that he believes I am a Spirit Elemental and will not be returning to Visaran."

It was all truly happening. If everything that he and Dimitri had said about the unseen elements was true, Queen Cheralin had no claim to any unseen Elementals within her country. The king believed she had relinquished those rights when she exiled and killed her own people to rid Visaran of unseen Elementals. Mylan would want to show that he is aware of Sayr's gifts by having her wear the gown in front of the queen.

"But you are not a Spirit Elemental, Sayr," Marenda argued and dropped the note. "This is going too far. All this will do is anger Her Majesty more and make it worse for you when we return."

Sayr chose her words slowly, carefully. "Do you want to return to Visaran?"

Marenda opened her mouth to answer, then closed it. Her eyes drifted between the dress and the note several times.

"Do I have a choice?" she asked. "Do either of us have a choice?"

She finally looked over at Sayr and that look on her face told Sayr exactly what she had meant. They had both found a sort of comfort here. Sayr had learned more about herself, and her gifts here than she had in seventeen years in Visaran. And Marenda was perfecting remedy healing in order to become a remedy healer herself. And they were both growing closer with members of the King's Court with each passing day.

The door to Sayr's chambers opened and the two turned to see Dema pop through the doorway.

"Pardon me," she called softly into the room. "I have a healer with me to check on Sayr's injuries. His Majesty is hoping you are completely healed by now."

Marenda stepped back and began placing, or rather shoving, the gown back into its box. Sayr hopped onto the bed and let Dema, and the healer look over her injuries. She had indeed healed almost completely since the incident with Lilith and hadn't seen the girl inside the palace since.

Marenda returned to her own chambers as the healer inspected Sayr. The bruising all over her body had disappeared a few days after Marenda had given her the vial that she'd made herself, and she no longer felt sore, only a bit stiff at times. The healer noted that her injuries were much improved and that she could be considered at full health once again.

Once he had given her his approval to attend the ball, the healer left. Dema remained in the room, wringing her hands nervously as she had been doing since she arrived, grounded to her spot near the bed.

"What is it?" Sayr asked lightly.

Dema bit her lip nervously. "The Visarian royal family has arrived."

Sayr sat on her bed, waiting for Dema to say more. When she didn't, Sayr remembered her vision. She wasn't supposed to know the royal family was in the palace yet.

She jumped from her place on the bed. "What? When did they arrive? Are they here on the guest level?"

Dema put her hands out as if to stop Sayr from running out of the room. "You cannot go looking for them. I wasn't supposed to tell you anything of their arrival."

Sayr halted. "I won't go looking for them."

She stood stunned, surprised that Dema would assume her reaction was one of excitement and not fear.

She needed to stay as far away from the royal family as possible until tomorrow. She could not risk Her Majesty finding her before then and keeping Sayr within her grasp until the Harvest Ball, and even after when the queen returned to the Eastern Palace. She needed to know where the royal family was staying, so that she could stay as far away from that level of the palace as possible. She wanted to see Ev, to talk to him, but not until the ball when she could sneak him away from his mother.

"You must be careful from now on, Sayr," Dema urged. "Both royals are going to try to keep you as close to them as possible. His Majesty has already ordered members of his Court to keep close to you until the Visarian royals leave to ensure that you do not leave with them. These next three days will be filled with many fights among the royals."

"Why are you telling me all of this?" Sayr asked. "You are part of His Majesty's Court. You have no loyalty to me or the Eastern Queen."

The young girl gave Sayr a sympathetic look, as if Sayr was the child between the two.

"I see much of myself in you. You are a good person, but I fear that other's manipulations of you will affect you more than you know. There are bad people within both Courts, I just hope that you find the ones that you can truly trust. Those who will not use you for your abilities."

Sayr's nerves ignited as Dema finished speaking. "You mean my abilities as a Spirit Elemental?"

Dema gave her a knowing look. "Your abilities, whatever they may be."

How could she know? Sayr's thoughts screamed.

This young girl who lived in the palace as a lady's maid. She was a member of the Creobian Court, but not the King's Court. How could she know what was being said by the king behind closed doors?

Sayr had feared that someone would find out her secret, that someone in this palace would uncover what she truly was, yet nothing swayed her to refute what Dema already knew. An odd sense of relief washed over her. If someone were to find out about her, at least it was Dema; sweet, quiet Dema.

"How do you know?" Sayr whispered.

"You have been keeping many secrets, but His Majesty has kept secrets of his own," Dema admitted. "After the Harvest Ball, once the Visarian royal family departs, I'm certain His Majesty will tell you everything. For now, be patient, and I promise that your secret is safe with me."

Sayr's chest tightened, and her eyes burned with tears that threatened to spill down her face.

Someone finally knew.

Her body took over as she reached for Dema and pulled her into a tight hug. The young girl wrapped her own arms around Sayr and hugged ger back.

"Thank you, Dema," Sayr cried as the two remained embraced.

Sayr carefully plucked the rollers out of her hair and curled the strands through her fingers. Marenda had carefully heated each roller for her and listened to her directions on how to roll small pieces of hair around the rollers and fasten them to her head with pins.

Sayr had been giddy with excitement all day. Her excited nerves hadn't just been for the ball, though. She'd received a letter from Julen this morning stating that he'd found a lead on the whereabouts of her father and requested her to meet him in the Department of Records at noon two days from today. Julen had signed the letter, but she knew who it was from as soon as she read the first short, blunt sentence.

She could barely contain her happiness. She had come to Creobe with only one intention, and yet her mission had spiraled and morphed into a series of plots for herself. She had found more about herself in the past few months than she had in seventeen years, and she was only beginning to scratch the surface of who she was.

A key jostled in the chamber's door lock and Marenda entered the room. Ever since Her Majesty had tried to find Sayr in her chambers, Marenda had insisted she be given a key to the room in case of any emergency.

Marenda had gone to have her braids redone for the ball last night, and after six hours of meticulous handwork, she'd returned with her beautiful red and black braids nice and sleek. She'd styled her own braids into a half-bun, leaving the bottom braids down to flow along her back and the few strands in front to frame her face.

She was already dressed in a beautiful, fitted gown. The bodice of the gown melted from darkest black to a burnt orange at the waist. The skirt was made of soft red silk. She looked as if she were made entirely of autumn flames herself.

Sayr finished unfastening the rollers and twisting her hair, setting the style into soft waves, much softer than her usual style.

Marenda and Sayr each darkened their lashes with charcoal and applied different makeup to their lips and cheeks to brighten their features. Once her hair and makeup were both finished, Sayr began to undress and lightly stepped into the gown His Majesty had gifted her.

The blush gown fit Sayr's form perfectly. The beaded bodice revealed her neck and collarbones while remaining modest. The sheer sleeves were elegant and light, freeing her arms for moving and dancing. The lines of pearls magnified the curves of her body as they stretched and swirled all over the dress.

A servant had brought her a pair of pearl-white slippers to go with the outfit, practical but beautiful. When she finished dressing, Marenda fastened the pearl buttons at her hips that made up the back of the dress.

"It's beautiful," Marenda remarked as she stared at the dress, then back up at Sayr. "You look beautiful, Sayr."

Sayr smiled at her best friend. "I look nothing compared to you. You look like the flames of the setting sun come to life."

Marenda snorted, averting her eyes from Sayr in embarrassment. "You're becoming too poetic for my taste."

Sayr let out a small laugh and turned to look at the two of them in the mirror. She linked her arm with Marenda's as they stared at one another's reflection.

"Will you have to be with Her Majesty throughout the night?" Sayr asked quietly.

Though they still remained in Creobe, it seemed their roles in the Eastern Palace were sneaking up on them quickly as the inevitable reacquaintance with Queen Cheralin crept near.

Sayr wasn't so sure she wanted either of them to return to their roles; living under someone else's domain, being at other's beck and calls, training and serving for such long hours each day that they barely had enough time for themselves.

She had experienced freedom here in Creobe.

Yes, she was still trapped in this Court for now, but she had left the palace on her own terms without guards watching over her. She had slept in on long mornings and wandered through the halls of the palace without the harsh looks and whispers that she had become accustomed to for so many years. Other than Lilith, she had been treated mostly with respect and kindness, she had developed true relationships here in Creobe. The thought of leaving all of that behind so soon made her throat tighten with sadness.

"No," Marenda answered.

Her somber expression seemed to tell Sayr that the exact same thoughts were swimming through her mind as well. "I've met with Ajax; he says two other guards have taken my role as personal guard during my absence. Apparently, the queen intends on keeping them during her visit and hasn't called for me to return yet."

She turned towards Sayr, and the usual, cocky smirk returned to her face. "I guess we'll see what the queen has in store for us both when we see her."

Sayr threw her friend a reassuring smile and squeezed her arm. "Let's go."

26

The ballroom was already crowded with people talking with one another, eating at the tables around the outskirts of the dancefloor, and dancing in the center of the commotion. A large band played different tunes of whimsical music that rang throughout the ballroom and out into the halls. The doors of the exterior glass wall had been opened to let guests out onto the large, multi-level balcony outside.

Air Elementals were hard at work during the ball to let tiny amounts of mountain air inside to keep the ballroom from becoming hot and stuffy, but not too much to have the guests catching a chill.

Waxless candles burned in the chandeliers high above by Fire Elementals lingering around the room, igniting the large room in jumping golden light.

Marenda and Sayr entered the ballroom together, taking everything in all at once. The banners blew lightly in the faint breeze through the room as if they, too, were dancing to the thrumming music from the band.

The smells of the food swam high above the crowds of people and made both of their mouths water instantly. Servants weaved through the crowds of guests with silver trays of small plates and different drinks.

A servant approached the two girls lingering on the outskirts of the crowd with a tray of long flutes filled with bubbly golden liquid. Marenda grabbed two glasses, thanking the servant, and turned towards Sayr.

"You know I don't drink," Sayr scolded, eyeing the two drinks in Marenda's hand.

Marenda instantly gulped down the first drink in her hand.

"I'm well aware," she said as she took a long sip from the second glass.

Sayr let out a laugh. The fullest, happiest laugh she had let out in a long, long time.

She and Marenda walked further around the ballroom. Sayr plucked a small dish of cheese pastry from another servant's tray as they walked. They continued to linger at the edge of the dance floor, watching the many guests dance through perfectly choreographed dances. Many guests watching clapped along to the quickening tunes of one song, and Marenda and Sayr clapped along as well.

They shuffled their feet as the beat of the song grew quicker and more intense until they were inevitably spinning one another. A loud laugh belted from Sayr as Mar almost tripped over the train of Sayr's gown. Marenda pulled Sayr into the dancing crowd as they continued to spin and spin.

"We don't know this dance," Sayr laughed.

"Just keep spinning to the beat of the music," Marenda shouted over the growing beats.

The girls took turns spinning one another around the dance floor, switching leads with every spin. Marenda took the lead next and lifted Sayr up off her feet, taking a full spin around the floor. Sayr howled with laughter and closed her eyes as she spun.

The music began to slow and fade as Marenda dropped Sayr back onto the ground and she opened her eyes once again. The rest of the dancers clapped as the music faded to a stop and Marenda and Sayr both gave a playful bow to one another.

Marenda's eyes left Sayr's face and locked on something behind her. Sayr turned to see Callum and Addy talking at the edge of the crowd, Callum's gaze locked on Marenda.

Addy wore a white lace gown; the corseted bodice revealed her neckline and shoulders, and the long thin sleeves flowed over her arms to her wrists. Callum's suit was an opposite depiction of Addy, deep black and trimmed with delicate white lace on the cuffs and lapels.

Sayr smiled and turned back to Marenda, who was still frozen in place. Her eyes remained locked on Callum.

"It's a good thing you've had one dance to practice," Sayr teased. She stepped out of the way to clear a path towards Callum.

Marenda's eyes finally looked back at Sayr, the question in her eyes clear.

"I'll be okay," Sayr reassured her. "Go. I've got someone to find, myself."

Marenda flashed a knowing grin at Sayr and quickly pulled Sayr into a brief hug. "Are you sure?" she asked.

"Of course," Sayr answered. "Go."

Marenda gave her one more grateful smile before walking off the dance floor towards Callum. Sayr watched as the two of them took in one another. If Marenda embodied the flames of the setting sun, Callum was the night sky that enveloped those flames.

Elements, she was becoming too poetic.

Sayr gave one turn around the ballroom, quickly glancing through the surrounding crowds. They'd easily spotted Addy with Callum, but she hadn't caught sight of Willa in the crowds or Tomas or Ryon around the ballroom. She stopped pretending to act curious about their whereabouts as an excuse to look for Dimitri, but she hadn't spotted him yet, either.

A young man with shaggy blond hair approached her in the crowds, offering his hand for a dance. Sayr took his hand as the music started up again and a new, softer tune played through the ballroom.

The young man led her through the different steps of the dance, pulling her gracefully to his side as they danced around other couples on the dance floor. Sayr giggled as they danced and twirled around the ballroom.

The music and the dancing had made her giddy with so much happiness that she laughed and smiled and danced and danced through each song.

After several songs and different dance partners, Sayr decided it was time to take a break.

She weaved through the crowd to the outskirts of the dance floor to catch her breath. She leaned against the wall and watched the people dancing to the never-ending music. She watched as couples flirted shamelessly with one another in the corners of the ballroom, children ran through the crowds chasing one another and laughing, and servants wandered through the crowds with unlimited trays of food and drinks.

Sayr caught the smallest glimpse of Marenda and Callum dancing in the middle of the dance floor through the crowds of people and she smiled, resting her head on the wall as her breathing slowed once again.

Several dances had passed before she peeled herself off the wall. She straightened herself, brushing a hand over her gown, and continued to walk through the crowds. She had made it to the main entrance of the ballroom just in time to catch Dimitri make his entrance.

Dimitri was dressed in a charcoal black suit. His hair was neatly styled, and his suit jacket was decorated with a blush pink handkerchief in the breast pocket, the exact same color of Sayr's gown. He took in the ballroom, assessing the crowds, before turning to look down at the girl on his arm.

Dema.

Dema was at Dimitri's side, her arm linked with his. She wore a beautiful sage green gown with pink and white flowers decorating the bodice, the same shade of pink as Dimitri's handkerchief.

She looked so small next to Dimitri. So innocent next to the mercenary towering over her small frame. Yet she did not look afraid as she looked around the ballroom, one arm resting at Dimitri's elbow. Dema took in the ballroom, eyes wide in amazement, before she smiled up at him.

Dimitri returned the look with a smile of his own before he looked up from Dema and turned to take in the rest of the ball.

His eyes met Sayr's.

He froze as he took her in. His eyes roamed from her face to her hair to the gown that hugged her body and back up to her face. A different smile spread across his lips, and he took a few steps toward her, pulling Dema with him as if he had forgotten she was on his arm.

Sayr walked towards them as well, meeting them halfway. She held her hands close to her body as she approached. Her eyes took Dimitri in fully, then Dema.

Dema peered up at Sayr, then at Dimitri, and back at Sayr. She smiled sheepishly at Sayr before taking a step back and releasing her grip on his arm.

Dimitri barely seemed to notice as his eyes remained locked on Sayr.

"You look beautiful," he said, his voice heavy with emotion.

"Thank you," Sayr smiled. "You clean up rather nice, yourself."

She glanced briefly at Dema again. "I wasn't aware that you knew my lady's maid."

Dimitri finally looked back at Dema, as if just remembering that she was there. "Yes. I'm sorry I haven't made any introductions, though the two of you already know each other. Sayr, Dema is my sister."

Sayr's eyes widened as she looked back at Dema, still standing a step behind Dimitri.

The similarities all hit her all at once. How could she not have noticed?

The matching hair, the same eyes—only Dema's was a deep brown instead of light hazel, their similar face shapes, both of their names even started with the same letter, for element's sake! Though Dema stood over a foot shorter than Dimitri, the resemblance of the two was uncanny when they stood side-by-side.

Dema had mentioned that she had a brother that worked in the palace months ago. And Dimitri had told Sayr about his family, his sister, in the king's quarters while he looked after her. Sayr had never made the connection that the two of them were referring to each other.

"I had no idea," Sayr whispered, both breathless from the news and at the information about her that both of them held.

Dema had revealed that she knew of Sayr's true gifts. Maybe not what they were exactly, but she knew that they were not Elemental gifts. Had she shared that information with her brother?

Dema must have seen the panic rising in Sayr's face and she softly shook her head.

Did she know what Sayr was thinking? That she feared Dema had given her away to a member of the King's Court, even if he was her brother?

"I'm sorry I didn't tell you earlier," Dimitri said quietly, bringing her attention back to him. "As you know, my position in the palace can be dangerous and I didn't want to bring any of that danger in Dema's direction. When I brought her to the palace for the position as a lady's maid, we made a plan not to speak to one another in public. We were to act as if we did not know each other, for her protection. I never wanted an enemy of mine coming to the palace in search of me and finding my sister instead."

"We still meet secretly each week," Dema continued for Dimitri. "It would be miserable being so close to one another and never getting the opportunity to see or speak with each other."

She looked over at Sayr again. "When you told me that you were having daily lessons with Tri, I was truly surprised because he hadn't mentioned these lessons to me when he and I met a few days prior. In truth, I was afraid for him and you. You seemed kind, but you were new, and Visarian. I was afraid for what may happen between the two of you if you were to continue these lessons, as I'm sure Tri's made his dislike for the Eastern Court very clear."

The three of them spoke in low voices, finally sharing their secrets with one another.

"What I didn't expect to happen," Dema continued, "was for the two of you to start bonding, developing a closer relationship. I am happy, of course, but a bit afraid."

"Everything frightens you," Dimitri laughed at his sister. "You jump at the smallest sound."

Dema elbowed him in the side. Sayr smiled, watching the two siblings tease each other. Dimitri looked completely happy, getting to be with his sister in a public setting once again.

All the pieces were fitting into place in Sayr's head.

The Harvest Ball was the perfect place to bring anyone as a guest, everyone danced with everyone. No one would assume the two of them were siblings or had any sort of close relationship simply because they danced and spent time with one another at the ball. Guests spent time with other guests all night and then never spoke a word to each other afterwards. The Harvest Ball was a perfect disguise for the two of them to get to spend a full evening together.

Another song began to pick up, the beat soft and slow, and the three of them turned their head towards the dance floor. Sayr watched the guests begin to couple up to start the dance and she looked back towards Dimitri and Dema to encourage them to dance and enjoy their night, but Dema was already walking in the other direction.

"She's not much of a dancer," Dimitri explained with a grin and held his hand out to her. "Would you care to dance with me?"

Sayr smiled as she looked up at him and took his hand. He wrapped her hand around his arm and led her through the crowd and onto the dance floor. The two of them stopped at a spot on the floor and broke apart, facing one another.

The tune continued slow at first, the strumming of instruments and slow graze of strings on a violin filled the room. Dimitri and Sayr both bowed low to one another, then returned upright again, and brought one hand high together between them. They followed the rest of the dancers, circling around each other as the slow tune steadily continued on.

Dimitri's movements were automatic, leading Sayr through the motions and weaving her through the crowd of dancers. A drumbeat started along with the tune, speeding the song up ever so slightly and the two came together. Dimitri's one hand still held Sayr's up, while his other arm wrapped around her, his hand resting on her back. The light in his eyes intensified, his breathing quickened as his hand met her skin. He spun her slowly, keeping his eyes locked on hers as they moved in tune with the music.

The tempo of the song slowed again. Dimitri spun Sayr slowly and caught her, bringing her closer to him. Their noses were barely inches apart as he leaned down towards her. The drumbeat returned, slowly at first, then quicker and quicker. The guests watching began to clap to the beat until each instrumental chord met one another in a high tempo chorus.

He pulled away slightly, only to lift Sayr into the air as he spun her. The music exploded into a beautiful melody, the steady beating of the drum and tune of the violin singing their own song to one another. Dimitri spun and spun Sayr, the two laughing as the train of her dress wrapped around his body. As the music began to settle, Dimitri gently set Sayr down, spinning her once again, much slower.

The music began to fade, only the strings of the violin now played. Dimitri dipped Sayr low, their faces so close she could feel his breath. Her nose filled with the familiar sweet scent of clove and peppermint.

The crowd clapped as the song ended, and he slowly brought her upright once again. He remained close to her, his lips almost touching hers. His eyes flickered between her own deep blue eyes and her lips. His hand cupped the back of her neck, and he pulled her closer.

A trumpet sounded and every soul in the ballroom turned towards the staircase, where King Mylan now stood. The two of them broke apart as the crowd all looked up towards the king.

"Presenting His Majesty, King Mylan of Creobe."

The crowd applauded wildly for their king as he took center stage on the stairs and bowed.

Dimitri pressed his lips to Sayr's ear. "I need to be with the king, I'll return for you soon."

Sayr nodded and smiled as he pulled away and made his way through the crowd, meeting Addy and Willa, dressed in a magnificent plum gown, at the base of the stairs.

"Welcome to Creobe's first ever Harvest Ball!" King Mylan announced, lifting his arms high as the crowd cheered louder. "We honor the traditions of Visaran and have been eager to bring these traditions here among our own. Now, may I introduce the royal family of Visaran who have traveled all this way to enjoy the Harvest festivities along with us?"

His Majesty stepped aside and turned as Queen Cheralin emerged from the halls and to the top of the staircase leading down to the ballroom.

"Her Majesty, Queen Cheralin of Visaran."

The crowd applauded and bowed to the queen. Her Majesty wore a silver gown with long sleeves and a high neck. The dress was covered in beading and gems, glittering at every angle in the candlelight above. Her hair was done up and pinned around the crown placed atop her head.

Queen Cheralin bowed her head in greeting.

"Thank you, King Mylan," she said before addressing the crowds below. "I am forever thankful to be here with you all to celebrate our Harvest season coming to an end. My people have been hard at work for the past several months, but I could not refuse the chance to come and see my people who have been working just as hard here, in the presence of King Mylan."

Refuse the chance? Sayr almost laughed aloud. *Cheralin made her chance to come here.*

"I have brought my own children here with me," the queen said.

Queen Cheralin did not move aside as Mylan had but remained standing and gestured for her son and daughter as they approached behind her.

"Prince Everett, Crown Prince of Visaran. And Princess Elanor, Princess of Visaran."

More applause sounded as the two waved to the crowds.

Lanni was breathtaking as always in a deep blue gown. The thin straps and tight bodice were beaded in blue gems and led to a tiered skirt that flowed to the floor. Her hair was neatly placed behind her back and a silver tiara was placed on her brow.

Everett was just as stunning in a deep blue suit of his own, decorated with silver stitching and bright gems on the hem of his lapels. His blond hair was slicked back out of his face and a silver crown of his own was placed on his head.

Sayr couldn't help but smile in glee as she looked at her oldest friend.

His eyes scanned over the crowd as he and Lanni waved, passing over her just briefly before bouncing back and landing fully on her. His smile grew as he took her in.

Sayr took a small step back and gave a spin. She could see him laugh, but the crowd was too loud for the laugh to reach her and all too soon the royal family was being ushered away from the stairs.

"Please," King Mylan spoke again. "Enjoy this night as a night of celebration!"

The crowd began to disperse as the music picked back up. Sayr craned her neck to catch a glimpse of where Ev may have gone, but he had already disappeared.

She'd become swept up in the crowd of people dancing and laughing. Her lungs began to constrict from the closeness of people crushing in on her and she began to elbow her way through the masses. She couldn't catch sight of Marenda, Dimitri, Dema, or Willa.

She tripped when someone stepped on the train of her dress and turned to pick up the massive fabric before pushing her way to the edges of the crowd. The outskirts of the dance floor were less occupied and gave her room to breathe at least. She took a few deep breaths and turned to check on the train of her dress. She couldn't find any rips or tears and smoothed out the fabric with her hands.

The song ended once again and a new, swift tune began to play. Sayr swayed along with the music as she watched the people around her. She needed this, needed a moment to breathe, a moment by herself.

A hand lightly touched her waist and Sayr froze.

A voice whispered behind her. "Looking for me?"

The nerves encapsulating Sayr immediately melted as she spun around and wrapped her arms around Everett's neck. She could feel the laugh reverberating through his body as he hugged her back.

"I can't believe you're here!" she said, tears making her vision watery.

"Neither can I. I thought I might never see you again." He pulled away from her slightly to look at her. "Look at you, you're beautiful! You look strong and healthy, too. Have they been treating you well here?"

"Yes," she said, refusing to tell him that she had been covered in bruises only a few days ago. "They've treated us all incredibly well, actually."

"I'm glad to hear it. Though, I'm sure the king knows we would expect nothing less of him."

"How long are you staying for?" Sayr asked.

"One week." Everett's smile fell ever so slightly. "But I promise you will come back with me. I won't let them keep you here any longer, it's time for you to come home."

Sayr stepped back and smiled weakly.

She hadn't accomplished her mission yet, Everett had to know that. Her Majesty wasn't going to just let her leave without tearing apart the King's Court like she had been ordered to do.

She meant to tell him just that, but he quickly looked around and leaned in close to her. "Let's go outside, somewhere private."

He took her hand and led her to the other side of the ballroom where the doors were propped open to let guests in and out of the ballroom. Everett led her out the doors and into the brisk night air. The sleeves of her dress were not built for the cold, and she shivered as the cool air danced along her arms and exposed back.

Everett led her out through the connected balconies. Couples sat around the railings and at tables on the balcony together. The two of them made their way past and down a staircase to a set of lower balconies. The far balconies were left abandoned by guests who didn't want to stray too far away from the party, leaving the two of them alone. Everett leaned against the railing and looked out into the distance.

"It's quite a sight to behold," he murmured.

"Yes, it is." Sayr looked out into the mountains. The stars were completely exposed, painting a beautiful sky over the peaks of the mountaintops.

Everett turned towards her. "I can't tell you how happy I am to see you," he began. "After Her Majesty told me about her plan between the two of you, I was worried sick that you would be caught or that you wouldn't be able to make it back home."

"Your mother told you about the mission?" Sayr asked, stunned.

Everett nodded. "Everything's going to change for the better when you return," he said. "She has great plans already in place for us."

"Then you know what she has asked me to do while I'm here?" Sayr asked.

She didn't care about the rewards Her Majesty was willing to give her if she succeeded, she already knew she could never go through with any of it.

"Yes, I do," Everett said grimly. "But her cause is far greater than one mission. The plans she has for us, for our country, after all of this is beyond just you or me or a few Creobians."

"She is asking me to *kill* someone, Ev," Sayr said.

Everett took her hands in his own, gripping them tightly. "I know, and I'm so sorry that the responsibility has been put on you, but you are not the only one that has had to experience death at their own hands. So many people have had to kill to succeed or advance their status and save their country."

"Did you not hear me?" Sayr's voice rose. "Do you even know me? I am not a killer, Ev. I cannot kill him. I *will not* kill him."

"Him?" Everett's voice tightened. "You've found out who the king's mercenary is?"

Sayr clamped her mouth shut.

"If you know who they are, you need to tell me. You don't understand the sacrifice you are making for our kingdom, Sayr," Everett continued. "The reward you will receive for doing what needs to be done."

"I-I can't," Sayr stammered. "So much has changed. Everything that I've learned during my time here. Who I am, what I am, what I could become. Everything has changed."

Everett didn't seem to be listening. He looked down at her, his hands still tightly holding onto hers. "She wants to make you queen, Sayr."

Sayr remained so still she thought her heart had stopped beating. "What are you talking about?" Sayr whispered.

Everett looked behind Sayr and his expression changed to icy stone as he backed away, bowing low.

Sayr turned to see what Everett had seen. Her gut twisted and her heart raced. She no longer felt the chilling cold, her body had gone numb the moment her eyes landed on Queen Cheralin standing at the base of the stairs to their platform.

Two Royal Guards flanked the queen. Sayr looked towards the top of the stairs. Three more Visarian Royal Guards stood at the top, keeping her with the queen and prince and blocking the way for anyone else to come down to their platform.

"You have been hiding from me, Sayr." The queen's voice was as cold and sharp as the icy look in her eyes. "Why is that?"

Sayr stepped away from the queen and towards Everett. "I've done nothing of the sort," she said slowly, calmly. "I had no idea you were in the palace until recently. And even then, the king has deliberately kept me away. If I have been hiding, it was by no will of my own."

"Please, Your Majesty," Everett spoke up from behind Sayr. "Tell her what is waiting for her back home. She will understand once you tell her everything."

The queen's gaze briefly darted from Sayr to look at her son. No warmth changed her icy expression as she looked at him. "Why don't you tell her everything?" Her Majesty asked. "It is what *you* have wanted all this time, after all. She will be *your* queen one day."

Sayr turned back towards Everett. He looked from the queen to Sayr and stepped closer to her. His eyes bored into hers and a small smile grew on his lips. He gently took her hands in his, holding them tightly close.

"We will be married," Everett practically cooed. "I know you've never thought about becoming queen, but you have been by a queen's side since you were a child.

And you and I are already so close, we would be a powerful force as king and queen."

"And you want this?" Sayr asked.

Everett's eyes scanned every inch of her face. "I do."

Sayr glanced back at the queen, then at Everett. There was no point in pretending anymore; pretending that she didn't know the truth of Visaran's history or pretending that her loyalties hadn't shifted.

"Everett, you are my oldest friend, and I love you dearly, but not like that. You have no idea what I've learned since coming to this palace. The parts of history I've discovered that have been hidden from me back in Visaran."

Everett's expression darkened as he listened to her, and he glanced back at the queen. "What do you know?"

"Did you know about your parent's exile of the unseen elements in Visaran?" Sayr asked. She turned to glare at the queen as the words left her.

The was a pause of silence. The queen remained unphased by Sayr's words, continuing to stare icily at her. She broke their stare first, turning towards Everett, her oldest friend.

His eyes searched hers, looking for something, before he let her go and turned towards the railing once again. "When you left, I figured you would eventually learn about the unseen elements."

"You knew," Sayr said accusingly. "All this time, you knew everything."

Everett's head fell to his chest. "Yes. I knew."

The pain in Sayr's chest felt like a knife had been twisted into her heart. Her oldest friend, the one person that knew everything about her and never judged, had always held the secrets that he knew she was looking for.

"All this time, you've known that your parents exiled and killed them all off." Sayr took a step away from Everett, away from the railing. "They are not gone here, none of the unseen elements are."

"The unseen elements are dangerous." Everett whirled around to face Sayr, and she took another step back. "They were a threat to my parent's throne. There was talk of rebellion, how else do you extinguish that kind of flame?"

"You don't kill an entire population of people!" Sayr's voice ached as she yelled. She swiveled back towards the queen. "Is that why you kept me so close? To make sure I could be used as a weapon instead of becoming a threat?"

"She did not know what would become of you, but she wasn't willing to risk the chance," Everett answered, drawing Sayr's attention back to him. "Now look at what you've become, you are a strong, gifted woman who should be proud and honored to one day wear a queen's crown."

"It is a crown of blood, Everett!"

Tears formed in Sayr's eyes. "How can you not see that? I have never wanted a crown, I never wanted to be a queen. I still don't want those things. I have always been unsure of my future, but a crown has never been and never will be a part of it."

"Do you see now, Everett?" The queen's voice was closer now. She stood directly behind Sayr.

Sayr stood directly between the two royals. She didn't want to be any closer to either of them. Her head turned back and forth as she cast heated glares at them both, willing herself not to cry.

"If you become queen, Sayr, no one will question you or your place in Court any longer." Queen Cheralin tried soothing Sayr's anger. "The Court will be yours; you will be worthy of a crown. Everyone will find you worthy."

"I don't want the praise of your Court," Sayr shot back. "I don't care what your Court thinks of me. Not anymore. I define my own worth. No one else. I am a gifted Seer, with powers unheard of by anyone on the continent. The wicked glares and whispers from those in your Court mean nothing to me anymore."

Cheralin's eyes darkened as she glared down at Sayr. "This is not a choice, Sayr. If you do not come back to Visaran and rule by Everett's side, you will die. If you somehow make it on your own outside of the palace, you will be hunted down and killed once others find out what you are—that you are unnatural. But if you do come back, you can reveal yourself and your gifts. You can claim to be an unseen Elemental, an unseen Elemental queen."

Sayr barked out a humorless laugh. "So you can earn the favor of unseen Elementals in Visaran? You won't use me to secure your family's place on the throne. I won't solve the problems you caused years ago for you."

Sayr took a step forward, fully facing the queen.

"I don't want your praise, or anyone else's for that matter." Her voice was final as she spoke. "I don't want your crown, and I will not serve as your dutiful, future-seeing lapdog anymore. I do not serve you anymore."

The queen lifted a hand and struck Sayr hard across the face.

Sayr stumbled backwards a few steps. Stars burned in her vision and her cheek stung in icy pain. She blinked rapidly to try and clear the stars from her vision.

"This is what I tried to tell you, Everett!" Cheralin screamed at her son. "She is dangerous, unpredictable! She has learned too much for you to be able to control her."

In one swift motion, Everett grabbed Sayr's shoulders and bent down so that they were eye to eye. "This is not something you can argue against, Sayr. You will see things differently when we get home, I promise. You will see how lucky you are to be given an opportunity like this."

"Let go of me, Ev." Sayr tried to yank herself from his grip.

"And when we get home, you will accept Her Majesty's proposal. One day, you will be Queen of Visaran, ruling by my side."

Sayr shook her head, tears spilling onto her cheeks. She needed to get away from him, from this future he was trying so hard to force her into.

She yanked back again but Everett only held on tighter, fingers digging into her arms. "Ev, please don't-"

"Well, this is not the type of mood I was expecting for a party."

They all turned their faces up towards the upper level of the balconies.

King Mylan leaned against the railing of the platform, looking down at them. His chin was propped in one hand that leaned on the railing. The feline grin returned to his face, as if he were enjoying the altercation down below.

Dimitri, Tomas, and half a dozen Royal Guards stood closely behind their king.

Dimitri's eyes were narrow, and his jaw was set. He stood with his arms behind his back, standing deadly still. His eyes never left Sayr. He did not look at the Eastern Queen or her son. He only looked at Sayr, surveying every inch of her body.

"Leave us, Mylan," Queen Cheralin called up to the balcony "She is my subject. I will speak to her and take her whenever and wherever I wish."

"She is still under my domain," Mylan said and waved a hand to his guard.

The guards stepped towards the top of the stairs, where Cheralin's guards remained. The Visarian Royal Guards tensed as the Creobian Royal Guards approached.

"Call off your guards, or I will have my men kill them," Mylan called down casually, too casually. "You agreed that Lady Sayr would serve in my Court, and her service is not over yet. I do not think you want to go back on your word. You do not want the truth getting back to your people."

"We agreed if I offered my troops as aid, you would no longer use any sort of blackmail against me and my kingdom." Cheralin's voice was murderous as she looked up at the Western King.

"And I plan to keep that promise, for me and all of my people," Mylan said. "But I said nothing about *your* people blackmailing you."

King Mylan gestured down the platform at Sayr. The queen's eyes trailed down from the king, narrowing as she took in Sayr. Sayr returned the queen's icy stare, the challenge clear in her eyes. She refused to back down before the Eastern Queen.

Cheralin stood as still as stone, but she nodded her head to her guards. Those at the top of the stairs stepped aside to let Mylan's guards down to their platform. Three Creobian guards and Tomas remained with their king. The other three guards and Dimitri slipped down the stairs onto the platform where Sayr and the Visarian royals stood.

Dimitri was instantly at Sayr's side. His arms wrapped around her, and he led her towards the balcony steps. He kept his eyes on Everett, then the queen, while they passed and climbed the stairs. He brought her behind Mylan, keeping her at his side.

"Take her away," Mylan said to Dimitri in a low voice. "I will deal with this."

He nodded and turned Sayr towards the ballroom. They walked back towards the large glass doors, leaving the royals on the balconies.

27

$\mathcal{D}$imitri's grip was firm but gentle as he led Sayr back into the palace. The music of the band lulled in her ears once more and the warmth of the palace tinged her frozen skin.

The ball was still in full swing with people dancing, drinking, and talking. Some of the guests were quite drunk, and one made a spectacle of falling onto one of the linen tables set around the room, breaking a series of champagne flutes in the process.

"Are you all right?" he murmured to her, his eyes still on everything but her. "Are you hurt?"

Sayr shook her head and wiped at the tears falling down her cheeks. "No, I'm all right."

A hand lightly grabbed Sayr's arm and Dimitri turned, stepping forward to block Sayr from the threat. Marenda grabbed Sayr. Callum stood close behind her.

"What happened?" Marenda asked, taking in Sayr's tear-stained face.

Dimitri looked behind her at Callum. "Take her to your chambers and lock the door," he instructed. "I'll let Addy know about my orders. Do not leave until the morning."

He didn't wait for a response before he led Sayr out of the ballroom and through the many levels of the palace. He shielded Sayr from any guests lingering in the halls, holding her close to his own body as they walked.

"I'm taking you somewhere safe," he had told Sayr. "Somewhere the Visarian royals won't come looking for you."

Dimitri opened the door to his own chambers to led Sayr inside. The layout of the chambers was close to hers, only much more cluttered. Various armor stands were placed on one side of the room, holding various kinds of leather and steel armor. A weapons rack was placed near the stands, filled with different weaponry. A large desk sat at the opposite side of the room, stacks of papers and books piled high on top of it.

The smell of him was even stronger here in his own chambers. The scent of clove and peppermint filled Sayr's nostrils. Sayr blushed when she eyed the bed. Green curtains hung from each side, offering privacy if Dimitri were to need it.

The moment they entered the room, a weight seemed to fall from his shoulders. He looked down at Sayr, his eyes roaming over her face and body for any sign of injuries. Sayr offered him a light smile to show she was all right.

"I apologize for the mess. I wasn't expecting company in here," Dimitri said lightly.

"I apologize for intruding," Sayr countered.

He chuckled and left her side to open his wardrobe. "If you're not too tired, there's somewhere I'd like to take you," he said as he filed through the wardrobe.

"Is this place appropriate for a ball gown?" she asked.

Dimitri looked at her from the wardrobe, a hint of mischief gleaming in his eyes.

"Not at all," he said.

He shuffled through one of the drawers of the wardrobe. Sayr walked over to the desk, eyeing the different books on the table. She didn't recognize any of them, the titles were all foreign to her. Dimitri pulled out a small pile of clothing and offered them to Sayr.

"These should fit you," he said as he offered her the stack of clothes. "I believe you and my sister are close in size. You can change in my washroom if you need."

Sayr nodded and made her way into the washroom to change. The clothes were simple yet warm, though Dimitri had given her double of everything. A thin pair of shorts underneath thick fur leggings, a light shirt over a wool sweater and heavy cloak and a pair of boots. Sayr ran her fingers through her hair after she finished dressing and left the washroom.

Dimitri was dressed in a similar fashion, thick pants, a wool shirt and heavy cloak, and leather boots. He carried a small pack on his back and grinned as she entered the chamber. "Let's go."

Leaving the palace was surprisingly easy with Dimitri. He had led them back through a secret hall and down, down, down several stairs. At the bottom of the many stairs was a single door. Pushing it open, he revealed the forest outside. Sayr stepped out, taking in the chilly darkness of the night. She looked back at the door; it had been hidden as part of the mountainside; rocks and moss concealed its shape. Sayr's wonder must have shown on her face because Dimitri chuckled.

"There are many different ways out of the palace in secret," he said. "In case His Majesty or any of us ever needs to evacuate."

Sayr clutched the hood of her cloak as they quickly made their way through the woods and down the mountain. The frosty night air stung her lungs, and she breathed heavily in excitement for wherever Dimitri was taking her. The steep decline of the mountain seemed to last forever until the terrain finally evened out.

The wind died down the farther they descended the mountain, making the air feel a bit warmer. They entered a clearing of trees at the edge of a large lake. Looking up, Sayr could see the palace towering high above them in the distance. This was the lake she had seen from her balcony the first day she'd arrived. The edges of the lake glowed a vibrant blue in the night.

"Why are we here?" Sayr turned to ask Dimitri but stopped as he began disrobing.

Without an answer, Dimitri shucked off his cloak and removed his heavy shirt, pants, and boots leaving him in his shorts. Sayr hadn't realized she'd been staring until he had finished undressing, and looked away quickly, though she couldn't help but sneak a peek again.

His body was rippling with muscles from his torso down to his legs. Sayr noticed thin black marks running from his waist down his upper thigh. A tattoo of tree branches intertwining with one another jutted from his ribs, past his shorts, and stopped just above his knee.

Sayr looked up and noticed him silently watching her, he adjusted his leg so she could see the tattoo better.

"It commemorates my nickname," he commented.

"Tri?" she asked.

He nodded. "When Dema was an infant, she could never say my full name correctly, so she opted for calling me Tri. The nickname stuck and not long after, anyone close to me called me by the name."

Without any more explanation, he sprinted to the edge of the lake and jumped in. Sayr watched in shock as the water glowed bright blue where Dimitri had jumped. Another spot of blue glowed further in the center of the lake as his head emerged from the water, lighting his features as he smiled at her still on the edge of the lake.

"Come on!" he called to her. "The water's fine."

Sayr glanced at the glowing water and bent lower to dip her hand in. The water was warm, much warmer than the air around her. Without hesitating, she flung off her cloak and began removing the thick leggings and sweater.

The thin shorts and shirt left her feeling exposed in the cold and she quickly walked to the edge of the water. Dipping a foot in, she realized she stood on a ledge that ended in deep water.

"Jump in!' Dimitri called.

She smiled wickedly and dove into the lake.

Her entire body was engulfed in warm water. Even with her eyes closed, she could see the glowing water shift behind her eyelids where she jumped in. She swam up to the surface, gasping for air as she broke through the water and looked around for Dimitri.

He was no longer where he had been when she jumped in, and she turned in every direction to look for him. The water around her glowed with each movement she made, one side glowing brighter as something below the surface lightly touched her foot and grabbed her, pulling her under.

Sayr barely had time to scream as she gasped for breath before being taken under. A set of arms wrapped around her, and she felt legs kicking against her own as she once again broke the surface. Sputtering water, she turned around and shot Dimitri a glare as he laughed.

She splashed him with water as she treaded with her feet, and he coughed.

"Oh, you shouldn't have done that," he teased and lunged for her.

A delighted scream escaped her lips as Dimitri brought the two of them under the water again. They broke apart and emerged on the surface.

Sayr laughed and looked at the glowing water around her.

"How is this possible?" she asked. "The water glows when we move."

"The water here is bioluminescent. It glows when it gets stirred up."

Dimitri floated on his back and looked up at the sky. "When I first came to the palace, a group of Royal Guards had invited me here. I didn't realize it at the time, but it was some sort of hazing ritual, throwing the new guy into the lake. They didn't know why the lake glowed like this and believed it was some curse on the lake and whoever was thrown into it would be cursed, too. Apparently, none of the new guys told them that the water was always warm, no matter the climate. They all ran as soon as they threw me in. Once I became part of the King's Court, I stopped the hazing ritual, mostly because I wanted this lake all to myself."

Sayr shifted her arms in the water, watching as it glowed with her movements.

"It's beautiful," she said and leaned back in the water so that she was floating on the surface, too.

The stars were bright in the sky like still fireflies dotting the black canvas. The moon itself shone so bright it could have ignited the lake without the glowing bioluminescence. Sayr and Dimitri continued swimming in the lake, splashing each other and racing from one end to the next.

A small cave opened into the lake at the far side and the two swam in. The air of the cave was warm and dry. Sayr sat on the edge of the water, lapping her feet in it and watching it glow with each kick. Dimitri pulled his upper body over the edge and leaned up to her.

"This place is amazing," Sayr said as the glowing faded.

"The lake is one of a kind," Dimitri agreed.

"No, I mean Creobe altogether," Sayr admitted. "I've been told about this cruel and cunning country to the west of Visaran since I was a child. We're told as kids not to trust anyone from Creobe, not that we would ever get the chance to meet a Creobian with the ban on visiting the country. Being here now, it's nothing like I ever thought it'd be. Your people are so different. You don't fear being different or showing strength in your abilities, and you don't use one another for your benefit. Well, not all of you anyway."

Dimitri slid closer to her, leaning his upper body further onto the ledge.

"Do you like it here?" he asked.

"I do," Sayr answered. "It feels different. I don't see a world where I'll ever be free of a royal, given my ability, but I feel freer here."

Dimitri gave her an encouraging smile. "His Majesty is not like your queen; he won't keep you here just because of your gifts. If you are a strong Spirit Elemental, it will be your choice whether or not you serve the king in his Court."

Sayr looked down at Dimitri, still halfway in the water. Until the Harvest Ball, she had no idea what she really wanted out of all this. She knew she didn't want to return to Visaran and be queen, she wanted to be free. And staying here offered her that small piece of freedom. But she couldn't be completely free if she still hid herself from everyone.

"I'm not a Spirit Elemental," Sayr whispered. "I'm not an Elemental at all."

*D*imitri's face remained unreadable while Sayr told him everything.

"I didn't go to the Eastern Palace to become an apprentice. My father took me when I was young after I'd had a vision of King Luzan's death. The royal family turned us away… until a few months later when the king fell ill. After his death, Her Majesty ordered my father to bring me to the palace each month and tell her about my visions. After a few months, she had a suite cleared out for me in the East Wing. My father left me to live in the palace, but he would visit me every so often until one day he never came back. I've been living in the palace as the queen's Seer ever since, informing her of any new visions."

Dimitri's eyes were glassy and blank as she finished. "You've been living in the Eastern Palace, offering your visions to the queen all this time?" he asked slowly.

Sayr nodded reluctantly, her heart pounding. "There is no one else in Visaran like me. I've had to keep my abilities secret from everyone else except the royal family and Marenda. Everyone else in the palace believes I'm the apprentice of a Council member, the same lie we told all of you when you came to Visaran."

"Does anyone here know of your ability?" Dimitri asked.

Sayr began to shake her head but stopped.

"Your sister does," she answered. "I have no idea how she figured it out, or how much she knows, but she at least knows that I don't possess Elemental abilities. That my abilities are…different."

Dimitri's head quickly shot up to look at her and she spoke faster before he said anything that would stop her.

"I have no idea why Lilith's influence didn't work on me when I ran into her in that hallway. Nothing like that has ever happened before, my gifts have only ever included visions of the future. When you told me about Space Elementals and how they have visions of the past, I thought that might be the closest I'd ever come to finding Elementals like me."

Sayr quickly shut her mouth, not knowing what else to say, what other explanation to give. She had plummeted over the edge and confessed herself to Dimitri.

She couldn't tell him about the mission the queen had given her, she was never going to go through with it. She did not serve Queen Cheralin anymore. She didn't know where she would go, but she would never go back to the Eastern Queen.

"I shouldn't have lied, or I should have told you sooner, but I didn't know who to trust. I still don't know who I can trust. For eight years, I have been told that I'd be hunted and killed because of my gifts, I had no idea why until I came here. I've grown up fearing what others might do to me if they were to find out that I possessed gifts outside the elements. But after coming here and seeing everything that's been hidden from me for so long, I don't feel as scared anymore. At least not when I'm here. I'm confused, more than anything, but at least I'm not being fed more lies."

Dimitri pushed off the ledge and moved closer to her until he was right in front of her. With ease, he pushed his upper body out of the water again, one hand on her leg and the other on the ground next to her.

"You shouldn't have to live your life in fear. You won't be harmed here in Creobe, I won't let anyone harm you. If you stay, I will be by your side always protecting you. If you wish it, then no one else has to know about your abilities, it can be our secret. If you don't want to stay in the palace, we'll tell the king that you wish to leave his Court, and you can live your life how you want."

"I don't think it'll be that easy," Sayr said.

Nothing in her life was ever that easy. Her life was never easy at all. As much as she wished for this one thing to be easy, for her to get her way just once, the doubt of finally getting something that she truly wanted sat in her stomach like a boulder at the bottom of a depthless ocean.

"It certainly won't be that easy. His Majesty will likely want both of us to travel to the palace occasionally to offer our services, but he will fight for you to remain in Creobe. Her Majesty and her children will never be able to use you again. You can have a life here. If you stay. Will you stay?"

They both stared at each other for the longest moment. Sayr had established a life in Visaran, she had friends, and a role to play, but her life was not real. None of it had been real. In Creobe, she could live in the Royal Sector, and live her life however she wanted, and she could have Dimitri at her side.

Without a word, Sayr gave Dimitri a small nod.

Yes, she would stay.

His eyes ignited, and his lips parted into a wide smile. His hand grasped Sayr's leg, the other reaching around her back, and he pulled.

Sayr gave a squeal of surprise as she was pulled into the warm water, strong arms around her keeping her afloat.

Dimitri's lips met hers and he kissed her.

Sayr gasped at the kiss and leaned into him. One arm kept them afloat while the other wrapped around Sayr's back, his hand in her wet hair.

He kissed her softly at first, then harder and she tangled her own hands through his hair. His teeth gently bit down on her lower lip, and her body ignited into flames. His arm kept her tightly locked against him and she wrapped her legs around his hips. His lips were soft as he kissed her, the taste of champagne still on his tongue as he deepened the kiss. Sayr melted into him. She kept one hand in his hair and the other ran down his chest.

Sayr felt as if she were melting away, blending into Dimitri's own body as they held each other tightly. Her pulse raced and her breathing quickened as Dimitri leaned down to kiss her jaw, then her neck, then back to her lips.

They broke apart, both breathing heavily.

Sayr's eyes were wide as she looked at him, then down at his mouth, and up again. His smile was one she had never seen on him before. He no longer looked fierce or dangerous; his eyes were calm, and his smile was joyous. The cool stone had been chipped away from every piece of him. Finally, Sayr fully saw Dimitri for who he truly was. For the first time since she'd known him, he looked genuinely happy.

"We will tell the king that you're willingly choosing to stay in Creobe tomorrow." Dimitri kissed her jaw. "He will fight against the Eastern Queen for you, I promise."

Sayr's pulse skipped a few beats, both from the kiss and the promise of tomorrow. Could she really be freed from her life of servitude so quickly?

"I'm terrified," she admitted.

"You have nothing to be afraid of. You hold the power here, what you do from here on out is completely up to you."

He looked up at her and gave her a mischievous grin. "They should be afraid of you, my little imposter."

Dimitri and Sayr exited the glowing lake quickly after leaving the cave. Dimitri had brought towels in his pack and they quickly dried, dressed, and made their way back to the palace. Sayr's hair was still damp when they arrived back in the palace halls.

Dimitri brought her back to his chambers. He called servants in to run a bath for her and gave her space while she dropped the damp clothing and entered the tub. The heat of the water felt incredible on her skin, she could have stayed in the tub until the water ran cold if it weren't for the man waiting for her outside the washroom door. She quickly scrubbed at her skin with soap and washed the lake water out of her hair. She was out of the bathtub quicker than she usually liked and wrapped a robe around her body.

A knock sounded at the door as she was brushing through her hair and a servant popped in with a fresh set of clothes for her. A pajama set of loose silk pants and a silk top with thick wool socks. Once she was all dry, she changed into the pajama set, gave herself a once over in the mirror, and headed into the chamber.

Dimitri sat on the sofa by the fireplace, a roaring fire had already heated up the room. He must have heard the door open as he looked behind him to where she stood and rose from his seat. He picked up the blanket and wrapped it around her before going to take a bath himself.

Sayr sat on the sofa, wrapped in the blanket and staring at the fire. She thought about Mar while she waited. Would she stay in Creobe with Sayr? Would she be given any choice, given her position as the queen's personal guard?

Sayr doubted so, but Mar had formed her own connections during their stay in Creobe, and Sayr knew she would likely fight to keep them. Maybe she could include Mar in the bargain with King Mylan. She would do anything to have her best friend remain in Creobe with her, to see Mar get to finally live a life of her own, too.

Dimitri returned from the washroom, and the two sat in front of the fire talking and kissing for the rest of the night. He had told her stories about growing up in his village, mainly about him and Julen growing up together.

Julen had wanted to be a soldier like Dimitri, but he wasn't a fighter and didn't have a vicious bone in his body, he had said. He'd always loved literature and history and became a records keeper when Dimitri left to join the guard. He talked about Julen like they were brothers, and Sayr could see Dimitri loved him like his own brother.

Sayr smiled and continued listening to his stories until they were both entwined together, quietly staring at the fire. Sayr's eyes grew heavy with the break of dawn just beginning to peek over the mountaintops and she briefly shut them, just for a moment.

The following day had been cleared of all lessons and duties, besides those of servants and Royal Guards. It seemed that everyone was too tired or hungover to take on the day's usual schedule.

When Sayr woke, she had found herself in a bed that was not her own.

After falling asleep, Dimitri had carried her into bed and had taken the sofa for himself. He had woken earlier than her and had clothes retrieved from her chambers. They spent the morning ordering breakfast and Sayr sipped her coffee while he went over some paperwork for the king.

The two remained in Dimitri's chambers for the remainder of the day. Sayr requested a guard to bring her *The Elemental's History of Magic* and she sat on Dimitri's balcony, wrapped in a warm blanket, as she pushed through the pages. After a short while, Dimitri came out to the balcony.

"I need to question the rebels from the attack," Dimitri said. "Would you like to come with me?"

Sayr raised an eyebrow at him. "They haven't been questioned after all this time?"

"Willa has had her spies down there almost every day trying to get them to speak, but they won't budge," Dimitri explained. "She has asked me to visit for a bit more… persuading."

"I see," Sayr said.

"I'm glad you see; now can you speak?" Dimitri teased. Sayr threw a pillow at him, and he laughed. "Alright, alright. In other words, I would like you to come with me so I know you're safe while I'm there. Will you?"

Sayr smiled. "That's much better. Yes, Tri, I'd be delighted to join you on your interrogation."

Dimitri lightly flicked her nose. "Smart mouth," he quipped and kissed her.

Sayr and Dimitri made their way down to the dungeons. Sayr had never been to the dungeons, the area was dark and cold and damp. Each rebel was kept in their own cell, separate from one another. Sayr stayed near the entrance of the dungeon while Dimitri strolled up and down the aisle, inspecting each prisoner.

"Who should we start with first?" he pondered to himself. He stopped in front of a cell where a young girl sat in the corner. Her knees were pulled close to her body and her face was buried in her arms.

"You."

Dimitri unlocked her cell, and two Royal Guards pulled her up and out through the open door. Sayr followed close behind as the guards led the girl to a separate room. Dimitri watched as the guards chained her to a pair of shackles bolted into the floor and left. They each took a moment to watch her, to see how she reacted to the shackles and the new environment. She did not speak. She barely looked around her and instead sat on the floor with her knees against her chest once again.

"What's your name?" Dimitri asked. The girl remained silent. "Why have you come into our lands?"

Dimitri pushed and pushed, but the girl did not utter a word. She did not look at him or Sayr. Dimitri let out a frustrated breath and unsheathed his sword. He walked closer to the girl, staying out of arms reach, but close enough for her to see the glint and length of the sword.

"I will only ask you once more," Dimitri said to her. "Why have you come into our lands and destroyed our homes?"

The girl's face was slacked with fear, but still, she did not speak. The smallest glint of disappointment flashed across Dimitri's face, then it was gone. He looked at Sayr for a moment while he lifted his sword, silently begging her to forgive him for what he was about to do.

"Maybe the others will talk more after they hear you scream," Dimitri said to the girl.

Sayr's mind flashed through memories, to Antoine and his fear of being discovered for knowing about those in the north and what they may have possessed. Dimitri was about to bring his sword down when the words rushed out of Sayr.

"What do you know about those with gifts outside of the natural elements?"

The girl came to life. She swiveled towards Sayr, turning as far as she could while shackled to the floor.

"You know?" she asked in a breathless voice. "You know about people like us?"

Sayr took in the girl's appearance. She looked younger than Sayr, and she was so thin. Her body shook slightly, either from cold or hunger, Sayr wasn't sure. Sayr walked closer to the girl and sat down, just outside of reach.

"I am someone like you," Sayr admitted. "I have gifts outside of the natural elements."

The girl's eyes went wide with astonishment. "A healer?" she asked.

"No," Sayr answered. "I am something else, entirely."

"What are you doing here in the palace?" the girl asked. "How have they not killed you?"

"They don't know," Sayr said. She watched the girl's eyes drift behind Sayr to Dimitri.

"But he knows?" she asked.

"Yes," Sayr answered for Dimitri. "He knows."

Sayr sat up straighter and the girl looked at her again. "Can you show me what you can do?"

The girl clutched her hands close to her body. She stared at Sayr, then Dimitri, then back at Sayr. She took a deep, trembling breath and opened her hands out towards Sayr.

"May I have your earring?" she asked.

Sayr lifted a hand towards her earlobe. She'd forgotten she still wore the small pearls she'd put on for the Harvest Ball. She took out the earring and placed it on the ground. She rolled the earring over to the girl, and she picked it up. The earring sat in the palm of her hand, and she folded her fingers over it, covering it completely. When she opened her hand again, four identical pearl earrings sat in her palm.

"They call us duplicators," the girl said. "We can duplicate objects, as long as they fit in our hands."

"That's amazing." Sayr was breathless and she looked up at Dimitri. Dimitri stared hard at the pearls; his face was unreadable.

"What can you do?" the girl asked, drawing Sayr's attention back to her.

"I have visions," Sayr admitted. "Visions of the future."

The girl gasped and dropped the earrings to put both hands over her mouth. "Are you the traveler?"

"The what?" Sayr asked. "I'm just a Seer."

"You must be the one Naz is looking for. He must know you're here. He is looking for you." The girl was growing frantic. She twisted in her chains to try and free herself.

"I don't know who you're talking about." Sayr tried to calm the girl, but she only twisted and yanked harder.

"He must know you're here! You have to go to him! Get away from here! Get away from here!"

Dimitri pulled Sayr up and wrapped his arms around her. "Let's go," he said and turned her towards the exit.

"No!" the girl screamed after them. "You have to find him! Find Naz! Get away from here!"

Dimitri slammed the door on the still-screaming girl. The two guards looked at Sayr, then Dimitri with unspoken questions.

"Leave her in there," Dimitri ordered. "Keep her separated. Don't let her speak to any of the other prisoners. I'll be back tomorrow."

Neither of them said another word while Dimitri led Sayr out of the dungeons and back to his room.

"I can't believe this!" Sayr paced around the room. "The healers are one thing, but His Majesty knows about people with gifts outside the natural elements?"

Dimitri sat on his couch, his hands over his face. "His Majesty does not know what you are, Sayr. It's likely he would have told you about these people if he did."

"But why is he keeping them secret at all?" Sayr pushed. "And that girl asked how I wasn't dead yet. Would the king kill me, too, if he knew what I was?"

Dimitri lowered his hands and steadied a look at Sayr. "The king is not a killer. He would never lay a hand to his own people. We don't know everything just yet. I'm sure there is an explanation here that we're not seeing."

"I can't wait for an explanation to come to me, Tri," Sayr said. "I need answers now."

"You shouldn't just go marching into this blindly," Dimitri advised. "You need a plan first."

"You're right, you're right." Sayr took a deep breath and stopped pacing. "I need to find Mar. We need to speak with His Majesty together."

29

$\mathcal{M}$arenda, Dimitri, and Sayr stood outside the king's quarters.

They had found Callum, Mar, and Addy in Callum's chambers. Addy had stayed with them all night after receiving word from Dimitri. She had sent Callum away the moment Sayr mentioned the rebels. Mar hadn't been pleased but she let him go. Sayr told them both everything she had uncovered in the dungeon, and while Addy didn't look surprised when she heard about the healer's gifts, she was surprised by the prisoner's abilities.

"So, you didn't know about the rebels possessing other abilities?" Marenda had asked.

"No," she answered. "And I doubt the king knows or he likely would've suspected that rather than assumed these rebels were his own people attacking one another."

Addy hadn't come with them to the king's quarters. This deal consisted of only the three of them. Sayr nodded to the guard stationed at the door and he turned the knob, letting them inside.

King Mylan sat in front of the fireplace with a drink in his hand. He stood while they all filed into the room and took their own seats.

"Thank you for meeting with us," Sayr started.

"Of course, Lady Sayr." King Mylan sat with the rest of them. He leaned forward and propped his elbows on his knees. "Your request sounded urgent; I did not want to keep you waiting."

"It is urgent, and I believe it has a great deal to do with the rebels and this upcoming war." Sayr looked at Dimitri, then Mar. She breathed in deeply and said, "I don't mean to push, Your Majesty, but certain information has come to my attention, and I need some questions answered before I can decide if I'm ready to stay in the Western Palace and serve you."

"I understand," Mylan said. "What is it you need to ask me?"

"Do you know about any Elementals that would have gifts that are outside the natural elements?" Sayr asked.

Mylan stared at her for a moment, his expression frozen. His searching eyes darted to Dimitri, then Mar. "I assume this means you know about the extent of the healer's abilities."

"Yes, but it's not just that," Sayr said. "I would like to know why you have hidden these people, though. Why can't the healers speak about their gifts?"

"It is not to harm or undermine them in any way," Mylan clarified. "I have them keep their abilities secret for their own protection. There are people outside the palace, throughout the entire continent, that would kill anyone with unnatural gifts just to keep the elements pure."

"So, you are aware of other's possessing abilities outside of the elements." Sayr fought to keep her voice calm, but her blood began to sing with rage. This was exactly what she had left the Eastern Queen for. She would not serve under another royal who would keep her or others like her a secret. She crossed her arms and leaned back in her seat.

"I have heard rumors before, but I have not seen another person with unnatural abilities since I was young, aside from the healers," Mylan explained. "And I did not make the rules for the healers on my own. I met with all the head healers, and we came to this conclusion together. They believed keeping their abilities secret from anyone outside of my Court would be safest. We did not want others visiting and finding out their abilities only to want to have them killed."

"And what if a healer wanted others to know about their abilities?" Sayr asked. "Would they be killed?"

Mylan's expression turned dark. "I would never lay a hand on anyone in my Court."

"I'm not saying you would be the one to do it. I am asking if they would die for refusing to stay hidden," Sayr said.

"No." Mylan's response was instant. "But they could not continue their practices in my palace. I could not let them put the rest of the healers at risk of being found out by those outside of this palace."

"And what about your Court?" This time Mar spoke up. "How do you keep them from outing anyone with abilities outside of the elements?"

"They must swear to secrecy in order to remain in my palace," Mylan said. "Every single person in this palace is sworn to secrecy, and to betray anyone who would out these people and their secrets is treason."

"So, secrets and betrayal. That is how your Court operates?" Sayr asked.

Mylan saw the decision in Sayr's eyes. He slowly shook his head, his voice calm and slow once again. "That is not how my Court is run, Lady Sayr, but you must know secrets are sometimes necessary to protect the ones you love."

Sayr looked away from the king. She did know that. Even now, she was keeping a secret from the king and Dimitri. His Majesty did not know why Sayr cared so much about these people, or about her true abilities. And she still hadn't told Dimitri about why she had initially come to Creobe, that she was sent here to kill him.

"I hope this does not affect your decision, or your opinion of me," the king said to her. "I am trying to do right by everyone. But believe me when I say it is near impossible, if not completely impossible, to do so."

The king rose from his chair. "It is dangerous to be speaking of this with the Visarian royal family still in the palace. If they knew what we were discussing and what lies ahead in the future, I cannot imagine what Queen Cheralin might do."

Sayr nodded. "Where is the Visarian family? Where are they staying in the palace?"

"Queen Cheralin and her children are staying in one of the lower guest levels," the king said. "They have access to three levels, and that is all. After the scene during the Harvest Ball, I had to restrict the royal family's access."

"When do they leave?" Sayr asked the king, though she looked at Marenda.

"They will depart in seven days," King Mylan said. "Assuming Her Majesty does not prolong her stay or try to leave early with the members of her Court."

Sayr uncrossed her arms and sat up taller. She knew what she needed to do.

"I will not serve the Eastern Queen any longer. I still wish to remain in Creobe but my decision on whether or not to serve in your Court is still undecided, and this new information only makes my decision harder," she told the king. "I will not serve in a Court that keeps secrets just like the Court I have left. I want to remain in Therod for the next seven days, along with Mar and Dimitri. I know this is a lot to ask, but I will not risk the royal family coming to look for either of us and I would like Dimitri to come with for protection... in case anyone decides to leave the palace and come looking for us."

The king's gaze bored into her. "And what do you plan to do once those seven days are up?"

"I have some people in Therod that have information I'm looking for. After I find what I need, I'll make my decision," Sayr said and looked at Mar. "I want Mar to remain here, too, if that's what she wishes. But we both need time away from here to discuss and decide for ourselves."

The king pondered their request for a long time. The group sat in absolute silence, waiting for a response. If the king refused their request, Sayr did not know what she would do or where she would go to stay away from the risk of Queen Cheralin taking her back to Visaran by force.

The king's eyes roamed over the three of them, then settled on Dimitri. "I assume Dema is included in this deal?" Mylan asked Dimitri.

"I assumed that was without question," Dimitri answered.

The king breathed in and sighed deeply. "Alright, I will grant your request," he said. "I will have a townhouse prepared for you for seven days and six nights. Once those days are up, you all will return to the palace and Lady Sayr and Lady Marenda will tell me personally what their next steps are."

Sayr's heart bloomed with joy and her nerves sizzled, but she kept her features neutral and calm. She looked to Dimitri, then Marenda, whose face reflected Sayr's, but her eyes burned with excitement.

"Thank you, Your Majesty," she said.

The king only said, "You leave tonight. I suggest you begin packing."

Sayr stared out into the streets of Therod from the balcony of their townhome. The house was already fully furnished and ready for them when they arrived. Three bedrooms, two baths, a full kitchen, dining room, living area, back porch, and front balcony made up the home, though Mar and Sayr knew they would only need one room for themselves. The two girls wanted to be separated as little as possible. Once they had arrived and unpacked, Dimitri left to get food and goods for the next seven days and gave Sayr and Mar some time alone.

The girls laughed and cried over their newfound freedom. Even if it was just seven days, they were free to do as they wished and make their own choices and decisions. Neither of them spoke of what they would do once these seven days were up. Sayr didn't think either of them truly knew what they would do once they went back to the palace. That decision would be made sometime during the next week, but not now.

The door to the balcony slid open and Sayr turned to see Dimitri step out onto the balcony. She smiled as he approached behind her, put his arms around her, and planted a kiss to her hair.

"Where's Marenda?" Dimitri asked through her hair.

"She went to bed early," Sayr said. "Where is Dema?"

"In the bath," Dimitri answered. "I doubt she'll leave that tub within the next hour."

Sayr laughed and Dimitri hummed a response, his lips in her hair. The two of them remained embraced, watching the people of Therod strolling through the streets. Oil lamps ignited the streets, and the talk and laughter of families and children floated up to them.

"What are you thinking about?" Dimitri asked.

Sayr let out a small sigh. "I can't stop thinking about a vision I had in the palace. About a young man sitting on a throne who said he was searching for me. And the girl who said I needed to find Naz, whoever he is. I can't help but feel that they're connected in some way."

She turned to look at Dimitri. "I think I need to find him. Not now, I can't add another task while the royals are both scheming and fighting over my future. But once I make this decision, I need to find him. I need to know why he's searching for me."

Dimitri ran a hand through Sayr's hair, and she arched her neck in response. "Then I will go with you," he said. "I will go wherever you go."

"I wish I could just stay here forever," Sayr admitted and looked back out towards the glowing city. "No responsibilities, no looming war. Nothing at all."

Dimitri rested his chin on the top of her head. "You will have that someday," he promised. "I'll make sure of it."

Sayr let herself smile at the thought, but it was fleeting. "No matter what decision I make, this war will affect both kingdoms."

"Do not let the war with the rebels make your decision for you." Dimitri reached around and lifted her chin so that she was looking at him. "No matter what choice you make, I will be by your side if you'll have me. I will protect you, always."

"I can't take you from your sister," Sayr said.

"If war comes, I will send Dema home, or to the Obsidian Coastline with Hoshi, or out of the continent if that means she is safe. She is not made for war." Dimitri reached for her hand. "But us, we can fight. We are made for war."

"I never wanted to be made for war." Sayr looked below them into the street. How many people would die if war reached them? When war reached them?

"None of us want it, but we are called to it. We are called to fight when others can't. And I promise I will always fight for you, Sayr."

Sayr turned to Dimitri again. His hand cupped her cheek, and he leaned down to kiss her softly. His hand moved to her hair, and she wrapped her arms around his neck.

"We will go through this together," Dimitri said against her lips.

Sayr pulled apart ever so slightly to look up at him. There was so much she needed to do. She needed to meet with Julen, to find out what he had uncovered about her father. She needed to try and see if anything new might come to her about the young man on the broken throne, or about Naz, whoever and wherever he may be. And she needed to decide what laid ahead for her future, what she would do after these seven days were finished and what her role would be in this upcoming war.

"We will," she agreed. "We will face this war and these royals and whatever else comes tat us. Together. But for the next seven days I want to experience what a normal life between us could be like. No warriors, no royals, no roles. Just you and me."

Dimitri smiled. "I like the sound of that very much."

Sayr kissed him again and turned back towards the streets. The two of them remained embraced as they continued to watch the busy streets of Therod.

Continue the journey

with an exclusive sneak peek of…

THRONE OF EXILES

Therod's city square brimmed with shoppers and residents enjoying the midday sunshine and entertainers performing throughout the square. The voices and laughter of children and families all partaking in the spectacles floated on the cold autumn wind, through the square, and into Hoshi's tent where Sayr sat cross-legged on the ground.

Sayr breathed in deeply through her nose and out her mouth. She squeezed her eyes shut while she focused and willed her mind to remain empty of any intruding thoughts. Her legs had grown numb while she sat waiting for the familiar tug at her core. The tingling sensation that crawled up and down her lower body continuously pulled at her focus, and she shifted slightly in discomfort.

A child's delighted scream pierced through the thin folds of Hoshi's tent, followed by a series of giggles. Sayr's stiff body deflated, and her eyes flung open to look irritatingly at Hoshi, sitting directly across the low table and monitoring Sayr closely.

"It's too loud here," Sayr said. "I can't concentrate long enough to see anything with all the noise outside."

Hoshi simply shrugged her shoulders. "The noise becomes unnoticeable after some time. Besides, you will need to get used to using your gifts when there is noise around you. There will be circumstances where you will need to use your gifts while distracted, just as any Elemental would."

Sayr let out a frustrated breath, but obediently closed her eyes again. She sat straighter and lifted her head high. She breathed deeply in and out, trying to empty her mind. Yet no matter how hard she tries, her thoughts raced with the events of the last six days.

She had left the Creobian Palace six days ago along with Marenda, Dema, and Dimitri to stay in Therod until the Visarian royal family left to return to their own palace. She had denounced her role in the Eastern Court at the Harvest Ball and told the Eastern Queen that Sayr no longer served her. She had chosen not to follow through with the queen's plan to find and kill the king's mercenary, the second-in-command in the King's Court, after learning that Dimitri, the man she had fallen for during her time in the Western Palace, had been the king's mercenary all along.

During her time hiding away in Therod, Sayr had met with Julen at the Department of Records on the possible whereabouts of her father. Julen had found a possible lead, records of a man named Jespon living outside a small village in Creobe near the Silia River. Julen hadn't found any death records or any records at all in the past three years. No one knew if the man still resided there or if he was long gone. Once things had settled down in the Creobian Palace and she settled into whatever her new role might be, her first task would be to go to that village and begin the search for her father.

Sayr stirred as she sat on the ground. She couldn't let herself hope too much. After so many years, could she truly see her father again? Even if she were able to find him, would he want to see her? Would he be thrilled to have her back, or had he abandoned her in the Eastern Palace for a reason? If the Jespon living near the Silia River happened to be her father, had he fled to Creobe to get away from her and the problems her and her unnatural gifts likely caused him? Was he content living the rest of his life in Creobe without her?

Sayr shot up from her spot on the ground and stood before Hoshi. "I can't do this," she griped. "Not today. I'm not going to be able to see anything with all the noise."

Hoshi didn't rise from her spot across the table. Her eyes, one pale blue and the other a deep brown, followed Sayr as she walked toward the entrance to the tent and swung the flap aside. "We will try again tomorrow. You cannot prolong a message from the stars forever."

"I'm returning to the palace tomorrow," Sayr muttered. She stood before the threshold of the tent. The cold autumn air rushed inside, flickering the candles and sending goosebumps over Sayr's body. She grabbed her cloak off a cushion and wrapped it around her shoulders.

"Then you will need to visit me soon, and often." Hoshi shifted and rose from the low table. Sayr turned to glance at her as she gave a nod of understanding. "You have much on your mind. We will begin again once the Visarian royal family is gone, and you have settled into your new life here."

Sayr's body trembled at Hoshi's words. She truly was starting a new life. Starting tomorrow, her life would be entirely different and entirely her own. But what kind of life would that be? King Mylan hadn't sent word for her in the last six days, and even if he did, Sayr didn't know if she would willingly serve in his Court. She still didn't have the answers on why King Mylan had kept the healers in the palace hidden away from the rest of the kingdom, or why the healers were so terrified to be found out that they threatened to kill each other if any of them slipped and revealed their secret abilities. Once the Visarian royal family left the Western Palace and Sayr returned, she would meet privately with the king and demand answers before she submitted herself to any sort of service to him.

"I'll see you soon," Sayr promised Hoshi before stepping out of the tent and into the chilling square.

The bright sun shone high above in the sky and Sayr lifted a hand over her eyes to shield them. She turned expectantly to the side of Hoshi's tent where Marenda stood, patiently waiting while Sayr met Hoshi inside. She was bundled in a heavy fur coat, thick pants, and heavy boots.

"How did it go?" Marenda asked. She peeled her body away from the tent and walked in step with Sayr as they made their way through the thick of the square.

"Awful," Sayr admitted. "I can't relax enough to see anything. And even if I did see something, what would I tell Hoshi? She still thinks I'm some sort of Space Elemental who has visions of the past like her. Even if I was able to call on a vision, it would be of the future, like all the rest. What am I supposed to say to her?"

Marenda scrunched her nose while she thought. "Have you seen anything since that vision on the balcony?" She spoke quietly enough that passersby in the square wouldn't overhear them.

Sayr shook her head. "I haven't had any new vision, and now I can't seem to call on them either. I haven't been able to successfully use my gift at all, it's like it's not even there."

The two girls exited the square and turned towards an outer street. "Have you told Dimitri?" Marenda asked.

Her voice still held its usual disdain when mentioning Dimitri, but Sayr had noticed the two of them warming up to each other over the past six days, ever so slightly. Once again, Sayr shook her head. "He has enough on his mind without me springing my problems on him."

"Did he tell you why he was leaving today?" Marenda pushed.

"No," Sayr huffed. "He was gone before I woke up. I don't doubt it's all the same business as before."

Dimitri had traveled back to the palace on two occasions since they'd left. Once to speak privately with King Mylan and another time to try and question the rebels in the dungeons again. He would leave Sayr, Marenda, and Dema in the care of another member of the King's Court while he was gone. Sayr hadn't minded too much, she knew the toll his role as the king's mercenary took and how big of a hole that he'd likely left in the Court these past six days. She didn't particularly enjoy his last departure, though, when she'd woken up that morning to find Tomas laying out his recently caught game on the kitchen table. He'd taken the free morning to go game hunting, he'd said, and was more than eager to spend the day preparing the game for dinner.

Sayr had wanted to go with Dimitri, but she couldn't bring herself to return to the palace just yet. Not while the Eastern Queen and the crown prince and princess were still within those walls.

Everett's words from the Harvest Ball rang in her ears and her heart cracked all over again. Her oldest friend had always known about the unseen elements, about people with gifts so similar to her own, and had kept that knowledge from her for eight years. He had watched her struggle with her identity as someone unnatural and unwanted, all while knowing he could have helped her. Everett had never truly wanted the best for her, he only wanted what was best for him and his family and the crown.

Sayr forced the painful thoughts away as she and Marenda reached the townhome, their temporary have while in Therod. Together, Sayr and Marenda climbed the steps to the front door but before they could ascend half the steps, the door burst open.

"Took you long enough!" Addy bounded out the door and down the steps. "You were supposed to be back eight minutes ago."

"Are you monitoring every minute that we're gone now?" Marenda asked, though she ended the question with a laugh.

The girls had awoken that morning to find Dimitri already gone once again and Addy sitting at the kitchen table in his place. Addy had pouted when Marenda refused to let her go see Hoshi with her and Sayr, claiming Dema needed someone to keep her company in their absence.

"Under His Majesty's orders, I am to monitor every second; especially when you're gone longer than you say you'll be," Addy answered. "I would have dragged Dema out into the streets with me if it weren't for the delicious muffins she has in the oven."

Addy reached into her pocket and lifted a small paper in her hands, teasingly waving it before Marenda. "I have a little letter here from *Callum*."

Sayr's eyes lifted back to the door of the townhome where Dema leaned against the doorframe. Her long black hair was in its usual braid down her back, and she wore a long apron that was coated in flour and sugar. She smiled softly and Sayr broke away from Marenda, leaving her to fight Addy for the letter.

"I'm guessing he's still away, if Addy's still here?" Sayr asked.

Dema nodded and looked down the steps at Marenda and Addy, already deep in their own conversation. "He is. Lady Adelaide says she will be staying with us tonight to take us to the palace tomorrow. His Majesty's orders. Though, I don't think any of us mind, Lady Marenda least of all."

"Haven't they both told you to stop addressing them as 'Lady'?" Sayr joked.

"Yes," Dema answered, "But to be fair, it seems unfitting to simply call Lady Marenda by name, and Lady Adelaide secretly likes it."

Sayr let out a laugh and she and Dema stepped inside the townhome with Marenda and Addy following not far behind. The place smelled divine, like warm sugar and baked fruit. Dema hurried into the kitchen and opened the wood-burning stove oven. Wrapping a cloth around her hands, she pulled out a batch of steaming muffins and sat them on the counter.

Dema had begged Marenda to help her light the stove oven their first morning in the townhome. The oven only needed fire to light the wood chips at the bottom, but having a Fire Elemental in the house that could monitor the flames willingly had Dema begging for Marenda's assistance. Since that morning, Dema had spent most of her time in the townhome baking and trying new recipes for the group.

Addy swiped at one of the muffins, but Dema shooed her hand away with a hand towel. "Let them cool," she ordered. "They are for dessert after dinner. Go wash up and we can eat."

Addy crossed her arms in defiance but obeyed, muttering to Marenda as they climbed the stairs to the second floor, "Who knew the youngest here would be the bossiest of us all."

The four girls sat around the kitchen table; each had a muffin plated in front of them. Marenda had already taken a hearty bite of hers and held it up towards her face, inspecting it closely.

"And what's in this?" Marenda asked through a mouthful of muffin. "Not that I don't trust your baking skills, they're exceptional, but I've never tasted a fruit like this before."

Addy answered before Dema could open her mouth, "They're plum muffins. Plums are like peaches but smaller and with a firmer outer skin, they're sweet and tart. Any sort of plum sweet is a delicacy during our colder months."

"These are sugar plum muffins," Dema added. "A vendor near the square had a few batches at his stall."

Sayr took a bite of her muffin, savoring the taste. The plum fruit was warm and delicious mixed with the sugared top of the muffin. Once again, Dema's baking skills had exceeded Sayr's expectations. "I hope you made enough to have for breakfast tomorrow, too."

Dema smiled, but before she could answer, the front door to the townhome burst open and Dimitri stepped into the room.

"Tri..." Dema rose from her seat and Sayr followed suit, but neither girl moved as they took in Dimitri's face. His eyes were wide and searching as he took in each girl in the room. The cold had left his nose and cheeks rosy, making him appear wild and severe.

"Is everything alright?" Addy asked, still seated at the table.

Dimitri's shoulders dropped. "Everything is fine, though no progress has been made on securing information from the imprisoned rebels."

"They're still not cooperating?" Addy grumbled.

"What about that girl?" Sayr interjected, remembering the imprisoned rebel who had been able to duplicate her earring. "The one I spoke to?"

Dimitri shook his head. "She's shut down. They've all shut down completely. Not only have they refused to speak, but they're also refusing to eat or drink anything. They've resorted to starving themselves in silence."

Marenda swallowed the last of her muffin. "You have Spirit Elementals in your palace, right? Why can't you bring a Spirit Elemental down there with you and have them use their gifts to persuade them into feeling guilty or as though they can trust you enough to confess?"

Addy stared at Marenda, wide eyed. "That wouldn't do any good. For them or for us."

"Why not?" Sayr asked.

"Influencing another being's physical or emotional state, willing or unwilling, is highly illegal," Addy explained and turned to Sayr. "Lilith may not have liked you but even she knew not to use her influence on you during your trainings."

"She used her influence on me in Visaran, though," Sayr reminded them all. "When the King's Court came to Visaran for the first time. You were there, Addy."

"Yes, and she faced punishment for that. Albeit punishment from Queen Cheralin rather than any of our law holders," Addy said.

"And besides the legalities of elemental manipulation on another being, having any sort of elemental influence on someone can cause irreparable damage," Dimitri chimed in, switching the conversation back to the topic at hand. "The consequences of Fire, Air, Earth, and Water are obvious, but Spirit and Space are different."

"How so?" Sayr asked.

Dimitri leaned against the front door and looked down at the floorboards. "An Elemental's influence always has some sort of effect, whether mental or physical. Earth, Air, Water, and Fire Elementals have physical effects from their manipulation. Spirit and Space Elementals have more… mental effects."

Dimitri looked at Sayr. "Space Elementals task their own bodies every time they manipulate their element. You've seen how Hoshi's gifts affect her. Manipulating her element takes a toll on her physical and mentally each time she has a vision, but that is an effect implemented on herself due to using her gifts."

"Spirit Elementals are the opposite, they influence their gift onto others instead of themselves," Addy cut Dimitri off. "Their gifts affect the Spirit Elemental, but they mostly affect whoever is being influenced. Having a foreign element manipulate a being's mind without their consent or control can cause that person's mental state to start to crack."

"You mean a Spirit Elemental can ruin a person's mind?" Marenda asked.

Addy shrugged. "In some cases, yes. But again, it's highly illegal. No one has done something so cruel in years, if not decades, as far as I'm aware. It would be barbaric for us to even consider using such a method on the rebels, even if they are imprisoned and under interrogation. His Majesty would never allow for something like that."

Sayr and Mar shared a quick look. They both knew from experience that Queen Cheralin would take an opportunity like that without a second thought if it meant gaining the information she needed. Shame burned both girl's cheeks for having the same thought.

"The Spirit Elemental would have to be incredibly strong." Dimitri spoke as if that part was supposed to be comforting, and not a dangerous threat. "But it would take multiple attempts from the Spirit Elemental to manipulate the person's mind."

"We'll find another way to make them talk," Dimitri finished. "Once we return tomorrow and I can consistently interrogate them, I don't doubt that I can find a means of making them talk."

"Have you spoken to His Majesty about what is expected of us tomorrow?" Addy asked.

Dimitri nodded but gave nothing further. "I assume you're all packed and ready for tomorrow if you're all lazing around the dinner table."

"You left before any of us woke up," Marenda countered, her tone once again icy. "If you had orders for us, you should've waited to tell us."

"I expected a 'thank you' for sending Addy in my place, not a lecture on the time I left. Least of all from you." Dimitri walked into the kitchen, clearly not wanting to start a fight with Marenda.

Marenda, though, looked as if an argument was exactly what she was trying to start. She glared at Dimitri as he walked away and opened her mouth to slight him some more.

"Mar," Sayr warned quietly before Marenda could start. Marenda looked at Sayr, slammed her mouth shut, and rolled her eyes.

Sayr and Dema followed Dimitri into the kitchen, leaving Marenda to seethe and Addy to finish her muffin. Dimitri leaned over the basin, his back to the two of them."

"You were gone for a while," Dema started. "Are you sure everything's okay?"

Dimitri sighed and faced the girls. He kept his hands gripped against the basin and leaned against it. "It's been a long day, and we have a lot to do before we return to the palace. Tensions are exhaustingly high in the palace; but I shouldn't be taking my frustrations out on any of you." Dimitri hung his head. "I'm sorry."

Dema and Sayr shared a concerning look, both over Dimitri and the endless possibilities of what could be occurring inside the Western Palace. "The Eastern Court is still in the palace?" Sayr asked.

Dimitri nodded. "They're scheduled to depart at sunrise tomorrow, though Queen Cheralin is fighting tooth and nail to delay the departure."

"What's happening in the palace?" Dema asked,

"Fighting and threats mostly," Dimitri, said. "Threats between the royals, fights between the guards. Like I said, tensions are high and when a guard hears constant threats made against their king or queen, brawls are bound to break out."

"How is the Court doing?" Dema pushed.

Dimitri lifted his head, and his tired gaze lifted towards the ceiling. "As best they can. They've been with His Majesty most of the time. Cheralin hates the King's Court. I think she hates how outnumbered her and her children are here. She wants to be gone and back in her own Court already but is fighting hard for Sayr and Marenda."

Sayr's body ran cold at Dimitri's words. She knew the queen saw her as an important asset to the Eastern Court, but she hadn't expected the queen to fight so hard for her. Queen Cheralin had let her go so easily when King Mylan had requested her, but that was when Sayr was on her side. Sayr realized that, once she abandoned her role in the Eastern Court, she had become one of Visaran's biggest threats. Queen Cheralin had never shared much information with Sayr besides what she'd heard in Council meetings, but Sayr had so much knowledge of the Eastern Palace and its Court that Creobe could use against Visaran. Visaran would no longer have the upper hand in any political disputes between the two kingdoms. Creobe would know everything Sayr knew. And Sayr knew quite a lot.

Dimitri looked at Sayr, reading the panic written all over her face. The queen wasn't fighting to bring Sayr back to Court, she was fighting to get Sayr back in her grasp and do whatever necessary to keep those secrets hidden for good.

Dimitri's face hardened with resolution. "She will not get to you," he promised. "But we need a plan. We need to be prepared for anything."

Dema stepped back towards the dining room. "I'll go speak with the other two," she said. "We'll start packing, and then we can begin our preparation for tomorrow."

Dimitri nodded to his sister, and she quickly left the kitchen. Once she was gone, Sayr approached Dimitri and hesitantly lifted a hand to his cheek. He leaned into her touch and lowered himself to grab her around the waist and pull her close.

"She will not get to you," he repeated. "We will wait for word from His Majesty that the Visarian royals are long gone before we leave here. If we don't hear from the palace, we don't leave."

Sayr nodded against his body. "Thank you."

The comfort of his arms around her body felt like an extra layer of protection had been placed around her. The threat of the royals and the events to come tomorrow felt eons away as Dimitri held her tightly. He shifted his body to lift her chin and face him but did not let her go.

"His Majesty wants to meet with you privately once we arrive back in the palace," he said. "Have you thought about what you'll do moving forward?"

Sayr's mouth tugged down in a scowl. "Why privately? This matter concerns Mar, too, if she's going to stay in Creobe. Why doesn't His Majesty want to meet with her?"

"I don't know," Dimitri admitted. "I didn't ask questions, in truth I got out of there as quickly as I could. But from what I do know, Marenda will likely resume some role in the king's Royal Guard, whereas you could become a member of the King's Court."

Dimitri lowered his head, his voice softer, as he continued, "You are also the only one with unknown gifts. His Majesty still believes you're a Spirit Elemental, but your concern for the wellbeing of the healers and any others with unknown gifts has raised his suspicions. It's possible he wants to speak with you on that matter, too."

"And I want to speak with him about that just as much as he does," Sayr confirmed. "I won't serve another royal who uses people for their gifts and then forces them to hide themselves. I've dealt with enough of that to last the rest of my life. I left the Eastern Court in hopes that Creobe would be different."

"If I serve King Mylan," she continued, "I want to do so as I am. I don't want to have to hide my own abilities again. The secrets and lies are becoming too much. I need to know the king's intentions with the healers before I can decide what I'll do for him and his Court."

Dimitri pulled away slightly. "I know but give the king a chance. Hear him out. I've served him for years now, and I can honestly say that he is a good man, a good ruler. He cares for his people and his country. Whatever reason he has for keeping the healers hidden in the palace, I'm sure it's for the benefit of everyone."

Sayr nodded again, but a seed of doubt sparked in her gut. She'd dealt with royals long enough to know they often served their own interests before anyone else's. She hoped the Western King was different, but she wouldn't know for sure until she spoke with him the next day.

"We should prepare to leave tomorrow," Dimitri said. "I want to leave the moment we receive word from the palace. No stalling. We'll take the quickest path from Therod, and we won't stop until we are back inside the palace walls. If all goes well, we'll be back in the King's Court by dinnertime; but we must prepare for the worst. Are you ready?"

Sayr tried to offer him a smile. "I'm ready."

Dimitri kissed her head, then gently kissed her lips. As he pulled away, he whispered, "Be ready for anything."

Sayr leaned her forehead against his and breathed in deeply. Her thoughts crowded with every little thing that could go wrong the next day. They had one chance for things to go right. Whatever happened tomorrow would set her future; her future with Dimitri, with Marenda, and Hoshi, and Julen, and the rest of the King's Court. She could picture the life she'd yearned for, a life she never thought could be possible for her/ No matter what, tomorrow would be the beginning of a new life.

And she would be ready.

Acknowledgements

Writing and publishing this novel was one of the toughest and most time-consuming tasks I've ever done. And it was so worth it. I've had an amazing group of people that have cheered for me since the beginning.

First, I want to thank God. Nothing would be possible if it were not for Him. Every blessing that I have been given is because of Him, and I am eternally grateful.

I also want to thank my parents and sister. Not only were the three of you my biggest support, but you also each helped me get through this process in different ways.

Madi, thank you for letting me blab about my book ideas and read different scenes aloud to you even when they came with no context and made absolutely no sense half the time. Your excitement in the story and in me as a writer kept me going, especially in times when I strongly doubted myself. Having you to talk to and feeling your excitement and support helped me more than you know.

Mom, thank you for shouting about this book to the world and everyone you know. Even before this book was completed and ready for publishing, you were yelling to the masses about this story and gathering readers for me from the get-go. I never would have had the major support that I received without your help and support.

Dad, thank you for all of your help in getting this book out to the world. I truly wouldn't have been able to bring this book out of my head and onto paper without all your help. You gave me all the business knowledge I needed to successfully publish my first ever novel. Even before then, you, Madi, and mom listened to me go on and on about writing a story about people with Elemental gifts for years. I know you'd say the same thing you always say when I thank you for your help, that you wish you could do more. But you've always done more than enough for Madi and I and neither of us would be where or who we are without you or mom.

To my friends and family, thank you for your never-ending support! I have so many of you to thank for supporting this book and my journey as a writer.

To my readers, thank you for taking a chance on this book. I hope you've loved it just as much as—if not more than—I do. I originally wrote this story to get it out of my head where it had been swimming for years and onto paper, and I'm so happy that this story now gets to be in each of your hands.

To my fellow writers, keep going! Thank you for all the advice and support in my different writing groups and even my fellow writers that I've connected with through social media. Having each other has given me so much confidence to publish this story.

Finally, thank you to Michael. You sat with me through much of the stresses of this writing and publishing process. Towards the end, you saw how much I stressed and gave into nerves about publishing this story, and you always lifted me back up when I doubted myself. You sat with me while I talked about this story over and over again and shot idea after idea at you and called on friends and family for support. You became the rock that I needed to stay grounded and determined through this process.

About the Author

Alley Rehfeldt was raised in Ohio with her mom, dad, and twin sister. She now lives in South Carolina with her husband, Michael, and their two dogs. She has taught high school English for four years. She received her BA in AYA–Integrated Language Arts and her MA in English. When not teaching the youths of America or divulging herself in her writing, you'll likely find her at her favorite coffee shops, playing the Nintendo Switch with her twin, Madison, out on the water somewhere, or walking along the beach with her puppies and husband. Check out her website at www.alleyrehfeldt.com!